W9-CFL-284

THE BACK OF
BEYOND

Tor/Forge Books by Stuart Fox

The Back of Beyond
Black Fire

THE BACK OF BEYOND

Stuart Fox

A TOM DOHERTY ASSOCIATES BOOK
NEW YORK

THE BACK OF BEYOND

This book is printed on acid-free paper.

A Forge Book
Published by Tom Doherty Associates, Inc.
175 Fifth Avenue
New York, N.Y. 10010

Library of Congress Cataloging-in-Publication Data

Fox, Stuart, 1950–
The back of beyond / Stuart Fox.
    p.   cm.
"A Tom Doherty Associates Book."
ISBN 0-312-85366-1
1. Investigative reporting—Australia—Fiction.
2. Australian aborigines—Land tenure—Fiction.
3. Journalists—Australia—Fiction.   I. Title.
        PS3556.O9557B3   1994
    813'.54—dc20   94-126
                CIP

First edition: May 1994

Printed in the United States of America

0 9 8 7 6 5 4 3 2 1

To my friends:
Larry Sargeant and Keith Nunn
In the best of times

And to my Aussie mates:
Brett, Dean, Vin, Jamie and Doug

CONTENTS

THE BACK OF BEYOND

A spirit-filled land is Australia,
Raw, rugged; and rare its mammalia.
But should you abscond
To the Back of Beyond,
Then the land or the spirits will nail ya.

"The Back o' Beyond? Ey, I kin tell ye where tha' is. Once ye're outa the city ye're in the bush, roight? Ye pass the farms an' the sheep stytions an' ye gitta the outback, a million square moiles a dust an' droidup lykes. Ere ye still wiv me? Ye're naw' even close yet. Thar's a far, far plyce cawld the Bula-bloody-makanka whar the country remynes loike it was thousands o' years before in the dreamtyme. Some sye this plyce doesn't exist. Others sye it does . . . and that beyond the Bulamakanka, ye'll foind somethin's cawld the Black Stump. This stump's whar the Back o' Bourke begins. A sor' ova never-never land. If ye was to maykeet through the Back o' Bourke ye'd cometa the Back o' Beyond. Anywhy that's wot some sye. Nobody really knows. 'Cause no bloke's ever found it an' come back to tell the tyle."

—Alvin Cockie

1

Welcome to Oz

I'll admit to an attitude.

No first-string player likes warming the bench—that's what I thought this art show amounted to.

And it's true I said something about starting a fire.

Big deal.

Who would've guessed they'd make such a fuss about it? But then, who would've guessed our host was ten minutes away from being cremated alive, that his art exhibits would go up in flames, or that the Sydney Opera House would come within an ace of being burned to the ground?

Not me.

And I sure never figured those clowns would try to pin the blaze on yours truly.

I'm a reporter. I specialize in the offbeat and my beat is Sydney, the closest thing to an Emerald City in this upside-Down-Under land the Aussies call Oz.

My name?

That's what the uninformed security cop wanted to know.

"Doyle Mulligan," I informed him, "Eastern News."

"Identification?"

I had my Australian Journalists Association membership card ready. Security was air tight.

"Never 'eard of yer rag," he said.

"Eastern News isn't a rag," I growled. "We're a press service for the American and European papers."

"What're you doing 'ere? I didn't know this art show was that bigga lurk."

Neither did I.

But I wasn't about to tell him that my bosses had sent out two
B Team bozos to cover the biggest yarn in Australia since the
prime minister put his paws on the queen while I, the office's
MVP, got assigned to an art show. So I said:

"You haven't heard?"

"Heard wot?"

"About the fireworks."

He cocked his head. "Wot fireworks?"

"I can't say any more. But do yourself a favor. Keep your eyes
and ears open and get ready to move on the jump."

Now he was glaring at me.

"Ye're flash as a rat with a gold tooth, ayn't ye?"

I winked, to let him know I was kidding. But he missed it. He
was glancing to one side.

A second guard was notifying a soaring black-faced and
black-skinned pro-basketball type—looking as uncomfortable in
his jacket and tie as I'd look wearing a crotch sheath—that he
couldn't go in.

Either the big aborigine didn't understand or he didn't believe
it. In any case he wasn't happy. As I watched, the guard ner-
vously fingered his holstered revolver. That kind of tension was
common these days. Relations between blacks and whites here
had sunk about as low as they could get, but the shooting wasn't
due to start for another week. Six days to be exact. Like everyone
else in Australia, I was doing a countdown—next Wednesday
was D-Day.

The first rent-a-cop was keeping an eye on them just in case.
He wasn't worried about what his pal might do; he was worried
about what might get done to his pal. You see there were only
two black guys in the room, and that aborigine was both of 'em.

Eventually the big black moved away.

The security cop breathed.

"The abos don't want them pictures shown," he explained to

me, jabbing a thumb over his shoulder at the poster-board sign
mounted on an easel:

COPLEY ABORIGINALS
presents
The Ularu Cave Paintings
"Artists of Antiquity /
Guardians of the Sacred Land"

* * *

Media viewing: 3:00
Open admission: 3:30

He said:
"Even setting 'r white eyes on them pictures is taboo, ye see?"
Suddenly he stood up and ordered an ABC cameraman to put
out his cigarette. Australian Broadcasting Corporation. "No
smoking 'ere or in the auditorium!" he snapped.
"Then how'd he get 'em?" I said.
The guy turned back to me and screwed up his brows.
"Wot?"
"Arthur Copley," I said; "he's white. How'd he get the pic-
tures?"
My question and I were dismissed with a single shrug. "Bug-
gered if I know," he said. "Ask 'im." He looked away, calling out,
" 'Oo's next?" to those journos yet to sign in.
I stepped aside.
"Better yet," said a deep voice behind me, "whyn't ye drive up
there yerself and ask them Ularu."
I rolled my eyes.
Another voice two octaves higher and twice as obnoxious
added, "Cause 'e ain't got the knackers, that's why."
The low voice had come from high over my head; the high
one had come from below. So I didn't have to turn around to
know who was talking. But I turned around anyway.

That was my first mistake.

They were a couple of Jack Anderson wannabes who wrote for The Picky. *The Sydney Daily Pictorial*. One was six feet seven and the other was five feet flat, but except for that they were twins. They both had mustaches and long noses and they were supposed to be a witty writing team, I suppose on the theory that two halfwits adds up to wit.

Their names were MacMutton and Geoffers. I called them Mutt and Jeff. Not to their faces.

Incredibly enough, they had their own column, a kind of behind-the-scenes-Sydney, a muckraking thing and an example of journalism at its most jaundiced. I'd given it a glance once or twice but never got very much out of it. Alvin Cockie—you'll meet him later—used to say it read better if he was "two shandies shy of the horrors," but whenever he found himself feeling that way he would order a double to put himself out of his misery.

As I turned around I was rewarded with twin expressions of surprise. Maybe they didn't think I had the knackers to face them either. At any rate, they were jolted. But I got a surprise too. There were three of them instead of two and the third was a friend of my favorite sex. But what she was doing with the likes of them I couldn't imagine.

"Look!" squealed the little one, Jeff. "It ayn't . . . It's the bloody seppo. What are you doing here, seppo?"

You'd have to understand Australian slang to get that. It's called strine—a way of rhyming and playing with words that's almost like a new language. A glorious home becomes *Gloria Soame*; a slide rule turns into *sly drool*; a babbling brook is a cook; and *grey day* is grade A. It takes getting used to. An American is a yank, is a *septic tank*, or *seppo* for short.

I ignored Jeff. He was too small to hit and too nasty to step on and if he'd run for dog catcher of Munchkin City he'd have come up short. Besides, we weren't alone. There were nosy news types all around. Not to mention my friend.

So I grinned up at MacMutton. What a piece of work! Everything below his beak was overbuilt: a cavernous mouth, a jaw the size of Ayers Rock . . . neck, shoulders and the rest of him all scaled to the same dimensions. But they'd shortchanged him above the nose. His eyes were too small and too close together. His forehead started sloping back too soon and didn't stop until it reached a tiny thatch of fur on the top of his cranium. The resulting cavity wasn't half large enough for the average-sized brain though I doubt it cramped his too much.

"That was pretty good," I said, still grinning at him, "the way you said that without moving your lips. But how did you get the dummy's mouth to open?"

"Very funny," Mutt muttered in his New South Welshman's eccent. "But ye dint answer 'is question. Wot are ye doing here?"

"Oh, I just came for the barbecue."

That was it.

A perfectly innocent remark. And my second mistake.

Mutt frowned.

"Barbecue? What barbecue?"

"You know, the barbie. Paul Hogan. 'Come'n say, G'day.' You Aussies invited us Americans over, remember? You said if we stopped by you'd throw another shrimp on the barbie."

"So?"

"So," I said, looking at Jeff and digging into a pants pocket, "I thought it might be the little munchkin's turn." I held out my hand. "I even brought along extra matches in case they have trouble getting a fire going under him."

Mutt balled an oversized fist and started forward. "Oi got 'alf a moind to stretch you out," he snarled.

I took a step back. In Mutt's case, half a mind made it unanimous. Jeff—the other half—was shouting: "Lay 'im down, mayte."

"Hey look . . . !" I started.

Suddenly the uniformed guard shoved between us.

" 'Ere now, what's goin' on?"

"Nothing," I said quickly.

"This bloke's a bloody firebug," whined Jeff. " 'E's got matches an' says 'e's gonna start a fire."

Facing off with me the guard demanded my name.

I heaved a sigh. "I already checked in," I said. "Doyle Mulligan. You took my name down. Don't listen to these guys, they're just trying to start trouble."

The guard aimed an unloaded index finger at me, told me they wouldn't stand for any trouble, holstered his finger in his fist and then moved warily away. The current climate, racial as well as seasonal, had everyone at each other's throats.

Meanwhile Mutt smiled a back-handed smile.

"Ye shuda thanked 'im, seppo. Next toime 'e mightna be here to save ye. You won't be so lair with a bunch o' fives in yer eye. Then we'll see if ye know 'owta 'andle yerself."

I started to ask him, who was he kidding? Fighters run in my family. But I figured, why waste a good line on a halfwit? So I smiled back and, with a glance at my friend, walked away.

And I thought that was the end of it.

But, like I said, I didn't know Arthur Copley was going to get himself cremated. I didn't know his blow-ups of the eons-old rock paintings in the Ularu cave would be destroyed. And I didn't know this theater, this symbol of Australian vision and drive, an architectural wonder and one of the most immediately recognizable buildings on earth, would soon be the scene of a five-alarm fire.

From a distance the opera house looks like a futuristic schooner unfurling its sails. It appears less to have been built on Bennelong Point so much as docked there and if the lines should ever be cast the billowing structure threatens to glide off into the harbor with Captain Nemo at the helm. Closer, the canvas takes on a feathered pattern as though it were the wings of some whopping big swan. In fact, it is neither canvas nor feather, as you can see by standing right below the eaves, but precast-concrete-sphere slices covered in ceramic tile.

The original drawing—which I'd seen on display in the foyer on my way in—called for a roof that looked more like a shell with shallower, more graceful slopes and sides that were scalloped from front to back. It proved impossible to build.

There are other design flaws too. Incredibly, nobody thought to leave room for a parking lot until it was done.

The main theater, I'm told, has wonderful acoustics but it lacked proper staging—there was no provision for wings—so they turned it into a symphony hall. Opera is confined to a secondary theater which seats half as many and which has a stage scarcely a third the size of most other opera houses.

However, I'm not an architectural critic. Neither do I write op-ed, Who's Who or movie reviews. And I don't, except on very bad days, cover art shows.

Which made today a very bad day indeed.

I'd followed the signs to the auditorium—neither the main nor secondary hall but one of two smaller halls behind the others for chamber music and art exhibitions.

Once through the security station and past those two halfwits I joined the several dozen members of the media in the grand auditorium—junior journos, freelance fotogs, and society sheilas.

Huge tapestries covered the walls. Faired in lighting reflected off a bizarre collection of ceiling detail. And the color was wildly Art Deco. Not so much flashy as it was Flash Gordon with overtones of Mongo. I stood there rubbernecking. Forgetting for a moment the artwork on the stage, which was as ancient as the opera house is modern.

"Iz nit luvly?"

I turned and said that it was. After all, they'd paid for the thing. Ten years behind schedule and a hundred million over budget, the opera house toppled a state government, and brought Sydneysiders onto the streets in protest before it was finished, paid for entirely by special state lottery which was only appropriate, this being a nation of "punters."

"I don't know how they could have mistaken you for anyone else," she told me. "Who but Doyle Mulligan would come to a fancy art do wearin' sandshoes . . ."

I glanced down at my tennies.

". . . and," said the young woman, poking a finger in the loop of my four-in-hand, "with his necktie not even snugged up?"

I tightened the knot.

"Who did they think I was?"

"Some bazza, I s'pose. You left without saying hi."

"Hi, Maggie."

"Oi, Blue."

Margaret McDowel was a feature writer for *Woman's Day,* which despite its name, is a weekly—not to be confused with *Australian Women's Weekly,* which is a monthly. She was also, in the vernacular, a "corker," as well as being friendly and bright, and being as she hailed from Brisbane she managed to turn the Queen's English into something called Queenslander, which is more of a slur than a slander.

"Why'd ye run off?"

I shrugged. "If I hadn't left when I did, you know, it wouldn't've been pretty. That rent-a-cop stepped in just as I was about to clean some clocks."

"My, I'm impressed." She made a valiant effort to look impressed. "I didn't know you were a scrapper."

"Are you kidding? Fighters run in my family."

She laughed. Because the line wasn't wasted on her.

I laughed with her, but actually, there was more truth to that statement than I cared to admit.

I'd run to Australia from Hong Kong eight months before when a lulu of a story I'd written about the Chinese communists pissed off Beijing and darned near got me killed. It's not that I'm chicken. I'm not. I've just got a passion for law and order. I believe it would be a crime to deprive the world of Doyle

Mulligan and therefore any move that keeps me alive is in order.

So I'd moved to Australia. Run, really. I had no way of knowing that in about ten minutes I'd be running again.

"How do you know those guys, Maggie, and since when are you keeping company with scandalmongers?"

She stepped closer.

"I didn't keep it," she said smiling. "I traded it for you, didn't I? That's an urge I get whenever I see you."

"Naturally. I have that effect on women. You couldn't help yourself."

She moved right up next to me, tipped her head back and said, "Now that I'm here I've got another urge."

"Help yourself."

Maggie and I were engaged. Not to each other. She was engaged to a lawyer in Brisbane and I was engaged to a girl in Bangkok—at least that's what I'd thought—so anything she and I said to each other was strictly in fun.

At least, that's what she thought.

"Not until *you* tell *me* something."

"You too, huh?"

"Me too?"

"You're wondering what an internationally-known Pulitzer Prize–winning writer like me is doing at a crummy art show. Right?"

"You didn't win the Pulitzer Prize."

"Now that you mention it, I guess it must have been the Nobel Prize."

"You're not internationally known."

"My mother knows me. She's in Chicago."

"Still, you're right, it is a daggy art show."

"And you want to know what I'm doing here."

"Ey. I'm surprised you're not in Canberra covering the riots? Or down in The Gong. The aborigines are having that demonstration today."

"You call those riots? You should've seen Los Angeles after

the Rodney King verdict. Those were riots! Canberra? That was
a warm-up. The same goes for Wollongong. Wait till the High
Court makes its ruling. When Killian comes out on top, you'll
see riots in spades . . . sorry, no pun intended."

"So why aren't you up in the Top End interviewing Rush
Killian?"

"Don't you read the papers? Killian can't stand reporters. He's
never granted an interview in his life. The man surrounds himself with an army of bodyguards and attack dogs and . . . have
you heard about his pet?"

"What about it?"

"Some kind of lion dog. It's even got a mane."

"Fair dinkum?"

"Yeah. They say it eats reporters."

She smiled.

"Well then, why not drive up there like MacMutton suggested,
cross into Ularu Occupied Land and talk to the aborigines?
That's more your style, isn't it?"

"I hear they eat people, too."

She gripped my arm with surprising strength.

"If you're on a big story, Blue, whyn't ye let me in on it? You
can trust me. I'd give anything to get out of this society news
stuff." She had my sympathy. "Tea pahties and comin' ups," she
went on, unnecessarily exaggerating her accent. "The lightest
fashions. Silvert'iles and tall poppies. 'Ave anothah cuppa,
deyar?' I swear, I'm ready for somethin' more."

"D'you mean it?"

"Dinkie die."

I turned serious. "This might be dangerous."

"All the more for it."

I looked carefully around. There was no one in earshot.

"Well I'll tell you," I said, lowering my voice all the same.
"You know those wild stories we've been hearing about up
there? Screams. Howling in the night. And that tourist who got
attacked?" She'd heard all about it. I was practically whispering

by then. "We've got evidence Arthur Copley may be tied in with that."

"What evidence?"

"I've talked to his barber. The man gets his hair cut once a week. He gets a shave twice a day. A manicure, too. They can't keep up with his fingernails."

"What of it?"

"According to Copley's dentist he's getting a little long in the tooth."

"So?"

"Six inches long! And tonight, the moon's full."

She was shaking her head.

"He's a bunnyip," I said, throwing out my hands.

"Raw prawns!"

"No, think about it. All that boogeyman stuff up there in the Top End started when he went up to take pictures."

Maggie shook her head in disbelief.

I should explain that the bunnyip is sort of an Aussie Loch Ness monster and Bigfoot rolled into one, with a little UFO thrown in for good measure. One or two good sightings a year is normal. But in the last couple weeks there'd been a dozen or more, all of them up in the Northern Territory, all within several miles of the Ularu Occupied Lands and Killian Development Property. Even then nobody showed much interest until an old woman got dragged into the desert while she and her husband were sightseeing up near the Devil's Marbles and the old man decided it must have been a bunnyip. After that, folks in the Territory began locking their doors at night.

"It's bun-yip," she chided me. "Not bunny-ip. And they don't change back and forth like werewolves."

"They don't?"

"No, you nit."

"Well," I said in disgust, "there goes my big story."

I took Maggie's arm and escorted her forward where a hundred or so 11″ by 14″ color prints rested on tripod stands in

neat rows atop a platform stage. The stage was roped off except
for a front center stairway carpeted in wine-colored shag. Only
a brass chain kept us from ascending this stair before twelve
o'clock.

A number of lamps had been suspended from the ceiling
directly over the displays to provide natural lighting. But most
of these were turned down. The photographs themselves stood
in near darkness.

Almost on the dot of three the lights waxed into brilliance. As
one, we newsmen turned to the platform and there stood a
black-tie-and-tail'd Arthur Copley surrounded by his pictorial
display. The truth is, he didn't look much like a bunyip. On the
other hand, he also didn't look much like a spelunker. He was
too old and too fat to go sneaking around Ularu Occupied Lands,
scrambling inside a legendary cavern—the existence of which
was only a rumor and its whereabouts a centuries-old mystery—
and high-tailing it back with snapshots of ancient rock paintings
dating back untold thousands of years. But if he didn't do it he
was sure grabbing a lot of credit from the guy who did.

Now Copley had a microphone in one hand. The other was
raised like a circus ringmaster's.

Journos pressed forward.

I spotted Mutt and Jeff making a place for themselves near the
platform and knew I'd missed my chance to see Mutt boost the
little shrimp on his shoulders.

Suddenly Copley's baritone filled the auditorium.

"Ladies and gentlemen of the press!"

We fell silent.

"It gives me great pleasure," he boomed, "to present this
advance showing of my fabulous photographs."

I whispered to Maggie, "—reprints of which will be on sale
at his studio by the first of next week."

"Hush."

Copley paused. "And now . . . welcome, one and all, to the
Dreamtime! Let us travel together through the millennia of Aus-

tralia's farflung past. To a time when dark hominids and eerie beasts roamed a lush landscape of—"

The audience's silence ended abruptly.

"How did you foind the bloody cave, mate?" blurted an ABC reporter.

"Ey," called out another. "Is it true them Ularu 'as put a curse on yer 'ead?"

Welcome, I thought, to the irreverent Aussie press.

Copley's hand was up again.

"Please, gentlemen, please," he pleaded. "I'll be glad to answer your questions after the showing."

Someone shouted from the back:

"Any o' them cannibals try to eat ye, mate?"

Before long everyone was barking out questions. Except me. I thought about asking him what the hell I was doing at his crummy art show, but I decided he wouldn't know any more than I did.

"Gentlemen, gentlemen, please," said Copley, "Hold your questions. I'm a dealer in art, not a peddler of fantasies. I can assure you—"

He stopped assuring us.

Bit by bit the decibel level came down.

One by one, heads had turned to the opposite side of the stage.

Copley turned too.

Maggie clutched my sleeve.

A tall bony figure, black as licorice and wearing a hideous face mask, had appeared from a side chamber.

Except for a swath of wallaby hide around his waist he was naked. His skeletal arms and legs—long and narrow and dark— were covered by nothing but white stripes which made him look even more like a walking skeleton. His bare chest was criss-crossed by the same white paint.

His mask was the kicker. It appeared to be carved out of wood. The eyes gleamed. The mouth was a vicious gaping maw. And the ears stuck out six inches on each side of the thing. It would have been right at home crowning some very tall totem pole.

He was a frightening spectacle and a flamboyant figure if I ever saw one.

At first I thought he was part of the show. Something Copley'd cooked up for excitement.

To make a splash in the headlines.

But no.

One look at Copley's face was enough to make me forget that idea.

I turned back. Like everyone else I found it hard to look away.

His hands weren't hands at all but furry gloves which had claws for fingers. In his left he held a bone, a long white human femur bone was my guess. In his right he held some kind of talisman.

He let the drama go on until utter silence had fallen over us.

Then slowly, he extended a slender arm and an equally slender hand and shook the talisman in Copley's direction.

"Yoo know the why I come!" he said in a full baritone with plenty of volume behind it.

"How did you get in here?" Copley barked into his microphone. Even with the amplifier to back him up his words didn't go through us as the aborigine's had.

"Yoo know the why, Copley. For yoo have offended the Dreamtime spirits."

"You can't frighten me!"

I looked back when I heard Copley say that and I said to myself, *the hell he can't, buster, you're scared stiff!* He wasn't alone. I got a glimpse of Mutt and Jeff watching with their eyes as big as silver dollars and I figured they were both scared out of their wits. But then don't forget, they were halfwits, so they didn't have as far to go as the rest of us.

"Your name has been sung," the skeleton figure shouted and this time his left hand extended pointing the bone like a pistol at Copley's head.

"The *kadi makara* are angry!" he cried. "The *kadi makara* will have their revenge." And then he started speaking in aborigine: "*Nogatu ki tonanu ano lo tehano kadi makara naru bori!*"

I tried to get the sounds down on paper. Of course the radio and TV stations were recording everything.

"*Ngai toki wota poturu yana dai dai otye.*" That's the best I can do. He jabbed the bone at Copley one last time. "*Tobraka* turn loose the beast that it may devour his body," he hissed.

And then he wound up his right arm and threw the talisman across the room. If he was aiming for Copley he missed. The thing landed right at my feet.

I heard Copley asking for someone to fetch the security people but he was too late. I bent down to pick the talisman off the floor and when I looked up the flamboyant figure had booked. His bony arms and legs were flying through the doors to the foyer.

The place started buzzing.

In my hands I held an animal skull about the size of a cat's with—at a guess—emu feathers stuffed into the mouth and eye sockets and the whole thing wrapped in string.

"All right, all right," Copley's voice called over the public address. "An unfortunate interruption but it's over now."

Copley turned his gaze to me.

I thought he wanted the darned talisman. Maggie, too. "Better toss it to him," she said. So I did. I lobbed it onto the stage.

That's when all hell broke loose.

Pow!

The stage—Copley, the pictures . . . everything—exploded! Like a volcano. The whole platform erupted in a huge column of fire; flames shot as high as the ceiling. I was standing twenty feet away and I felt like I'd just stuck my head in a blast furnace. I threw my arms in front of my face. A lot of other people, those who hadn't fallen down or turned away from the explosion, were doing the same thing.

Maggie had fallen. I picked her up and wrapped my arms around her, keeping my back to the inferno.

I heard her cry: "Oh, Blue, look!"

I looked around, through a living curtain of flames, and saw Arthur Copley turn into a torch. He was living too, but not for long.

He screamed. The scream of the damned.

I'd never heard anything like it.

I hope I never do again.

But there was no saving him. When he fell to the stage floor we couldn't even see him any longer and most of us had stopped looking. There was a general exodus for the doors, not orderly.

Almost immediately the flames ignited the drapes behind the platform; they leaped for the ceiling. I heard the hiss and felt the spray of the automatic sprinklers coming on but I knew it was too little too late.

Everyone was screaming by that time.

I grabbed Maggie's hand and together we raced into the foyer, past the security guard's table and toward the front entrance stair.

Smoke was already spilling out of the auditorium behind us. Alarms were going off. The whole place was a madhouse.

As I raced arm in arm with Maggie toward the main doors I heard:

"Stop, you!"

I looked around and saw my rent-a-cop pal pumping his arms behind me.

"Come on, Maggie," I shouted. "Let's amscray."

The guard locked eyes on me and raised his pistol in the air.

But he didn't shoot.

And I didn't stop.

I bounded from the opera house with him still screaming to the crowd:

"Somebody stop that thinny red-headed bloke!"

2

Two-Up and Away

I'll have to leave Maggie alone in front of the opera house, give Mister Flamboyant a little head start, and hope my rent-a-cop pal doesn't miss me too much, while I go back and help the rest of you catch up. Copley's murder was the second crime I witnessed that day. The first one was only a misdemeanor, but it was responsible for my getting kicked off my big story and so it shouldn't be overlooked. Maggie will wait. As for flame-boy getting away or the rent-a-cop nailing me, no sweat. I'm the one wearing tennis shoes and runners run in my family, too.

Golden Australian-style sunlight flashed over Sydney's glass towers which rose into a cobalt Australian-style sky.

It was June. Winter in Australia but still very warm. The past summer—they call it The Wet—wasn't, but it sure was hot. And now winter—called The Dry—was, and heating up more and more as we counted down the days.

Horns sounded as I jaywalked across town.

No one I passed looked me in the eye. All people did these days was check a man's skin color before hurrying on their way.

Everybody, it seemed, was up in arms. It wasn't just blacks against whites even though that's the way it played out in the foreign press. Most of the rural folks were in Killian's corner, true enough, but a lot of people here in the cities of the east coast were sympathetic to the aborigine position. Greenies, the Australian conservationists, had announced their support. So had other minority groups.

None of that mattered.

Killian was white; the Ularu were black.

The Minister of Aboriginal Affairs, an aborigine, had brought
suit against Killian on behalf of the Ularu tribe. Australia's quarter of a million aboriginal citizens stood firmly behind them.
That's the point. For the first time since Captain Cook dropped
anchor in Botany Bay, thousands of native tribes scattered across
the continent had united in a common rage. The Ularu's cause
was hopeless and they knew it. Every day brought fresh assur-
ances that the High Court would have to rule against them. This
only made them angrier. The country had become a time bomb
with a six-day detonator. Nobody could stop it.

All anyone could do was find a hole to hide in. An oasis and
bomb shelter in one.

Fortunately, there's one on every street corner.

I headed for ours—the Black Stump, a typical basement beer-
ateria in the Sydney city centre. Inside, the temperature dropped
ten degrees C. The atmosphere turned friendly too. I gave the
barmaid a smile and a "guhday" and made straight for the rear
of the room. Past the bar, the booths and the dart boards, all the
way to the back where a game of Two-Up—though strictly
illegal these days—was going full swing.

No less than a dozen Aussies stood in a circle calling out
wagers and waving their fists or their bets in the air. Their heads
rose in unison as the two shiny coins flew, and their twelve
heads fell as one when the coins hit the floor.

In the unnatural silence that followed I heard my footsteps
along the wooden floor and the pennies spinning round and
round as I got closer. But the silence ended abruptly. I could
count half a dozen Bloody-this or Bleedin' that and an equal
number of Beauts and Sweets! Money changed hands. More bets
got made, the coins flew again, and twelve heads rose and fell.

I pushed through the outer circle. And because that's where
I found my two bosses, I might as well introduce them.

Percival Newman and Alvin Cockie could hardly have been
more unalike in appearance or character . . . from each other or
anyone else. Meet "Percy" Newman, the *spinner,* now aligning

two pennies on the end of his wooden kip. He's a university fossil, all bones and brains, a former professor with a post-Oxford accent. Next, say hello to "Alf" Cockie, the fat man kneeling beside him—today, as all days, the game's *ringer*. For settling any disputes which arise he gets ten percent of the winnings and occasional spirits. Alvin Cockie is a one-time bushranger, a some-time sheep shearer, and an all-time ocker whose brogue is as broad as his belly.

"Roight!" he called out. "Chuck'em up."

Newman held the loaded kip over his head and flicked it so that the coins popped even higher before falling straight down between his feet and Cockie's.

One of the coins landed almost immediately heads up. I could tell that without stooping because the engraving of Queen Elizabeth had been burnished so brightly it gleamed.

The other exposed its dull side, bearing a likeness of the feather-tailed glider, Australia's smallest marsupial.

Cockie called for a rethrow with all the pompousness of Solomon. The coins must land both heads or both tails up to win. Everyone knew this. But Cockie was earning his beer.

Newman scooped them onto his kip as some of the Aussies groused about the "new money." The old English pennies were bigger and heavier, they recalled, and didn't float like the new ones. I smiled when I recognized the voices—two fellow journos named Mickey and Nevil who were hardly older than me and who had still been in diapers when the pounds-pence system got converted to dollars.

I tapped Cockie's shoulder.

He turned. "Ey, Blue!"

Let me get this "Blue" stuff cleared up before I go any farther. That's what they call people like me. I've got blue eyes, yes, but that has nothing to do with it. It's the red hair. Red heads are called Blue. I don't understand it myself. I said:

"I've heard you've got two seats on a cargo plane going up to the Top End."

"That's roight."

"Who's the lucky neophyte?"

"Oo?"

Before I could answer, the hubbub of bets won and lost drowned me out. I waited for silence.

"Who's going to sit at the master's side?" I said. "To transcribe his wisdom for the masses; to bask in the warmth of his radiance, carry his bags and shoo away the riffraff who flock at his feet?"

Cockie contorted his face in confusion.

"Who's coming with me?" I snapped.

"Mickey and Nevil are leavin' this arvo."

"What!"

"Mickey and Nevil are—"

"What about me . . . !?"

"There's only two seats."

"You're not sending me! I don't believe it!"

"Ey, but Mickey 'n' Nevil've been ta the outback before 'n' you 'aven't. They know 'ow to handle them aborigines up there. 'Ow ta talk to 'em. You don't. It's no plyce fer an outsider loike you, Blue."

In the clamor of voices that followed and the flurry of money changing hands I looked across the circle. Mickey and Nevil were raking in cash.

"Mickey Fine," I said, "took a holiday to Alice Springs when he was eight years old; Nevil Cross played Aussie Rules in the bush league. That doesn't make them Daniel Boone and Davy Crockett." I hated myself for saying that because the fact was I had nothing against either man.

Mickey had a club foot, and his left eye didn't see eye to eye with his right but he could turn out a tale if he had to. His chum Nevil stopped playing football when a soft spot on the side of his skull had forced him out of the sport. He also had a soft spot for tattoos and plenty of spots to sport them. Still, he was house-broken and completely loyal, and I liked him. But it was *my* story.

Newman, waiting a signal from the ringer to toss, began looking from Cockie and me to the other two journos.

I could have appealed to him if I'd wanted to go over Cockie's head but of course I never would.

Technically speaking Newman was bureau chief and Cockie was second in command but in fact the two men ran the Sydney branch of Eastern News Association much like the Australian government. Cockie was prime minister. He made ninety percent of the decisions. Newman, like the governor-general—the ENA's (not the queen's) representative—stepped in when things got out of hand. The two men were "cobbers." Mates.

Like Nevil and Mickey.

"They've been around the aborigines all their loives," Cockie said.

"So?"

"They can deal with 'em."

"That's silly."

"Ye don't know, Blue. They don't think loike you an' I do. Not logical. If ye don't know 'ow to handle 'em ye can woind up karked. But it's not jist the aborigines. It's the land. The heat. The vast distances. No water. No conveniences. And no second chances. If ye knew wot it was loike up there, ye wouldna be wantin' to go."

But I did. Want to go, that is. I waited while Cockie oversaw a toss and then I went after him again. I was determined.

Suddenly Cockie did the unexpected. He called to Nevil and Mickey. "Ey, Doyle 'ere wants to tyke yer plyce on the floight, mates. There's only one w'y to settle it. What'll ye 'ave, 'eads or t'iles."

I started to interrupt but Mickey cut me off.

"Heads," he said smiling.

Nevil smiled too and nodded. "Heads, it is."

"Chuck 'em up, Percy."

Newman didn't like it any more than I did but he went along all the same.

The two coins went up, fell down, spun. When the first lay over wobbling with its dull side showing Cockie reached across quickly and scooped them both up. "Illegal throw," he snapped, playing Solomon again. "A bit 'oigher, Percy."

Newman retossed.

The next thing I knew the two coins were lying on the floor with their brightly polished heads staring me in the eyes. I'd lost the pot to a pair of queens.

"You can't do this, Alvie."

"Now cop it sweet," chided Cockie. "No bloke loikes a whinger."

Cockie swept his eyes round the group and for a second I thought he was going to poll the blokes to see if any of them liked a whinger—whatever that was. But all he said was: " 'Oose shout is it then, ey?"

"Yorse, Alf," called Mickey.

"Roight you are!" Cockie lofted a fat fist to signal the barmaid, " 'Another round over here!" He looked inquisitively at me: "You'll join us in a turp, won't ye, Blue?"

"No."

"Per'aps a middy then?" he said, holding up a thumb and forefinger spread ten ounces apart. "Or a shandy."

"I'm quitting, Alvie."

Horror twisted his face. "Ye're quitting the grog!"

"No, I'm quitting this job." I started to push through the circle.

Newman moved to block my way. "Now don't act hastily, Doyle."

"Ye can't quit," said Cockie.

"Give me one good reason."

"If you quit," Newman replied, "you'll have to leave the country. That's the law."

"Besides," said Cockie. 'Oo'd we get to cover that art show?"

My voice rose an octave.

"Art show! You're pulling me off this story to do an art show? Anybody in the office could handle that."

"There ayn't no one in the office," said Cockie.

"Alf's right," agreed Newman. He stopped talking and I moved aside as the barmaid showed up with a tray of pint mugs. "We sent Peter to Canberra to cover those riots," he said, eying with delight the vessels of chilled amber fluid being passed around.

"And Duff drove down to The Gong," added Cockie, placing a wad of orange and brown, and green and yellow Aussie notes on her tray. "That leaves the art show fer you."

"The art show," I replied, "has nothing to do with the story."

"Sure it 'as," Cockie assured me. "It's a sacred thing, just loike the land. Them Ularu don't want us whites lookin' at their 'oly paintin's any more 'an they want the loikes of Rush Killian runnin' beef an' punchin' 'oles in their 'oly ground."

"Sidebar stuff."

"Not 'ny more. They've boasted their ancient spirits won't allow the pictures to be shown. They've said Arthur Copley will pay with 'is life fer trespassing in that cave and taking those photos. Don't ye see, Blue? It's like a test of their power. And what 'appens at that art show can make all the difference to Killian's mob 'cause they've put the same curse on 'im."

"I thought you didn't believe in the curse."

"I don't."

"Or ancient spirits."

"Roight. But them aborigines do. A lot more'n they believe in our legal system."

Newman laid a hand on my shoulder: "Be honest, Doyle; who's the best journo in Sydney?"

"That's easy," I said. "I am. But even if I was twice as good as you think I am, which is half as good as I think I am, I still couldn't dig up anything at that art show that was worth sending out on the wire."

"A good reporter has to do more than dig," said Newman. "He must recognize a gemstone in the rough. He has to know how to cut it. Grind it. Polish it. Only then does he end up with a jewel. You think you're the best journo in Sydney. Very well, the art show's right here in Sydney. This development business now, the spooks and ancient spirits, that's so far out in the outback it's beyond—"

"It's the back o' beyond," added Cockie.

Newman pressed the point home:

"Killian's got himself a thousand square kilometers of desert surrounded by a million square kilometers of desert. There's nothing up there but roos and aborigines. Why not let Mickey and Nevil handle that end of it, Doyle? You can cover the art show."

"Ey," said Cockie hefting the schooner to his lips and inhaling the aroma: "The art show, that's yer cuppa."

As Maggie and I reached the Cove Road in front of the opera house, I looked back over my shoulder to see plumes of vile darkish smoke spiraling up off the opera house roof. It belched out the doors.

People by the hundreds swelled onto the road behind us. Many were coughing and gasping for breath.

Maggie pulled me around.

"You knew . . . !" she was shouting. "You knew all along, didn't you?"

"I did not!"

"Then why's that wowser chasing after you, ey? And why are you runnin' away?"

I stopped.

The security guard was ploughing toward us through the still growing mass of newsmen, art patrons and tourists. He hadn't caught sight of us yet but he would pretty soon if we didn't get moving. There wasn't time to explain how things are. I may not be a fighter but I am a reporter and I never run away from a story. So I told her, "I'm not running—I'm chasing. Did you see where he went?"

"You mean. . . ?"

"That aborigine—witch doctor, whatever. He was ahead of us leaving the building!."

"He's not here." Maggie scanned the sea of frightened faces. "He must've run into the park, ey?"

She turned wild eyes to me. "But, Blue, we can't just shoot through. That guard thinks you had something to do with this mess. What was that thingo you threw at Copley? What made it blow up?"

"Search me!"

"You've got to explain."

I pulled a twenty-cent copper coin from my pocket.

"Okay then, I'll toss you for it. Heads, we head after the witch doctor. Tails, I'll turn in my tail to that guard and try to talk our way out it. Fair enough?"

A toss had gotten me pulled off this story and a toss could by-god! get me back on.

Maggie nodded.

I spun the coin high, caught it with the right hand and slapped it onto the back of my left. "Here you go," I said, holding my wrist out for Maggie to see. "You're the witness. What is it?"

"It's a duck-bill platypus."

"I know it's a duck-bill platypus!" I shouted, "I mean is it heads or tails."

"It's t'iles."

"That settles it," I said. "We tail the witch doctor."

Maggie's eyes radiated excitement. "Ye'll take me with you?"

Suddenly the guard spotted me. He began pushing people aside to get to us. He was calling, "Hey, you!" at the top of his lungs and, "Somebody grab that man, there; he started the fire!"

"Please, Blue."

I told her to take the Circular Quay Road and that I'd check out the park. "Meet you at the traffic circle."

With that I dove into the shrubbery.

This may be a good time to explain that I'm no fan of wilderness. The hundred acres of the Royal Botanic Gardens south of the opera house on Bennelong Point is the biggest park in the city. As far as I'm concerned trees belong in the forest; any park you can't see across is a jungle; and if it hasn't got thoroughfares, stoplights, signposts, and sidewalks . . . it's got no business inside the city limits.

Mother Mulligan's boy Doyle is no eagle scout. I crashed into a hedge of thornbushes, fell over it head first, landed on my hands and knees, rolled, sprang to my feet and dashed on again without breaking stride.

Shrubbery and trees hemmed me in on all sides. Wattles, coolabah, eucalyptus, and gum trees. Suddenly I pushed through some bushes and there, right in front of me was Government House, surrounded by manicured lawns and flower beds. And people.

Pencil pushers, tall poppies, and pollies were pouring out of the building. Rushing toward me. They were staring wide-eyed and pointing over the treetops at the thunderhead of smoke mushrooming over the opera house.

I could hear distant sirens now.

Government Drive was empty. The lawns to the south, east and west of Government House were bare. If he'd run that way he was long gone. But I didn't think he had. He couldn't have risked being seen by all those suits and ties.

I took a deep breath and dove back into the garden.

Before I got near the western boundary I'd used up that breath and a lot more just like it, falling into flowerbeds, hurdling hedges and tripping over tree roots.

I almost tripped over the mask.

It was lying right there on the ground at the base of a large tree. I picked it up. In the bole of the tree, where the wood was hollowed out, I found his clawed gloves and the white bone, too. It was ten to one he'd had clothes waiting for him there. He'd left

the park wearing western attire and no one was the wiser. I
stuffed the mask back in the hole, with the idea of coming back
for it later.

That's when I heard Maggie calling.

Her voice was coming from the other side of a thicket. It was
too thick to see through. But it was also too wide to hike around
and too high to jump over. I guess I wasn't thinking too clearly
by that time. I just lowered my head and plunged inside, grabbing at the sharp, thorny branches and pulling myself through.
My head poked out. Then my arms and shoulders came free and
I fell to the ground along with an afterbirth of broken twigs and
leaves.

"Are you all right, Blue?"

With Maggie's help I staggered to my feet. Then she steadied
me with a hand on my arm.

Fleets of fire engines were screaming by us. Ladder trucks,
pumpers, cherry pickers, and ambulances. Cars weaved among
them and each other ignoring those threnodic sirens and horn
blasts. Pedestrians filled the sidewalks. More people were now
rushing toward the scene of the fire than were trying to get away.
Many had tears in their eyes. Smoke can do that and so can
seeing the loss of a treasured landmark when you know it's only
the first of many to be lost. That it's only the beginning.

Out on Jackson Pond a Harbour-Sights ferry loaded with
tourists had anchored off shore, front row seats to see the opera
house burn. Those guys were getting their ten dollars worth. A
motor sailer joined them and other vessels were heading that
way.

But some couldn't wait. Scheduled ferries were making for or
leaving the nearby quay, jetcats were revving their rocket-like
engines for the high-speed run to Manly. Out of sight but not far
away were the underground subway and overhead monorail
which shuttled people around the city—a city of three and a half
million people, or one out of every four on the continent, living
in a metropolitan area larger than London or greater New York.

Somewhere out there was my witch doctor.

"We've lost him," said Maggie.

"Oh, no we haven't," I snapped. "Now he's in my park."

I raced down to the ferry piers with Maggie hanging on to my tail. In three blocks we reached the south end where Sydney Cove and Port Jackson meet the downtown.

There were five piers. Each pier had assigned ferries currently boarding, debarking, coming or going. From here he could get to any of a dozen destinations in and around Port Jackson. But that wasn't all. The Cahill Expressway thundered as hundreds of cars every second blew by overhead heading to the eastern suburbs or north across the Sydney Harbour Bridge. Below, the Circular Quay Railway Station, part of the loop that serviced downtown traffic, could have taken him anywhere in the downtown. He might have picked up a cab from that taxi rank down the street, strolled onto a busy avenue and lost himself in a shopping arcade, or just stepped behind any one of hundreds of columns holding up the overpass and waited for me to go by.

I'd just sent Maggie across the street to look around when I spotted a soaring black-skinned athlete leaping off the pier and onto a departing ferry. The guy looked as out of place in his jacket and tie as . . . as he'd looked thirty minutes ago when I'd watched him arguing with the security guard.

"Over there!" I shouted.

By the time Maggie came running over the ferry was already well out in the pond, heading for the Harbour Bridge whose single long span and immense trussed arch had earned it the nickname Coat Hanger.

"Where's it going?" she demanded between breaths.

"That's the Darling Harbour ferry," I said. "Come on!"

I passed up a City Service cab because they don't have radios and flagged down a DeLuxe that was across the street. We hopped in, told the hackie to beat it to Darling Harbour, and I added, "if you make it fast, you'll get your best tip of the week." I didn't settle back. As the cab headed south, I said, "No, no, take

York Street to Market. It'll be faster this time of day. We'll use the walkway. Hurry!"

"You'll get there," he said, easing out into traffic, but the notion of a fast blast through town didn't seem to arouse him. I pulled out a wad of bills and peeled off a violet-colored fiver. Aussie money looks like something out of a Monopoly box and no bills sport the faces of politicians. Aussies don't care much for pollies. More often than not they vote against whoever's in office just to . . . "give the other mob a go." The guy who incited the Rum Rebellion got his phiz on the two dollar bill. On the five is a naturalist and explorer who sailed here with Captain Cook. A World War I aviator's mug is on the twenty.

I stuck the five over the seat and introduced the cabby to the explorer. "This is my friend Joe Banks," I said. "He likes to go places."

The cabby's lips curled into a sneer.

"It'll be more than that, myte," he said without taking his eyes off the road.

I peeled a red and yellow bill off my roll. A twenty. I showed him the aviator's profile. "This is Colonel Smith," I said with feeling, "another friend of mine. He likes to fly."

We took off.

Unfortunately, his initial burst of speed didn't last.

I told him I had other friends in my pocket who wanted to meet him and would he please call up his dispatcher and order a cab sent to the Darling Harbour ferry pier as fast as it could get there.

He reached for the handset.

"Who's it for?"

"For me."

He glared over the seat.

"But I'm takin' ye there, myte. Wot d'ye need another cab for?"

"Because I'm not sure," I growled, "that you're gonna get me there in time to pick me up!"

He thought that one over, decided that I was either a lot
deeper or a lot more dangerous than I looked, and made the call.

"Tell the driver he's to keep his eyes peeled for an aboriginal
man who's getting off the ferry, wearing a suit, upwards of seven
feet, two hundred pounds plus. See where he goes and then wait
for me to get there."

"Abo. . . ? What's going on?"

"Just do it."

As I sat back Maggie whispered to me:

"You're very clever, aren't you."

I smiled. "I try to hide it, but . . . I'm only human."

She humphed loudly.

"If that was s'posed to sound 'umble, it f'iled."

"Oh, humility," I said; ". . . that goes without saying."

We moved through the downtown. Slowly. Barring Los Angeles, the ratio of cars to people is higher in Sydney than anywhere else in the world; traffic here is the worst bar none.

It seemed to me we were losing a lot of road to other vehicles.
When the cabby slowed down to let another driver merge near
the Sydney Stock Exchange I said, "Can't this bucket go any
faster?" and he replied that it couldn't because it had "a gove'-
nor." I decided what the car had should be called a prime
minister, because it seemed to be making at least ninety percent
of the decisions. When we neared Wynyard Park, a jungle from
the north or south but not so intimidating from the east side, and
the cabby passed up a hole my mother could've pulled a bus
into, and then, if you can believe it! stood on his brakes at a
yellow light, I offered to get out and push. He didn't answer.
Finally, as we crawled under the monorail at the State Theater,
I cried, "Watch out for that old lady with the walker," and the
dope looked around like he expected to see her. "Where?
Where?" he asked, "Is she gonna hit me?" "No," I replied
blandly, "She's passing you."

With a tug on my jacket, Maggie pulled me back against the

seat. For the rest of the run I just sat there glaring at the darn cabby in the rearview mirror.

He could've turned right on the red down Market Street, which is one way, but he waited for the green light instead. "I'm not really a slow driver," he explained when I made the suggestion—about turning, I mean—"it's just that I'm not a fast driver."

"Let's agree you're a half-fast driver," I muttered.

By then I was pissed off. The ferry had already landed and the witch doctor was getting farther away every second.

Needless to say by the time he dropped us off in front of the Western Distributor walkway, it was all I could do to keep my mouth shut. But then, before I'd taken two steps, he called me back, pushed his palm out the window, and reminded me I'd promised to let him meet some more of my friends.

I dug into a pocket. I placed a copper nickel in his hand, the queen's face down and the little echidna face up. "This," I said, "is my friend Icky. He likes to crawl."

I don't expect you to believe this but the guy left ten feet of rubber when he took off.

Maggie and I raced over the pedestrian walkway. The curb in front of the Sydney Aquarium and ferry pier was as bare as a church pew on Melbourne Cup day.

"Looks like it didn't work," Maggie observed.

I jumped to a telephone, called the DeLuxe dispatcher and read her the riot act. But she already knew about the act; she'd read it and seen the movie, too. She quoted it chapter and verse. My taxi had been dispatched as ordered. It had checked in at the pier. It had picked up the fare.

"Where did they go?"

"Central Station," she said.

"Can you get another cab over here on the double?"

She assured me she had cars in the immediate vicinity and hung up.

I passed on the news to Maggie who stood grim-faced, watching the sky grow darker and darker as the smoke piled high above Bennelong Point.

"Oh, Blue!" she sobbed.

"Forget it. We've got work to do."

I called the Black Stump.

When the bartender answered, I told him to let me talk to Alvie fast. I listened to mugs hitting the bartop, news of the fire being shouted over orders for beer, Two-Up bets won and lost, and I told myself not for the first time that this was the problem with operating a press business out of a pub. Telephone service is lousy.

Suddenly Cockie's voice was in my ear.

"Ye bloody yank! What're ye up to? Did ye know every bleedin' walloper in Sydney is after—"

"It's okay, Alvie," I told him, "I've dug something up. But before I start grinding and polishing, I'm cutting out."

"Where d'ye think ye're going?"

"I think I'm going up to the Ularu Occupied Lands, but I won't know for sure 'til I get there—no, just listen up. Who do you know over at the Central Terminal?"

"Wot's that? Central Stytion?"

"Ticket sales."

"Patty Walker. 'E's head of ticket sales. But ye—"

"Call him up, pronto. Tell him there's an aborigine coming in to buy a ticket. Tall, very dark, and athletic looking. I want to know where he's going and, if possible, get two tickets on the same train. The same car would make it even nicer. Be sure to tell him Eastern News is picking up the tab. I'll be there in fifteen minutes to claim 'em."

He was still sputtering when I rang off.

Our wheels pulled to the curb and as I led Maggie over I was practically strutting. Of course I'd told Cockie and Newman I couldn't get a lead from the art show even if I was twice as good as they thought I was, not even if I was half as good as I thought

I was. But I'd forgotten to allow for the possibility that I was fully as good as I thought I was, which apparently I was.

I opened the back door of the cab, took one look at the driver, and froze.

It was him—my half-fast friend.

"Not yoo!" he said after one look at me. " 'Oike."

I shoved Maggie in quick.

"No, no, it's all right," I said jumping in beside her. Maggie smiled as I peeled a twenty off my roll and handed it over. "I made a mistake," I told him with my jaw clamped so tightly it ached. "About little Icky, I mean. I realize now there are times when you have to crawl."

"Well . . . where're ye goin'?"

"We need to get to Central Station the fastest way—"

His glare stopped me.

"—but," I said, "we'll settle for a half-fast way."

That's the way we went.

3

Indian Pacific

The final call came for the Indian Pacific as we ran to the passenger platform. It was bare except for an oncoming stream of redcaps wheeling their empty baggage dollies back to the station hall. All the other passengers had boarded.

I swept my eyes down the length of gleaming carriages.

The Indian Pacific.

Australia's Orient Express.

My ticket book was stamped "Adelaide." Just over a thousand miles west of Sydney on the southern coast of South Australia was Adelaide. It's another thousand miles north by air to Alice Springs, and four hundred more by road to the Ularu Occupied Lands where I was sure the witch doctor would lead us. This was only the beginning.

The departure time flashed on the indicator board: 16:30 . . . 16:30 . . . 16:30 . . . NO DELAY.

A whistle blew.

We found Car 89 midway among the first class sleepers. Maggie hopped aboard first. When I grabbed a stanchion and pulled myself up I could feel the hum of the locomotive far ahead.

From the vestibule at the head of the carriage I passed into a corridor and gave my ticket coupon another look.

"Single Roomette," it said, "Car 89; Compartment Four." Maggie stopped at Compartment Three.

I found Four half way along the corridor. But I didn't go in. The door to Six was standing open but Five, Seven and Eight were closed. I kept going. There were just the eight compartments, but also shower closets for SHEilas and HEilos at the far end. When I reached the vestibule that led to the next carriage I turned around and headed back. Passing Eight this time I leaned against the wood paneling. No voices, no sounds. Nothing.

Just then I spotted Maggie sticking her head out of her compartment.

I moved quickly back to Four and went in.

My roomette was a compact affair in plastic wood-grain veneer. It had a Pullman-style bed above the settee, a two-by-three window with a panoramic view of the passenger platform and a wardrobe that doubled as a linen cupboard. In the corner by the door was a miniature "ensuite" complete with a sink, mirror and commode but no shower—the shower, a poster informed me, was located at the rear of the carriage, as I'd already discovered for myself.

A full-length mirror hung from a third door across from the seat between the wardrobe and the toilet. This door led to the adjoining compartment.

I knocked. It slid aside at once. There stood Maggie grinning like a kid at the circus. I grinned back and told her:

"We'll have to start meeting like this."

She waved me inside.

Her berth was a mirror image of mine. I looked it over but didn't overlook Maggie.

"Isn't this to die, Blue?"

I agreed that it was. Nothing, I observed, compared to seeing the Sydney Opera House burn down, but still, more fun than an art show.

Her smile evaporated. "Do you think it has? Burned down, I mean."

I was instantly sorry I'd said it.

"Maybe not. The fire crews got there pretty fast."

Without warning the train lurched. The two of us fell back onto the seat.

Maggie squealed with delight. She put an arm around my shoulder and gave me a squeeze. I took it for a big-brother little-sister kind of squeeze; after all we were just fellow journos out to grab the big scoop.

With a couple more lurches the train started rolling out of the station. We sat there as it gathered momentum, not talking, just listening to the clacking of the wheels, feeling the sway of the coach, and watching the high-rises of south Sydney, Ultimo, and Surry Hills glide by.

"You're quite a girl," I said, "to come on a trip like this without so much as a toothbrush."

She shrugged. But I could see the reality of the thing was just now catching up with her excitement.

"It'd be a lot more fun if we had a change of clothes and some toiletries," I said, adding quickly, "Of course we can pick some things up in Adelaide."

She nodded. "Maybe sooner. I'll ask the attendant."

"Good idea. Get a feel for the guy. I'm gonna hit him up about checking out our *flame*boyant friend. He can do it without arousing any suspicions."

"That man frightens me."

"He scares me too. That's why we'll let the attendant do it."

"What do you mean, check him out?"

"Just see that he's there and if so, with whom."

"You think he may have someone else with him?"

I shrugged.

"Alvie's friend said he asked for that compartment. But it connects with Seven just as these two connect. I'd like to know, that's all. Anyway it won't hurt to have somebody else on our side, too."

Unfortunately it didn't work out that way.

The attendant turned out to be a miniature version of the witch doctor, a cocoa-colored half-pint with a chocolate chip on his shoulder. Actually he was half-blood, somewhere between chocolate milk and milk chocolate but there were no half measures about where he stood on the question of black/white relations. He took one look at me and saw milk. Skim milk maybe, but one hundred per cent, Grade A, pasteurized, homogenized, vitamin A and D fortified milk.

I heard him leave Maggie's room. He knocked on my door and before I opened up Maggie popped her head in through the connecting door to give me the bad news.

She was right.

The guy looked as agreeable as chocolate cheese. With a sneer he informed me that the buffet car, which was seven cars ahead, would begin serving at five o'clock. Meanwhile the club car, four cars up, he said, would open at six. If we cared to enjoy a formal dinner, the dining car, which was right behind the buffet car, would open at seven. Was there anything he could do for me?

He was really giving me the once over.

"Eat, up seven at five; drink, up four at six; dine, up six at seven. Right?"

"Yessir." More sneer. "Will there be anything else?"

I said forget it.

Don't get me wrong, I've got nothing against chocolate. It'd be a bland world if vanilla was the only flavor around. Olive is nice, and cinammon is spice, and butterscotch is . . . well, I almost married her but no dice. However. The chocolate chip was more likely to tell flameboy about Maggie and me than he was to tell us about him. If you follow my antecedents.

When the attendant left me, the Indian Pacific was flying through a kind of hinterland, neither city nor bush but a sparsely populated zone between Sydney's outskirts and the outback.

Before long the suburbs of Sydney had fallen behind us. Aboriginal and English villages rolled past. Ashfield and Flemington, Blacktown and then Emu Plains. Sheep farms soon dominated the countryside. To the south lay Lake Burragorang and Warragamba Dam. They were places I'd read about but had never seen. The railroad followed the Great Western Highway through the Blue Mountains into the vast, mostly uninhabited and largely uninhabitable interior.

Maggie came in with a drink she'd ordered from the club car. I was looking her over again. What had she done to her hair? Nothing, she replied. She'd just combed it. It was long and golden, the color of Australian sunlight. However it did things sunlight doesn't do.

Her eyes were cobalt, the color of the Australian sky.

I guessed she'd touched up her mascara and lipstick at the same time for her lashes were darker than I remembered, her lips were fuller and redder, and my mouth was drier. She was also wearing a scent which may or may not have been French but definitely wasn't Australian.

"What's this?" I asked of the glass pressed in my mitt.

"Rum. Didn't you have your hand out?"

"Oh that," I said; "that was my tongue."

"Lap this up first."

I took the drink and we ended up sharing. How was the trip so far?

She pronounced it "foine."

Then I indicated the settee and said, speaking of laps, why don't we make a couple. She chuckled as we dropped down together.

Maggie started out by asking me about my girl Sung and I said I understood she was getting along just swell and then I asked her about the lawyer in Brisbane and she replied that Donald was doing all right, too. We talked about the United States and about Australia and news reporting in general as well as some of our recent assignments in particular.

She kept working closer to the opera house story and at the same time, working closer to me on the seat.

"Tell me, Blue, do you really believe in bunyips?"

"Sure. Why not?"

"Have you seen one?"

"No, but I've seen lots of strange things. Things you wouldn't believe even if I swore they happened."

"You're talking about Hong Kong?"

"Yeah."

"That's why you moved to Australia, isn't it?"

I nodded, and gave her a few of the highlights. While after that lulu of a story I mentioned earlier, I came within an ace of doing an interview with St. Peter—the Pearly Gates being the object of the viewing and Doyle Mulligan being the subject of the interring. The King Kong of killers tried to take me apart limb from limb and I'd lost a thumb and a hand before a stiff-lipped, hatchet-faced British inspector named Hawthorne saved my neck by killing King Kong, then racing me and my parts to a hospital in time to be sewn back together. *That's* why I'd moved to Australia. To avoid a repeat performance.

She wanted to know what happened to the Brit inspector.

"He went back to London. You know, Maggie, if you and Donald have a falling out this Hawthorne might be just your type. He cinches up his necktie and he wears leather shoes and he feels the same way you do about yanks who don't."

"What makes you think you're not my type?"

"Am I?"

"You might be. Tell me somethin' else, will you, Blue?"

As she said it she scooted over so close that her lap and my lap practically overlapped.

I said to myself, *Uh huh, here comes the payoff.* She probably wants to know what I know about the Northern Territory end of the story. And what I was doing at that silly art show.

But that wasn't it.

"Do ye hold yer breath when ye kiss?"

It caught me completely off guard.

"What kind of a question is that?" I stammered.

"I want to know," she said, and she leaned in so close I could have whispered the answer in her mouth. "Do ye hold yer breath when ye kiss or don't ye?"

"Some guys may," I said. "I've never thought about it."
I moved back and she moved in.

"Think about it now."

Don't think I wasn't.

"Wouldn't it depend on how long the kiss lasts?" I said.

"Come on, Doyle."

"Well, I . . . not as a rule, I don't. Why?"

She sat back, folded her arms and compressed her lips.

"Donald does," she said.

So that was it.

"Holds his breath when he kisses, you mean?"

"Yes. As a rule. It's his rule."

"Huh."

"Now don't go tellin' anyone. It's not the kind of yarn a woman likes to have yakked around." I nodded and she went on: "He won't kiss any longer than ninety seconds. That's as long as he can hold his breath and that, so he says, is long enough for any kiss. Can you believe that?"

"It's pretty incredible. Ninety seconds, huh?"

"Ey."

"He must have a great set of lungs."

"Better than mine."

My eyes automatically fell and when I looked up she was smiling.

"What do you say, Blue?"

If you think she was hitting me up for a demonstration I'd have to say thanks for the compliment but why here? Not that I wouldn't have loved to kiss her. Ninety minutes would've been about right.

But I wasn't holding my breath.

I mention that little episode for one reason only. If she hadn't started me thinking that way I wouldn't have let down my guard, we wouldn't have had those last drinks after dinner, and maybe, just maybe, we wouldn't have seen what we saw.

However, that's getting ahead.

I stood up and suggested we go to the dining car. We shared a little table near a window and watched the sun setting behind the tops of the Great Dividing Range. I wondered if we were in the outback yet or just the bush, or if there was really a difference. Certainly the landscape looked wild enough. Utterly unexplored. But not nearly as desolate as I'd expected. It was hard to believe only four hours had passed since I'd been whinging about a routine assignment. And now here I was sitting down to dinner with a beautiful Aussie while chasing a wicked witch doctor across Oz aboard a first-class train and sipping something robust from the Coonawarra wine-growing region of South Australia.

I thought about Mickey Fine and Nevil Cross.

They'd had two or three hours aloft in an uninsulated, unheated prop-driven cargo plane. By now they'd have landed at the Killian Development site. It would be hot there, and they'd probably get a meal out of a tin can before going to bed on a couple of cots.

I turned away from the window.

Maggie was looking me over the same way I'd done to her in the cabin. Why?

"I'm just tryin' to figger out what that security guard was talkin' about," she said.

"How's that?"

"When he called you 'thinny.' You remember. He called you a thinny red-haired man. Did he mean you have thinning red hair? Your hair's not thinning."

I agreed it wasn't.

An ornery sparkle shone in her eye. "He must have meant skinny, ey."

"No, he didn't," I snapped; "he meant thin."

She giggled because she knew she'd gotten me that time.

"Why don't we order," she suggested, changing the subject, "so you can tell me about this big story of yours and what you were doing at that daggy art show."

This then was the payoff. But it was all right. I'd already made up my mind to tell her everything.

"How much do you know about Rush Killian?" I asked her once the waiter had brought us our entrees of broiled snapper and barramundi and we'd switched to the national drink. I like wine, especially champagne, and they say that nobody beats the Australians at making Australian wine but with me it's like the old saying, *in vino vomitas*, after I've had more than three and even one can give me the whirlies.

"Killian? He's a pseud, isn't he?"

"A what?"

"A pseud. Pseudo-intellectual. Pseudo-aristocrat. He knows all the right people but he doesn't like them and they don't like him. He's a grunt in a three-piece suit."

She took a bite of snapper, chewed slowly, put a thumb and fingertip to her mouth, pulled out a fishbone, and then washed it down.

At her suggestion we were drinking "fives" of Queensland's Castlemaine XXXX, which she'd ordered as: "Four Ex." (Somehow the Australians are able to say "Castlemaine" with only one syllable although it takes them two to say "beer.")

"Down the gurgler," she toasted.

"Fill the pagan hatch," I said, raising my mug. After we'd drunk I asked her about Killian's project up in the Top End. What did she know about that?

"Just what everybody else knows," she said; "just what I've read in the papers."

"Okay, sit back and listen for a while."

Rush Killian was the kind of man who gets his kisser on money down here—one of the larger denominations, of course.

He'd erected half the skyscrapers in Sydney.

He'd piled up a pile in the process.

Then, seven weeks ago, he'd turned his back on the city and invested everything he owned in a big chunk of ground in the Northern Territory. Like Newman said, a thousand square miles of sand, scrub, and kangaroos, surrounded by a million square miles of desert.

He told the federal government when they'd sold him the land that he wanted to subdivide the valley into cattle and sheep stations. That he was going to make the desert bloom.

Not until after he'd moved in his equipment, set up a base camp and begun surveying his acreage had his neighbors, the Ularu aborigines, informed him that the land was sacred ground. It had been sacred for thousands of years. It was also theirs. And they wanted it back.

Naturally Killian refused.

There were threats.

Killian ignored them.

At first.

But as the days became weeks and word of his sacrilege spread, the resulting furor gathered momentum. Rumors began to filter back that his construction crews had lost several men to Ularu attacks. Killian denied it. Still, something must have happened because suddenly and without explanation he extended an olive branch. He offered to trade land with them. He'd take their occupied lands. They could have the sacred land he'd bought. The problem was the Ularu could no more live there than they could allow him to stay. It was forbidden to them too. If they gave away their land they'd have nowhere to go.

Nevertheless, the gesture paid off with a load of good press. It didn't settle the dispute but it put the majority of Australians on his side once the case went to court, which it did almost immediately.

The Minister of Aboriginal Affairs had filed a suit on behalf of the Ularu, who didn't have any lawyers and hadn't ever heard of the legal system. Their case was doomed from the beginning. The government itself had approved the sale. No records indicated that the land had belonged to the Ularu or to any aboriginal tribe. The lawyers failed even to get an injunction to stop Killian from moving in and setting up shop and within a matter of days the territorial court rubber-stamped the transaction. Killian had won.

The effect of this was to outrage the whole aboriginal population. Across the country they held demonstrations of black solidarity. They met. They marched. They picketed. They occupied federal offices. There was talk of a nationwide strike and even threats to burn down all the buildings Killian had erected, whether or not he still owned them. The situation quickly reached a boiling point.

That's when the High Court agreed to hear the case and make a decision by the end of the month.

Wednesday.

It was just a temporary cease-fire and all it had done was give both sides a chance to draw battle lines and ready their forces for war.

Tensions soared.

Police departments in every major city cancelled leave time and hired on extra men.

The prime minister put the army on standby.

The Governor-General went so far as to call London and ask them to send someone around to assess the situation for possible British intervention.

That was unheard of. And predictably, when word of it leaked out, tempers flared all the higher.

Meanwhile, the Ularu, who many doubted even understood what was happening in the rest of the country, gave Killian and his crew until the full moon—a deadline which came and went while more work crews came and stayed—to get out. Or suffer whatever agonies the spirits brought down upon them. There were no specifics, but the curse and the conflict had logged more television and radio time, more space in the papers and on our wires, than any other story since the death of Phar Lap.

Forgotten in the uproar was Rush Killian himself, and his plans.

"I think there's something going on up there," I said, "A big story. But not like anything we've been reading and hearing about."

"There ayn't much that 'asn't been written about."

"Well then let me ask you this. What is Rush Killian up to?"

Maggie pinched her lips. " 'E's building 'imself the grandest station in all of Oz, that's wot."

"No, I mean right now. What's he doing?"

"I dunno."

"I don't know either. But I've got a pretty good idea of what he's not doing. Turning a thousand square miles of desert into productive sheep and cattle stations takes a lot of sheep and cattle. I can't find anybody who's sold him a single ewe or calf. I can't find anybody—breeder, rancher, not anyone—who's even been approached by Killian about selling livestock."

"There's nuthing odd in that," said Maggie.

"How so?"

"What's the use of bringing in all that livestock if he can't feed 'em?"

"Right! First he needs to turn the desert into grazing land." I gave her a wink instead of a pat on the back. "Now I've talked to the Minister of the Northern Territory and to the Agricultural Department and they assure me the ground is marginally suitable for pasture grass and clover, once a few essential nutrients and chemicals are added to the topsoil—mostly phosphate, copper and zinc."

"Well then. . . ?"

"So I did some checking with firms that wholesale these chemicals and none of them, anywhere, have made any sales or are negotiating to sell any of these to Rush Killian. I ran into the same thing with the cultivators. Killian's going to have to clear, level, and then plow hundreds of thousands of acres. But I can't find anybody set up for this kind of job who's been contacted by Killian's people, let alone anybody who's contracted to do it."

"I 'eard he was movin' out his own machinery."

"He is. But he's a commercial, industrial developer. He's got plenty of heavy equipment—earth-moving stuff—but not the kind of farm tractors and cultivators needed to sow land."

Maggie took a sip of her beer.

"You know, Blue, I think you're making too much out of too little. Isn't it possible he's jist goin' to subdivide the land . . . parcel it out to individual investors, let 'em plant and stock it themselves."

"I suppose so. It's not his style—he's the type who likes to own things. Still, it's possible."

"Then he wouldn't have to do any planting himself."

I acknowledged that. "But," I said, "he'd still have to survey it. If the land's not properly surveyed he's got nothing to sell." I leaned across the small table. "Okay, so I checked and sure enough, he has got a surveyor working for him out there. Just one, as far as I can learn. A man by the name of Hector Boyle." I was warming up now. "This guy Boyle's got an office in Sydney. But from what I hear, he isn't thought of too highly. Apparently he runs a small operation, just himself and a couple of minimum-wage slaves as rodmen or whatever. Killian's never used him before. I talked to the surveyors he normally hires, a large firm out of Canberra, and they've been left out entirely."

"What are ye saying? That he's pinchin' pennies?"

"I'm saying it would take a guy like Hector Boyle ten years to survey a thousand square miles, if he could do it at all."

"I see your point."

"There's more. Say this Boyle does survey a few of the parcels. Before Rush Killian can interest anyone in acreage he's going to have to find water. Without water for fields they'll be no pasture. Without water for stock the pastures won't mean a thing."

" 'As he done any drillin'?"

"Apparently so. A couple of wells, according to the federal people. But they've come up dry."

"Maybe he's waiting for things to cool down."

"Maybe. But I don't believe it."

Maggie leaned forward as I'd been doing and one of her elbows slipped off the table. She recovered slowly.

"So you tell me," she said, "wot's goin' on up there?"

"I don't know. That's why I want to go up. It's why I'm following our flamboyant friend. The Ularu settlement is just across the mountains from the Killian Development Camp. I've learned as much as I can from down here."

The waiter was hovering nearby. I sent him after two more beers just to get rid of him. I didn't need any more to drink. When they came, I drank anyway. I was still warm to my subject, inside and out.

And that wasn't all.

I'd begun catching signals from Maggie she wasn't even throwing. When she reached over suddenly and cinched up my tie I practically blushed. After her foot brushed my leg I lost my place in the story and didn't get back on track for five minutes.

Now she puckered her mouth.

"Okay, Blue; now how about that cuhse?"

I jerked up.

"In here?"

"Wot? Not kiss. Cuhrrr-se."

"Oh. That. Well, you gotta admit it worked on Arthur Copley."

"An' those bunyips?"

"What's the curse to do with bunlips?"

"Bun*lips?*"

Maggie told me later my face turned four shades of red.

"Bun*yips,*" I said. "I said bunyips."

She gave me that smile again.

I grabbed my mug and up-ended the last of my beer.

By this time it was quite dark outside; the dining car was practically deserted. Our dinners had long before been cleaned up and the plates cleared away. I'd had four beers on top of my limit of wine, so even forgetting the cocktail in my compartment beforehand, I was understandably buzzy.

Eventually the stewards shooed us out and we walked arm in arm back through the train to our own carriage.

I should have realized sooner that something was wrong. In the first place, none of the corridor lights were burning. What light there was came from a boomerang-shaped moon that shone through the corridor windows. It wasn't much.

I felt my way along. When I came to a door mid-length of the car I searched for a knob.

That's when Maggie screamed.

Not a shrieking, ear-piercing, Fay Wray kind of scream. Maggie's was more of an arm-clutching, there's-something-behind-you, turn-around-quickly-before-it's-too-late kind of scream.

I turned around quickly.

It was the witch doctor in full dress again. Or rather, undress. He had the same white lines running down his black legs and arms and the same cross-hatching white lines on his chest. In the moonlight this made him look more than ever like a walking skeleton. Moonlight also illuminated a pair of fiery red eyes and a gaping snout full of wolfish white teeth—a mask. A match for the one he'd worn at the opera house show.

He started chanting:

"Nogatu kai lo tehano Kadimakara tonanu-ano bori naru."

We stood there watching, Maggie and I, with our backs pressed against the wall.

Soon he was stamping his feet and shaking his fists at us. He must've had something in them, rattles or castanets of some kind, for I heard a clicking sound. But it was too dark to see what.

I was scared, I can't deny it. Something about the guy tied my stomach in knots, and having Maggie there beside me gripping my arm and shaking didn't help matters any at all. Still, I might have been much more scared if I hadn't just attended his premiere performance a few hours before. I was also a little upset because apparently our cover was blown and he wouldn't lead us anywhere now.

Add to that six servings of liquid courage downed over a three-hour period.

That's the only explanation I can offer for what I did next.

He was shouting, *"Ngai toka wati noa bori!"* at the top of his lungs.

I shouted back: "Ackjay and illjay went up the illhay, to etchfay a pail of aterway!"

And I'll be darned if he didn't stop!

He held out one fist to me.

"May *Tobraka* turn loose the beast. Set *Gol* free among the desecrators. May their bodies be opened; their blood be drunk; and their hearts torn from their chests and devoured." He slowly opened his clawed fingers as he spoke.

I mustered my mettle.

"We know; we know!" I said. "The *kadi makara* will have their revenge. We caught the matinee. Come on, Maggie, let's go inside."

I turned back to my door and brought Maggie around too.

I heard a thumping, scuttling sound mixed with a half-human breathing from the corridor behind us.

She pulled away from me.

And screamed.

This was a real shriek, an ear-piercing, heart-stopping Fay Wray kind of scream.

I turned around again.

The witch doctor was gone. Some ghastly thing had taken his place.

I saw it.

And I'm not certain I didn't scream too.

There's no way to describe it. It was quite indescribable. Any resemblance to that monster and the world that I knew, the real world, simply didn't exist.

It was eight feet tall at least, maybe taller. It had two legs and four arms—I swear to God it did—a gorilla's body but as big as a bigfoot. It had no eyes that I could see, but its teeth, twice the

length of those on the witch doctor's mask, reflected the moonlight like stainless steel knives. Its claws shone the same way.

My first thought was that I was having some kind of a drug-
induced dream. Alcohol being a drug. The dream being a nightmare.

It was too damn crazy to be real. But it was also too real to be
a dream. And Maggie was dreaming it with me.

"Doyle! Come on! Come on!"

She grabbed my arm and started pulling me down the corridor.

The thing stamped right after us, lumbering along with a gait
so heavy it shook the floor under our feet. Its snarls drowned out
the rumble of the wheels. Its four arms slashed in circles, hack-
ing at the darkness with four sets of almost incandescent claws.

When we reached the end of the corridor and came up against
the vestibule door the claws slashed toward my face. I must have
turned at the last moment. They sliced through my shoulder
instead.

I did scream then. I know I did. The pain shocked me sober.
This was no dream. And no hallucination.

Before we knew it, Maggie and I had backed right inside the
vestibule. I closed the door behind us and put my weight to the
bar. I had no illusions I could hold it for long for my left arm was
in agony and the thing, whatever it was, had to be three times
my weight.

Maggie was screaming that the door to the next carriage was
locked. She was hammering her fists on the glass.

"We just came through there!" I shouted.

"It's locked! I can't push it open. Try the outside door, Blue.
Hurry!"

"The train's moving! We can't—" Suddenly a battering ram
crashed into my door. I was knocked back so hard it's a wonder
I didn't black out. The compartment door swung open and in it
came.

"Jump, Blue!"

Four arms reached out for Maggie.

I grabbed her out of its claws. We were shoved to one side. Against the outside door. The thing moved in for the kill. But then I heard the crash of glass and a hurricane-force howl in my ears. I found myself falling outward into space with Maggie still wrapped in my arms. I felt a warm, night wind in my face, and then the whole world went black.

4

Bump in the Night

I broke my neck.

I cradled my head in my hands and slowly cranked it to the left. That was okay. I could lower it, too. But if I tried to lift it or turn it to the right the pain was unbelievable.

"My neck's broken. I broke my neck!"

"Your neck's not broken."

I sent Maggie a withering scowl. She was five feet above me, and off my right shoulder. I was down in the culvert.

"How can you stand up there and tell me my neck's not broken. It's my neck. I ought to know when it's broken."

I did know.

There were no doubts in my mind. It hurt the same way it had back in high school when I'd broken the thing playing football. Or at any rate, it hurt the way it would have if I *had* broken it playing football, which I hadn't—played football, that is, because mother Mulligan felt sure if I had played football I'd've broken my neck. So I hadn't. But now I had—broken my neck, that is.

"If it were broken," she said, "you wouldn't be moving it around."

Just like a woman.

"If I weren't moving it around, how would I know it was broken? Anyway what would you know? Did you play football?"

"Yes."

"You did!?"

"Ey."

"And did you break your neck?"

"Of course not."

"There, you see," I muttered as much to mother Mulligan as to Maggie. "I was right all along."

She lowered a hand. I took it and climbed out of the culvert. We brushed ourselves off.

I asked her if she was okay though I knew she couldn't have been hurting too bad; she'd climbed out on her own.

"My back's a bit sore." Did she want me to take a look at it?

"No," she said, "It'll keep 'til mornin'. How about you?"

My shoulder hurt like hell. The jacket and shirt were badly torn and so was the skin. Blood was dripping down my back. There wasn't much to be done about it though and considering the sympathy I'd gotten for a broken neck I decided not to bring it up.

I didn't want to bring up the monster again either but I had to know.

"What was it, Maggie?"

"What?"

"You know what. That . . . thing."

"I've told you a dozen times, Blue, I don't know?"

"It's your country. If we were in the States I'd tell you: Oh, that was a Bigfoot. Or a Sasquatch. If this were the Himalayas they'd say we just saw an Abominable Snowman. But we're not. We're in Australia. You're Australian. You ought to know what monsters you've got prowling around down here."

"You said you believed in bunyips, didn't you? Maybe that was one of 'em."

"That was a *bunyip?*"

"What else could it have been?"

"They ride trains!?"

"I don't know? I've never seen one before either."

I didn't believe it and said so. Buses? Maybe. Everybody knows the kind of animals you see on the bus! But on a train? Not even the economy section. First class!

"Oh, Blue." She sat down on the rail and lay her head in her hands.

"No, think about it. We're stranded here in the middle of nowhere in the middle of the night while some prehistoric ape with six legs is sailing over the outback in our sleeper car."

"I was never so frightened in my life."

"For all we know that thing may be breaking down one of our cabin doors right now. Sleeping in our bed!"

"At least we're still alive."

"Maybe even charging meals to our compartments."

"It's lucky we're no worse off," she said. "The train must've been moving slowly through the mountain pass."

We made circles, the both of us, surveying the terrain.

The boomerang-shaped moon was almost directly overhead; nothing it illuminated looked too encouraging. Low, sloping, and treed hills on each side of the tracks was all.

I asked her which way should we go from here. Did she know where we were? What town had we passed last, and how far back was it? How far ahead was the next one?

She didn't know. She thought we must be somewhere in the Blue Mountains . . . near Springwood and Lithgow someplace.

"How far apart are they?"

Long silence.

"A hundred kilometers. Two hundred."

"Should we go east or west, do you think?"

"East," she said, "The towns are closer together that way."

I started walking.

"Blue?"

"What?"

"East is that way."

If I reported everything Maggie and I went through in the next twenty-four hours I'd need another book instead of a chapter. It'd be nice if I could just report: Twenty-four hours later we walked out of the outback . . . even though that fails to describe the rather roundabout route we took. But I can't. We didn't walk out alone and the character who led us has to be introduced since he became an integral part of the story.

We considered walking through the night. It was about ten o'clock then, so obviously we'd lain in that culvert for close to an hour. Dawn was eight hours away. But midnight hadn't struck yet when we sat down to rest. We didn't move again until daybreak.

Friday.

Five days to go until D-Day.

I woke up with a headache, a hangover and a lump on the back of my head as big as a fist. I'd spent the whole eight hours dreaming about two-legged four-armed monsters starting fires all over Australia.

Maggie was already awake and ready for what she called a "walkabout." An aboriginal custom, she informed me. Was I feeling up to it?

I told her I didn't even want to talkabout.

We checked each other over in the gathering light.

Her head was okay. She'd been very, very lucky, not even tearing her clothes in the fall.

She let me know the gash on my shoulder could use some stitches but ought to hold together until we reached Sydney, a prognosis that sounded overly optimistic to me since she didn't know how far that was or how long it would take us to get there.

I remember doing another slow circle. The picture was disheartening to say the least. It was a parched-looking landscape I surveyed, and no signs pointed to relief.

We started walking. We stuck to the railway tracks at first, as we had the night before, but within an hour or so and at my suggestion we left them.

Another train might not come along for days and when it did, it wouldn't stop. If we just headed east, we'd have to come to a town. That was my reasoning.

I took a sighting on the rising sun.

"Blue."

I stopped.

"Not that way."

"That's east, isn't it?"

"That's north. You're in the southern 'emisphere now. Sun comes up in the northeast, not the southeast. Go that way and you'll end up in the Wollami National Park."

"Look," I said, "were you serious about that football stuff?"

"What?"

"Did you really play football?"

"Ey."

"Soccer or rugby?"

"Footy. Aussie Rules football."

I tried not to look impressed but I was. Aussie Rules is a pretty tough sport. They like to say down here if you go to a brawl before long a game of Aussie Rules will break out. Still, you have to ask yourself, if it really is such a tough sport, why do they call it footy?

The rough ground was no good for walking. Dry washes wound through rolling terrain, covered with scrub trees and sharp stones, spinifex grass and cacti of every conceivable variety. I spotted a land rise about three miles away that looked like a good place to take a sighting, and headed for it. From then on everything was uphill.

The terrain wasn't even the worst of it.

Mosquitoes and blowflies descended on us in living black clouds.

Australian mozzies are bigger than other varieties and meaner too, but the blowflies are even worse. I spent most of my time trying to scare them away. When one got through my defenses I'd try to smash it quick before it could sting me. I kept count of the ones that escaped. That's okay for a little while, but after three or four hours and a hundred bites it's enough to drive you crazy.

They especially liked my shoulder. Something about the blood drew blowflies like . . . well, like flies.

The wound was starting to bother me. Not just the pain either. I felt if it didn't get treatment soon, it would be a prime candidate for infection. Already it had the rotting flesh smell of gangrene. I made the mistake of mentioning it to Maggie and she told me I ought to get a smell of my other shoulder. "Ye're a bit whiffy on the lee side," she kidded. I pretended to laugh, to let her know I hadn't lost my sense of humor even though hers was sadly misplaced.

"If you're really worried," she said, "quit scaring the blowies away. Let 'em lay a few eggs. The maggots'll hatch in only a day, and they say them little sprogs will eat the infected tissue and leave the healthy flesh alone . . . mostly."

I stopped and turned.

Maggie's hair was mussed to the max. She'd collected a bunch of bark scraps and tied them to long strands of hair so that they swung back and forth in front of her face as she moved.

"It keeps the mozzies off," she explained.

"What position did you play?"

She frowned and shook her head.

"Footy. What position did you play? Quarterback?"

"There ayn't no quarterback, Blue. I played for'ard."

"In that case, why don't you lead for a change?"

She did, and I slapped at the blowflies in peace.

I stepped on so many cactus spines I spent half my time hopping around on one foot, or hauling myself up off the ground. The first time I stumbled into a wombat hole and fell flat on my face it was maddening. The second and third times, too. I would swear something awful, pick myself up, and dust myself off. But after a while it just wasn't worth it—I was too darn dirty to get any worse. I didn't bother to brush myself off after that and I didn't have enough wind left for swearing.

It was 10:25 by my watch when we left the tracks. It was noon when we reached the top of the hill so it couldn't have been three miles away and probably wasn't even two, not with the pace we were keeping. My jacket was largely to blame for that.

The houndstooth check. I was suffocating with it on, that and the shirt and tie but I was unwilling to leave them behind for fear I'd freeze if we had to spend another night out there. So I carried them all the way up.

At the top, I dropped them in a pile.

Maggie was already scanning the horizon.

I shaded my eyes with a dirty hand. There was no sign of life. Not a highway or a house. Not a hint of humanity.

Another higher hill in the distance looked promising.

We never got there.

A dry watercourse wound across our path, cutting a kind of canyon through the valley. We climbed down easily enough but couldn't get up the other side. By following the riverbed we had some easy hiking for a change but when we finally emerged, the hill had disappeared over the horizon, and the landscape had changed completely.

With hopeful hearts Maggie and I headed for some fence posts in the distance, our first hint of civilization since abandoning the railroad tracks. Only once we got there, we found they weren't posts at all but termite mounds six feet high and as thick as tree trunks. Their mottled regurgitated-mud walls were as hard as bricks. It occurred to me I'd swallowed enough dust to fill my stomach and I grew suddenly afraid if we ever did find water it'd turn my intestinal tract into a solid lump of adobe. As soon as I turned away from the mounds this fear subsided. Nevertheless, the idea continued to haunt me and hours later I was still breathing with my mouth tightly closed.

By midafternoon my mouth tasted like shoe leather, my breath was coming in gulps and I couldn't decide which hurt more, my head or my feet. I was falling farther and farther behind.

"Don't answer me if you'd rather not," I sang out, "but I've been giving it a lot of thought and if I'm going to die out here in this wasteland, which seems likely, I'd like to settle something first."

She turned around. "Like what?"

I wet my lips with my tongue. To clean off the dust. All I succeeded in doing was caking my cheeks with mud.

"When you're kissing somebody who's holding his breath, and he opens his mouth—you know how you do sometimes—well, how do you keep the air from coming out?"

"Oh, Blue!"

"What!"

"You promised you wouldn't talk it up about that."

"I'm talking about it with you; that's not the same as talking about it."

"That's absolutely silly."

"Why?"

"What you said before is silly."

"No, it's not. Not really. Suppose we try it right now. You be you and I'll be Donald. I'll take a big gulp of air and you see if you can make me breathe when my mouth comes open. Of course I can't hold my breath for any ninety seconds. I'll try for thirty the first time. Maybe I could work up to sixty with a little practice. No fair tickling. I'm ticklish. If you goose me I'm sure to start breathing."

"You dill!"

"Better yet," I said, "I'll be you and you be Donald. That'll be a better test. But you can't—"

"It's silly," she said evenly, "because we're not going to doy out here."

I laughed aloud. *Doy.* You know they can pronounce the word if they want to. Everytime they say "day" it comes out "die." So why, when they say "die" does it sound like "doy?" *That's* silly.

Like I said, I haven't enough space to tell everything that happened to us. The ant hill that seemed like a nice place to sit down and wasn't. The ravine which took us two kilometers off our route by promising to lead us to water. And didn't. The handy foothold on the side of the mountain which looked hard, and the rocks at the bottom which were.

Two hours later Maggie and I were dragging our shadows across a valley surrounded by steep-sided hills—basically a frying pan, except we were broiling under the sun instead of frying. I remember seeing a small stand of trees in the distance and thinking that if we found some decent shade it might be a good place to spend the rest of my life. Or an hour, whichever came first.

I have no memory of reaching the trees.

Liquid ice trickled over my forehead. It flowed still frozen down my cheek. A gentle breeze passed over my body. I was pleasantly cool. My feet even felt cold. Numb. Not numb from pain but a satisfying kind of numbness that comes once the hurting stops. I opened my eyes. Leaves fluttered high above me. When I raised my head and looked myself over I found dapples of shade dancing across my bare chest and a fresh mat of green grass beneath me.

Nearby, in the shade of another tree, lay Maggie. She was on her side with her legs bent and her arm folded under her head for a pillow.

I started up.

A reddish cloth—my T-shirt folded into a compress and soaking wet—fell off my back. I stared at it in disbelief. It had fallen into the water beside me. My feet lay in the same pool up to the ankles.

I couldn't pull my eyes away.

It was ten feet across and half that again from one end to the other. A foot or two deep. Grass grew around it and several large trees provided the shade.

The aborigines call it a billabong. A pool of water in a river that no longer flows but hasn't completely dried up.

I rolled to the edge of the pool, dunked my head under and drank. I didn't stop until I'd run out of air. Then I took two whooping gasps and went down again.

When my stomach could hold no more I lay back and closed my eyes.

I thought about going to sleep. About sleeping for a week before waking again. I thought about staying here by this pool until I recovered enough to go on. Another week yet at least, or maybe a month.

My thoughts began to drift.

I don't know when I first realized Maggie and I weren't alone. I didn't hear anything, or see it either. Yet something made me look up.

There, in the hollow of the biggest of the shade trees, one of those bottle-shaped trees, I saw him. The trunk was split so that it formed a kind of dugout near the base, six feet high and surrounded on three sides by wood. That's where he was sitting, hunched down with his arms folded around his knees. He was as black as a man can get; he was bigger than any man ought to be; he had a bowling ball head and a face like five miles of bad road. Blacktop. I couldn't have described him any better than that.

"Who are *you?*" I cried.

My voice actually croaked.

When he didn't say anything, I asked again.

He came out of the dugout. He stood up. It was something to see. Even when I thought he was up, he wasn't, he just kept coming. And then he was standing there before me. Tall. He wasn't as tall as the tree that stood over him, not quite, but he looked like a tree standing over me.

That's when I got my first good look at him. A carpet of hair hugged the top of his bowling ball head like black lichen (if there is such a thing). His lips were the same violent black, and his eyebrows, too—or so I thought until I looked closer and realized that what I was seeing was the black of his skin. He had no eyebrows.

Without a word he started toward me.

He was wearing only a loincloth of soiled cotton around his

waist and a sleeveless shirt open across the chest exposing an ebony body of sharp-edged planes and grooves gouged to the bone. When he moved, the muscles of his thighs flexed eagerly. His washboard belly heaved. With arms and legs as long as his he should have looked awkward but he didn't. He looked like a statue come to life, a statue hacked from coal with a miner's packax.

Closer, I could see a lot of scars across his stomach. Ridges in equally spaced rows about two inches apart. They looked like they'd been carved with an ax, too.

When he got within a few feet of me—an arm's reach for him or a single stride—he stopped. He balled his fists and folded his arms on his chest.

That's when it hit me. I knew him.

I leaped to my feet.

It was the witch doctor!

My *flame*boyant friend; except he wasn't a friend and he wasn't flamboyant, not any more. He was just frightening.

"What are you doing here?" I practically screamed it. In the back of my mind I guess I'd hoped to wake Maggie.

Seconds slipped by. The guy didn't utter a sound and I couldn't turn my eyes away.

I'd seen him four times. Twice he'd been wearing that mask and once, leaping onto the ferry, his back had been to me. But that first time, squaring off with the rent-a-cops and looking as big as both of them put together, I'd gotten a good look at his face.

No question about it. It was him.

Now, without his clothes, he looked even bigger.

What was I to do? There was no way I could outrun him. I'd little enough chance to outfight him.

I crouched, waiting for his attack.

But half a minute passed and he still didn't move.

I tried to keep my voice steady. "What do you want?" I demanded.

He shook his head and said nothing.

"Now, look here! We're not your enemies. As a matter of fact, we're on your side in this thing. You know, about Killian and the sacred land? We're with you."

His blackish eyes suddenly gleamed. His lips drew back, revealing two rows of brightly polished ivory, broken only by a cavity where his left upper incisor ought to have been. I couldn't tell if he was snarling or smiling. He just stood there looking me up and down. But mostly down.

"My name is Doyle," I said. "Doyle Mulligan. I'm a reporter."

"Doyle . . . Doyle?"

"That's it! Doyle. Doyle Mulligan."

"Doyle Doyle."

I risked a quick glance over my shoulder. Maggie was still fast asleep.

"What's your name?" I stalled.

He thought the thing over. Then he rumbled:

"Jim, Jim."

I glowered at him. "Jim . . . Jim?"

He nodded back. "Jim Jim."

Whatta ye know! I thought. Two black guys and both of them are him; two names and both of them are Jim. It wasn't that funny. But for some reason I felt like laughing. And once I got started, I couldn't stop.

At first he just glared. Then his lips cracked into a smile and the next thing I knew he was laughing right along with me. His laughter sounded like a distant explosion. Or maybe like a mine caving in deep below ground.

When I stopped, he stopped at the same time. His face looked like it had never smiled at all. And never would.

I asked him if he was lost too, and he wordlessly wagged his big head.

"Do you know the way out of here?"

He nodded.

I went over to wake Dorothy. Now that we'd met up with the scarecrow, it was time to get back on the yellow brick road.

To make a long story short Jim Jim wasn't who I thought he was. He hadn't torched Arthur Copley, or burned down the opera house. It's true, he was there, but he wasn't the guy I was chasing. Oh I chased him! But only because I thought he was who he wasn't.

Maybe I'd better let him tell it.

Jim Jim talked slow but to the point for he didn't know enough words to talk around it.

"I went to Sydney to warn the people," Jim Jim told us. "I did not want to hurt anyone."

"Warn them of what?" I asked.

"About . . . the danger."

We were walking along side by side with Jim Jim in the middle. Maggie had shown no surprise when I woke her because, as she told it, the two of them had practically carried me into the trees.

"Danger of what?"

He shrugged. I mention his shrugging because tossing those giant shoulders of his ought to have qualified as an event.

"You're Ularu?" I asked.

"Yes."

"You live on the Occupied Lands."

"Yes. I am a Dongo."

"Dongo? What's that?"

"I don't go from our land."

"But you did leave. . . ?"

"Yes."

He was starting to clam up again.

"Who was the man in the costume?" I asked him.

"His name," grunted Jim Jim, "is Black Tom. He is our mulla-mullung."

"Like a witch doctor, right? Or a shaman."

He nodded. "Yes. He is very powerful. He knows many spells."

I asked if he knew whether or not Black Tom was the one who started the fire in the opera house. "Did he come down here from Ularup just to burn Copley?"

Jim Jim remained still for a moment. Then he shook his head: "No."

"He didn't?"

"I don't know. Black Tom has many powers but even he cannot stop the spirits. I tried to warn the people about the forbid pictures. So they would not be hurt. But that man would not let me—"

"You mean the security guard?"

"Yes, that man. He would not let me talk to the man."

"You mean Arthur Copley?"

"Yes."

"What happened?"

"I left the building. I saw Black Tom run out of the building and I followed him. He went into the trees near the building. There he took off the *keowa*—the ceremonial headdress and gloves. He put on some pants and shirt that he found in a tree. He put the headdress and gloves in the tree. Then he ran out of the trees."

"And you followed him?"

"Yes."

"Why?"

"I did not know what to do. Where to go. I followed Black Tom because he knows."

I didn't buy that. I didn't believe Jim Jim was being completely honest with us. However I didn't have any lever to pry the truth out of him—nothing lighter than a crowbar would have made a dent in his skull—besides which I needed him conscious and congenial if he were going to lead us out of this wilderness. So I swallowed my suspicions and said: "You followed him to the

quay, huh? And when he got on one of the ferries you jumped
on at the last second."

"Yes."

"It was you I saw then. Instead of this . . . Black Tom?"

"Yes."

"After it docked you took a taxicab, right?"

"Black Tom got in a car. I ran behind the car for many
blocks."

"To the train station?" He nodded. "And what happened
there?"

"I had no money. I slipped onto the train. One of the men
working on the train is from the Arnhem Land. A Gangra tribesman."

Maggie piped up suddenly: "Our attendant!"

Jim Jim nodded.

"He said I could stay in his . . . his box until we got to the
town. He watched Black Tom for me. He also watched the two
men who were with Black Tom."

Once again this didn't ring true. Why hadn't Jim Jim just
bunked in with Black Tom if the two of them were that close?
But I didn't ask him that; I was too interested in the rest of what
he'd said.

"Two men!" I exclaimed.

"Yes. Two white men."

"One was in Compartment Seven?"

"One, yes. And one in Five."

I turned to Maggie. "That explains it. If they had a man in Five
he could have overheard us talking. He heard us going over our
assignment, our plans . . . everything."

"Yes," said Jim Jim. "I told the Gangra to watch you, too. To
see that you did not get into trouble."

"So that's what you're doing here."

"He came to me in the night. He said that you and the girl
were not in your boxes. He said a window was broken, and he
was afraid you had fallen off of the train. You may be hurt. But

he was afraid to tell his bosses on the train. If he was wrong he would lose his job. So I jumped off the train and walked back to find you. But I had to wait until morning to find your tracks."

"You must have been miles from us by then."

"Yes. I followed the rail for many kilometers before I found your tracks which went into the bush. You should have stayed on the railway, you know. You should have followed them to Sydney."

He reminded me of my mother, making me promise not to step off the sidewalk.

"One more thing, Jim Jim," I said. "You've lived your whole life in the bush, right?"

"Yes."

"I'll bet you know all the animals out here."

"Yes."

"The strange ones, too?"

"Many strange ones."

"We saw something—"

"—A bunyip," Maggie interrupted me. "Have you heard of that?"

"Bunyip?"

She pressed him.

"Come on, you know what I'm talking about. Those big ugly creatures. Mean. Sharp teeth. Don't tell me you've never heard of them."

He dismissed the description with a shrug.

"Maybe you have another name for them," she persisted.

"Maybe."

"What do you call a thing like that? It looks alien . . . you know. Like it comes from another planet. It certainly doesn't look like it's got any business out here."

"Ah . . . that."

"You know what I'm talking about."

He nodded.

"What do your people call it?" she demanded, giving me a smirk.

Jim Jim fixed his eyes on her.

"White man," he said.

An hour later we came to the highway.

My thumb got us onto a farm truck and the truck got us to a jerkwater called Blaxland. We bummed a ride as far as Penrith. There we caught a Countrylink bus back to Sydney.

Maggie and Jim Jim sat together while I curled up in a pair of seats behind them and slept. She told me later the two of them talked the whole way back. They didn't keep me awake. Before I dropped off Maggie poked her head over her seat back and asked me, now that we were going home, what I thought of the bush and I, not wanting to hurt her feelings replied that it's a nice place to visit but I wouldn't want to die there.

"At least now you can tell everybody you've been on a walk-about, can't you?"

I agreed, with reservations. "In my case," I said, "I think it should be called a lie-about."

She laughed.

"Loy-about! You make it sound like you spent the time loafing around. You barely came out alive and . . . let's face it, Blue, your performance was nothing to brag of."

I didn't even open my eyes.

"You're right," I said, "that's the part I'm gonna lie about."

5

Come A-Waltzing

That was Friday night. Ten hours later, with two days shot and only four to go, I caught a City Hopper bus to the Ballarat Building, crossed to the elevators and pressed the down button. ENA coughed up two big ones every month for a luxury suite on the twentieth floor, but if those magoos at headquarters ever knew how little they got for their money, heads would've rolled. The suite was okay—that wasn't the problem. There were two private offices and an open arena, seven desks, a five-line switchboard with six extensions, a mainframe computer tied in to HQ Seattle and four terminals. The problem was nobody used it. For two thousand dollars we had an art deco mail drop and a very fancy place to pick up our phone messages. That day I found the gang as always in the basement, at our permanently reserved table in the back of the Black Stump Pub. I swear, if Alvin Cockie and Percy Newman could've arranged for a private phone line down there they'd have closed up the office altogether.

The two of them generally headed downstairs about nine for what they called a "heart starter" and ended up staying for lunch. Around one-thirty they'd toss to see who made a dash up in the elevator to check on the blokes. Whoever it was, he wouldn't hang around long. He'd be down before two to join the mob for a "smoke-o" which, since neither smoked, was really just an Australian version of afternoon tea.

They didn't drink tea either.

All official meetings—brain-storming sessions, assignment briefings, story rehashes, etc.—convened in the Black Stump.

We toasted our victories there, found consolation in our failures and somehow there were more of the one than the other. Incredibly enough the system worked. More incredibly yet, it worked because of them.

Percy Newman had been a professor of advanced economics at Sydney University. After twenty years of theorizing he'd finally been given a fellowship to test his financial ideas. He invested the money right and left—none of it right; none of it left. He bought into booze. When he showed up stewed at a lecture he'd promptly gotten himself canned. Someone at Eastern News thought he might make a good editor-in-chief of the Sydney Branch and, by God, he did! He turned out to be better at overseeing money than investing it, maintained the regional books in his head, and composed wire-ready copy off the cuff.

Within days Newman had put his old drinking buddy Alvin Cockie on the payroll. This might have seemed like nepotism at its worst since Alvin (Alf to his mates and Alvie to me) had no education to speak of and didn't know a subject from a predicate. What writing he did was unreadable. Covering important events was out of the question for he didn't own a suit or tie and his one hat, an *akubra* that he never doffed, had been made out of wallaby skin. Cockie had only one thing going for him: He liked everybody. And it was impossible for anybody not to like him. He knew every mover and shaker in Sydney, and they knew him. Not the bigwigs, the leaders of business and government, the stars of sports and screen, the ones who sneer at reporters and say things like, "No comment," or, "My attorney will answer that." He knew the little guys. Guys who move the bigwigs around in their cabs and trucks; the ones who move furniture from one house to another, cargo from the docks to the ships, or garbage from the back street to the landfill. He knew the people who shake when the bigwigs start screaming: the butlers and butchers, barbers and barmaids, bellhops and bellydancers. For every cheese with a secret there's a secretary, a bookie, a cabby, a cop or a crook who knows all about it. People who wouldn't be caught dead walking into a newspaper office would saunter into the Black Stump any time of day or night and tell their yarn to Cockie over a schooner of beer. As a result, we got everything hours before the networks or other wire services found out about it.

To see them together was to laugh for Cockie was Humpty Dumpty to Newman's Jack Spratt.

I tried to explain that to mother when she'd called me long distance from Chicago soon after I'd come to Australia. It didn't work. "Well, it's like this," I told her. "Newman looks like Chips Rafferty except he's thinner and taller and doesn't have as much hair. Cockie, on the other hand, looks more like Paul Hogan, except he's fatter and shorter and has a lot more hair."

"Yes," she said, "but who is Chips Rafferty?"

"Don't you ever watch old movies? He's the archetypical Aussie. The one all Australians would like to look like and none of them do."

"What about Paul Hogan?"

"For crying out loud, mother, you have to know him!"

"What does he look like?"

I shook my head and controlled my voice before sending it ten thousand miles with an edge.

I said: "He looks just like Chips Rafferty."

"Oh," she said.

I didn't tell her that I thought the world of the pair of them. Cockie especially. It sounds corny to say he was something like the father I never had because I've heard my mother describe my father, and Alvin Cockie wasn't anything like him. But he was certainly something.

It was ten o'clock on a Saturday morning . . . the last peaceful weekend before the big blow-up was due to hit. The boys should've been having some fun with their families, sailing off the Manly coast, surfing Bondi Beach, or perving the girls down at Dawes Point. Instead they were sitting in a pub with Newman

and Cockie knocking back beers and playing scissors-cuts-pa-
per-wraps-rock Australian style for the tab.

I'd called that morning to let them know I was back but even
so, my appearance created quite a stir.

"Well, well," someone called out, "Look oo's 'ere."

Twelve hours had made a new man out of me. I'd showered
not once but twice, shaved, eaten two sizable meals, brushed and
flossed my teeth after each one and gotten nine hours of sleep.
Some aspirin for my head, some iodine and gauze on my shoulder, and a fresh set of duds had managed to relegate my outback
adventure into the unpleasant past.

"What in buggery 'ave you been up to?" Cockie growled.

But there was relief in his eyes.

Maggie and Jim Jim and I had picked up a taxicab at the bus
station. I'd had the driver drop Maggie off at her flat in Paddington and saw that she made it inside before giving him directions
to my place in Woolloomooloo. Jim Jim had no place to stay.
Which meant he was staying with me, at least until we found
some way to get him back up to the Territory.

Mine was a typical Sydney "unit"—small bedroom, living
area, bath, and kitchen/dining room in one—too little space
going for too much every month.

When I threw open the door, Jim Jim and I stood on the
threshold. He, for not having seen anything like it before; I, for
not having expected to see it ever again.

"You can sleep on the couch if you bathe first," I told him.
"Otherwise, you can sleep on the floor."

I'd said it half in jest but I noticed he was thinking it over.

"What about you?" he asked.

"I'm going to sleep in my bed."

I pointed to a closed door at the end of a short hall.

"Are you going to . . . bathe?"

"Yes," I said. "First."

When I came out of the shower I found him nosing around

my collection of classic films on video. He passed these up and began studying some of my vintage movie posters. Jim Jim looked very large in my small apartment and very much out of place. He stopped between *The Adventures of Robin Hood* and *The Defiant Ones.*

Staring.

I said: "Errol Flynn lived right here in Woolloomooloo when he was a kid. Did you know that?"

He ignored me.

It turned out he was looking at the other poster.

"This one looks like Ularu tribe," he observed.

By golly, so he did. Jim Jim was a little darker and not quite as handsome but the resemblance was noticeable.

"Could be," I said.

"Do you know him?"

"Everybody knows him. He's a Hollywood movie star."

"Sid-ney-Po . . . Po—"

"Poitier."

"Sidney . . . I've heard of him."

"Good for you."

His head nodded in appreciation. "He must have been a very great man if they named this big city after him, don't you think so?"

"You better believe it," I replied though I knew good and well they'd named the town after Sydney Greenstreet. I told him it was his turn to shower.

Wide eyed and wary, he tiptoed into the bathroom as though he were stalking some slavering, carnivorous beast.

While he was in the shower I found some clothes someone had given me which were two sizes too large for me and would only be two or three sizes too small for him. I set them out. Fully half an hour later, as I was transferring grub from the icebox to the table, here he comes, as dark as ever but now as shiny as my black leather shoes after a liberal application of neatsfoot oil.

"I like showers!" he announced.

I stifled a guffaw.

"The sleeves are okay," I said, "but your arms are a little long." In addition to that the trouser legs didn't quite cover his shins. "Tomorrow, I'll make a stop by the local Big and Tall outlet."

"I have no money."

"Don't worry about that. You'd still be wearing your suit if you hadn't jumped off the train to help me." Which was true, though he'd still had the suit on when he jumped. Jim Jim admitted he couldn't walkabout fully dressed. He'd taken off the jacket, trousers, shirt, and tie, rolled them into a ball and hidden them under a rock.

He made another admission now. "The suit did not fit well neither," he said.

True enough. And it had been far from new. I decided a trip to the local second-hand clothes store would be more in line with his tastes and my budget. Or, better yet, the local army surplus for a slightly used two-man tent.

"How does a guy get a name like Jim Jim?" I asked him between bites of cold chicken and canned peaches. I thought I was hungry but he was shoveling in two mouthfuls to my one and his mouth was twice as large as mine.

"Jim means big."

"In Ularu?"

"Yes."

"But why Jim Jim?"

"Jim Jim. Two big."

"You mean two big? Or too big?"

His browless forehead furrowed and his big bowling ball head shook back and forth as he wrestled with an all two-too subtle distinction.

"Forget it," I said, "It's the same thing, isn't it?"

Abruptly he stopped eating.

"What," he asked, "does Doyle Doyle mean?"

*   *   *

Cockie looked me up and down with a fatherly eye before wondering if I knew the police had been hunting all over New South Wales for me.

I'd been afraid of that.

"They've a warrant out for your arrest," said Newman.

"And they're up in the office roight now," added Cockie as he made room for me on the booth beside him.

It was a squeeze. And yet he always saved me the seat. They say of a man like Cockie that he has a heart as big as Phar Lap, referring to the New Zealand-bred racing sensation whose heart was found to be half again normal size. Alvie's was, too I'm sure. But that wasn't all. He also had a lap as big as Phar's lap which took one and a half times as much seat space as everyone else's. Which is why it was always a squeeze.

I said, squeezing in:

"Don't tell me—they're manning the switchboards so you and Percy could blow the heads off a couple of brews."

"Goin' through yer desk, that's wot."

"My desk!"

"Ey. Lookin' fer evidence."

"And you just let 'em do it!"

"They had a search warrant."

"You could've kept an eye on them anyway."

Newman broke in: "We came down here, Doyle, to keep an eye out for you."

"What do they want?"

"Wota they want! They wanna know why ye troied to burn down the op'ra 'ouse, that's wot they want." Cockie pushed a fat forefinger at me. "I'm a bit curious about it myself."

"Very funny, Alvie. Did it burn down? I mean did they get the fire put out before. . . ."

"They saved the building," he said. "But there's a lot of smoke and fire damage. You got plenty to answer for."

Cockie called to the barmaid who came bumping over.

We hi'd each other.

"Blue 'ere wants some neck oil," he said.

"No, never again," I sighed. "Maybe some ginger ale."

After the maid left the guys contented themselves with small talk. But when I had my drink they wanted more. And I didn't blame them. I knew exactly how they felt. With a little ginger ale in my belly I leaned back in the seat and got comfortable because I didn't want to miss a single word of what they got out of me.

I laid out blankets and pillows on the couch but when I returned moments later Jim Jim was stretched out on his back on the carpeting with no pillow under his head and no covers at all. Naturally I asked why and he replied that the couch was small. I looked again. Brother, did I feel like a louse. Small-small was more like it. His feet would have stuck out a foot off the end.

The decent thing to do was take the couch myself. But I frankly didn't want him on my bed for the fact is I still thought of him as a kind of savage thing, not mean but wild. He did nothing to dispel this impression when he volunteered that he and his brothers and sisters had a little two-room humpy in Ularup, but still bedded down in the back yard six nights out of seven. Everybody did that in Ularup, he told me.

If he wanted the floor, I thought, let him have it.

"Answer me one question before you go to sleep," I said to him.

His eyes came open.

"Last night—on the train—Maggie and I saw something. She calls it a bunyip. Maybe it was or maybe it wasn't but we saw something. I know that. One second we were looking at that mulla-mullung of yours . . . that Black Tom. We turned away, and when we looked back—"

Jim Jim's chiseled black face showed no emotion.

"—he was just gone," I added, "and something else was standing there in his place. Does any of that make sense to you?"

His head dipped once.

"A mulla-mullung is very powerful. Black Tom is more powerful than most."

"How does he do it?"

"Some say a mulla-mullung can dive into the ground and reappear wherever he wants. In another place in this world or even in the spirit world."

"Have you seen him do it?"

"No. But it is said."

"That monster—"

"It is said he can come back in the bodies of spirits."

"What spirits?"

Jim Jim hesitated.

"Which spirit, Jim Jim."

"Gol."

"That's it!" I said, "he used the name Gol just before it appeared."

Jim Jim remained stone faced.

"Have you ever seen this Gol?"

"No."

"Has anyone in your tribe seen it."

"Yes."

"Who?"

"A tribal elder, also a chief of the council of ten, and my father."

"What did they see?"

"They?"

"Start with the elder. How did he describe it?"

"He did not."

"How do you know what he saw?"

"I know."

"What happened?"

"Another tribal elder took his place on the council of ten. The council chose a new chief. I buried my father."

"Oh, you mean the chief was your. . . . I'm sorry Jim Jim, I

really am." I waited for him to go on. When he didn't, I asked
him if he wanted to talk about it.

His head moved once from side to side. He didn't trust me
enough to say more. Maybe one day he would, but not now.

"Why didn't you tell this when Maggie was with us?"

"Yes."

"Huh?"

"She was with us."

"I see. Well, tell me more about Black Tom."

"It is also said the mulla-mullung can cure sickness by suck-
ing evil from a man's body. That he can take his eyes from his
head and look death upon his enemies. This I *have* seen Black
Tom do."

"Like a whammy, huh?"

"A whammy?"

"You know, the evil eye. A hex." Jim Jim nodded understanding but without conviction. I asked him where Black Tom came
by these powers.

"He has joined the *kadi makara*. When he first became a
mulla-mullung, skeleton spirits carried him into the spirit world.
There they cut open his body and took out his bones and his
organs. The spirits dried the organs. They filled the bones with
magical substances. Then everything was put back into his body.
They put a crystal in his head, like a strong eye. With this he can
see beyond time and space."

"I see."

"He can even leave his body to see things happening far away.
In this state he cannot be harmed. He can touch hot coals
without being burned and remain under water for a long time
without drowning. Even spears cannot pierce his skin."

"And your people believe this?"

Jim Jim stirred uncomfortably.

"Some do," he said; "mostly Dongos. More and more they
doubt; mostly Bentoos."

"Who are the Bentoos?"

"Bentoos have seen the white man's city."

"And what about you, Jim Jim?"

"I am a—" He stopped. Then he wagged his head. "I was a Dongo," he said, "but now. . . ."

"I meant what do you believe?"

He shrugged mightily. "I don't know what to believe. The white people want us to accept their beliefs. Their legends. But I have to wonder if one myth is better than another. At least ours . . . are ours."

"That crazy witch doctor—that mulla-mullung," I said, "his name is Black Tom; he's the one who did it. Ask anybody who was there."

Cockie wagged his Humpty Dumpty head.

"That's the problem. There was forty, fifty journos 'oo was watchin' 'im. They all say he didn't do it. They say the fire didn't start till after he left. The coppers think some bludger close to the stage must've set it off. You was close to the stage, you an' that sheila from *Woman's Day,* an' you chucked somethin' at Copley jist before the fire."

I waved it away.

"Wot was it, Blue?"

"A skull and feathers."

One of the boys asked what it was for.

"The feathers," I explained, paraphrasing Jim Jim, "aid the mulla-mullung on his magical flight to the spirit world. The bones symbolize his mastery over the realm of death. It wasn't a firebomb if that's what you're thinking."

"It's not what we're thinking, Doyle," offered Newman. "It's what the police are thinking. They think the performance of that shaman was just a diversion for somebody else to toss a thermite device . . . a fire bomb, to use your words, underneath the platform. They suspect that talisman was in the nature of a hypergolic igniter. Like oil and potassium nitrate which combust spontaneously in the presence of acid. There are many such chemical possibilities."

"You mean someone may have placed some other chemicals on the stage beforehand."

"It's possible."

"I don't know anything about it."

"As Alf has already pointed out, you were close to the stage."

"An' the security coppers say you told 'em there was goin' to be fireworks," added Cockie.

"That was just talk."

"Ye told those two nits from the Picky ye was goin' to start a fire. The security coppers 'eard that, too."

"More talk. You know me, Alvie, I talk."

"Ye ran out."

"Everybody ran out."

"But you didn't stop when you got outside."

"I was chasing Black Tom. Look, Maggie McDowel was with me all the time, you can ask her."

"No doubt the police will want to talk to her, too." said Newman. "But you're still going to have to face them."

He was right.

I asked how much time did I have.

"Not long," Cockie said; "I promised to let 'em know the minute ye came in."

I started to get up.

With a hand on my shoulder Cockie eased me back down. He said to a fotog across the table. "Did ye make a note of it, Peter?"

"Ey. It was noine minutes to ten, Alf."

Cockie smiled. "Well, we'll 'ave to let 'em know that, won't we?"

"What can you tell me about Gol?" I asked Jim Jim. "Is it an animal? A ghost? A monster? What do you think it is?"

Jim Jim's black gaze bore at me.

"Nothing," he said.

"It's nothing?"

He shook his head.

"I can *tell* you nothing."

"Why not? Is it forbidden? Are you afraid? Of Black Tom and the spirits? Maybe you just don't want to tell me. Because I'm white, is that it?"

"Yes."

"It's because I'm white?"

"No."

"Then you're afraid of Black Tom?"

"No."

"Why not tell me then?"

"Because it is forbid."

I was starting to figure him out. Not his thinking but his way of answering questions. He picked out the part that seemed to him most important and ignored everything else.

"What's forbidden about it?"

"Gol is one of the *kadi makara*," he said suddenly.

"The *kadi makara* . . . they're spirits?"

"Yes. Spirits of the Dreamtime. Of all the *kadi makara*, Gol is most powerful."

I eased myself onto the couch.

"Remember you told Maggie and me that you tried to see Arthur Copley?" Jim Jim nodded cautiously. "You said you wanted to warn him about some kind of danger. What danger? Did you mean a danger from an ancient spirit?"

He nodded again even more carefully.

When the meaning of this struck me, I couldn't keep the astonishment from my voice: "Then . . . there really is a curse, is that what you're saying?"

"Yes."

"Is it . . . like a prophecy."

He frowned and I tried again.

"It's not just another of Black Tom's stories?"

"Oh, no! My people have knowed of this for thousands of years."

"Rush Killian's people, they're in danger from this . . . this prophecy, just like Arthur Copley?"

"Yes."

"What's going to happen to them? Can you tell me that?"

"It is too late."

I checked my watch.

"You mean it's too late to tell me?"

"Too late for them."

Something about the way he said it almost made me gulp.

"What kind of curse is it, Jim Jim?"

The big guy propped himself up on an elbow.

He eyed me strangely; I did my best to meet his glance squarely. Whatever I did must have worked.

"Long ago my people made a promise to the Great Goanna. A part of that promise was never to walk upon Gol's hunting grounds, nor to allow any other man to walk upon them. The other part is to guard the gate through which Gol can enter our lands from his. We have kept him imprisoned within his abode—in the forbid land—since the days of the Dreamtime."

"His abode. The cave Copley found?"

"A sacred place. Even I cannot enter. Every year for thousands of years our mulla-mullungs have gone to the cave to record on its walls the proof of our promise-keeping. In this way, the Great Goanna continues to protect the Ularu."

"I'd like to hear the story, Jim Jim."

But it hadn't worked that well.

He shook his head. Nothing doing. "You will not understand." His voice was hard; his jaw, set.

"I'll do my best."

"If you understand, you will not believe."

"Try me. I've seen some things in my time, some pretty wild things. I've learned to keep an open mind."

"It is not good."

"You came here to warn someone. Because you didn't get to talk to him, he was killed, and the opera house caught on fire. If we put your story in the paper then lots of people will be warned. They won't all understand or believe but at least they'll know why you and the Ularu believe what you do and why the land Killian bought is so sacred to you guys. If we can stop the violence before it happens—isn't that something to try for? You know what's going to happen if nobody does anything, don't you? A bloody war, between your people and mine. This story might help to stop it."

"The story is not written down. It is told from father to son; from brother to brother; from man to man."

"You mean you could tell me if I don't print it?"

Jim Jim turned full on me and not for the first or last time did I consider just how intimidating a creature he was. The longer his silence lasted the more ominous he seemed.

"Aren't we friends?" I asked finally.

The black eyes in his rich chocolate face blazed at me.

I think he was seeing only skim milk. Like the Gangra attendant on the train. Like most aborigines saw when they looked at white guys these days. Somehow I had to do something to make him trust me. Somebody had to trust someone.

He said nothing.

I let it go. "All right, you like Maggie, don't you?"

"Yes. She's nice."

"You could tell her and I'll listen."

"No, I cannot tell her. She wanted me to tell her but I could not. The sacred stories are for men alone."

"Well then, can't you tell me? I'm a man, aren't I?"

Again his darkling gaze swept over me.

"Maybe," he said.

I hadn't the nerve to ask him which of my questions he'd answered.

* * *

Cockie, Newman and the guys only interrupted me once, when I was describing the creature that had attacked me and Maggie on the train.

A couple of the boys were chuckling. They could afford to. They hadn't been there at the time.

"Actually," I said, "it's easy to see in hindsight what they tried to do. By turning out all the lights and locking the doors to the carriages behind ours they kept anyone else from stumbling through. When Black Tom slipped out he must have gone forward and locked that door behind him so Maggie and I couldn't escape."

"Sounds like a bloody whowie!" exclaimed Cockie.

"A whowie?"

"An aborigine playabout."

I shook my head.

"It wasn't any man in a monkey suit if that's what you mean. I don't see how it could've been anything other than the real McCoy. It's true I was pretty whirly at the time. But—if it was just a stunt—whoever pulled it off couldn't have counted on us getting drunk."

"No," Newman observed, "but they might have seen you drinking."

I told how Maggie and I had gotten ourselves lost out in the bush and how Jim Jim had followed us, found us, and then led us to the nearest burgh where the three of us had picked up a bus back to Sydney.

"Now ye know," said Cockie, "why I din't want ye to go bush—it's no playce fer an outsider loike yerself. No sir, no playce at all."

"I'm beginning to believe it's no place for any white man."

"You sound loike one o' them."

"Do I? Wait'll you hear the rest of it."

Cockie showed surprise; Newman, keen interest.

"You got him to tell you about the curse?"

I nodded:

"I got him to tell me about the curse. I understand now why the Ularu believe Rush Killian's land is sacred, and why they're so anxious for him to get off. The same with Arthur Copley. When he took those pictures he violated a thousands-year-old agreement the Ularu had made with their spirits and they believe he's put all of their lives in danger."

Think of the Dreamtime as a kind of Australian Big Bang and you won't be too wide of the mark. This was long before man, even the aborigines, came to the continent. The desert was covered by forest back then. A Tarzan set from coast to coast with rivers and lakes galore. According to aboriginal lore, strange, long-dead and long-forgotten beasts abounded. When they died their spirits, the *kadi makara,* were born again in the bodies of other animals, plants and rocks in an unending totemic recycling of life, just as aborigines today are totemically related to the fauna, the flora and features of their environment.

I offer that synopsis because it took Jim Jim half an hour to explain it to me. He said the whole thing had been clear to him since he'd turned six years old.

"In those long ago times the Great Goanna, he ruled the land like the queen she does today," said Jim Jim.

"Goanna, now that's a lizard, right?"

Jim Jim stretched out his long arms as though he were trying to encircle the trunk of a baobab tree and said:

"The Great Goanna was many times bigger than any goanna living today. But he was not the only big boss. In the air was the Rainbow Serpent. The water, that was the territory of Tobraka, the goanna fish and brother to the Great Goanna. Gol ruled in the treetops. In those days each of the beasts remained in his own abode and did not trouble the others."

"Okay, let me get this straight. You've got the Great Goanna who's like Godzilla. His brother is half fish and he lives in the water. The Rainbow Serpent flies and Gol lives in the trees."

Jim Jim accepted this with a scowl and said: "Things began to change. The air grew hot. Rivers began to dry up. Lakes shrinked. Tobraka, the goanna fish, looked around one day and did not like what he saw. He called to his brother, the Great Goanna, and said, 'All is not right. As my water becomes smaller, your land becomes larger. We must share.' But the Great Goanna did not like sharing. He told his brother the goanna fish he must accept what he. . . ." Jim Jim paused.

"You mean he could like it or lump it?"

"Yes. So the goanna fish he told the Rainbow Serpent there wasn't enough water for rain. No water, no rain; no rain, no trees. Soon the forests began to disappear. And before long there was little left but land."

And how about Gol?

Let me paraphrase Jim Jim: Gol wasn't about to take up residence in the air or the water so he went to Godzilla and said pretty much the same thing as the lizard fish: Godzilla had to slice up the neighborhood like it or not. Oh Godzilla liked that . . . you bet he did! However, Gol was more powerful than the lizard fish. He and Godzilla went at it hammer and tongs. They each took plenty of lumps but neither could make the other cry uncle.

"Okay, I got that," I said, "what happened then?"

"Finally," said Jim Jim, "the Rainbow Serpent summoned the Mighty Marsupial and together they divided the land with a mountain so high and wide that neither spirit could get to the other. So the Great Goanna ruled on the near side while Gol remained on the far side."

I was slumped back on the couch then, just hanging on. As much as I wanted to hear him explain about a two-legged, four-armed monster, I was so beat it was all I could do to keep my eyes open.

"Is that the end of it?"

"No. Goanna fish and all his waters were with Great Goanna. Gol tricked the goanna fish, who was still angry with his brother goanna, into carving a river through the mountain. Now Gol was free. Each night, while the other *kadi makara* slept, he crawled out and fought with the Great Goanna. Each morning, before they awoke, he crawled back into his abode."

"Where does the curse come in?"

"Many years passed. My ancestors moved into the land. At first they were enemies of the *kadi makara*. They hunted and were hunted by the Great Goanna and his brother goanna fish. And at night, Gol would come into their camps, too. He would drag children, women and even men into the desert, tear open their bodies, and devour their hearts. Sentries who kept watch over the camp would themselves be devoured. Not until the Ularu learned to build fences and gates were they freed from him. We do not like fences but we learned. Only Great Goanna threatened us when we left our campsites during the day to hunt. And even he was losing strength. The Great Goanna, tired of warring with Gol, made a treaty with the early Ularu. If they would put a gate across the passage then Great Goanna agreed not to harm them or their children. And so it was done. My people sneaked into the cave early one morning after Gol had returned. They sealed off the opening. Each year they went back into the cave to see that the gate still held. As proof they had done this, they painted each year a new picture on a wall of the cave. The Great Goanna knows by this picture that my people have kept their promise. For many centuries the Ularu lived in harmony with the *kadi makara*.

"And then came the white man. . . ."

"And that's it?" Newman asked me.

"Pretty much," I said. "I fell asleep soon after that and woke up nine hours later on the couch. The curse says if anyone wanders around to the other side of the mountain, they're liable to be attacked by Gol. Or if a man enters the cave without understanding the evil that awaits him, he may open the gate and loose the spirit of Gol upon himself and the Ularu people. Arthur Copley sneaked into the cave without getting Godzilla's permission. He's dead. And Rush Killian trespassed on Gol's abode. The question is, what's happening to him and his men."

"What does your native friend think is happening?"

"He doesn't know. But he's scared. And so are all of his tribe. As far as they're concerned the only difference between this Gol and the Black Plague is that they've never heard of the Black Plague."

I caught Cockie checking his watch.

"Ye ought to be goin' upstairs 'fore long."

"I'm going. But before I go, I want to say something. Maggie and I would probably be dead now if it weren't for Jim Jim. We owe him. And that's not all. We were working for ENA at the time so you owe him too."

"Wot's 'e want?" asked Cockie.

"He wants to go home. If the cops get their hands on him they'll lock him up and throw away the keys. We can't let them stick him for any of this mess."

Cockie grunted.

"That may not be easy. Yer story gets you off but it gets 'im in. The coppers want 'im too. Where is 'e now?"

"He's still at my place."

"Will 'e stay there?"

"He'll stay put for a while but not long. He wants to go back to Ularup."

"An' ye want me to put 'im on a plane, is that roight?"

"A train . . . a bus. It doesn't matter. Just get him out of town. Meanwhile, I'll hold off the cops for as long as I can. A couple of hours. That'll give you time to make your arrangements."

"Ye're gonna loy . . . to the coppers?"

"I won't lie exactly but I'll figure some way to stall. Two hours. That's all I can promise."

"Good as done, Blue."

"You'll have to move fast, Alvie."

"She'll be apples." His eyes fell to his schooner and his face lit up when he saw the frigid froth which had sunk barely halfway down. He hefted it in his fat fist. "Well, down the gurgler, mates."

Everyone drank.

Except me.

I watched them, without moving.

Cockie set the mug down empty. He surveyed the other empty mugs hitting the tabletop one by one. When the last mug was down he thrust a fist into the midst of them. One by one, the others extended their fists the same way until these formed the hub of a five-spoke wheel. Then the fists began to hammer the tabletop in unison. On the third blow Cockie's fist came down in the thumbs up position. Others came down with the index and middle fingers protruding and another with the fist still balled. A few fists withdrew. In the end it was just Cockie and Bobby. Cockie came down thumbs up again which everyone there knew he did six times out of ten because he liked to think of his fist as a bomb.

Bobby pinched Cockie's thumb between his two fingers. "Scissors cuts fuse," he said; "you shout."

Cockie did a slow turn around the table adding up the mugs. When he came to me he stopped, apparently surprised that I was still hanging around.

"Would ye like a stubby before ye go up then, Blue?"

"No, I'd like to see you do something about Jim Jim."

He smiled.

"No hurry, Blue, no hurry. We're all just a bunch of working stiffs, ayn't we?"

"You're getting stiff," I agreed. "But I seem to be the only one working and Jim Jim's the one being stiffed."

Cockie whirled to Newman.

"Wot's 'e mean?"

Even I rarely stumped Percy Newman.

"I think he wants you to do something, Alf," he said.

6

Auld Acquaintance

There are three kinds of facts.

There's the kind you look up, the kind you make up and the kind you testify to in court.

It's a fact, for example, I've been arrested six times through the years. The record proves it. It's also a fact they were all in the line of duty and I never spent a night in jail—I can swear to that. This time I darned near took the fall. I walked, but only because I met an old acquaintance downtown who pulled the right wires and convinced the right people that if Doyle Mulligan didn't write the thirty dash on this story it wouldn't get written. That's a fact, too. I'll admit I never checked into the thing and I can't swear it happened that way but, even so, it's a fact. Take my word for it.

Here's how it went:

Those city cops were waiting for me upstairs—openers, that's all, just a pair of jacks.

They were happy to see me. They insisted on giving me a ride downtown. I was willing to find my own transportation but they wouldn't hear of it. They even offered to put me up for a few days courtesy of the city of Sydney. We went down in the lift arm in arm, their hands on my arms and my hands in handcuffs.

The first cop was an easygoing Aussie with three chins and a sense of humor. He and I got along fine. His partner was another matter. An athlete. One of those square-jawed, Vic Tanny types with overactive hormones and his brains in his fists. Also his ears were too big and his head was too narrow. I swear he could have hidden behind a salute. He'd clamped the bracelets on me a lot tighter than necessary and he liked to walk behind me and push.

We made it downtown without coming to blows. But hold on, the blows were coming.

Sydney Central Police Station is an old brick building with historic murals on the inside walls. I remember one of convicts being herded ashore from a three-masted ship in the harbor. Another mural showed a shirtless prisoner tied to a seven-foot tripod frame around which British soldiers stood at attention and the flogger cracked his whip. The convict's ankles were bound to two legs of the triangle. He was suspended by a chain from the triangle's apex. His back looked like something hanging in a meat locker.

This, the painting seemed to say, was waiting for me if I didn't wise up.

My escorts prodded me into an office. There was a desk and a filing cabinet and three chairs. I was ordered to sit down in one chair. Vic Tanny propped himself up in a corner while his chinny-chin partner dropped down behind the desk.

"They tell me ye're a broight un," Vic announced with a sneer. "Izat roight?"

I admitted it.

"A real wonder, ey?"

"I'm one of 'em," I said; "I've never claimed to be all seven."

He didn't think that was very funny.

"Say something broight," he challenged me.

I grinned.

"Robert R. Goodman, American Vice-Consul. Two-six-one, ninety-two hundred."

When I finished, the silence seemed to go on forever.

Finally:

"Are you saying," asked the friendly one, "that a smart bloke like you needs legal counsel? All we want are answers to a few questions."

I held up my manacles.

"What about these?"

"Oh, I guess those could come off—" he started to say. But the other guy nixed it. First I had to prove I could be "cooperative."

"Just whose side are you on, yank?" Vic Tanny wanted to know.

"I'm not on anyone's side."

"I think you're siding with the abos."

"Think again. Reporters aren't allowed to take sides."

"Don't give me that; reporters are just like everybody else. I think you're an abo lover."

I said I hardly knew any aborigines.

"But I bet you don't much like Killian and his mob."

"I've never met him. It's he who doesn't like reporters like me. Haven't you heard? He keeps a lion dog around just to keep reporters away."

"A lion dog?"

"Yeah. It's got a mane and everything."

"Don't get smart, Mulligan. Just answer questions."

I told him to just ask questions instead of making accusations.

After that things got businesslike fast. They wanted to know everything I knew about the opera house fire. About Arthur Copley and his pictures of aboriginal cave paintings. Next they surprised me by wanting to know everything I'd dug up on Killian's development project. That was odd because I didn't think anyone but Alvin Cockie and I had made the connection.

I didn't volunteer much but I supplied a few facts, all of them the first kind of fact, the kind you look up. That's how I'd gotten them—I'd looked them up.

Then they changed direction.

For the next half hour we went over the same questions Newman and Cockie had asked. Why did I position myself near the stage? What was that thing I'd thrown? Why did I run? Why didn't I stop running when the rent-a-cop ordered me to stop? What had I meant when I told him there were going to be fireworks? Why did I tell two reporters from The Picky I was going to start a fire?

I answered with more facts, the third kind of fact, the type you can testify to in court. I could have, too, I just hoped it wouldn't be from the prisoner's dock.

Suddenly they shifted gears again. Now they wanted to know who was the sheila who'd run from the opera house with me. Where did we run to and what had we been up to for the past forty-two hours?

I told them I didn't know what woman they were talking about. I'd run after the aborigine who'd started the fire, but I'd lost him and didn't know where he'd gone. I'd spent the whole night as well as the next day and night trying to pick up a new lead. Even to me it didn't sound believable, and I've always said I trust me implicitly. The truth is I trust me explicitly but I'd never say so in so many words.

"What koind of tale is that?" Vic wanted to know.

"It's a fact," I said.

"What koind of fact?"

"The kind you . . . the second kind."

Three chins took over the questioning before Vic could delve deeper into that.

"How well did you know Arthur Copley?"

"I don't. I didn't."

"You'd never met him?"

"Never laid eyes on him before that day. Never even heard of him before."

"Then why did you tell the security guard that you had to talk to him? To warn him of trouble unless he cancelled the showing."

I knew a little something about police interrogation procedures but this was a new one on me. I just sat there shaking my head.

"Do you deny saying that?"

"I am denying it. I didn't say anything of the kind."

"We can bring the security man in here."

I told them to go ahead because I thought it had to be a trick and anyway it would eat up some time. Unfortunately it wasn't. Ditto it didn't.

Two minutes later the security guard pops in the door and gives me a smirk. My wearing handcuffs and sitting on the hot seat seemed to amuse him more than it did me.

"That's him," he announced.

"This is the man who told you there was going to be fireworks?"

"Ey."

"I said I said that," I said.

"And," said three chins, "he's the bloke who demanded to see Arthur Copley. He said he had to see Copley before the show started. Right?"

"He wanted to, ey."

I spoke up, "I think I know what you're talking about. I asked you how Copley had gotten his pictures of the cave art and you told me to ask *him*. Remember?"

Vic Tanny growled for me to shut up.

But the rent-a-cop was nodding his head.

"I think that's right," he said. "This bloke's about the same size. Same height and thinny like him. Same hair and eyes, too. But this one had an AJA card. The other'ne didn't."

"Thinny? You mean skinny?"

"He means thin," I sang out.

"Shut up!" Vic turned on the rent-a-cop. "You said he threatened Copley."

"It was more like a warning. He said Copley'd better cancel the showing before he got hurt."

"That was this man?"

The guy glommed me good.

"Could be. Could be the other bloke, too."

Vic Tanny swaggered over. "You can't say for certain that this is the man who threatened Copley?"

"He wanted to see him. They both wanted to see him."

"And that's the best you can do!"

"I think this is the one who started a fight with them other two journos."

"Go on. Out!"

Three chins showed him the door.

About that time Vic Tanny and his hormones had a fit. He paced circles around me while smacking his fist in his palm. He screamed in my ear. He pushed and slapped a lot and occasionally even knocked me out of my chair. His pal always stopped him before things went too far. Every time three chins left the room Vic Tanny would swoop down on me in a rage, ranting and swinging until his partner returned and cooled him off.

Once, after three chins brought me a glass of water, Vic knocked it out of my hand. Then, without warning, he leaped on me, got my shirt in his fists and began shaking. His partner managed to calm him down before he did me any real harm.

"Maybe I can keep him away from you," said three chins when Vic went out for a smoke. "Would you like that?"

"If it's not too much trouble," I said.

"All you have to do is cooperate, Mulligan."

I swallowed a choice remark.

But I wasn't upset.

In one way, I enjoyed it—this was a police procedure I did recognize, and I never saw the good cop/bad cop routine done better. It was a pleasure to watch. But in another way it was an insult to my intelligence.

I mean, I may have been born in the day, but it wasn't *yester*day.

Anyway, Vic Tanny went out for a smoke, and chins and I had a heart-to-heart talk. He'd be going off duty in little while. I'd be stuck with Tanny and his overactive hormones, which weren't the only things overacting—that ham! He said if there was something I wanted to get off my chest I should do it now. He

couldn't hang around if I didn't open up. It was all I could do
to keep a straight face.

By then it had been two hours and more.

There was no point in holding out any longer.

I waited until he left. When Vic Tanny stormed in, I rushed
over.

"Please, please," I said. "I'll tell you anything you want to
know if you promise to keep that guy away from me."

It more than met expectations.

He looked over his shoulder.

He looked at me.

"What's wrong?" he whined.

"That guy," I said, "I can't stand it any more."

"Ye mean. . . ?" He was incredulous. "It's *'im* you don't like!"

I twisted up my face. "He's just so darned . . . *good!*"

From that moment on, he knew that I knew what they had
been up to. I'd won. And he knew it.

"Go to buggery!" he growled as he went out to fetch his acting
partner.

I told them about the witch doctor. I told them about Jim Jim
and Maggie and all the rest. The only thing I held back was the
part about the monster. They wouldn't have believed me anyway
and after all the lies I'd already told I didn't dare to put them to
the test. Before I knew it they had bundled me into a squad car
and shot me across town at what, for any citizen under any
circumstances at all, would have been a criminal speed.

I figured we were headed to my apartment and I prayed that
Cockie had done his job but no, we headed in the other direction. To the city meat locker.

Sydney's morgue is a modern building. It's carefully maintained. I've never been in there when janitors weren't busily
scrubbing the floors and washing the walls. On top of that an air
conditioning unit blasts away day and night. But it stinks. It reeks
of formaldehyde.

There was some confusion about which body they wanted me

to identify. Several John Does had come in at one time. Three from Tennant Creek, and another from the tracks just outside of Lithgow.

My ears perked up when I heard the Tennant Creek part. But it was the Lithgow body they wanted me to see.

They especially did not want me to see the other three bodies. Three chins led me into a room. There was a gurney out on the floor.

I told my stomach to hang on.

A dead object starts out as a corpse. Somewhere on the way to the coroner's it turns into a cadaver and by the time a priest gets into the act it's "the remains."

I didn't know if this object had been carved up yet. As far as I was concerned what he showed me was just a stiff.

A sheet covered it from head to foot.

"Just tell me if you recognize 'im," said three chins.

"I've already told you—I never saw the witch doctor's face. I have no idea who he is or what he looks like without the mask."

"Then how do you know he's not the same bloke as this black friend of yours?"

"I just know. Black Tom's a lot thinner. Jim Jim is solid muscle. Ask anyone who was there."

"Well, look at 'im anyway."

He pushed me to the head of the gurney and pulled back the sheet. The vacant eyes of an aboriginal face stared up at me. And surprise! I did recognize him.

It was a cocoa-colored face somewhere between chocolate milk and milk chocolate. Alive, the guy had had a chocolate chip on his shoulder but now, of course, I knew why. Jim Jim had told him that Maggie and I had followed Black Tom on the train. He was keeping an eye on us.

"It's him," I said.

"Black Tom?"

"No, no, the attendant on the Indian Pacific."

"The train guard?"

"Whatever."

"Do you know his name?"

"No, I . . . I never asked."

"You're sure it's him?"

"Positive."

"You don't know anything about him?"

"Nothing more. Wait. He's from Arnhem Land—a Gangra tribesman. That's what Jim Jim told me. He was keeping an eye on Black Tom and the two white men traveling with him."

"Two white men? You're sure?"

"That's what Jim Jim said."

"But you didn't see 'em?"

"No."

"And your black friend was bunkin' in with this man?"

"So he said. But Jim Jim didn't kill the guy. He was still alive when Jim Jim jumped off the train."

"How do you know that?"

"Well . . . because Jim Jim told me."

"Is there anything else you remember?"

"No, nothing."

The good cop led me back out to a waiting area. He sat me down, told Vic Tanny to keep any eye on me, and then left to make a call and fill out some papers.

"What now?" I asked.

"Just wait," Vic Tanny growled.

He was back in character. In addition to a narrow skull and a narrow mind, he had a narrow repertoire. I decided he played the bad cop for a reason. Typecasting.

I waited a while longer before standing up and holding out my hands.

"I'd like to do something. How about taking off these cuffs?"

"If I was you, sport, I'd just si'down and shu'up," he snarled.

"*Were* you," I snapped.

He strolled over and stood right in front of me.

"Wot?"

"Not if I was you. It's if I *were* you. You're in the subjunctive mood, see? When you're bullying a member of the press, you have to watch your grammar. What you say may end up in the morning paper."

He shoved a muscular finger in my face.

"And what *you* say may end up on the floor along with yer teeth. If you want somethin' to do try twiddling your thumbs."

"A fellow like you," I snapped back, "ought to twiddle his ears."

He bunched both of his fists.

"What's that supposed to mean, yank?" he demanded. He stood over me, defying me to reply. He wanted me to repeat it. So I didn't.

I shrugged my shoulders.

"I should wiggle my ears, huh?" he demanded.

"No, I said twiddle, not wiggle." I held up my hands with the fingers interlocked and the thumbs twirling about one another. "Anyone can wiggle his ears. I once dated a girl who could flap her ears." I fanned my elbows up and down to demonstrate. "She flapped them so hard she raised a breeze. Believe it or not, officer, she could put out a candle from two paces. I'd have married her, just for the novelty of it, if she hadn't kept giving me head colds."

I felt his hot breath on my face. I can't say for sure what the guy's mood was right then but I doubt very much it was the subjunctive.

"An' I should twiddle my ears, ey?"

I shrugged again.

"Are ye sayin' my ears are too big, yank?"

"Nobody's told you?"

"Told me what?"

This time he really didn't want me to answer.

So I did.

"Mostly," I said with a grin, "they're just too close together."

I never saw it coming. His fist came out of nowhere and

caught me right on the nose. My brain did a backflip inside my skull and I fell in a broken pile on the couch.

By the time I got my eyes open again he'd backed off.

My nose was bleeding like crazy. I staunched it with a finger and mumbled something about needing to get to a bathroom. I must have sounded pretty desperate.

He pointed to a door down the hall.

I guess he realized he'd gone too far.

I staggered out, letting the corridor walls hold me up. I made it look good. Cops aren't the only hams. Inside, I used a wet paper towel to stop the bleeding. Then I let the faucet run while I went to the door and peeked out.

The guy had stuck both his brains in his pockets which, at least as far as I was concerned, was the only safe place for them. When he wasn't looking I cat-footed down the hall.

An official at the front door had seen my handcuffs and that meant I'd never get past him alone. It didn't matter. I didn't want to get out. I slipped into the second autopsy room.

Two coroners were busy on the far side.

There was not one, but three gurneys in this room. All were covered by sheets. Either the coroners had completed their autopsies or they hadn't yet gotten started.

I moved in a crouch to the first one. It had a tag on the side with a typed code number and BOYLE, HECTOR? in all caps— the question mark was theirs, not mine.

I raised a corner of the sheet.

What I expected to find, I don't know; all I know is I didn't find it. I got a glimpse of skeleton, some brownish tissue and a few scraps of skin. Not even enough for me to be certain the body was that of a white man or an aborigine . . . a man or a woman.

I swallowed hard and raised the sheet higher.

"See here! What are you doing?"

I whirled.

One of the coroners was closing in from the side.

I started for the door but it swung open and in marched good cop, bad cop, and another guy who turned out to be none other than top cop, Lug Webber, Sydney's pugnacious chief of police.

I froze.

"Who is this bloke and what the bloody hell is he doing in here?" Webber demanded.

I'd recognized him at once—anyone would. Webber had a formidable physiognomy and a physique to match. Nobody, but nobody, not even the premier, messed with Lug Webber.

A fourth man had stepped in behind them. Him I'd have recognized too if I hadn't been busy trying to figure out A: who I was, and B: what the bloody hell I was doing in there. As it was I barely noticed him.

"I left him with Sergeant Ek, sir," said three chins.

"Ek?"

Narrow-mind saluted and, sure enough, for a moment he vanished behind the edge of his hand. If the door had been left open even a crack he'd have vanished into the hallway.

"I thought he was using the loo, sir."

Webber turned his pugnacious phiz on me.

"Well?"

Before I could answer, someone else spoke.

"His name," said a voice I ought to have recognized as easily as the face, "is Doyle Mulligan. He's a reporter, a correspondent for the American press, and he's doing what he always seems to be doing—meddling in matters that are none of his business."

I looked over Lug Webber's shoulder.

I started to say that meddling in matters that are none of my business *was* my business. I never got the words out.

Now I recognized the face and the voice.

It was my old ally and savior from Hong Kong. Scotland Yard Inspector Llewellyn Hawthorne.

I was saved again.

*   *   *

He was tall and lean with quick angular movements. But his face was the thing. Back in Hong Kong I'd described him as hatchet-faced. He had a razor-edged nose, a pointed chin and a forehead like the business end of an axe. He also had a way of bobbing his bean up and down when he got angry that made him look like he was chopping cordwood, but was capable of cleaving skulls just as easily.

To top it off, he had cream, almost-yellow, hawkish eyes that were now narrowed to mere slits.

I smiled hugely.

"Well, I'll be damned!"

"What *are* you doing here?" he demanded.

"Small world!" I cried, starting forward. "Inspector Hawthorne! Holy cow, it's good to see you." I stuck out my hand. Both of them, in fact, since they were still manacled together.

He ignored them both. Probably he thought I wanted to have them unlocked and of course he didn't have a key.

From behind me came:

"D'you know this man, superintendent?"

I turned.

"The inspector and I," I let Lug Webber know, "are old pals."

The chief dismissed the three chins and Sergeant Ek, who closed the door on his way out by giving me a last lingering glare through the crack until finally even his narrow face was pinched off. Webber was glaring too.

"This is *Superintendent* Hawthorne, Special Branch," he chided me.

I raised my brows.

"And we are not . . . pals," added Hawthorne.

I grinned up at him. "So it's Superintendent now. Gee, doesn't that have a nice ring?"

He snorted.

I turned to Lug Webber.

"You know," I said, "it's not going too far to say that everyone

. . . the whole world but particularly those of us here in the East, owe this man a great debt of thanks."

Webber nodded. "I know of his service in Hong Kong."

"No, I mean for saving my life. If it weren't for him, I wouldn't even be here."

But Lug Webber couldn't see a joke except by appointment and he'd be late for that.

"I apprehended a criminal," Hawthorne corrected me. "It had nothing to do with you. Now see here, Mulligan, are you involved in this mess as well?"

"It looks that way, don't it?"

The police chief broke in.

"This is the man who's suspected of trying to burn down the Sydney Opera House. We think he's working hand in glove with the abos."

"Abos? Sir, are you referring to the aboriginals?"

"Ey," said Webber and then added with a sneer. "Indigenous persons."

But Hawthorne shook his head. "I don't think so, Chief Webber. Mulligan is just a bumbling reporter who can't stay out of trouble. All right, Mulligan, what's your story this time?"

"Honest, Inspector—I mean, Superintendent—I was just covering the art show. The thing got out of hand, that's all."

"Naturally. Let's have it."

I let them have it. The works. This time I even threw in the part about the monster. Maggie's bunyip, or whatever it was. In fact I started there.

Hawthorne stopped me before I'd done more than start.

"That's enough of that!" he snapped.

"I'm not making it up, Inspector; I saw what I saw."

"Well I don't have time for nonsense."

"He's admitted being drunk," explained Webber.

"Not that drunk!" I cried.

"Go on then, but start from the beginning."

I've said it before and I'll say it again, Hawthorne's the worst audience in the world. I remembered back in Hong Kong—after the plane I was flying in had a hole blasted in its side and the guy I was following got himself defenestrated at thirty thousand feet—Hawthorne did his best to make me out to be the bomber. Then—as now—he'd circled around me nodding his head like an executioner's axe. Now—as then—his pale face turned whiter and whiter as a sure sign that his temper was flaring.

"If you telephoned your office," he said, barely holding his voice to a low roar, "then you could easily have called the police. You could have alerted the railway security when you knew that man was on the train."

"We would have had some men waiting at Lithgow," added Webber.

There was nothing I could say about that.

That's what I said.

"I've a good mind," Hawthorne said, "to let the police put you behind bars until this whole thing is over. In any case I doubt if I can stop them. Surely, you can see why you're their principal suspect. You were there at the opera house. You disappeared immediately after the fire, and didn't reappear for two days. You failed to notify the authorities of what you learned. If it were anyone else, Mulligan, you'd be locked up right now."

"I know. It's great having friends in high places."

He snorted again. "I wouldn't count heavily on that."

Hawthorne spoke to Chief Webber. He suggested that I step into the waiting area with Sergeants Ek and Willoughby while he and Webber conversed in private for a few minutes.

Ek was in another mood but three chins, Willoughby, was still enough of a good cop to unlock my handcuffs. I sat on the couch and tried—not very hard—not to look smug. I knew what was going on in there. Hawthorne was pulling the right wires and convincing the right person that if Doyle Mulligan didn't write the thirty dash on this story, it wouldn't get written.

That's a fact!

I knew it. So did they. Which is why Ek was in a mood and

why Willoughby took off my handcuffs. It was also why I tried not to look smug . . . even though I did, because I didn't try very hard.

Finally they called me back in.

Webber was standing in a corner with a sour expression. Hawthorne, with his back to the cadaver I'd almost gotten a look at but not quite, was grim-faced, too. But to be fair his face always looks grim to me.

"I've made a suggestion," he announced.

I took one more shot at Lug Webber's sour puss and just had to smile.

"I like it already," I told him.

"Be quiet and listen, Mulligan. Do you know those two reporters who've gone to the Top End?"

"Sure. They work for ENA, too. Their names are Mickey Fine and Nevil Cross."

Hawthorne turned to Webber for confirmation.

"I thought you said they were columnists for that daily paper. . . ? The *Pictorial*?"

"That's right. MacMutton and Geoffers are their names."

My brows soared.

"Mutt and Jeff! They're up at Killian's?"

"So I understand. Chief?"

"Yes."

"If they're as bad as I'm told, the sooner we get some responsible reports coming from out of there, the better off we'll be," he growled. "They're spraying gasoline on a fire and it's getting hotter every day. Mulligan, if you've been here for more than a week you know this country has all the ingredients for a first-class race war."

"I know," I said.

"The very factors which led to rioting in your country in the sixties and seventies, not to mention Los Angeles in '92, are at work here today with the aborigines. Unemployment six times the average. Life expectancies twenty years shorter than whites.

High infant mortality; high incidence of disease—diseases, most
of them, introduced by white men. Too many aborigines live in
substandard conditions. They're sixteen times as likely to wind
up in prison—"

"Superintendent, this isn't the time."

"I know. I know. I'm only pointing out the potential for
trouble has long existed in Australia. It's needed only a flash to
ignite it."

"There are twenty-five million blacks in the States," argued
the chief of police; "we have scarcely a quarter of a million of
them and we can handle—"

"And fifteen million whites. You're right, this isn't Los Angeles. There, inner-city blacks rioted after a black motorist was
beaten and the five white policemen responsible were turned
loose by an all-white jury. Think what would've happened if the
circumstances had been reversed. What if a white population
suddenly turned on a minority of blacks in a murderous rage?
That's what you should be concerned with. How do you suppose
the white majority is going to react to this?"

With that, Hawthorne pulled back the sheet on the first
corpse. The one I'd gotten half a look at myself.

It wasn't Boyle. Maybe it was at one time but not any more.
What it was now, I had no idea. It wasn't exactly a corpse. Or
a cadaver. Judging by what was left, it didn't even quality as the
remains.

While I stood there, transfixed at the gruesome pile of bone
bits, organs and tissue heaped on the gurney, Hawthorne moved
around behind me and pulled the other two sheets from the
other two gurneys.

They were in much the same condition.

"Jesus Christ!" was all I could think to say. "What happened
to them?"

"We don't know. When found, these parts were strewn across
several acres of desert. They collected everything they could find
but, to tell the truth, we're not even certain we've divided them

all up properly. One of these is—or was—a man by the name of Hector Boyle, a surveyor hired by the Killian Development Group. We believe the other two were men who worked for Boyle. Which are which . . . we don't know."

I couldn't turn my eyes away.

"They look like they've been thrown in a den of lions."

"If this were Africa, I'd agree with you."

"The official report," broke in Chief Webber, "and the media release . . . will say they were attacked by dingos."

"Dingos!" I exclaimed.

"Wild dogs," explained Hawthorne.

"I know— Look, dingos didn't do this."

"Until we have evidence to the contrary," said Webber, "it's dingos."

Hawthorne said, "The fact is there are no creatures in all of Australia capable of this. Not any more. Australia has no wolves, no true bears, and no big cats. In fact the only large meat eaters still around are the crocodiles and, as these men were murdered in the desert, that's ruled out. Nevertheless something's ripped them apart. You can see the skin has been literally slashed to shreds, they've been disemboweled, and the muscle tissue has been wrenched from the bones. Most of the bones have been splintered. Even the skulls are crushed."

I said softly: "Their bodies opened, their blood drunk and their hearts torn from their chests and devoured."

"What's that?"

"That's what Black Tom said would happen to those who violated the sacred lands. He called them the desecrators. He said the spirits would—"

"Spirits don't butcher people," snapped Webber. "This is the work of a madman."

I shook my head. "No. I don't believe it was dingos. But I don't believe any man did it either."

The three of us regarded the human piles. I don't know about them but I was looking for any sign of a heart. I saw none.

Hawthorne's voice remained flat.

"You're correct, of course. No one man could do that to another. It would take a mob, armed with waddies and native knives. The waddi can break bones; the native knife can cut and tear flesh just as savagely as a lion's claws if wielded by a small army of black warriors."

"You believe the Ularus did this?"

"Somebody did," he replied.

"Or some *thing*. Like that thing I saw on the train—"

"Oh, please, Mulligan!"

"There *is* a curse on that land. The Ularus claim—"

"That's enough!"

There was another pause just then. This one was very much the pregnant kind and midwifed by revulsion it nearly delivered a full blown period.

I found myself looking over one set of remains.

My eyes had caught sight of something that made all of Hawthorne's words fade.

A dismembered foot on one of the bodies was badly mutilated. Not by the killers that had torn him apart but by a mistake of nature.

I stepped closer.

My heart fell into my sneakers.

"Hold on!"

Hawthorne crossed to me. "What is it?" His voice was still flat but he knew that I knew that something was wrong.

"This man had a club foot."

He scooped up the autopsy report.

" '. . . congenital talipes.' "

"I'm not Dr. Scholl, for Chrissake!" I cried, "It's a club foot!"

"What of it?"

"My God. Mickey Fine."

"You know him?"

"Hell yes! I know him. He was a reporter. One of the guys ENA sent up to Killian's."

I pushed by Hawthorne and pulled the sheet farther back on the third victim.

As strange as it sounds, I found myself repelled by the sight and drawn to it. Both at the same time. A head, but no face. The chest was completely open. I searched the arms and leg pieces that had been placed beside it. I found tattoos. One there on the forearm. Another on a hunk of shoulder tissue.

"Can you identify this one?"

I nodded dumbly.

"Yeah. Nevil Cross. He and Mickey Fine went up there together." I couldn't turn away. I could talk all right—but the sight was so ghastly I stared at it spellbound. So did he. "It was my story from the beginning," I explained. "I should've gone. But Mickey and Nevil won it in a Two-Up game."

"Two-Up, you say? That's illegal."

This set me free from the spell. I broke away to stare at the chief of police. And what a relief it was! Even Lug Webber's ugly pug was a welcome sight after that.

7

The Follow-up

"Ye've heard 'em called whistlecocks, ayn't ye?" Alvin Cockie put to me suddenly.

I frowned at him, then at Percy Newman.

"Yeah, I've heard it," I said; "I don't like it."

"Do you know what it means?" he demanded.

"It's like nigger, isn't it."

"Ey, but I mean, d'ye know where it comes from?"

I admitted I didn't.

It was just the three of us there at our table because I'd wanted to break the bad news to Newman and Cockie before everyone else found out. It hadn't been easy. They ordered Fosters. Five schooners. Two of them went untouched. What became of them I never learned. Cockie made a toast to old chums without mentioning Mickey or Nevil by name. Poor Alvie was taking it badly. "We'll 'ave a whip-round jist as soon as I've spoke to their woives," he said.

Newman nodded. "Do you want me to handle it, Alf?" Cockie pinched his lips and shook his head in reply. He would do it. On that occasion I *had* known what they were talking about. A "whip-round" is their way of passing the hat. It can be done anywhere, anytime, but in a pub among one's mates is the usual practice. A hat gets filled quickly down here for Aussies are generous to a fault. Except with those who aren't. The first time a bowl was put under my nose Cockie muttered, "Dig deep, Blue, they're collecting fer a postie's widder." I hadn't argued. But after the guy left I'd asked Cockie what would happen if a man didn't chip in. "Well," he said, "we'd collect fer *his* widder next."

But that was another occasion and another Cockie. Today he was telling me about "whistlecocks" though he surely knew I wouldn't like it. He may have had a heart as big as Phar Lap and he may have had a lap as big as Phar's lap but there were times when Cockie could be a real horse's anatomy and I could take him about as far as I could throw him. Which was not phar.

"The abos have a ceremony—"

"I don't like that word either," I said.

He glared at me. I thought for a moment he was going to put me in my place, and so did he, but at the last second he changed his mind. He showed the glare to Newman.

"Neither do I," said Percy.

Cockie fumed sulphurously. "They butchered Mickey and Nevil, didn't they? Blue saw 'em!"

"I saw their bodies. I didn't see who killed 'em. The police are saying it was dingos."

"Bah! Dingos! They're not loike wolves. They're small dogs and small game hunters. Oh, they'll get a sick roo now and again but it would take a dozen of them to kill and maim three grown men and they only hunt in pairs. Anyway I doubt there's a dozen of them in Killian's whole valley. They're practically an endangered species."

"If anything did it," I said, "it was that thing I saw on the train."

"Yer whowie? Don't make me larf!"

Newman came to my assistance. "Even so," he said, "how can you be so sure it was aborigines?"

"I was tryin' to tell ye!" he said.

"Go ahead and tell us."

"They 'ave a ceremony involving subincision. Not circumcision, they take care of that when their males are still at an early age. That's bloody enough. Later, while a young male is away from the village by 'imself, hunting perhaps or on a walkabout, 'e's set upon by several of the elders from the troibe, wrestled to the ground and held down by his arms and legs. His clothes are ripped off. His skin is ritually slashed with a crude knife. The chest. Abdomen. It depends on the troibe. But all of them end the same way. They grab the young man's penis and slash it from . . . from end to end as deep as the urethra. Just like a whistle, ye see?"

When he paused, I cleared my throat.

"What's your point?"

"They've another initiation ceremony. In this one the elders mutilate themselves. They toie off their upper arms, encircle a young male and begin lancin' the veins near their elbows. Blood floies out in a stream. They all direct their spray at the youngster until he becomes virtually covered in the stuff. It's a roite of courage."

Newman and I exchanged doubtful glances.

Meanwhile, Cockie was going on:

"Wait till you see them roo hunting. The old way, I mean, on foot without rifles or knoives. Killing the roo is bloody enough. To dress it out they drag the poor creature 'cross the desert floor, one mile, two miles or more, until the fur and the skin are torn from the meat. They throw it into a coal pit, viscera and all, cook it and pick it apart with their fingers."

"You're talking about a hundred years ago," I said.

"I'm talking about twenty or thirty years ago for some of the troibes. The Ularu are different. They cling to the old w'ys. Oh, they've got a few old vehicles and they live in some government-built tin humpies but their way o' loife hasn't changed much in forty thousand years. Don't make the mistake of thinking the Ularu aren't up to that kind of violence. They are."

"This doesn't sound like you, Alvie; I've never thought you were prejudiced but—"

"I ayn't. But I ayn't bloind neither. I've seen 'em. When they're noice they're as noice as can be. But if they git mad ye don't know what they'll do. They can't even git along with each other.

Why d'ye think they've got no political power? 'Cause they foight with one another as much as they do with us. An' not jist troibe against troibe. Each family quar'ls with the next. Families in each clan quar'l with other clans. The troibe's divided into two moieties an' even they can't get along."

He had a point. Killian had managed to do what no one and nothing before him had done—to unite the aborigines.

"White men fight with each other too," I said.

"We don't do to each other wot got done to Mickey and Nevil. Bloody savages! No white man ever did that."

I could've said: Baloney! But I didn't care to.

I would've said: What kind of a horse's lap are you? But I didn't dare to.

I should've said: Have you forgotten about The Rocks? So I did. The Ballarat Building stood a stone's throw away from the first convict barracks built in Australia. It was bad enough there, the savagery that white men had inflicted upon one another. It was worse up the coast in Moreton Bay and worse yet down in Tasmania—what was then known as Van Diemen's Land. But it was pure hell at Norfolk Island nine hundred miles to the east. Norfolk Island became the death sentence for convicts who got out of line over here. Dying was better than Norfolk Island. But, once there, dying was the only way out. In fact the convicts, most of them Catholic and barred by canon law from killing themselves, drew lots for the prize of being killed by a mate. The winner got a quick death. But both men would escape the brutality and butchery of their fellow whites since the killer would be sent back to Sydney to hang. I reminded Cockie of that. I'm so good at explaining things he didn't have to ask me a single question when I was done.

I went on to remind him how the white men, British and Aussies alike, had hunted the aborigines, the same way they hunted kangaroos and koalas, to the point of extinction.

"That," Cockie said evenly, "was two hundred years ago. We've changed."

"Maybe some of us have. Not Rush Killian. Two hundred years ago he'd have been a member of the squatocracy, making a fortune off of convict labor and treating them worse than the British ever did. His cut-throat tactics are as savage as anything the aborigines came up with."

"He don't kill people."

"Tell that to Arthur Copley. Somebody turned him into a Roman candle."

"An aborigine!"

"Come on, Alvie, be reasonable. You're overlooking the fact that Rush Killian is up to something and probably something no good. Black Tom had help killing Copley. You said so yourself. Whoever it was . . . he must have been white. Not only that, those guys on the train with Black Tom—they were white."

" 'Ow d'ye know?"

"That's what the attendant told Jim Jim."

"Both aborigines. One's dead and the other's run off."

Now we were back where we'd started.

Jim Jim had disappeared. This, as much as Mickey and Nevil, was responsible for the friction between Cockie and me. Because he'd reported to me before I'd made my report to them.

Cockie had arranged for an air ticket for Jim Jim and he'd sent Bobby over to my flat, but by the time Bobby got there, Jim Jim was gone. I'd felt it coming. "What do you mean, gone!" I'd challenged him.

" 'E was jist gone."

"In other words he's either in jail . . . or wandering the streets alone trying to find some way to get home?"

Cockie didn't know. "Maybe the cops got there before we did. 'Oo knows? Sorry, Blue. We did our best." But Cockie hadn't sounded very sorry to me, and now I couldn't blame him. He'd lost two reporters. He, not I, would have to inform their wives and parents. I didn't envy him. Oh sure, I'd felt bad about the boys and their families. But it had been our job to take care of Jim Jim. At least that's how I saw it. And we'd blown it.

However, there was no point in rehashing old news.

Cockie signalled the barmaid by raising three fingers.

"Not for me, Alvie," I said, "I've got to go."

I slid my schooner aside.

"Ye 'aven't finished yer turp."

"Later. There's a couple things I haven't told you yet about my trip downtown."

"Loike wot?"

"First, there's a man I've got to find. I heard about him while the cops were slapping me around. He's about my height and weight and he even has my red hair and blue eyes. I think he must've been at the art show. Something he said to the security people got credited to me. He knows Copley. And he had some reason to believe Copley was gonna be hurt."

Newman and Cockie shook their heads.

"It's not much to go on . . . d'ye know 'is name?"

"No. But I think he knows those two Picky reporters, MacMutton and Geoffers."

"Wot makes ye s'y that?"

"Those two halfwits approached me at the art show. The way they did it . . . I thought at the time it was strange; they seemed surprised when I turned around and traded wisecracks with them. I think maybe they mistook me for this other guy. Even Maggie thought so. He and I must look something alike. At least from the back."

"Have ye asked them about it?"

"No!" I was emphatic. "I wouldn't. But I couldn't ask them anyway because they've gone up to that Killian Development Camp to cover things for The Picky."

"Ye don't mean it!"

"The cops say so. I don't think they've found this guy yet. But they may not know that he knows Mutt and Jeff. If you check with your contacts down at The Picky—"

"I'll ask around," Cockie promised. He said it quickly as though seizing upon this as a way to make up for what had happened with Jim Jim. "No worries, Blue. Wot's the second thing?"

I took a deep breath.

"I met an old acquaintance downtown. I've spoken of him before. Inspector Hawthorne of Scotland Yard. Remember?"

"Ey."

I looked at Newman.

"The fellow who saved your life in Hong Kong?"

"That's the guy. He's going up to the Top End—to look around a little. And he's asked me to go with him."

"Where!" Cockie could not contain his surprise.

"I told you. Up to the Killian camp."

"We can't let ye go," he declared.

"Now look, Alvie—"

"No, Blue, you look. Look at what's goin' on up there. Look what happened to ye that last toime ye went bush. And look what happened to Mickey and Nevil. No sir, as long as those aborigines are on the warpath—"

"Somebody has to cover it!"

"Somebody 'as. Ye jist said yerself that MacMutton and Geoffers are up there. We'll let them take the chances. We can get what we need through The Picky."

"You'd rely on Mutt and Jeff?"

"I don't loike it; but it's better than losin' any more people to them black butchers."

I couldn't believe this was happening. "I'll promise to stay away from the Ularu if it'll make you feel better."

He humphed and replied that he'd given Mickey and Nevil the same instructions.

"Yeah, but I'll have Hawthorne with me."

"Bah. Hawthorne don't dare go in with an army and nothing less than an army can keep him from getting chopped up like the others. Them Ularus don't know any difference between Scotland Yard and a coupla journos." Cockie wasn't budging. "I'm sorry again, Blue, but they'll have to foind someone else."

He still didn't sound very sorry.

"Is that your final word."

"I'm afr'id so."

I turned to Newman. I couldn't appeal to him but why should I have to? He was sitting right there. And saying nothing.

I stood up. "Okay. That's it."

"For chrissakes, ye're not quittin' again?"

"Clock me out, add up my time and send me whatever I've got coming."

"Don't come a gutser, Blue; ye can't quit now. Not with Mickey and Nevil gone. We're short-'anded."

"For what? Two-Up?"

"Anyway, I've got something for ye to look into."

"What is it this time . . . a fashion show?"

"As a matter of fact, it's a dinosaur exhibit going on over at the Powerhouse Museum. The man you want to talk to, his name's Rolly Melsum. 'E can str'ighten ye out about that whowie ye saw on—"

"Forget it, Alvie!"

"I've already told 'im ye'll be there. Don't ye want to know wot it was—?"

"Get Mutt and Jeff to talk to him when they get back." I said and I stood up to leave. As an exit line it was all right but I didn't get a chance to exit.

Bobby and Peter, our fotogs, were marching through the tables to get to our booth. The newspapers in their hands and the expressions on their faces brought me up short.

"Alf. Percy. All bloody hell's come callin'. Take a squint at this!"

They stood over our table. Bobby slapped down a copy of the afternoon *Daily Pictorial* in front of Cockie and me. Atop the fold but below the masthead was a banner headline in sixty point type. A screamer.

BLACK CANNIBALS BUTCHER KILLIAN SURVEYORS

"And that ain't all," stammered Peter. "There's something in here—about Mickey and Nevil!" Newman reached out for his paper while Cockie and I swept over the text. There was a smaller subhead. A teaser. But none of us was laughing.

> TWO ENA JOURNOS MISSING, FEARED DEAD
> BY PICTORIAL REPORTERS
> E.L. MACMUTTON & D.O. GEOFFERS

(Tennant Creek, N.T.) Aboriginal violence has claimed the lives of at least three white men and threatened many more at the Killian Development Station in the Northern Territory where overwhelming black forces now hold a handful of construction workers in siege as each night turns out more victims and more evidence of human butchery.

Among the dead are a surveyor, his assistant, and a guide. According to officials on the scene, their bodies were horribly mutilated, disemboweled and dismembered, and scattered across a hectare of desert. The surveyor, from Sydney, has been identified as Hector Boyle. The other two have not as yet been identified.

Boyle and his men were reported missing after failing to return to camp Tuesday evening. No one is allowed out of camp after dark. Search teams discovered their ravaged corpses this morning near the mountain range that divides Killian's property from his neighbors, a tribe of warlike aborigines known as the Ularu. So badly were their bodies mutilated they were hardly identifiable as human. Many of the searchers were sickened by the sight.

"We're dealing with animals here," said one of the men assigned to gather the bits and pieces of his chums in plastic bags. "Animals, pure and simple.

What else could be responsible for this?" Searchers collected the human detritus and flew it by police plane to Sydney for analysis and identification.

An Ularu cannibal clan calling themselves the *Dongos* have taken credit for these mutilation murders. The *Dongos* have threatened more midnight attacks on innocent civilians and even more horrific "acts of sacrificial blood-letting" until all the whites have gone. "Anybody who stays will die before the week is through," the *Dongos* have boasted.

The Ularus assert that land legally purchased by Killian Development from the federal government is sacred ground. They demand that the developers evacuate at once. The case is now pending in High Court with a decision due Wednesday. Rush Killian is expected to prevail.

A shoulder blocked my view of the page. "The part about Mickey and Nevil is right down here," said Bobby, jamming his finger into the newsprint. "Look at this!"

Cockie and I started reading where Bobby had pointed.

In the most recent development, two reporters from the Eastern News Association have turned up missing. They also are presumed dead, victims of *Dongo* savagery. It is not known when or how they were killed. However the ENA reporters did take a utility truck and venture alone into the desert on Friday morning.

"God help them," said one searcher.

The pair of reporters arrived without invitation on a cargo plane Thursday evening. They spent the night in the camp and then left first thing in the morning. They have not been seen or heard from since.

Ironically, even as search teams overflew the desert looking for signs of the two ENA reporters, another

ENA journo has been taken into custody for questioning in connection with the near-disastrous burning of
the Sydney Opera House. Doyle Mulligan, an American assigned to the Sydney branch of Eastern News,
has steadfastly refused to turn over to the police an
Ularu aboriginal wanted for arson and murder resulting from that fire.

I stopped reading there, looked up and found a full mug of beer
in front of me. At some point the barmaid had come and replen-
ished our drinks, been paid and left, without my even noticing. I
gulped it down. "This is exactly the kind of reporting the cops
were afraid those halfwits would turn out," I announced.

"Those scunges." Cockie was as florid as I'd ever seen him.
"To run something loike that without even checkin' with us to
see if we knew."

"It's a ratbag trick," agreed Bobby. "Even if there's no truth to
it. . . ."

"It's true, all right." That was Newman. He gave the substance
of my report to Bobby and Peter, even throwing in my conviction that some creature was behind it and not the Ularu. Maybe
he wanted the other journos to understand why I hadn't cooper-
ated with the cops or maybe he wanted me to see that Cockie
had been right all along. It sounded a lot like "I told you so!" to
me. "Now listen to this," he said lowering his eyes to the newspaper. " 'The *Dongos* take their name from the mysterious balls
of light which are sometimes seen floating over the desert at
night and which, according to aboriginal legend, are lost spirits
seeking new souls to inhabit. They believe a *Dongo* appearance
presages death. "As the *Dongos* prey upon their victims," vowed
a leader of the cannibal clan, "so will we prey on ours. We will
steal into their camps by night. We will drag them into the bush.
We will feast upon their bodies." ' "

"But that's not right," I said. "Not according to Jim Jim. He
says the Dongos are Ularus who never leave tribal land."

"Yer friend Jim Jim 'as run away," replied Cockie. "By now he's prob'bly back with 'is troibe.'"

I raced outside to the nearest bus stop, hopped an express to Woolloomooloo, ran up to my apartment house, and took the stairs to my flat three at a time. Sure enough, Jim Jim was gone. There was no sign of him. No note. No nothing. Naturally, if the police had come looking for him and found a note they'd have taken it with them.

I called *Woman's Day*. Maggie hadn't showed up. I tried her place and got her on the first ring. "Don't go out!" I told her without even identifying myself; "I'm coming right over." I rang off before she could utter a sound.

Having missed the bus to Paddington I started running, sprang for a taxi somewhere in King's Cross and had it drop me off in front of Maggie's flat.

She answered the door on the first ring.

"Oi, Blue. . . ?"

She was wearing a yellow gingham dress. At any rate it looked like gingham to me, whatever that is. And now that I think about it, it might have been jasmine or saffron. When I looked up I caught her staring at me and looking even more troubled than I was.

"Have you seen Jim Jim, Maggie?"

"No—"

"I asked Cockie to get him out of town before the cops grabbed him," I told her, "but by the time someone got to my place, Jim Jim was gone. He was with me when we dropped you off and I thought he might have come here. You're the only other person he knows in Sydney." Finally, her facial contortions managed to stop me. "What's wrong?"

"I can't talk right now, Blue, I've got things—"

"This is important. I've just spent the whole afternoon downtown being grilled by the cops and I'm sure they'd love to get their mitts on Jim Jim."

That's when a tall figure moved in behind her.

"Come on in, Mulligan."

It was Inspector Hawthorne. I mean superintendent.

He ushered me into the apartment.

I went in and staked out the seat that Hawthorne indicated but I looked to Maggie and didn't sit down until she nodded her head because, after all, it was her place.

They'd been sitting across from one another with a tea table between them and two little cups already set out. It wasn't at all like the grilling I'd gotten downtown. "'*Ave anothah cuppa, dear?*" The afternoon Picky was lying on the table and Mutt and Jeff's story was staring me in the face.

I looked up quickly when Hawthorne said, "For your information we don't have your friend in custody."

"Thanks for telling me. Do you know where he is?"

"That's what I was going to ask you. As you pointed out, the Sydney police are very anxious to get their mitts on him."

"If I see him," I said, "I'll certainly advise him to turn himself in."

"Uh huh."

Since I reported what Maggie was wearing, I may as well mention that Hawthorne had changed his clothes, too. He was now sporting khaki bush drills, shorts and an outback shirt. His feet, in brand new hiking boots with leather laces, were sticking out from under the table. The topper was a "bushy" hat. It was hanging on a rack in the entryway but I'd never seen it on Maggie's head and never would. Somewhere between the police station and Maggie's, Hawthorne had gone shopping for some togs *a la* Crocodile Dundee. The only thing missing was the Driza-bone bushman's vest, as waterproof as oilskins and every bit as stylish, currently making the rounds around Sydney.

He asked me if there was anything else I had to say to Miss McDowel.

I told him no, but there was something I had to say to him.

"Me!"

"That's right."

"You're to meet me at the airport—" Hawthorne checked his watch. "—in less than an hour. What's so important it can't wait until then?"

There was no better time to break the news.

And no worse one.

I remembered the time I'd gone to the football coach to tell him I couldn't play. Not that he was hot to have me on the team but I'd told him I'd play and mother had vetoed it. Of course I couldn't tell coach the truth. I explained that I was an only child. If anything happened to me—if I broke my neck, for example— my mother would be all alone. A thing like that can get you out of military service. It got me out of football.

"I can't go," I said.

"What! Why not?"

Maggie asked where we were going.

"To the Top End," I explained. "But I can't. You see, we're short-handed at the office right now. With Mickey and Nevil gone, I mean. We can't spare any people—"

"It'll only be a few days."

"You don't understand. Cockie and Newman really depend on me. They'd be in a bind if anything happened. . . ."

"Now see here, Mulligan. You put me in a rather awkward position today. With the local authorities, I mean. Damned awkward."

"I know."

"The truth is . . . I was happy to see you. Really."

"Me too."

"Naturally, I had to play it down."

"Oh, sure."

"Under the circumstances I did the best I could for you. Arranging for you to fly up to the Territory with me was the most expedient way to have you released."

I told him I appreciated what he'd done.

"There's more to it than that." He indicated the newspaper

with a chop of his hatchet head. "Have you seen this? Today's paper?"

"Yeah."

"Totally irresponsible! It's . . . it's criminal! That's what it is!"

"You don't believe it?"

"What I believe doesn't—"

"But is it true or isn't it?"

"I don't dare to be quoted."

"Off the record."

He looked at Maggie and she nodded agreement. "Unfortunately," he said, "I think it's probably pretty close to the truth. That's why I was in such a rush to go up there. To get the persons responsible for this butchery in custody before the story was released. Now it's too late for that. Disastrous! Wait and see. The reaction will be swift and violent. That's why I say that to print this kind of thing at a time like this amounts to criminal malfeasance."

"Some of us have higher standards," I said.

He snorted, turning a shade lighter.

"Rot. You're all the same. Bunyips and beasties!"

"You weren't there," I told Hawthorne.

"No, but you've admitted being intoxicated; so has Miss McDowel. At least she has admitted that the 'thing' you saw was probably some black chap in a Hallowe'en costume."

Maggie and I exchanged glances.

"Did you say that?"

"Yes, Blue. In the light of day, it just doesn't seem reasonable that it's. . . ."

"What? A monster? Wait until you see the bodies down in the morgue. They weren't killed by any trick-or-treater."

"The superintendent told me about your friends."

"If anything killed Mickey and Nevil, and Hector Boyle, it must've been that monster. That bunyip. You saw what it looked like. What it tried to do to us! Tell him, Maggie."

"Whatever we saw, Blue," she said, "it couldn't possibly have gotten up to the Top End in time to kill Mickey and Nevil. Not unless it got off the train at Lithgow and caught a plane to Tennant Creek."

"There must be more than one. For all we know there's a thousand of them."

"I just don't believe it. I've made arrangements for us to talk to a friend of mine—a zoologist. Rolly knows every animal that's ever lived in Australia. I'd hoped you could go with me."

I faced Hawthorne.

What I saw in his eyes . . . it was the same thing he was seeing in mine. Neither of us wanted to go through what we had in Hong Kong. Not again.

"The Governor-General, representing the crown," he told me, "has asked Special Branch to investigate. As a Britisher I'm a neutral party down here. So are you. As a yank, what you report will be believed."

I thanked him for the thought but the truth is I didn't think much of this theory. After one look at Maggie, I knew she didn't think much of it either. I was a seppo. That was bad enough. But he was a *pommy*. "Ordinarily," I said, "I'd be happy to go. But the fact is the office can't do without me. Suppose there was an accident; suppose I broke my neck. ENA Sydney would go to hell in a hurry. How could I do that to Cockie and Newman?"

"That doesn't sound like you, Blue," said Maggie.

I shrugged.

What could I tell them? That I'd quit my job? That ENA wouldn't take any copy I sent back? Neither would any other paper or wire service in Australia. I could freelance. But Hawthorne needed a reporter with established connections and I didn't have any. Not now. So he spent a good ten minutes trying to talk me into going and then, when he saw it wasn't working, gave in.

"Well, suit yourself," he said sullenly.

"I'm really sorry."

"So am I. I haven't much time to find anyone else."

A sudden thought struck me. "You know, superintendent. Maybe you've already found someone else. You couldn't do any better than Maggie McDowel."

He eyed me sternly.

"Oh, it's all right for her to go, eh?"

"For her," I said, "not for me. She's not as vital to daily operations as I am. Anyway, she knows the bush better than most guys in Sydney. She's tough, she's gutsy, and besides that, I've briefed her on everything I know about this Killian business."

Hawthorne inspected her with his hawk's eyes.

"How about it, Miss McDowel? Do you want to go?"

Did she!

The only problem, as she explained it, was that she'd already made the date to talk to her zoologist friend over at the Powerhouse Museum. He'd been good enough to oblige her; she couldn't cancel now. Maggie appealed to me. Why couldn't I go and talk to Rolly? She'd planned to ask me to go along anyway; couldn't I describe the thing we'd seen as well as she could? Anyway it would only take an hour or so.

"Do you think ENA would be able to get along without him that long?" groused Hawthorne.

Maggie implored me.

"Will you do it, Blue? *Pleeeeease?*"

The only way to get out of it was to admit I'd walked away from Eastern News.

"It's the least you can do if she's going to go to the Territory for you," he said.

I asked if the guy's name was Melsum. Rolly Melsum.

She said it was.

"And he works in the archeological department over at the museum?"

"You know him!"

I told her no, but Cockie knew him. Apparently I was back on the job whether I liked it or not.

8

A Time of Dreams

I've already explained that, as far as I'm concerned, trees belong
in the woods; that, to me, any park you can't see across is a
jungle; and if it hasn't got thoroughfares, stoplights, signposts
and sidewalks, it's got no business inside the city limits. Imagine
my surprise when I walked into the Powerhouse Museum that
afternoon and found myself in a prehistoric forest surrounded
by creatures and plants of the sort which haven't been seen in
Australia for thousands of years.

Surprise doesn't cover it.

The woman at the information desk took my name, spoke into
a telephone, and then escorted me into a small office furnished
with a small desk and a small chair and occupied by a smallish
man who rose as I entered but didn't offer a hand. He looked like
the curator of a museum. Scholarly. Underfed. Underfoot. Even
if no one had told me he was a curator I would've known. Only
the wild tangle of hair on his head defied the description; he had
otherwise ordinary features and eyes that blinked behind bullet-
proof lenses. Myopic, no doubt. For him, anything farther away
than the pages of a book was a blur. In short, a worm.

"So," he said, "you're Maggie's friend."

His tone was cool.

"That's right."

"I don't really have time to talk to you," he told me, "but I
promised Maggie I would so I will." I thought swell, he may be
a worm but at least he's a worm of his word. Before I could utter
a sound, I caught a flash of disapproval from behind the thick

glasses and he bolted on. "So you're the bloke who holds his breath when he kisses?"

I goggled.

"No, I'm not," I snapped. "That's Donald. I'm Doyle. Doyle Mulli—"

"Oh, that's right. The two-pot screamer. Maggie told me all about you. Poor girl. Always looking for a man who can keep pace with her. I couldn't."

"What did you call me?"

"Huh?"

"A two-pot screamer?"

"Oh." He blinked. "That's a bloke who can't hold his likker."

I held my licker for that. "What else did Maggie say?" I asked him.

"She wants me to convince you that beastie you two saw couldn't have been a bunyip. That it was some sort of aboriginal trick."

"Was it?"

"Probably."

"It couldn't have been a bunyip?"

"I don't see how."

"You don't believe in them, huh?"

"As a matter of fact I do. There's something out there which the zoologists haven't identified yet and, for want of a more scientific title, we call a bunyip."

"You've seen one?"

"Well, no."

"Then. . . ?"

"I've never seen the Territory either but the evidence is compelling it exists. Too many people have seen it; too many strange things have happened. The bunyip is elusive—sure. It's also mysterious and dangerous. But it's there. I'd stake my reputation on it. When you've worked in paleozoology down here as long as I have nothing surprises you."

"Then. . . ."

"They're real enough; but they don't ride trains. I'm sorry I can't spare you more time," he said, "but I'm late for my next appointment. I warned Maggie I couldn't give you more than a few minutes. She suggested I direct you to some aboriginal experts who can tell you more. My secretary has their names and numbers."

He spoke into his intercom.

"Bonnie, what's my next appointment?"

"A Mister Mulligan. From Alvin Cockie's office."

He looked up.

"Nice to have met you, mister. . . ?"

"Mulligan," I said. "From Alvin Cockie's office."

He blinked twice.

"You're Alf Cockie's man!"

"Yes."

"The yank!"

I confessed.

"Well. That's more like it!" Melsum came from behind his desk and shook my hand with surprising energy. "Doyle, is it? Glad to meet any friend of Alf's. My name's Rolly. Rolston Melsum. Everyone calls me Rolly—there's no formality in paleozoology. Too many dead things looking over our shoulders." Apparently there weren't many secrets in paleozoology either because he was shouting loud enough to wake the dead things looking over his shoulder. He had, he said, known Alf for twenty years now. What a luvly man! What is it like to work with such a luvly man? He just had to know.

I said it was lovely.

"Alf says I'm to treat you right, give you the Cook's tour, tell you anything you want to know, and then share a couple of short ones before you go. Speaking of holding yer likker, there's a bloke who can drink. And what a newsman! I'm not piddling in your pocket, Doyle, you'll learn plenty from Alf Cockie."

I held my licker for that, too.

I had to.

Rolly Melsum is one of those guys who never runs out of words. They just keep talking until they run out of breath. In Melsum's case that wasn't often. In fact, I gathered this was what bothered him most about Donald. Not that he held his breath when he kissed but that he could only hold it for ninety seconds at a time.

"Sorry about trying to rush you off," he raced on without a pause. "I'm a bit of a blind Freddy when it comes to Maggie. But now that I know you're mates with Alf it's all right. He says you're okay. Not much of a fister and fast to cut out but okay."

"What else did Cockie say?" I asked him.

"Eh? Oh, he wants me to convince you that creature you saw on the train was a whowie."

"Was it?"

"Probably."

"Okay, what's a whowie? And what about that aborigine business?"

Melsum smiled hugely and ran a hand through his tangle of hair. He didn't look like a worm any more. Or scholarly either.

"Forget about that for a minute. What do you think it was?"

"I'll tell you what I think. Have you heard of things that go bump in the night?"

"Ey."

"Well that was the night," I said, "and we bumped into the thing."

Melsum threw back his head. When he got his laughter under control, I informed him I was already on record that what I saw was no man in a monkey suit."

"It wasn't, ey? Well, my friend, just come with me."

With a firm grip on my arm he led me out of his office and down a back staircase. We headed for a far door at the end of a service passageway—a time tunnel, though I didn't know it until we reached the end and he bade me precede him through.

I stood on the threshold and stared.

We had passed, not just into a different wing, but into a different world and a different eon.

On every side were broad-leafed ferns, head-high grass, and palm fronds the size of umbrellas. The trunks of hardwood trees I couldn't have wrapped both arms around soared into the vaulted darkness of the ceiling. A thick carpet of moss and creepers edged the walkways which wound like trails among the exhibits.

To my unhorticultured eye it looked very real.

Melsum took off down a trail.

I followed.

"Australia really looked like this?" I asked, a little disconcerted at how closely it matched Jim Jim's description of the early continent.

"Yes, a long time ago."

This part of the museum was devoted to ancient aboriginal culture. It featured displays of aboriginal artifacts as well as life-size dioramas of aborigines making camp and building fires, digging pits, wielding spearthrowers, boomerangs and knives, hunting and eating their prey. There was even one of a mulla-mullung type—white-painted chest, arms and legs as Black Tom's had been—at work on the wall of a mock cave.

The black mannequin had one outspread hand on the rock wall. His mouth, cheeks apparently bloated with air, was a few inches away.

Melsum gestured to this display without slowing down.

"That's one of the simplest and earliest forms of cave paint-ings," he told me. "They'd put paint in their mouths and then blow it over the backs of their hands. It made an outline on the stone. Some of the later stuff is much more detailed. I'd have loved to get several of Arthur Copley's Ularu paintings down here for display."

"Did you go?"

"Certainly. I waited with the general audience but the opera house caught fire before I got in."

"Too bad."

"Yes. As a supporter of aboriginal causes I sympathize with the Ularus' trying to sanctify those cave paintings but as an historian I couldn't resist the chance to see Copley's pictures. What a magnificent opportunity! To stare through a window to the past. It's ironic those pictures might have helped the Ularu claim the land Killian's developing."

I perked up when he said that.

"How do you figure?"

"It was just a chance. Buckley's chance, as Alf would say, but the only one them poor bludgers got."

"But how?"

Melsum stopped in front of a bush scene and faced me.

"Aboriginal land grants are made on the basis of traditional occupancy. That's how the Ularu got the land they're on now—they've always lived there. However, the High Court ruled they had no claim on the land to the west because they never have occupied it. The court wasn't impressed by their argument that it's off limits to them, too. After all, they could say the same thing about the whole Northern Territory; that shouldn't make it theirs."

"So how could the pictures have helped?"

"There's a small chance a few of those paintings would show something special about the valley across the mountain, something which predated the white man's arrival on the continent."

"I see."

"If it really has been sacred to them for thousands of years then it's at least possible this relationship is symbolized on some of their cave paintings. A thing like that might sway the court that there's a tradition of use behind the land even if they never occupied it."

"So that's why you went?"

"That was one reason. But it wasn't the only one. My specialty is ancient fauna. Imagine finding a ten-thousand-year-old drawing of an extinct animal species. Not merely a fossilized fragment

of bone but an actual picture. Multiply that by a hundred paintings. Thousands more Copley hadn't even photographed. How
could I stay away? Only digging up a Pleistocene camera and
finding exposed but undeveloped film inside could compare to
it."

"I wish I'd had a camera with me that night. If I had a
photograph you'd know I wasn't just dreaming it."

"Maggie said it had six legs?"

"Yeah."

"Did anyone else see it? Other than you and Maggie, I mean?"

"There was an aborigine in the car. A mulla-mullung. But he
left as soon as it appeared."

"Alf said there were two other blacks."

Apparently Cockie had said a lot.

"I don't think they were in the carriage at the time."

"One was a big bloke, right?"

"Yeah, Jim Jim's as big as two guys but he's only got one set
of arms."

"What about the other one?"

"The attendant?"

"Isn't he quite small?"

"It's *wasn't* he now—he's quite dead. But yeah, he was small.
Except he had just two arms too. Why? What are you getting at?"

"Just this. It was a dream, all right, Doyle. But not yours. Have
you heard of the Dreamtime?"

"Sure."

"The Dreamtime," he said, "is the aboriginal past. But it's also
a heritage that remains with them. They're inextricably linked to
it. They believe that the animal spirits of the Dreamtime eventually took the form of the present-day animals, to which present-
day aborigines are totemically related. It's all a big circus to us.
Our university-trained minds grapple with concepts which are
second nature to their six and seven year olds. The difference is
that we study it and they live with it. But it's more than that—
some things we've only recently discovered, creatures which, to

us, are the stuff of horror and science fiction, they've known about for thousands of years."

His timing was perfect.

As he said it, I found myself staring wide-eyed through the trees at a beast straight out of a Godzilla movie. With two long, clawed, battering-ram legs and a giraffe's neck it was almost twice my height. On top of that it had a beak as big as a garden shovel.

I stopped in my tracks; he stopped beside me.

"What the hell is that?" I said with something like awe in my voice.

"Take a guess."

"It looks like an ostrich on steroids."

Melsum laughed loudly.

"Emu," he cried, "There are no ostriches in Australia. Never have been. This bird weighed half a ton and reached ten feet in height. The heaviest bird to walk the planet. Its relative, the moa from New Zealand, only became extinct about a thousand years ago. Wiped out by early settlers. But this is just the beginning. Follow me."

A moment later, I was standing in front of another one. A nightmare kangaroo. It had powerful forelimbs, short hind legs, at least shorter than the modern variety, and a longer neck. It also had a skull as big as a bull's and a chest as big as a fifty-gallon barrel. I'll bet I could have crawled inside its pouch.

"This is a *Protemnodon*, an ancestor of the kangaroo; it died out about three thousand years ago." He pointed across the path to another stuffed monstrosity. "How about that one? Does it look familiar?"

This one was different. I recognized it right away. It was the size of a grizzly bear though it clearly wasn't a bear. It had spotted fur like a leopard, and was as heavily muscled as a large lion but it obviously wasn't any cat that still walked the earth. Not that thing. Yet I knew what it was the moment I saw that pair of six-inch daggerlike canine teeth projecting from its upper jaw.

"A sabre-tooth tiger!"

"Very good, Doyle."

"I didn't know they lived in Australia."

"The mammalian variety didn't. A marsupial cousin of the sabre-tooth—known as the Smilidon—migrated from North to South America. It disappeared in Pleistocene times, but another species appeared in Australia about the same period. Whether it's a case of parallel development or migration nobody knows. The *Thylacoleo Carnifex*. Quite a mouthful, ey? Marsupial lion's a bit easier, and that's what we call him."

"But it was a cat?"

"It was bigger than any cat. And much more savage. It ranged over most of Australia until eight or nine thousand years ago. Dry weather and the loss of its habitat forced it into extinction, just like the sabre-tooth. Both hunted large prey. They used their fangs like knives. Stabbed them into the victim's neck and chest. Not once—again and again until the animal died. Notice the powerful neck? Biting and chewing were their problem. Those long teeth only got in the way. Once they'd downed the prey they had to slash the bodies, rip the flesh into hunks small enough to be swallowed whole."

A shiver ran through me.

"How do you know what it looked like if it's extinct?"

"In the lion's case, we made an educated guess. Based on environment and hunting habits. The Tasmanian wolf is another story. We've got some old black and white films of the last captive specimen. It died in Hobart Zoo back in 1936."

"Isn't it possible there're still some around?"

"The wolf? There are sightings now and then in Tasmania's wild hill country. Occasionally even on the mainland. But nobody's ever brought one in, dead or alive."

"So you can't say for certain there aren't some still out there?"

"Certainly not. Remember the coelacanth? An ancestor to the first fish that crawled up on land. Scientists were sure it'd been extinct for six million years until a living specimen was hauled

out of three fathoms of water less than a hundred yards off the
Madagascar shore. Now we know that there are hundreds, perhaps thousands of them." He laughed. "But the Tasmanian wolf
is not your mysterious monster. It was hardly as big as a dingo
and only took mouse-size prey. Come on. We're getting closer
to the thing I wanted to show you. You'll catch my point in
another minute."

He took off.

We breezed by a mock-up of what looked like a hairy hip-
popatamus but then, almost as an afterthought, he brought me
back. It stood more than six feet high at the shoulder and it had
a hippo's head too.

"Can you name this one, Doyle?"

He laughed when I did.

"Ever hear of the mighty marsupial?" he asked.

"No. Now hold on! . . . Jim Jim said something about that.
According to him, a mighty marsupial made the mountain range
between Ularu Occupied Land and the sacred land."

"Of course we now know," said Melsum, "that just such a
creature existed. We call it a *Diprotodon*. Essentially, it was a
giant wombat. But its ability to move earth about must have been
prodigious."

As he started off I grabbed hold of his arm, pulling him
around.

"Wait a minute! Are you trying to tell me that there's something to these legends? That these ancient spirits they tell stories
about. . . ? They really existed?"

"That's the idea!"

"I wouldn't have believed. . . ."

"Neither did anyone else until we began digging up some of
these bones. Except the aborigines, that is. They'd been painting
pictures of fantasy creatures on the walls of their caves for
thousands of years. As far as they're concerned—spiritually and
totemically—these things still live today." He prodded me on-

ward. "One more exhibit to go, Doyle. Then you'll understand where I'm heading."

We trudged deeper into that chamber of ancient horrors. Abruptly he stopped. Right in front of a whale-sized reptile. It almost took my breath.

At first I thought it must be a dinosaur. However, the diorama depicted a handful of blackish Neanderthals fighting the thing and I knew that dinosaurs had died out millions of years before man showed up. So I settled on a dragon. That's what it looked like. Not something out of a Godzilla movie, but Godzilla himself. It had a crocodile's head. Except it was two, three times the size of any crocodile that I'd ever heard of. It had much longer legs too, and though it walked on all fours like a croc its belly was high off the ground.

Without stopping to consider the effect of my words, I muttered:

"Great Goanna!"

"That's it! Several Northern Territory tribes believe in the Great Goanna. This creature is undoubtedly the source of their beliefs."

"It looks like a dragon."

"It is. This, my friend, is *Megalania*. Second cousin to the dragon of Komodo Island north and west of Darwin. Of course this creature was many times bigger. Where the Komodo Dragon reaches lengths of ten feet and weighs maybe three or four hundred pounds, the *Megalania* of Australia once grew to thirty feet and weighed upward of a ton."

"Then early aborigines really did fight with these . . . these monsters?"

He nodded. "If they wanted to eat they did. Or keep from being eaten. Aboriginal legends told today are based on hunting trips and battles fought ten, fifteen thousand years ago. This creature for example. For the past hundred centuries—its bones were unearthed just a few years ago—*Megalania* has lived only in aboriginal tribal tales. Every tribe has their own name and

legend for it, but it's known commonly as a whowie. Some of the
tales describe the thing as having the body of an enormous
lizard with the head of a crocodile and six legs."

"Six!"

Melsum became uncharacteristically silent.

"Did you say six legs?" I said.

I was staring at the exhibit. It had only four feet—the back
ones with five toes and the front two with four—the two outer
toes were larger and seemed to carry most of the weight.

He basked in the moment.

"Yes, that's the part which should interest you. One legend
tells us the whowie lived in tunnels in underground caverns. It
would crawl out at night and devour kangaroos and wombats.
And aborigines too, of course. It would sneak into their camps
by night and swallow them whole, slipping away before the
others awoke. Not until several tribes banded together did they
defeat the whowie. They blocked the creature's tunnels with
tinder and wood and set them ablaze. The aborigines left one
tunnel open and when the whowie emerged, coughing and
half-blind, they set upon him with sticks and clubs."

I shook my head.

"The Ularu don't believe it happened that way. They believe
their ancestors made peace with the Great Goanna—that, working together, they were able to best another even more savage
spirit they call Gol."

"Very interesting," Melsum said. "I'm not familiar with any
spirit or creature named Gol."

"But those are just myths. Aren't they?"

"Of course. But that has nothing to do with it. The aboriginals
still believe. Many of them do, anyway. They celebrate their
victory over the whowie even today in special ceremonies."

"Like a corroboree?"

This, at last, was what he'd been leading me to.

"Something like that. Part of the ceremony is a ritual dance in
which tribal actors recreate this battle . . . or their tribe's own

version of it, by wearing elaborate camouflaging and make-up."

"Camouflaging?"

"Yes."

"You mean costumes, don't you?"

"That's right—rough by our standards but in many ways very sophisticated."

"I see." I should have found a little satisfaction in solving the mystery of the monster but I didn't. None whatsoever. "So," I said, "Maggie was right all along. Cockie too."

"I'm afraid so."

"Jim Jim fooled me."

"Don't feel bad. Aborigines are really extraordinarily good at this sort of thing. They've been doing it for thousands of years and it's amazing some of the appearances they can create."

"I don't mean just that. . . ." I shook the cobwebs out of my head. "But that, too. How did he do it? The four arms, I mean."

"Well, one of the two men—"

"*Two* men?"

"Certainly. Why do you suppose I asked you about that other aborigine? It takes two men to pull it off. One has to be very large. Tall as well as strong."

"And the second one . . . small!"

"That's right. One man, the tallest and strongest of the tribe, wears the mask and a pair of claw-like gloves on his hands. Another man, the smallest of the tribe, wearing a similar pair of gloves, is tied to him at the chest, both facing forward. Their waist and legs are tied together too. The short man's feet won't reach the ground. He wraps them behind the bigger man's calves. A grass or cloth covering is thrown over them so all four arms protrude but only the single masked head. In some cases the actors drop down and walk on all sixes; in others they walk upright, their forearms—if ye'll pardon the pun—are used for mock fighting."

I said: "I will be damned!"

"Seeing something like that in the dark, sober or not, who

could blame you for believin' it was real? But no such terrible creatures exist. Not any more. The outback today is basically a predation-free environment. The only really bad beastie left is man; and when it comes to savage, man's a pale shadow of what used to live there."

I told him he'd be surprised. The fact is, we'd both be surprised, but I didn't know that then. I was too busy kicking myself.

And then I was pumping Rolly Melsum's hand up and down the same way he'd done to mine, thanking him, and promising him that some day, some*how* I'd find a way to repay him. I don't remember anything more until I bounded into the Black Stump and began shouting to Cockie and Newman.

"Of all the bloody twists!" exclaimed Cockie after I'd reported in full.

"Didn't I tell you it wasn't any man in a monkey suit? It wasn't. It was two men in a monkey suit."

Newman asked if I had any proof.

"No. But Cockie can get it."

Cockie did.

He phoned *The Sydney Daily Pictorial*.

He spoke to someone he knew on the city desk and, under the pretense of finding out if Messrs. MacMutton and Geoffers could act as ENA field representatives, he found out the two of them had left Thursday afternoon for the Top End. How had they traveled? By train to Adelaide and a cargo flight from there to Rush Killian's camp. Which train? Why, the Indian Pacific, of course.

Cockie rang off and joined us at the table.

"Just loike ye said, Blue."

I lathered my hands with anticipation.

"Don't you see what happened? Black Tom was a distraction, all right. Mutt and Jeff slipped that firebomb under the platform while all eyes and cameras were focused on Tom. When everyone ran out they followed him. They recovered his gloves and mask in the park and went straight to the Central Station. Mutt must've been in Compartment Seven. Jeff took the berth next to mine . . . to protect Black Tom and maybe even give him a place to hide if the cops searched the train. It might've worked, too. If Maggie and I hadn't been following him. So they pulled that charade. It was undoubtedly Tom's idea but they did it and I got to admit they did a good job. They must have cut up the blankets in their compartments and used some of Black Tom's masks and gloves to make a costume. In the darkness, it was more than good enough."

"Now wot?" Cockie wanted to know.

"That's up to you. How did you make out with Mutt and Jeff's buddy? The one at the art show who looks like me."

He was ready. "The name's Brock Allitt," he said.

"That sounds familiar."

"It ought to. Allitt was the land agent who negotiated the deal between the federal government and Rush Killian."

"Now I remember!"

"The description fits. He's a bit older'n you but he's your size, red hair, an' yer two chums from The Picky did an interview with 'im four weeks ago. I called his office over in The Rocks. 'E's the nervous type."

"Scared?"

" 'Is knackers 're tremblin'. But 'e knows somethin'."

"Sure he knows something. He can tie this whole thing together. He knew Arthur Copley and Mutt and Jeff knew him. What's he got to say?"

"That's for you to foind out. He won't talk to me and not no one else either but he'll talk to you if you meet him tonight. Nine o'clock sharp. He says to be there on toime."

"Where?"

"At his office. Harington Street."

"That's The Rocks!"

"I told ye it was."

"Why there? And why me?"

"Ask 'im. Ye're the only journo in Sydney 'e can trust with 'is story."

"Who says?"

" 'E did. It's you or no one."

"He asked for me by name?"

"Dinkie die."

I turned to Newman. "You know," I said, "it suddenly occurs to me I don't get paid enough."

"Ye'll be lucky to get paid at all." That was Cockie, trying to sound stern, but his Humpty Dumpty face cracked a smile. "Ye quit, remember?"

"Yeah. But you don't have to beg. I know a repentant soul when I see one. Besides, how long could you guys last without me?"

"Ey. Don't forget, Blue. A bloke can't piddle in 'is own pocket without droppin' 'is strides. Allitt saw yer name in the Picky story today, that's all." He turned to Newman. "Wot'd'ye think, Percy? Should we give 'im another try?"

Newman winked at me.

"As long as 'e doesn't cut out again."

"Hang on," I said, "Doyle is through cutting. But he's got a little grinding and polishing to do."

9

Pale Shadows

The Rocks.

When the first convicts rowed ashore two hundred years ago that's all it was, a rocky promontory just west of what would become Sydney Cove. Convict laborers built their own prisons by quarrying sandstone into blocks and mixing mortar from lime found in vast deposits of mollusk shells off the opposite point. Barracks soon stood in rows like steps up the side of the hill.

Today The Rocks is a quaint quarter of nineteenth-century architecture. By day it nestles in the shadow of the Sydney Harbour Bridge, a collection of specialty shops and souvenir stores catering to the tourist trade. Across the cove the opera house sits in full view atop exhausted lime deposits.

Pinched between the Harbour Bridge ramp and the docks, The Rocks becomes a forbidding place once the sun has gone down. Shops close early. You may see a few street lights, but not many. Even the network of steps and walkways which led visitors through the historic quarter hours earlier has turned into a twisted labyrinth that entices few strollers. At night, a chilling inshore breeze carries with it a sense that the original occupants have reclaimed their land. These convict settlers had come to die, and in dying, their souls have earned a kind of quiet title to the rocky quarter that no king and no court could decree. Lost somewhere amid traffic rushing over Cahill Expressway and north onto the bridge, muffled by ferry horns on Circular Quay, come the faint cries of doomed men upon The Rocks.

I could almost hear them now.

Maybe it was my imagination. Maybe it was the sound of distant voices coming over the water . . . revelers on Bennelong boardwalk. It might even have been the gulls.

Maybe.

I'd been here before, though never at night. The place didn't look anything the same. It had exuded charm then and atmosphere. Not any more. The atmosphere now was the sort that made me shiver inside my jacket and hike the collar up around my ears.

I watched the tail lights of my taxicab, tires whining, wag south down Harington Street. The cabbie was as anxious to leave here as everyone else.

I crossed the deserted street.

Like the storefronts, the professional offices were all locked up tight. Allitt's little complex was no exception. No lights burned from any of the windows. This didn't surprise me. Around here even "achievers" knock off before nightfall. Allitt's office was as dark as the others.

No one answered my knock. I banged on the window but nothing stirred.

My watch said exactly nine o'clock.

Apparently I'd been stood up.

I glanced around.

There was a pay phone not ten feet away. I considered calling the office to let them know the meet was a wash but before I could make up my mind, it started ringing.

In three steps I was there; I scooped up the receiver.

"Yeah?"

The thing barked in my ear. *"Who is this!"*

A medium tenor with an edge of fear.

"Didn't your mother teach you any manners?" I scolded. "You're supposed to tell me who you are first and who it is you want to talk to."

"I want . . . no, not like that. Give me your name."

"I'll give you half of it," I said. "Doyle. If you're who I think you are, you can give me the rest."

"*Madigan. Doyle Madigan.*"

"Mulligan. But that's close enough. Okay, your turn."

"*Allitt. Brock Al— No. Like you did . . . you tell me!*"

The sap had just told me.

"I'll go you one better," I said. "I'll tell you what you look like. You're five ten and a hundred fifty pounds; you've got blue eyes, red hair and you're somewhat good-looking."

"*How do you know what I look like?*"

"Because you look somewhat like me. Okay, Allitt, we got through that. I'm me and I'm here and you're you and you're late."

"*I'm not late! Brock Allitt is never late. Ask anybody.*" It seemed to be important to him, his never being late, so I said okay, he was never late, so where the heck was he? I could hear him breathing; then he blurted:

"*Why didn't you give that abo up to the police?*"

"What?"

"*You heard me. Why didn't you turn that abo in to the cops?*"

Let me say at this point, I was feeling abused. A man who answers questions with questions does not make an ideal subject for an interview.

"I had my reasons," I said.

"*I have to know. If you want anything from me, you'd better tell me.*"

I took two seconds to look it over and decided to spill a little. "The truth is," I said, "I did give him up. I just stalled long enough to give him a chance to get away first."

"*Why?*"

"I owed it to him. Call it quid pro quo. You know, as in: You've had a quid's worth, how about giving me a quote."

"*All right. I had to know I could trust you. I've got to trust somebody. You're the one. God help me if I'm wrong about you. Look under the phone.*"

I thought he meant the receiver and eyeballed it first but then I bent down and checked the box. Sure enough there was a key taped to the underside.

"Okay. I see it."

"Do you know the Morisset Building?"

"Yeah. . . ."

"That's where I'm calling from. Suite Fifteen, second floor. I'm leaving an envelope for you in the top right hand drawer of the desk."

"What's in—"

"Just listen. I've sealed it. You're not to open it up. You've got to promise me that. Otherwise, I'll just tear it up and walk out of here."

"Who's it for?"

"It's for you. But don't open it up. Not for at least a week—that's the part I'm trusting you with. If you don't hear from me at the end of a week, then go ahead. There's a story inside the likes of which you wouldn't believe. You'll know what to do with it."

"You'll have to give me an idea of what it's all about. Maybe we can set up a meeting and—"

"No, no, I'm leaving tonight. I'll be back inside of a week. If I make it back. At that time we can meet and I'll pay you five thousand dollars for the envelope still sealed. But look—if it's been opened, you don't get the money."

"I don't want the money. I want a story."

"That's the deal, take it or leave it."

I took five seconds this time.

"The Morisset Building," I said. "Arthur Copley had his studio there."

"So does Hector Boyle. The envelope's in Boyle's room."

This was even better. Allitt was not only tied in with Rush Killian and Mutt and Jeff but apparently he knew Hector Boyle, too. I liked it.

"I don't like it," I said. "Why can't we meet?"

"Because we'd be seen. They're following me. If I met you they might suspect that I've given you the yarn and then they'd be after

you, too. Keeping your mouth shut is part of the deal. You can't let
anyone know you're holding this for me. Not anybody. What do you
say? Are you in or out?"
   "Who's following you?"
   "You'll find out in one week, Madigan. Not before."
   "It's Mulligan. And a week's too late. Don't you read the
papers? This country hasn't got a week. Wednesday's as long as
I can wait. If you know something that can stop all the killing,
I'll have to print it."
   "Wednesday?"
   "That's the limit, Allitt."
   "All right. Wednesday night at this time."
   "Wednesday noon."
   His tenor turned harsh. *"Wednesday noon—Wednesday night!*
What difference does it make? Do I have your word?"
   "Yeah. Okay."
   "Say it!"
   "Cross my heart and hope to die. Your secret's safe with me
or my name isn't Doyle Madigan."
   "All right, clown, I'll be seeing you."
   The phone clicked with finality.
   I hung up, smiling. I was whistling a little tune as I peeled the
key off the phone, gave it a glom, and then stuck it in my jacket
pocket. What a break! Allitt wasn't simply tying the thing to-
gether, he was wrapping it up with ribbons and a bow. All I'd
have to do was punch it into the computer and then wait for the
Pulitzer people to call.
   I stopped whistling about the time I stepped onto the sidewalk.
   Suddenly, that was one eerie avenue. There wouldn't be another cab in the neighborhood. The subways didn't run this far
north and the buses were down until morning. I was on my own.
But what the heck, I told myself, the Morisset Building was just
across the quarter.
   So I started walking.
   Whistling again.

Through the Opal Fields. Past the old archives.

The air grew more stale with each step. The street got darker. Featureless black buildings stood like barracks and sentry boxes all around me. Every time the wind whipped the tree limbs about it sounded like the work of the lashmaster. Even the immense frame of the Harbour Bridge loomed over the rocky point like a gallows.

I stopped beside a pillarbox across the street from the Morisset Building and looked the place over.

This was one gaol that hadn't come down in two hundred years.

But its hours, not its days, were numbered.

I crossed the street.

The front door was closed and locked.

My key slipped right in the keyway; it turned smoothly and a bolt slid back.

I went in. The vaulted lobby was the forecourt of the prison. Aged stone blocks rose to the roof. Hand-hewn timbers spanned the ceiling. The place had gotten spruced up a bit in two hundred years but a prison, even in pastels, is still stir.

A directory hung on the lobby wall.

Hector Boyle, so it read, had an office on the second floor. Suite 15.

I had to climb two flights of stairs altogether to get to the second floor because there was no "lift" and because the Aussies, like the British, don't count the ground floor. The solid sandstone steps were narrow and worn. The treads had been pitted by many years of abuse and hobnails to boot.

At the second floor landing I paused to survey.

The corridor was so poorly lit it looked like a tunnel. Rooms—former cells—gave off both sides. The original iron doors with their barred judas windows had been replaced by wooden jobs with glass panels. Several of the doorways had been blocked up and I guessed that the landlord had knocked down some dividing stone walls to accommodate larger suites.

A single shabby light fixture twenty feet down the hall threw its meager incandescence over Hector Boyle's entrance. His name was scribed in black letters across the glass panel of the door. Below that—*Surveyor and Geologist.* Someone had taped a sign to the inside glass facing out which read:

TEMPORARILY CLOSED
Please direct inquiries to
Allitt Estate Agents
Harington Street

The interior was dark but I knocked anyway.

No answer.

The key slipped in as smoothly as it had downstairs.

I cracked the door open, pushed my head through, and called out: "Hello. Is anyone here?"

Still no answer.

I stepped in. I fumbled for a light switch and turned it on. I found myself in a small anteroom furnished with a desk and a chair. The walls were from the current century. The decor was from the last one. But cheap. The reception desk had no drawers and no envelopes. A door off to my left led to a private office.

It wasn't much.

Another desk. Another chair. And a filing cabinet in the corner. A single bookshelf on the wall held perhaps a couple dozen books. Journals. Surveying handbooks and texts. Behind the desk hung an aerial photograph of greater Sydney.

I went to the desk, pulling open the right-hand drawer. This was more like it. Inside was a legal-size envelope with DOYLE MADIGAN written on the face in red ink with a nervous hand.

Inside the envelope was a letter and another envelope which was sealed. The words "To be opened in the event of my death" were written across the front and it was signed Brock Allitt. The letter merely restated the deal as he'd already explained it on the phone. If I kept the envelope without opening it up and without telling anyone I had it, he'd pay me five thousand dollars at the end of this week. If he didn't, I'd get to print what was inside. The same signature again.

I'd just pocketed the envelope when I heard footsteps in the corridor.

My first thought was that Brock Allitt had decided to meet with me after all. Swell.

I stood up.

But then I had another thought. This wasn't as swell as the first.

It could be the bozos who were playing tag with Brock Allitt. Had they been keeping an eye on the place? Maybe they'd seen me go in and mistaken me for him.

I turned off the room lights. Then, moving with care, I tiptoed back behind the desk and started to replace the letter and envelope in the desk drawer, but suddenly thought better of it and slipped both between the wall and the map so they didn't show.

I tiptoed to the anteroom and listened at the door.

Yes. Footsteps. One man. The sounds were fading.

I poked my head out and looked up and down. Nothing. For just a moment I wondered about going back and getting the envelope but I knew I dared not be caught with it on me. Better to come back in daylight. With help. I locked the office door and started toward the stairs. I paused at the landing.

More noises. Steps. Coming up!

I couldn't go down and I couldn't go back.

Only one place left.

I hopped up the third flight of stairs to the top floor where I found another tunnel even darker than the lower one. I cat-footed down it, feeling my way along, and trying every door I came to. They were all locked.

Until I found a door standing open.

COPLEY ABORIGINALS
Arthur Copley, proprietor

And then I saw a hand-lettered sign taped to the inside of the glass facing out. It said:

TEMPORARILY CLOSED
Please direct inquiries to
Allitt Estate Agents
Harington Street

I slipped inside, closing the door behind me. I stood with my back pressed to the wall. The light switch dug into my spine but I didn't move and I didn't turn on the lights. Slowly my eyes adjusted to the darkness.

I explored the place without moving. Another anteroom but this time the artwork was ancient. All of it aboriginal. Walls covered with native trinkets. Even more in a display cabinet. A table pushed into a corner. Upon it still more aboriginal artifacts. Samples of rock and bark paintings. Stick carvings.

The corridor remained quiet and I turned my attention back to the room.

Two doorways. One door, standing open, led to a small cubbyhole, most likely an office. Another door, just ajar, was off my right shoulder.

I stepped through this one.

The room was big. Thirty feet or more wide and twice that in length. At one time it would have housed fifty or sixty prisoners in a half-dozen cells. Now it was Copley's workroom, a hodge-podge of platforms and partitions, nooks and crannies, knick-knacks and artifacts. Walls filled with pictures, paintings and photographs. Easels stood in every open space and display cabinets filled with various styles of aboriginal craft lined the walls.

Moonlight coming through six tiny windows spaced along the outside wall lent a surreal quality to the chamber. It was an eerie collection of shapes and shadows in shades of black and grey.

There was only one other door in the workroom. At the far

end. As I got closer I could see it was a seventh cell whose stone walls still stood. The door was a massive thing and ancient. A crimson warning light had been mounted just above the lintel.

I was looking out one of the windows, staring down at the street, when I heard floorboards creak ever so softly.

I whirled. The anteroom door. I'd left it open for light, an oblong of grey-black against the sheer blackness of the walls. My heart stopped beating. The oblong of grey-black had vanished. The walls and the room were a uniform blackness.

My eyes strained until they ached.

No one. And nothing. Not a flicker of movement.

And then something.

A huge shadow moved. Without a sound it separated itself from the other shadows and slid menacingly toward me.

I practically jumped.

"Who is it!"

A low voice rumbled, "You are Doyle."

I identified the gravel a second before I recognized the grey features on the black face.

"I know who I am," I snapped. "Jim Jim, is that you?"

"Here I am."

He was just inches away now and still looked more like a shadow than anything else in the room.

"Dammit! Jim Jim, are you trying to scare me to death? What are you doing here? And where the hell have you been all day? Why didn't you wait for me to get you out of town? Don't you know the police are looking everywhere for you?"

"No."

I blinked.

"You didn't know?"

"I'm not trying to scare you."

"What about the rest?"

Even in the darkness I could see his massive shoulders rise and fall.

"I don't remember."

"You don't remember what you're doing here? You don't remember where you've been all day?"

"I don't remember the other questions."

He couldn't have seen my scowl but I scowled anyway.

"Well, what are you doing here?"

"Those pictures."

"Pictures? What pictures? You mean the ones Copley had at the art show? I thought they were destroyed in the fire."

"No."

I counted to ten and inhaled from my navel.

"They weren't destroyed?"

"Yes. But there will still be negatives."

My mouth came open.

Strangely though, no words came out.

I felt a little silly, standing there with my mouth open and not saying anything so I said: "How did you know about the negatives?"

"All photographs have negatives."

I could have argued the point. Polaroids don't. But Copley had had to enlarge his pictures. So he'd used film. No way around it. Probably 35 millimeter, maybe a portrait camera, but certainly film.

"It won't be out here," I said. "This place is cold."

I led Jim Jim to the back of the room, to the seventh cell whose stone walls were still standing. The relic of a door, solid wood and three inches thick, had a two-hundred-year-old deadbolt and a hinged doggy-door about knee height that was just big enough for a bucket of food to go in or a bucket of waste to come out.

More recently the doggy-door had been taped up. There was more tape around the edges of the jamb and below too to keep studio light from entering the dark room.

The "keep out" light was out.

So we went in.

When I threw the light switch a red safety lamp bathed the

darkroom in blood. Jim Jim's eyes grew huge. He froze and surveyed the place with the same kind of horror another man might the stairwell to Hades.

The room looked pretty big until I remembered that it had probably held ten or twelve men at a time. There was a floor-mounted enlarger, a large storage cabinet, a bunch of floor-to-ceiling shelves containing large carboys of every kind of photochemical including developers, stop-bath, fix, special washes, and even a thirty-gallon drum of photoflash powder which Copley had probably used for shooting his cave pictures, since it's more easily backpacked than electronic flash.

A massive developing bench occupied an entire wall and had four trays of chemicals, five film developing tanks and a color analyzer already set up for business. Several 35 mm film strips hung from a wire over the bench.

"Now we're getting warm," I said.

However, none of the films were cave pictures.

I went to the cabinet. The first shelf was camera accessories. The second was film, all right, but still in the boxes. I tried the third shelf.

"Getting warmer," I announced.

Jim Jim came over. I told him to help me look through the stuff. There were a dozen developed film rolls.

One by one I started pulling them out and holding them up to the light.

Jim Jim followed my lead.

"Arrrrrrr!" he said, after viewing the first.

"Find something?"

"It looks like the spirit world."

"A cave painting?" He passed it across to me. "No," I said and handed it back. "That's not it. There's a building in the background."

"Spirit world," he insisted. "In the spirit world the sun is black and it rises in the west. Rivers flow up into the mountains and the tops of the trees grow down into the ground."

"Terrific."

"As old men we enter the spirit world and grow younger and younger until we are ready to be born again in the real world."

"I gotcha. Look for cave pictures, huh?"

He looked but not for long.

While I finished the bunch he left, busying himself in poking around the far side of the dark room where the window had been bricked up to keep out the light. He found a space to explore between the end of the bench and the stone wall.

On a hunch, I went to the enlarger and pulled the negative holder. There was a single 35 mm negative still locked in the frame. As I held it up to the light I sensed Jim Jim at my side.

"Bingo!" I cried.

He rejoined me.

"What is bingo?"

"It means we're hot."

I brought the film over to the developing bench. Four trays were laid out. But they were empty. I crossed to the shelves, brought jugs of developer, stop bath, fix and wash and poured some of each in that order in the trays. I gave Jim Jim the job of stirring them while I moved back over to the enlarger and got the negative back into the film holder. Copley was set up to handle color and this film was a color negative, but I didn't have time for that. I just wanted a peek. Once I had it set up, I focused on the base, stopped it down, switched it off and grabbed a sheet of print paper from the cabinet. Any exposure, it didn't matter. I let it go for seven seconds before clicking it off, then threw the paper into the developer. I felt Jim Jim's breath on me as the white surface gradually went grey in spots and then the grey became black and the spots resolved into significance.

A pass through the stop bath, a minute in the fix and then a quick wash. We studied the picture in the blood-red glow of the safety lamp.

"Wow!" I cried. And then I added: "On second thought, make that Whowie!"

"Gggggggg!" said Jim Jim.

It was a single frame from the Pleistocene camera Rolly Melsum was hoping to find. The photographer—not Art Copley but the original painter who'd died ten thousand years ago—had known how to bring cave walls to life. He'd also had an eye for detail. His subject, on a bet Rolly Melsum's dragon and Jim Jim's Great Goanna, showed several variations to the one in the museum. For example, it had only a tiny tail and its head didn't look like a crocodile head because the snout was too short and the teeth were far too long. Besides that it had spots and what—granting the primitive workmanship of the artist—looked more like fur than scales. There was one other difference too. One that convinced me it was the *Megalania*. It had six legs. The painting also depicted a black stick figure beside it for scale—the monster stood shoulder high to the man—and showed what looked like a river flowing in the background and a distinctive cliff face behind that.

"This is hot stuff," I said.

"Bingo?"

"You're darn right, bingo. This came right out of the cave, didn't it?"

"Yes. We must destroy it, Doyle."

"Destroy it!"

"It is not good. It is—"

I didn't hear the rest of what he had to say. Because suddenly the darkroom door slammed shut.

We both started. I moved toward the door but only got close when the sliding bolt clanged home.

"Is somebody out there?" I called.

I pushed. The door didn't budge.

"Hey!" I shouted, "we're in here. Unlock this door!"

I could hear someone moving around out in the workroom but nobody answered my call.

Jim Jim stepped up beside me.

"Knock it down," I told him.

He stood back and threw his shoulder against it. If it had been an ordinary door he'd have reduced it to splinters. But this was no ordinary door. He couldn't even worry it.

After two shoulder-crushing tries I told him to stop.

Someone was still moving around in the workshop. What they were up to I couldn't begin to guess.

"I smell," said Jim Jim.

"What?"

He bent down. His fingertips raked the wooden floor and then went to his nose. Now I smelled it, too. When I dropped to a knee I saw a reddish liquid—red in the light of the safety lamp—flowing beneath the threshold.

"That's oil."

"Yes."

As we stood there a sheet of flames rushed under the door and into the center of the darkroom. I jumped out of the way. Jim Jim, too.

The cabinet near the door was the first thing to go. Flames surrounded it in seconds.

I shouted, "We've got to get out of here, fast!"

Jim Jim took a running leap and hit the door with bone breaking force. It didn't have any effect. Not any.

I hopped to the bench.

There was no water. Plenty of fluids but most of them, I knew, were highly flammable. On a chance I took the tray of wash and spilled it over the fire. If anything this made things worse. I don't think the wash was really burning but the stuff that was burning spread even faster.

By this time Jim Jim was going crazy.

He was hurling himself against one of the walls like a madman. But the walls were all stone. There was no hope of breaking through them. They had withstood more desperate men than us for decades.

We were trapped good and starting to sweat.

The cabinet had turned into a bonfire. Roaring flames pushed toward the ceiling. It was impossible to stand near the door it was so hot. I'd moved to the opposite end of the room and even there the heat was almost unbearable.

We hadn't more than another few minutes to live.

Even if we managed to extinguish this fire, we couldn't get out of the darkroom. The studio was probably in flames now and the whole building would soon be burning.

I reached for one of the carboys. It must have weighed two hundred pounds. I couldn't even pull it off the shelf.

I grabbed Jim Jim. He whirled around. His face was a blend of fear and fury.

When I took him by the sleeve he jerked loose.

"*Nglai tanga ku!*"

"Jim Jim," I shouted over the flames, "you'll never get out that door. Come over here. I need you." I tugged on his arm until we were standing on the opposite side of the room, in the niche between bench and stone wall.

"Behind this bench! It's the only safe place!"

"We will die!"

"Listen to me, dammit. Do what I tell you to do and then come back here. Behind this bench. Do you hear me?"

"I hear."

I steered him to the shelves. Right under the large carboy of flash powder.

"Help me lift this barrel!"

He didn't move. The flames were making so much noise by this time I had to shout to make myself heard.

"Dammit, Jim Jim, if you don't wanta die, do as I say! Help me lift this barrel. It's too heavy for me to lift by myself." I was screaming and shaking his shirtsleeves with every word.

I managed to get through to him.

He reached up with both hands and hefted it against his chest. I did the same. When it came off the shelf we held it between us.

The flames now had engulfed half the room. Smoke, too. Black clouds of it hung from the ceiling and roiled down as far as my head. Jim Jim was in it down to his chest.

I pointed to the other side of the room.

"Let's push it or roll it over to the door and then get back here fast behind this bench. Understand?"

His black head wagged back and forth.

"What will it do?"

"It might explode. It better. If it doesn't you and I are cooked."

He nodded.

And then without warning he leaned back and took all of the weight in his arms. "I can do it, Doyle. You go behind the table."

As I stepped back he somehow hefted the carboy over his head. He took a couple steps nearer the blaze.

I shouted for him not to get too close.

I don't think he knew what was going to happen. I know damn well he didn't know what was going to happen because it was my idea and I didn't know what was going to happen . . . not really.

He threw it.

The thing struck the door with an awful thud. I called for him to come back. He turned and started over.

And then just as he crawled over beside me the sky fell in and the bottom simply dropped out of the world. To me it sounded more like a volcano erupting than a bomb going off.

Several things happened in very short—not necessarily this particular—order:

My eardrums blew.

My consciousness went out for a walk.

The roof started raining down and the floor collapsed.

Jim Jim, I, the bench and everything else in the room plunged down into the lower level. It was lucky we weren't crushed in the bargain.

I remember feeling like my brain was on fire and a ton of debris was resting across my chest. That's all. I have a faint recollection of somebody digging me out, lifting me up and carrying me over a lot of rubble to the outside, but apparently it wasn't much of a memory because, according to the papers, I kept screaming there was someone else back in the building, someone else to be rescued. And there wasn't. Because Jim Jim was the one who carried me out.

10

News from Beyond

ABORIGINE BURNS HISTORIC SYDNEY BUILDING TO GROUND

Arsonist in Opera House Fire Strikes Again at The Rocks

A major fire in The Rocks last night resulted in the total destruction of the historic Morisset Building and the capture of the number one suspect in the Sydney Opera House blaze.

An unnamed aboriginal, described by emergency personnel as "bloody big," surrendered to police last night after allegedly setting fire to the two-hundred-year-old gaol, then carrying to safety the journalist who was investigating him, according to sources on the scene. Officials confirmed today that an Ularu native was treated for second degree burns, cuts and abrasions, and subsequently incarcerated after being identified as one of possibly two aboriginals present in the art exhibition room of the Sydney Opera House just minutes before that earlier near-disastrous conflagration which has so shocked the citizens of this city, the nation, and the civilized world.

Police fear the two fires may signal an early call to arms by aborigines who've been threatening nationwide rioting as soon as the High Court makes its expected ruling against natives in *Ularu Tribe versus*

Rush Killian Wednesday. As we went to press there were already alarming indications of trouble in cities up and down the east coast.

Yesterday's fire began soon after dark. Fire trucks were summoned at approximately 9.45 p.m. by an alert toll official whose booth on the Harbour Bridge ramp overlooks The Rocks.

Several residents recall hearing an explosion about half past nine.

Flames engulfed the Morisset Building before the first fire trucks responded to alarms and fire fighters began hosing it down. It proved to be an impossible task. They were forced to direct their attention to protecting neighboring structures and write off the converted office building altogether. No rescue people had dared venture inside as it was assumed to be unoccupied at that time of night.

However subsequent events proved that assumption to be erroneous.

"I thought I had seen something moving around inside," said fire chief Robson. "I called for a squad." That's when the aborigine stumbled through a blazing orifice that had minutes before been the doorway. "He was carrying a man in his arms. His clothes were afire and so was his hair; so was the man for that matter. He took us all by surprise."

Water hoses were directed on them.

Before collapsing, the aborigine laid the man carefully onto the pavement. At that point medical technicians raced in.

The injured man turned out to be a journalist whom police had earlier in the day interrogated in connection with the opera house fire. Apparently, he had followed the aborigine to the Morisset just minutes before the explosion. Papers on his person identified him as Doyle Mulligan, an American with the Sydney branch of Eastern News Association. He was taken by ambulance to St. Margaret's Hospital where he remains in stable condition.

Police officers took charge of the aborigine. He is still being held.

Copley Aboriginals was a tenant of the Morisset Building. Proprietor and dealer Arthur Copley had sponsored the Ularu cave paintings art show at the opera house. He burned to death in that fire. His studio on the third floor of the old prison is presumed to be the starting point for yesterday's blaze. The Ularus had declared that Copley's pictures must be destroyed. Authorities suspect that his negatives were the target of the fire.

I lay down the paper. Cockie and Newman, standing at the foot of my hospital bed, looked every bit as pained as I felt. More.

"This damned rag! Jim Jim didn't start that fire," I said.

"Nobody knows who started it, Doyle," replied Newman.

"Well, it wasn't Jim Jim. He was with me all the time. When are they going to release him?"

" 'Oo knows?"

"Well what's happening now? What's going on out there? I know it's all over the television. I can see it on everyone's faces when they walk by my door. But I can't get anybody to tell me."

"It's bad, Blue."

"I want to know."

"That's why we brought you the paper."

"This is Sunday's edition. Today's Monday."

Newman came to Cockie's aide.

"There's no follow-up on your story, Doyle," he said. "Subsequent events pushed it off the news pages."

"What events? I want to know about Jim Jim. Is he all right?"

"He's fine."

"Where've they got him?"

" 'E's still in gaol," said Cockie pronouncing the word to rhyme with "bile" which is what he called the process of releasing a prisoner on bond.

I asked him about it. Bail, not bile.

"We've troied. The coppers are hangin' on to 'im fer now. Which reminds me, they want to talk to you again, too."

"Get them in here. I'll talk to them right now if it will help get Jim Jim released."

Newman, turning to go, assured me that all would turn out for the best. "You just get some rest," he said. "We'll do everything that can be done."

"When are you coming back?"

"Maybe tomorrow," said Newman.

He looked at Cockie.

"Ey, we're kinda busy roight now what with everything that's goin' on."

That was Monday morning.

Monday afternoon the cops showed up.

A nurse woke me up to tell me that two police officers were waiting to get a statement. I told her to show them in without even stopping to think they might be three chins and Vic Tanny . . . Sergeants Willoughby and Ek.

Willoughby was one of them all right but, fortunately, the other guy was just a stenographer.

A doctor must've ordered them not to slap me around if they didn't like what I had to say because all they did was scowl.

I told them about Rolly Melsum and my conviction that Mutt and Jeff had started the opera house fire, as well as my notion that Rush Killian himself was behind everything. They asked me about proof and of course I didn't have any. When I finished my statement I inquired if any offices had been spared in the Morisset fire. How much had been saved?

"Nothing. It's all gone," said Willoughby. "What's on your mind?"

The proof. Brock Allitt's envelope.

It was the one thing I hadn't told them. How could I? After giving my word to Allitt. I'd just said that I had a meeting at Boyle's office and the party never showed up. To the question who, I replied it was only a voice on the telephone. You can imagine how much they liked that.

"Look," I said, "the paper got it wrong. I didn't follow Jim Jim there, he followed me. He was keeping an eye on me. I left the front door open and he came right in. There was someone else in the building. Somebody else started the fire. Trying to kill me."

"Is that right?"

"You're darn right, that's right. Jim Jim shouldn't be in jail. We're lucky to be alive and it's only thanks to him that we are."

The stenographer studied his notes.

Willoughby studied his nails.

"When do you think he'll be released?"

They stood up.

Willoughby said:

"Like you say, Mulligan, he's lucky to be alive. If it were up to me he wouldn't be." I guess I was still a little groggy. Did he mean Jim Jim wouldn't be released if it were up to him or that he wouldn't be alive? It didn't make sense either way.

When they left I thought about it for five minutes and then asked a nurse if she'd be kind enough to get me a copy of the morning *Daily Pictorial*. Five minutes later, she delivered; a glance at the front page was enough.

The Picky was full of it.

Bannered across the top in seventy-two point type was this story:

ABORIGINES ATTACK FEDERAL BUILDING IN PERTH

And below it, complete with pictures, was this one:

WHITE VIGILANTES RETALIATE!
GAGADJU SLAIN IN DARWIN

I started reading. But then another headline below the fold with the slug "EXCLUSIVE to THE PICKY" in red and green capital letters caught my eye, and instantly Jim Jim went on the back burner:

POLICEMAN, JOURNO MISSING, FEARED MURDERED IN TOP END

VICTIMS OF "CANNIBAL CLAN"

Tennant Creek (NT)—If the situation in the great Central Desert weren't terrible enough these days it just became more so with the disappearance yesterday of the British Special Branch detective appointed by Governor-General Smyth to investigate incidents of inhuman butchery, ritual slayings and native cannibalism by the Ularu tribe.

Also disappeared is the first female victim—a journalist. Air search teams and ground parties are making every effort to find the two but little hope remains that they will turn up alive.

Sydney Chief of Police L.B. Webber has called the news "an appalling development."

Superintendent L.M. Hawthorne and *Woman's Day* reporter Margaret McDowel were declared "missing and believed dead" after venturing into a "sacred" valley and failing to return to camp. They've been absent now for more than twenty-four hours.

Hawthorne and Miss McDowel, in the company of a police sergeant from Sydney, flew to the Killian Development Camp a hundred kilometers northwest of Tennant Creek Saturday evening by chartered plane. The pair signed out for a utility vehicle and went on a familiarization outing into the desert Sunday morning. They never returned.

Their disappearance brings to seven the count of persons attacked, dragged into the desert, then butchered by local aborigines.

Supt. Hawthorne was assigned to look into the earlier incidents: a surveyor and two unidentified laborers as well as two ENA reporters whose bodies were discovered in a ravine on the western side of the Murtchison Mountains literally torn to pieces. The mountains divide Killian's land from the Ularu cannibals.

Rescue teams described the earlier victims as having been gutted, dismembered and even partially consumed in a "loathsome cannibalistic orgy by indigenous persons unknown."

A cannibal clan which calls itself the *Dongos* and which has taken credit for past atrocities has declared that Hawthorne and McDowel have "paid the price for their interference." The *Dongos* openly defy the government and Rush Killian to halt their murderous spree. "All who trespass on sacred land will die," they have boasted. "Their bodies, like those of the English policeman and the woman, will be ripped open, their bones will be crushed, their hearts will be rent from their chests, and their flesh will be consumed."

Asked if aborigines would be likely to show a lady special treatment, a native expert discounted this possibility as a frail hope. "If anything," he said, "they would deal with her even more ruthlessly than they would a man. A quick death would be the best she could expect." He added, however, that "this wasn't apt to happen."

Two *Sydney Daily Pictorial* columnists staying at the

Killian settlement are now the last newsmen on the scene and since the only approach has today been closed by police blockade to prevent further loss of lives, everything they communicate will be an exclusive for *The Pictorial.* Veteran newsmen E. L. MacMutton and D. O. Geoffers will transmit communiques direct to *Pictorial* editors via radio as the news breaks. They vow to stay on and report "to the end."

I read the story in a kind of shock.

When I finished I set the paper down and told myself it was lucky for me I hadn't gone with Hawthorne, after all. I even congratulated myself on getting laid up so no one could fault me for not doing something about it. I reminded myself there was nothing I could do anyway.

I told myself that.

I guess I wasn't listening.

Because the next thing I knew the day nurse was trying to talk me back into bed by saying I couldn't leave without a doctor's permission. But, like I say, I wasn't listening. I signed a personal responsibility quit form and walked out of the hospital.

"So that," I told Cockie, sitting at our table in the back of the Black Stump Pub, "is why you didn't want me to see today's paper."

He'd offered me a beer but I'd turned him down.

"Ye're not off the turps again, are ye?"

"No. I want to do something beside sit here and drink."

"Loike wot?"

"Find out what's going on, for starters."

"All we know," said Percy Newman, "is what we read in the newspaper. The police have closed off the development camp. No one's allowed in. No news is coming out except what the Picky prints."

"That's another thing. Why aren't MacMutton and Geoffers under arrest?"

"Fer wot? There's no witnesses against 'em."

I stood up.

"I can't just sit around here doing nothing. I've got to talk to somebody. Interview somebody. It's what I do!"

"Whyn't ye try talkin' to the police?"

"I'll try. I doubt if they'll talk to me."

"Maybe I can help ye there. The chief of police owes me a favor. Ye can use my name if—"

"Lug Webber!"

"The very sayme."

"I don't have to talk to him. I know what he'll say."

But I went anyway.

"So," said Chief Webber, "it seems you were smart not to've gone with the superintendent after all." He couldn't help looking at me the same way the other two officers had. He'd only turned me loose because Hawthorne talked him into it, so as far as he was concerned I should either be in jail now or dead and if it were up to him I wouldn't even get my choice.

"Yeah. Smart."

"What do you want?"

His pugnacious phiz warned me that whatever it was, I wouldn't get it. Still, I had to try.

"I want to know what's being done to find Hawthorne. And Maggie McDowel."

He shook his head.

"Now that's not smart. If you'd wanted the story you should have gone. You've your own share of brass, Mulligan; I'll hand you that. Asking me for an interview after bowing out of the trip."

I didn't feel like brass. I felt like copper . . . about two cents worth.

"You'll get a press release along with everyone else," he told me.

I wasted five minutes of his valuable time in a brief review of

Hong Kong. How Hawthorne had saved my life. How he alone had shown the guts to stand up to a killer who was turning people into mincemeat and walking rings around the whole Hong Kong police force. When the killer kidnapped my fianceé and offered to trade my life for hers, Hawthorne had backed me up and saw to it that we both came out alive.

"If that's the case," said the Chief, "if you feel that way, why didn't you go with him when he asked you to?"

"I didn't know he was going to get himself lost. And I couldn't have helped. I get lost in a park if I step off the sidewalk."

His hard gaze hadn't softened.

"C'mon," I said. "Have a heart."

"I'm sorry, Mulligan, I can't spare you any more time. I've got a million—"

"Cockie said he's got a favor coming. He said I could use it if I needed to."

"You've used it. Tell Alf that. Why do you think I'd be sitting here talking with the likes of you when I've got the entire force and part of the army walking the streets. And the Governor-General is waiting to learn what I've done with one of Her Majesty's special investigators. Good day, Mulligan."

I took a cab to the *Woman's Day* building. After cooling my heels in an outer office for an hour and a half I finally got to see Maggie's boss. I didn't have to introduce myself. She recognized my cold feet.

"Oh," she said. "You're that one. The one who refused to go up there, right?"

"Yeah . . . the name's Mud. Doyle Mud."

"No, it's not. It's something Irish. Murphy. Wait. Mulligan. That's it. Doyle Mulligan. Maggie told me all about you. She's in trouble because she took your place."

"Didn't I say mud? Have you heard from her? Anything at all?"

An uncomfortable silence followed. Uncomfortable for me.

She took her time answering because she could see how it was.

"Why should I tell you?"

"You shouldn't," I said. "Maggie trusted me and look what happened to her. If you're putting together something for this issue I might beat you to the punch. You probably think I'm so low I'd have to climb on a stepstool to watch grass grow so why should you give me the time of day?"

As I spoke she'd turned away but now she was facing me again and giving me a grim little smile.

"You're very good, aren't you? You've got what we call gift of the gab. I suppose you'd say you kissed the Blarney Stone."

Another time or another place I might've said that and as a matter of fact I have said that . . . but not then and not there.

"I don't feel very good," was what I did say.

"You're not alone. We're worried sick about her. What *are* you doing here? Are you after a story?"

"No."

"You're not doing a story?"

"Well, I am . . . but that's not why I'm here."

"Then why?"

"Isn't it obvious? I have to know."

She shook her head.

"It's a shame really. I allowed Maggie to go because she was so eager. She's very ambitious. I doubt we'd have used the material. It's not our sort of thing. Maybe she could've sold it to another magazine or to a newspaper . . . I don't know. It was a chance for her, that's all."

"Did she contact you from the camp?"

"There are no phones—"

"But by radio. I understand Killian has a radio."

"No. I'm sorry."

"Did she check in . . . leave any messages?"

"No."

"Is there anything you can tell me? Anything at all?"

Another shake.

"Nothing you don't already know. It was just her bad luck. And your good luck. But then, you're Irish, aren't you? Don't they say that? Luck of the Irish? Maybe you get luck by kissing the Blarney Stone, too."

"If you do," I said, "I must've been holding my breath at the time."

She stared.

"Oh!" she said. "Are you that one?"

My next stop was the Picky building.

My contact was the city editor, the same guy Cockie had called two days before to learn that MacMutton and Geoffers had taken the Indian Pacific up to the Territory.

What I wanted, I explained, was some professional courtesy. His reporters up there were the only source for news. The police weren't talking and neither were Killian's people here in Sydney.

Of course that only confirmed what he already knew: he and his paper were sitting on the biggest scoop of the year and there was no percentage in letting me have a peek until after they'd used it first. In short, he saw the situation as a professional and to hell with the courtesy. I thought about telling him what I suspected: Mutt and Jeff's being involved in the Sydney Opera House fire. I decided against it. If he thought his journos were going to be implicated, he'd just clam up altogether.

"We only hear from them twice a day," he informed me. "Every twelve hours. It's not a radio Killian's got, it's a satellite link. Three in the afternoon and again in the morning, just before deadline."

I asked if he'd already gotten his report for today.

He had. Two hours ago.

Could I see it?

No.

"What about their reports from over the weekend?"

"What about them?"

"Can I read them?"

"What is it you want to know, Mr. . . . er, Mulligan?"

"I want to know what's being done. To find the woman and the British policeman who are missing. I need to know what's going on."

"That's what they're looking into right now, I presume; what's going on. We'll hear from them when they find out."

"You mean *you'll* hear from them."

"Yes. Tomorrow morning."

"How do I go about finding out what you hear."

His face brightened.

"Is that all you want?"

"Yes."

He became helpfulness itself.

"Why didn't you say so?" He jabbed his finger at me. "Are you familiar with the building?"

"I can find my way around."

"Okay, here's what you do. Take the lift to the ground floor. You'll see a sign pointing to the lobby. Follow it. The circulation department is straight ahead. Classified is on the right. Are you with me so far?" I said I was. "The doors to the street will be to your left. Turn left. As you exit the building take the footpath about twelve paces west. You'll come to our newspaper dispenser. Plug in seventy-five cents."

He was lucky I didn't plug him.

"Okay," I announced suddenly, "I'm going up there."

I expected an argument.

Maybe laughter.

What I got was silence. The Black Stump was practically empty. A conference at our assigned table was the only thing keeping the barmaid busy.

Newman broke the silence by saying: "You mean up to the police station again?"

"No. Up there. To the Top End."

"Ha!" laughed Cockie.

"Somebody's got to go."

"Somebody did. Mickey and Nevil went. Maggie and yer copper friend. And they've placed it off limits now, did ye forget that?"

"No, but there's thousands of square miles of desert up there. They can't rope it all off."

"They don't have to. There's only one road in, and the sayme road out."

"I'll cut across the desert then."

Cockie laughed again much louder than before.

"Remember wot happened last time, Blue? Yer wee jaunt through the bush. That was jist outsoida Sydney. Now ye're talking about the back o' beyond."

"The what?"

"The Mulga . . . west o' the Divide . . . the Wallaby Track—it's all the sayme thing, isn't it? Bluey, you may be the best journo in Sydney, but out there in the back an' beyond ye ayn't got Buckley's chance."

"I'm through talking, Alvie. I'm going."

"I can't let ye do it, Blue."

"You can't stop me."

Newman broke in. "It's not Alf," he said. "It's I and the whole ENA saying no. We let the Seattle people know what happened and they decided that no more reporters should even attempt to get inside the camp. They suggested that some of the press services chip in to send a representative to Alice Springs. There's a—"

I stood up.

"It's no good. I'm going."

"Don't make us sack you, mate!"

"Alf's right, Doyle. Don't forget, if you quit, or we let ye go, you've only got twenty-eight days before you have to leave Australia. That's the law."

"I'm sorry, Percy."

Without warning Cockie clapped his hand on my arm and said: "Tell ye what, Blue, we'll toss fer it."

Newman objected, "Alf, I don't think—"

Cockie silenced him by raising a hand. When he opened the fist there were two coins inside.

Again.

I took ten seconds to look it over. This was the only way I could go and still hang onto my job. It was worth the gamble. "Okay," I agreed. "But not Two-Up. Just toss one. A straight flip: Tails . . . I get my tail up to the Top End—"

"An' 'eads . . . ye use yer 'ead and do loike we tell ye."

I crossed my fingers.

Cockie's coin went up, fell to the tabletop and rolled round before falling in a puddle of beer with its gleaming regal face looking me straight in the eye.

" 'Eads!"

"Heads," seconded Newman with relief.

I uncrossed my fingers.

Heads.

"That settles it," I said; "I head for the Top End."

11

Down the Red Dust Road

"D'ye like abo jokes?"

"Sure."

"How many cops does it take to kick an abo down a flight of stairs?"

I stretched my neck to look over the seat backs in front of me. Window seat and aisle seat both occupied. The window seat was doing the talking—apparently he'd tired of staring outside because the airplane hadn't left the jetway yet and, quite frankly, there was little to see on the tarmac.

"I dunno. How many?"

"None. 'E fell."

The aisle seat chuckled.

I sensed myself getting upset. Not just at the joke. It bothered me because it made me think about Jim Jim. How I was going to try to help a man who had once saved my life and in the process, abandoning another man who'd just saved it twice.

"Those bloody 'eathens!" exclaimed the aisle seat. "I used to think we could live with them but I'm not so sure. Burning buildings. And all that butchery. Maybe somebody ought to round them all up before they have a chance to do any more. Send a regiment up there and clean out the whole place."

"They'll have to eventually. Have you heard this one? What do you call a *gin* who gets an abortion?"

A *gin* is an aboriginal woman.

"What?"

"Croimestopper."

More laughter.

I thought of Jim Jim once again, and despite my anger, held my tongue.

To say that I had the next twenty-eight days mapped out may be going too far. In fact, my plans for the next twenty-four hours were hazy at best. My immediate plans had gotten me out to Kingsford Smith Airport and onto an Ansett Airline flight first thing Tuesday morning. The flight would get me to Alice Springs. Beyond that I planned to make plans as the need arose.

Everything I'd brought with me was thrown into a flight bag which I'd carried on and stuffed into the overhead.

All the money I had in the world, about six hundred and fifty dollars, was in my wallet.

"Here's one," said the window seat suddenly, "Two abos and a galah were standing on the footpath when one abo said to the—"

" 'Ey, nip it."

"What?"

"—shhhhh."

The cabin lights dimmed. Or so it seemed at the time. I thought we must be getting ready to go but that wasn't it. Something made me turn. When I glanced up, I found myself once again in the shade of a tree-like form.

My mouth fell open.

"Can I sit here, Doyle?"

"Jim Jim!"

It was him all right. I didn't recognize the clothes—jeans and a denim jacket, God knows where he'd gotten them. The stuff I'd given him must have been burned in the fire—and he still had gauze bandages on his hands and antiseptic cream of some kind on his cheeks, chin and forehead, but it was him without any doubt.

He saw me examining his burns.

"Bingo," he said with his one-hole smile.

"Bingo?"

"Yes. Too hot."

I controlled my laughter. "Jim Jim, you didn't bust—?"
I stopped. If I could overhear my neighbors then they could overhear me.

I stood up, slid to the aisle, took him by the arm and coaxed him forward to the galley. I looked up and down the aisleway. "They let you go, didn't they? You're not on the lam?"

"Lamb. . . ? Like a jumbuck?"

"No. Like a jailbreak. You didn't bust out of jail, did you?"

"Yes. They let me go. I am going home."

A wave of unimaginable relief swept through me. Part of it was for him; he was free, and he was going home. But part of it was for me too. I won't deny I felt a whole lot better knowing we'd be travelling together.

I stuck out my hand. It was instantly swallowed up by his huge mitt.

We shook with feeling.

"The last I heard you were still locked up. Come on, give! Why did the cops turn you loose? Did somebody pull some strings? What happened?"

"A man named Mister Cockie."

"I knew it!"

"He had a lawyer. The lawyer told the policemen they did not have any evidence against me. The lawyer gave the police some money."

"Bail? How much? Who paid for it?"

"Mister Cockie."

"Well, I'll be darned."

"Mister Cockie told the police he was doing a story about me. A good story. He said the police would look bad in the story. He said if they let me go he would not run the story."

"That sounds like Alvie. What else did he say?"

"He wanted me to look out for you. He said you can get into trouble without any help but that you always need help to get out."

That sounded like Alvie, too.

"Anything else?"

"He said you are a liar and a Welshman."

Jim Jim showed me his one-hole grin.

"It's welsher," I said; "and I'm not—I had my fingers crossed." His blank face served to amuse me. "Come on," I said leading him back to our seats, "we'd better strap in."

He sat down beside me with his knees hitting the tray table in front of him and his shoulders cramped between the seats on each side until I leaned over and levered his seat back upright. He perched ramrod straight. I was so happy to see him it didn't occur to me that this was probably his virgin flight until after the plane started taxiing and I saw him take a mighty grip on the chair arms.

Sure enough, when the pilot ran up the engines Jim Jim closed his eyes and tensed every muscle in his body. Which made for a great deal of tension. I guess he felt the same way about visiting the troposphere as I did about visiting the wilderness, the way most people feel about visiting the back side of the moon.

As the jet began barrelling down the runway he inhaled a bushel of air. I asked him if I should let him know when we were up.

"No," he said, pushing the words out through clenched teeth. "Let me know when we are down."

But he didn't mean it.

When we reached altitude and leveled off I told him it was all right to look. Slowly his eyes cracked open and he peered around. I pointed out the window.

He leaned across my lap, putting his face against the Plexiglas. "Aaaahh!"

The sun was rising out of The Ditch, that part of the Tasman Sea which separates mainland Australia from New Zealand. Inland from the shore, as far as the eye could see, Sydney was a concrete, steel and glass landscape with only occasional splotches of green or brown to break the metropolitan monotony. We soared over the suburban sprawl following the same westward route we'd taken on the train only higher and faster. Soon, once we'd gained altitude and distance, the concrete inevitably dwindled away and the green and brown splotches inexorably grew and joined until they'd choked off all but the barest evidence of civilization and only urban outposts remained, linked to the city by tiny threads of concrete and asphalt. Of course in the beginning there was a certain orderliness to the bush: fields with geometrical shapes and boundaries marked with barbed-wire, dirt backroads which met at right angles, endless rows of cotton and corn, and tidy clusters of sheep being shepherded from paddock to meadow. But soon even these gave way to the wilderness. Pastures first lost their orderly shapes and then their boundaries. Villages grew smaller and smaller and clung to the highway for protection against the wild. Byways came to dead ends. Order succumbed to haphazard. As the land rose to the Blue Mountains, trees, rugged outcrops and ravines predominated. Beyond the mountains loomed the outback, two million miles of arid wasteland where only heat and hardship held sway.

For almost four hours we sat there the two of us taking turns at the window, watching the landscape—once beyond the dividing range—grow flatter and flatter, redder and redder, until we approached the sunburnt central plain of the continent and at that point I knew how the Red Centre had gotten its name.

There were times, particularly over the Simpson Desert, when the ground was as flat and featureless as the ocean—a sea of red dust from horizon to horizon. Only occasionally would a narrow gravel road or a single modest dwelling break the relentless red landscape like a lowly tramp steamer with its almost imperceptible backtrail that would soon disappear altogether. There were no trees. No bushes. No hills and no rivers. No stock. In fact no life of any kind. But it was a deceptive picture. The unpretentious homeowner might be the baron of a station encompassing as much as a million acres which could, after a sudden shower and virtually overnight, become a sea of grass.

Eventually they brought us some breakfast.

Jim Jim only nibbled at his while I gobbled mine down. When he passed his across I finished it, too.

He was pathetic.

By the time we got to "The Alice," Jim Jim knew me a lot better than I knew him. Something about either the plane or the altitude made him even more silent than usual. I used a half hour to bring him up to date on the latest developments at the Killian camp but he already knew from Cockie what had happened to Hawthorne and Maggie and there wasn't a lot more to tell so I spent most of the flight time talking about me, about my adventures in the Far East. He asked me where that was. I replied it was China and Japan and Korea as well as a few other countries of Southeast Asia. He said they weren't east. They were north. Those few words were the first he'd uttered in nearly an hour, so to keep the conversational ball going I put it to him where he thought the Far East was. He said he used to believe it was a place called Biggawindi but now he knew it was New South Wales. Twenty more words which had to last me the rest of the trip.

Eventually the seat belt lights came on.

We locked our tray tables up.

I looked out the window while Jim Jim assumed the white-knuckle, tensed, crash position and screwed his eyes shut.

Alice Springs is very nearly the geographical center of the continent; 25,000 inhabitants make it the only community of any consequence between the east and west coasts. Darwin, barely three times as large, is a thousand miles away on the north coast and there is nothing, to speak of, in between.

Rail service from Adelaide, a thousand miles south on the southern coast, ends here.

Our plane dipped, Jim Jim inhaled a huge draft of air, and soon we were skipping across the tarmacadam like a rock thrown into the River Todd and—like the rock—coming to rest in a splash of dust.

*   *   *

The desert air hit us like a blowtorch.

I couldn't believe the heat.

I carved a path through the airport crowd. Jim Jim had the build for carving but we hadn't got to his country yet. He followed me about like an overgrown puppy. Neither of us had checked any luggage—I had nothing but the one carry-on, and he had nothing—and so we gave baggage claim a pass and reached the car rental counter ahead of the rush. And then trouble. All three rental agencies turned up their noses at my Illinois driver's license. They insisted on an international ticket or an Australian license. I asked Jim Jim if he had one but he didn't even know how to drive. So we wound up going into town, saving nine bucks by shunning a taxi and taking the airport bus.

Twenty minutes later we got dropped off in front of the North End Car Hire Agency, pinched between a body shop and an outback pub. On the one side were "Smash Repairs" including "Top Quality Panel Beating." On the other: "Icy" cold beer and "Takeaway Foods."

We still had to pay mileage—there's no getting out of that in the outback—but the per diem was cheaper, and they gave us our pick of any car on the lot. Any of the three, that is, an F.J. Holden, and H.Q. Holden or a Holden, G.M.H.

I settled for the Holden, a Fosters, a hamburger and a side order of chips. Jim Jim had three—four counting mine. I seemed to be losing my appetite about the same time and at the same rate he found his. However, I gulped the beer down because it was liquid and cold. Both rarities in the bush. Not long ago they used to serve beer warm out here, but not any more, every pub has an icebox kept on the coldest possible setting.

While we downed our drinks we watched a dog chase a cat through town. Both of them were walking. That's how hot it was. And dry! It's so dry out here the locals like to tell tourists that the bushes follow the dingos around. Anyway, that's what they told me.

They wouldn't say boo to Jim Jim.

They just glared.

So we left with our food and filled the tank and it was still shy of noon when we started up the Stuart Highway, a straight, flat, blacktop thing with almost no traffic and only two hazards. The first is, you'll get so bored of the desert scenery you'll fall asleep at the wheel and drive into a ditch. The second hazard is road trains. One minute we'd have the world to ourselves and the next thing you know a semi-tractor rig hauling three or even four trailers would come screaming down on us out of a cloud of bull dust. If I wasn't ready, if I didn't grip the wheel with both hands and hang on, they'd have blown us right off the highway. Except for those times, it was a pretty dull trip.

Jim Jim sat in the suicide seat, more talkative now that we were back on the ground again heading for his neck of the woods. I let him talk. During the next eight hours he told me about the land and the animals, about his friends and his family, and about growing up as an aboriginal in the desert.

He called the landscape *jiba*, his word for a kind of stony desert. It wasn't exactly sand. Neither was it rock. There was some soil too, but not very much. Jim Jim thought of the dunes as being alive and it was easy to see why—they were forever realigning themselves to the elements, wind and rain. Parts were fixed by vegetation—the indomitable mulga plants being the most notable, a scrubby little acacia which can survive the worst droughts. But there were low-growing saltbush plants too and bluebush. Jim Jim pointed these out to me along with "tussock" grass, the major source of forage for kangaroos, and the rare hard-leafed evergreen gum trees.

We didn't see many roos but he assured me they were out there. He talked about the snakes and the spiders, too. And about some ants that could jump half a meter in the air.

He talked about almost everything. I tried to steer him into talking about Black Tom. I knew Tom was either the one man I didn't want to go anywhere near, or he was the man I'd have to go see about Hawthorne and Maggie in which case he'd still be the one man I wouldn't want to go anywhere near but I'd have to. I thought it would help to know which.

Anyway, he talked. You can do a lot of talking in nine hours of driving. Here are a few samples of the stuff I had to sift through.

Jim Jim was just nine or ten, he thought, when he saw Black Tom for the first time.

He and his older brother had crawled on their bellies to the top of a hill where the mulla-mullung was trying to heal an elder from the village. The man was their father. Everyone had said he was dying. Their father believed it, too. He had already made his farewells.

Three years before, their mother had died of a similar disease, one of many brought to Australia by the white man, diseases to which the aborigines had no resistance. She had gone to Black Tom to be healed but Black Tom had said there was nothing he could do. Sure enough, Jim Jim's mother had soon passed away. Their father had raised him and his five brothers and sisters alone.

Now it was his time. The old man had told his children goodbye and left to die alone in the desert.

"I thought you said he was killed by an evil spirit?" I cut in.

"Yes. This was long before."

"Then he didn't die of the disease?"

Black Tom, said Jim Jim, had declared that their father would not die.

He could heal him.

The elder was laid out on a bed of grass surrounded by stones at the very peak of the hill. A number of men stood outside of the stone circle. They were the other elders in the council of ten. Including the chief. No one else was allowed near.

Jim Jim and his brother had crept to within a few yards of the site when they looked out from behind a bush and saw Black Tom applying the last of the white ochre to his chest, legs and arms. The patterns they knew held totemic significance in invoking the spirits. Every ceremony called for a different set of markings. When he was done he gathered up his click sticks and other sacred objects with their sacred incisings, placed a head dress of cockatoo and emu feathers on his head, and stood. Then he did something odd. He reached into his ritual ditty bag. Some are made of wallaby skin, others of *pandanus* fibre woven so tight they can hold water for days. Not his; it was fashioned from a human skull! From it Black Tom produced a reddish bulb which appeared to the two boys to be a piece of *tlinga* root.

Just as he popped the root in his mouth a sound warned him of their presence and he spun.

He stared at them, Jim Jim especially. Though Jim Jim was the younger by two years he was already larger than his brother and he looked older too.

Both boys were too frightened to move.

Black Tom's gaze bore at them with unwinking intensity. His eyes got bigger and bigger. Suddenly they swelled from their sockets and seemed actually to hover in space between themselves and the mulla-mullung.

It was an awe-inspiring sight, one sure to propel even the staunchest skeptic into devoted worship but to the boys it was mind-numbing.

They remained in that numbed state, hidden, throughout the ceremony.

Black Tom chanted and danced around the elder while the others watched. Then he dropped to his knees and lifted the raiments from his chest. He placed his mouth just below the old man's ribcage. Gently at first, then harder and harder, he suckled with his lips. His jaw cranked in circles. His lungs seemed to heave. When he finally drew back there was a smear of blood red around the wound and more blood seemed to run down Black

Tom's chin. With a flourish the mulla-mullung spat the diseased tissue onto the ground.

Only the boys from their place of hiding could see that the tissue was in reality a soft piece of *tlinga* root chewed until its reddish juices flowed freely.

"You mean it was just a stunt?"

"Yes."

"Did you tell anyone?"

They did not. They didn't dare to. In the first place, Black Tom's eyes would have seen if they did. In the second place, no one would ever have believed them . . . not even their father who, as it happened, recovered from his sickness that very night.

Here's another sample. This encounter took place a few years later:

Jim Jim was out gathering bitter roots and goanna eggs one day when, with no warning, Black Tom and four other men joined him.

They came out of the underbrush without a word and made a circle around him. Jim Jim didn't move. He knew what was going to happen. The long-awaited ritual both terrified and thrilled him. He was only fifteen but already more than six feet tall and for this reason alone he was being challenged years ahead of his peers.

They pushed him down on the ground, pinned him there by his arms and legs. Black Tom himself wielded the ceremonial stone knife. Jim Jim tried hard not to call out. To cry or show pain of any kind was not allowed. But there was pain.

They performed the ceremony of subincision.

They cut slashes across his abdomen, deep ones, so the scars would be thick and wide.

Then, forcing his mouth open and using the blunt edge of the stone like a hammer, Black Tom pounded out Jim Jim's left front incisor.

When this was done the men got off him.

As Jim Jim lay there, too near unconsciousness even to rise,

Black Tom stood over him telling him that he was not to return to the camp until the new moon still ten days away. When he did return, if he returned, he would then be a full member of the tribe.

Having said that, they left him.

The first night was the toughest. He did little more than crawl on hands and knees to a cleft between some large rocks and lie there until the blanket of darkness enveloped him. His mind reeled with a pain so great that he suffered hallucinations all night. Jim Jim dreamed that the rainbow serpent came to him. It spoke to him in Black Tom's voice, urging him to be strong. When he woke in the morning an emu egg lay on the ground beside him. He drank and ate. Again the next night the serpent came, this time with Black Tom's face as well, hovering in the sky above him. It exhorted him to forget the pain and go hunting. At first light there was more food. A little scrap of dried meat and a cup of water. Jim Jim downed the water but offered the meat to the spirit. Then he fought to his feet and staggered off to hunt.

Ten days later, his wounds healed and his mind strong, he walked into Ularu.

And this:

More years had passed and times had changed. The white man's cities and wares had lured many of the young men from the tribe. Some of these "Bentoos" returned telling tales of fabulous things. Of modern miracles. Of money.

Jim Jim's father had by that time been elected chief of the council of ten. He had long spoken in favor of breaking away from the Ularu's traditional isolation and forging ties to the white people. The gifts of the spirits, he counseled, would bring prosperity to the village because the white men were eager to see the cave art Great Goanna had inspired and to share the water which flowed from tunnels bored centuries before by the lizard fish Tobraka when he released Gol from his prison beyond the mountains. The whites would pay well for these.

Black Tom would not hear of it.

Already there was talk that a white man had laid claim to the land to the west. Gol's domain. If nothing was done the Europeans would desecrate this sacred ground.

Jim Jim's father urged calm.

Even when Killian showed up with his men and machines, and the Ularu people—especially the Dongos—were outraged, the chief held his people in check.

Black Tom and the council chief often fought.

Their differences left Jim Jim confused for he was his father's son and yet he believed as Black Tom believed that the whites would ultimately destroy his people—as they had killed his mother. Jim Jim was a Dongo; he was the biggest, strongest man in the tribe and the best hunter, and yet he had never left the occupied lands.

Torn between his father and the tribe's mulla-mullung, he did not know who to follow. When they argued, he didn't know who to believe.

The last time the two men went together into the mountains to settle their differences among the *kadi makara.*

Jim Jim had watched them go.

Neither man returned. Black Tom was never seen again; the body of Jim Jim's father was found the next day outside the sacred cave.

I gathered from the horrifying picture Jim Jim painted in simple sentences and mostly one-syllable words that there wasn't much left. The old man had been brutally butchered. In much the same way Nevil Cross and Mickey Fine and Hector Boyle had been butchered.

Jim Jim ended the story there. I got the feeling that wasn't really the end. He was still holding back. He just didn't trust me enough yet to say more.

And finally this:

Since the death of Jim Jim's father weeks before, the Dongos had led the tribe and all talk of accommodation with Killian and the other whites was forgotten.

Every day there came more attacks, other deaths, and the Ularu lived in fear.

An emergency meeting was called of the council of ten. This meeting included Jim Jim. Rumors abounded that the ancient gate which had for centuries kept Gol imprisoned behind the mountain had been opened.

It was Black Tom's job to see that the gate was closed. Only he was allowed to enter the sacred cave.

But Black Tom could not be found.

And there was more.

Someone, some member of the tribe, had led a white man into the sacred cave. He had seen the rock paintings. This was bad enough. But now it was learned that the white man had taken photographs. And these photographs were going to be shown to hundreds, even thousands of other white people.

The situation was intolerable.

Someone would have to go to Sydney. This is where the photographer worked and where the art showing would be held. He would have to convince the white man to cancel the show, to warn him of the danger to himself and others of angering the *kadi makara.*

Sydney was far, far away. A strange and hostile place. Only a great warrior and a true believer could have any hope of succeeding on such a journey.

Jim Jim was their man.

They did the aboriginal equivalent of a whip-round for travel expenses, rounded up a suit and tie, gave him a ditty bag with enough dried fruits and damper to last another man for a day or an aborigine for a week, and saw him as far as the bus stop in Biggawindi, N.T.

The rest, he said, I knew about.

I asked him if he'd known that Black Tom had also gone to Sydney.

He had not.

"You didn't have any idea he'd be at the opera house . . . that he would try to kill Arthur Copley?"

"No."

I thought the thing over.

"I don't get it. Where does Black Tom fit in?"

Jim Jim shrugged mightily.

"Black Tom," he said, "was the one who'd led the white man into the cave."

The desert is an ocean, someone wrote, in whose waters no oar is dipped. During the day I'd failed to see any resemblance. It was too hot and the air was so dry you could crunch it between your teeth. I felt more like a man being escorted through hell with Dante or Faust as his tour guide. Night changed all this. The blackness of the Great Central Desert at night is a sobering thing.

There are no highway lights along this narrow ribbon of road. No distant city lights. No headlights or taillights from other travelers, since ours was the only vehicle on the desert. Only the stars were there to remind us that we were not the only souls left in the universe.

When the twilight ended we drove on into a blackness as big and as forbidding as any ocean.

We stopped to fill up the tank for the last time in the cross-roads town of Tennant Creek. Then we drove on.

The lights of the roadblock alerted us miles before we reached it. In that vast emptiness a candle would shine for ten miles. The police floods burned off to the west, like a Pleiades floating in a starless sky. There was no question of missing the turn. At least a dozen vehicles had gathered on the roadside. There were a couple of makeshift tents and a few campers, too.

I pulled off the highway near an aging plywood sign on which were painted the words "Ularu Occupied Lands" in sand-blasted bare red lettering. Below in smaller words it said: "Ularup village—43 kms." An arrow pointed off to the west.

There was another sign too. Newer, more professionally hung nearby, with an eye-catching type style that proclaimed: "Killian Development" but nevertheless pointed down the same primitive road.

No sooner had we come to a stop than two men in uniform approached our vehicle from either side. Their guns weren't drawn but they had guns and they were ready to draw them at a moment's notice. One, the guy off the passenger's side of the car, held back. He played a flashlight beam through the interior of the car, blinding our night vision.

And then, through my open window I heard, "An' where do ye think ye're goin'? What's yer business 'eyer?"

Jim Jim said only, "Take that light out of my eyes!"

"We asked where ye was going!" Another policeman came out of the darkness and I heard the words:

"Git 'em outa the car, ey."

"We're going to Ularup," I announced. "He lives there; I'm just visiting."

A cop rested his elbows on my window frame.

"You a reporter?"

"Nope."

It was true enough.

"Who 're ye?"

"I'm a friend of his. He lives in Ularup."

"Let's see yer license."

I passed it across for him to study.

"It's no place for a white man," he said as he turned his torch on my Illinois buzzer, "Especially a tourist. Not now, it ayn't. He can go through but not you."

"It's my car and he doesn't know how to drive."

"He can walk, canty?"

"It's too far. I've promised to take him."

"It ayn't safe."

"I'll be all right with Jim Jim."

They muttered back and forth to each other. What they were

talking about I couldn't hear but shortly the one guy strolled over again and handed me back my license.

"You know the road beyond Ularup, to the Killian Camp—it's off limits. You can't get on. They won't let you on."

"So I've heard."

"All roight, yank, it's yer neck." The policemen stood and moved away from my window. I fed gas onto the gravelled strip. One of them shouted after us, "Stay on the road and don't get out of the car!" as though we'd just paid our way into Lion Country Safari.

The road, an easement that marked the southern boundary of the tribal lands, was hardly more than two ruts with a hump in the middle. Often the ruts were so deep and the hump was so high the undercarriage of our little rental would drag bottom and I'd quick have to run one set of tires up onto the center or risk beaching ourselves until the tide came in. Driver's side low was bad enough with the driver—me—crushed against the door but driver's side high was even worse. I'd have to grab the wheel with one hand and the door grip with the other to keep from sliding onto Jim Jim's lap.

We ran into potholes as big as craters and cracks that looked like minor crevasses. According to Jim Jim, it rarely rained up here but when it did "come a drownder," it rained so hard that the roads were routinely washed out.

After sixty minutes and thirty miles of this we came to the turnoff to Ularup.

To the second roadblock.

And trouble. . . .

12

Black Blokes

We'd seen it coming, a small bright spot on the horizon that grew larger and brighter. Still a hundred yards off, I heard Jim Jim growl as the bright spot turned into a blaze. I stood on the brakes. It was a bonfire of scrub trees piled on the road and ignired. Several dozen half-naked black men caught between the fire light and the glare of our headlamps rushed toward us. They were spoiling for trouble—shouting, scooping up stones and shaking crude weapons in the air.

"Roll up your window!" I cried. "Lock your door!"

Jim Jim was slow to act, and I had to shout to get him to move.

"This is bad," he kept saying.

I barely got the Holden stopped before they were on us. A dark mob swarmed over the front of the car as well as both sides and the back. It was too late to get away. There was nowhere to go. Before we knew it they were hammering on the hood with their fists; they pounded on the windshield. They were grunting and barking, every one of them. Maybe it was a war chant of some kind but to me it sounded more like a pack of wild animals.

"Who are they?"

"Dongos."

Their savage faces filled every window, snarling, spitting, leering. Five miles of bad road. That's how I'd once described Jim Jim's face. But there was enough savagery here and enough bad road to take me all the way back to Sydney. It suddenly seemed like a good idea.

They threw their weight against the door handles. Somehow the doors held.

"Do you know them?" I cried.

"No. They are not from my clan."

"Talk to them!"

He said he could talk but added, ". . . if they listen."

By this time the car was rocking back and forth on its suspension; when they'd found out they couldn't get in, they tried to roll us over.

"Well . . . start talking!" I insisted. "But be careful!"

He shook his head at me: "Oh, they wouldn't hurt *me*," he replied and while I digested the obvious implications of that he muscled open his door. He had to push back half a dozen of them to do it.

Then he stepped out, closing the door at his back.

Immediately a bunch of the blacks gathered around him. His size didn't seem to intimidate them, not nearly as much as their numbers intimidated me. They swallowed him up. I could hardly see him after that and I couldn't understand a word of what he said to them. When they led him away I was surrounded by the blackness.

Seconds crept by.

Minutes.

More and more blacks converged around the car. One guy wore a crotch sheath and a two hundred dollar chronograph watch. Nothing more. Another wore a pair of designer jeans with the legs cut off so high that the pockets hung out. None had firearms—spears, clubs and knives but no guns—and yet I distinctly heard recorded music and once got a glimpse of a ghetto blaster sitting on the road near the fire. They moved restlessly. They leered and gestured constantly. While I watched, one of them slashed himself with a knife, sucked the wound and then spat blood at the windshield. More blood hit the other side. When I made the mistake of switching on the wipers they grabbed them and wrenched them off. A Neanderthal—dressed like a jackeroo including a familiar *akubra* hat—pressed his

Alley Oop face against the driver's window and mouthed obscenities through the glass.

Somebody pitched a rock through the right headlamp. As it winked out, a cheer went up. I turned off the switch before they got the left one but they broke it anyway and then proceeded to rake the body paint with sharp stones. The windows would go next.

What was taking Jim Jim so long?

What was he doing?

The side door swung open. I turned in a genuine panic, realizing I'd forgotten to relock it behind him. Chocolate brown hands reached in for me. I kicked and swore but there were too many of them and they were too strong. They pulled me onto the road. Two took hold of my arms and squashed me between them. I felt like the inside of an Oreo cookie until more pressed around me and then I felt like the inside of a Ding Dong.

I screamed. A chocolate hand covered my mouth. Other hands wrapped me up and dragged me swinging and kicking into the darkness.

They carried me several yards off the road to where an ancient flatbed truck was parked behind a rise. They hefted me onto the bed, hopped up after me and held me down flat by sitting on top of me. Somebody got the motor going. Seconds later we were flying across the desert like a bunch of kids on a joyride.

Which way we went, how long or how far, I've no idea.

We started off north.

But there were so many twists and turns I couldn't keep track of them. The truck bed shook so badly I couldn't even get a look at my watch. Half the time we spent in the air. I didn't need a watch to know that much. We flew over every ravine. Every boulder was a launching ramp. Rarely did we have all four wheels on the ground at the same time.

The funny thing was I didn't want it to end.

The farther we went into Ularu territory the worse were my

chances for being rescued. Or even for being found. But I had a feeling about what would happen to me when we did stop and so I prayed we'd just keep going.

I nursed a hope Jim Jim might be the driver because he wasn't on the back and if he wasn't in the cab either I was very much on my own. Whoever the driver was, he had at least two things in common with Jim Jim: he didn't have a driver's license and he didn't know how to drive. However he had real possibilities as a pilot. If he ever got his hands on a craft capable of sustaining flight he might never come down.

When we finally touched down for the last time and they tossed me off the truck bed, I looked around to see who came out of the cab.

I'll be darned if it wasn't Alley Oop. The guy with the jackeroo hat and Neanderthal face.

He deserved a second look so I gave him one. But I saw something then I missed the first time and a shiver ran down my spine. I swallowed hard. Now I had more than a feeling. I knew . . . knew what had happened to Hawthorne and Maggie, and that the same thing would happen to me if I didn't act fast.

I was led along a path, into a deep depression, and told to sit down in what turned out to be the bed of a river that was flowing off to my right. Not the river. The riverbed. The desert wind, cooler than before, was picking up dust and carrying it downstream in clouds so thick at times I could hardly see the opposite bank.

The whole mob of them followed us down. They gathered downstream while two blacks, Alley Oop and one other, kept a close eye on me and a third, a little fellow, dashed off up river.

While I watched, the rest got a fire going. I've never seen it done slicker. They gathered up some dried twigs and grass, made a neat pile and then produced some stones from a ditty bag and whacked them together. The spark caught right off, going from flicker to flame in mere seconds. Meanwhile, others were building a stockpile of dry wood. After that, a conference ensued. There were objections, motions and demurs but no consensus. I didn't understand a word but by the way they kept leering at me and feeding the fire, I gathered the gist of the argument was whether to serve me fried or fricaseed.

The little guy came back.

Not alone.

With him was a tall gangly jet-black man wearing jeans and a leather vest. A true troglodyte. He had a flat nose, wide cheeks, no chin at all, but a massive brow and eyes that reflected the firelight the way a cat's eyes do. Marbles—black clearies—buried in a bed of ashes. I'd never seen a face like his before.

His hands were wiry and gnarled, tendons and bones overlaid with burnt leather.

I'd never seen hands like his before either.

But I knew who he was.

What cinched it was the thing hanging from his neck by a leather strap. The ditty bag Jim Jim had told me about . . . it was a human skull!

He said something to a guy at the fire before crossing over to me.

I stood up.

When he was close enough to see my face, he stopped to stare. He recognized me, too. Of course he would. I hadn't been wearing a mask and gloves the last two times we'd met. "Yes," he growled, "it is yoo."

The voice cinched it.

He was Black Tom.

"Newspaper man, he say," he said. "And I knew it would be yoo."

"It's me all right," I replied. "What've you done with Jim Jim? There's only one way his men could've known I was a newspaperman and that's if Jim Jim had told them.

"He is not here."

"Where is he?"

"Jim Jim knows not this place. Only a handful of Ularu may

come here; no other black men. And no whites. Those who violate the spirits' abode must die. The last one, the only other white man, is dead. Yoo were there—yoo saw him die."

"Yeah," I said. "But you killed him."

"I warn him."

"Like you warned Rush Killian's surveyor? And those two reporters?"

"All were warn."

I screwed up my courage enough to say: "Those reporters were friends of mine."

His shrug of indifference was quiet eloquence.

"How about that Gangra attendant on the train? Did you warn him, too . . . before you killed him?"

His blazing eyes glared from beneath that immense brow. Finally he grunted, "The black man must suffer for the white man's greed."

"Is that right?"

"It is not right. But it is true. That is the truth yoo are here to learn. Are yoo strong enough to face death, white man?"

This was it then.

"Why me?" I asked. "What did I do?"

"Yoo talk too much."

I'd heard that before. But nobody'd ever tried to kill me because of it. Before I could say so he added:

"When yoo talk, much whites hear."

"Oh, I see. Well in that case you don't have to bother with me; I haven't the slightest idea what's going on around here so I've nothing to write about. Anyway, didn't Jim Jim tell you? I don't work for the papers any more. I'm through with all that. I'm not even interested. But, hey, I can give you the names of some people at Associated Press. . . ."

Suddenly his glare held nothing but contempt. And when he spoke, I knew it was no use arguing.

"Are you not a man?"

It was almost word for word what I'd asked Jim Jim four days before.

I swallowed a lump in my throat.

"We'll see," I said.

He rattled off some senseless syllables to my watchdogs and moved off into the wind. The pair of them grabbed hold of my arms and hauled me along after him. The whole crew of blacks followed us upstream.

It was useless to resist. In fact there was nothing to do but face up to things. I've said before I'm not chicken. I'm not. I'm not scared of dying either. I just don't see any reason for me to be around when it happens, that's all.

We hadn't gone far before the river narrowed. The bed steepened and the banks rose. At the same time, I felt the wind building. It turned colder, too. I started shivering and couldn't stop. When we entered a trough at the base of a cliff, a mountain loomed over us masking half the stars in the sky.

Black Tom drew up. He turned.

The rest of us gathered around him. I was shaking good about then, but I wasn't alone. So were the others.

On the cliff over our heads the rocks opened wide like a toothless ogre-ish black maw and gave vent to the belly of the mountain. Cold desert air rushed through us, a frigid wind that stank of rot and decomposing flesh. It seemed to pour from this hole. Perhaps it was just the cooler night air settling to the low elevation, spilling down the trough and following the river-course into the desert.

But that's not how it seemed.

Most caves breathe. At least, all of the bigger ones do. It's got something to do with barometric pressure and temperature variations. Air rushes out or in seeking equilibrium with the surface. But no cave ever howled like that one did. No cave ever exhaled such a putrid volume of air. By the time we reached it, the stench threw my head around.

I winced and covered my nose with a hand.

Was this the sacred cave where Black Tom had brought Arthur Copley? I looked away because I wanted them to know I respected their taboos. That they had no need to kill me because I hadn't seen anything and I didn't want to. Still, I couldn't help wondering what Copley had seen that meant he had to be killed and what was the chance I could get a peek at it, too . . . before they did it to me.

Black Tom stood there, his longish hair blowing wildly. I raised my voice above the wail:

"Is this where the others died? Did you bring them here too? Where are they? You can tell me that much, can't you? If I'm not going to live long enough to write the story, why not toss me a bone. . . ?"

His eyes were transfixed on mine. They protruded more and more from his skull until they were ready to pop.

". . . figuratively speaking," I added.

He stretched out a long narrow arm.

"There," he said.

I looked where he was pointing. Not up at the cavern but in the shadows behind a rocky outcrop. One of his men stepped nearer with a torch he'd brought from the campfire. He tossed it into the brush. The dry grass caught at once and in the sudden blaze of light whipped up by the wind I saw them.

Both of them.

I didn't take time to try to see who they were because they were in the same condition as those I'd seen before at the morgue. Scraps of flesh. Shattered bones. Torn cloth. Not enough to identify man from woman, black from white, or even Inspector Hawthorne from Maggie McDowel.

My brain was whirling.

Black Tom's cannibals closed in around me.

About that time my eyes turned up in my head, my knees buckled, and I crumpled to the ground in a small, windswept explosion of dust.

*   *   *

They wasted no time picking me up and carrying me back to the
campfire.

They dropped me onto the riverbed again.

Not gently.

Every once in a while one of them would prod me with a foot
or a spearpoint or raise one of my eyelids or pinch my nose for
a few seconds.

I didn't flinch.

I just lay there in the dirt. Not moving. Not daring to. Occasionally I'd crack an eyelid to see what was going on but I was
careful to make sure no one saw me.

The rest of them gathered around the fire and proceeded to
discuss the menu and placecard settings. It got so heated at one
point everyone was shouting and when I sneaked a peek around
I noticed no one seemed to be concerned about me.

Alley Oop and friend were looking away.

I couldn't go upstream because some of them might still be
back there. Anyway, that's where Hawthorne and Maggie had
gotten it. If I left the riverbed they would spot me for sure.
Downstream. No other choice.

I crept away.

I crawled on hands and knees to the far bank, into the thickest
part of the dust. The river wound to my left. By hugging the left
bank and running in a crouch, I soon moved out of their line of
sight. After a few seconds I stood up. I could see the light from
their bonfire but I couldn't see them and they couldn't see me;
they wouldn't know which way I went and they shouldn't be able
to follow me in the dark.

I took off.

Almost at once an alarm went up. A shout. And then a chorus
of excited voices.

That's when I really poured on the speed.

One time I crashed over a fallen tree and a dozen times I
tripped on stones. I couldn't see where I was going. All I could
do was put the wind at my back and run and pray that in the dark

they couldn't know where they were any more than I could or run any faster than I was. But that was wrong; I knew it was wrong. This was their park; they knew it better than I knew the city. And as for running, I jogged a couple times a week. They ran to survive. I'd heard stories of aborigines running for days across the desert . . . of them running down kangaroos. The fact is they probably ran ten miles just to jog their memories, while I've got total recall and after five minutes of my best speed I couldn't even remember what the hell I was doing out here.

The wind had turned hot again. I was sweating freely. I was also inhaling dust in huge gulps. About that time, I decided sticking to the riverbed hadn't been so smart after all, but now I didn't have any choice. I wasn't able to see over the banks any more and I doubt I could've climbed over them either. I ran on.

For the thirteenth time I stumbled. I pitched into the ground, scraped both elbows, but saved my skull from cracking against a boulder by half an inch.

For a hundred seconds . . . a thousand heartbeats . . . I lay there. Panting. Listening.

I could hear them behind me. Close. Coming closer all the time. They *were* tracking me in the dark. Other sounds reached me too. A low rumbling drone of many men singing a verse without words. The boombox? No. These sounds came from downwind. Some of them must have circled around me and were now lying in wait. I was trapped.

I crawled forward on my stomach.

When I saw the first of many black bodies blocking the riverbed I threw myself into a notch in the bank.

Wild cries broke the stillness of the night.

I heard the stomping of many bare feet and the clapping of many hands.

Carefully, I peered out from my hole.

The place was lit up like a Fourth of July celebration, not much illumination but plenty of dazzle. I saw two large fires inside a wide circle of smaller ones that were turning out more smoke than light and making three, four, as many as a half a dozen black shadows of each black. A hundred . . . no, two or three hundred aborigines were raising a ruckus of the most primitive sort.

I'd stumbled upon an aboriginal ceremony in full swing.

Whatever this was, it was serious business.

The banks here were high and wide. In wet weather it would be no place to linger because desert runoff would come rushing down these river beds in a solid wall of water. Deep scars gouged into the sides by current-driven desert debris gave evidence that it had happened here many times. For the rest of the year, the other three hundred and sixty days, it made an acceptable outdoor amphitheater and that's what these blacks were using it for. Along both banks sat an aboriginal audience of men, not lounging but squatting with their legs cocked under their bodies like coiled springs and their arms dangling between their knees.

But the real show was down below. Inside the circle of bonfires.

There were a couple of men crab-walking on their hands and feet with their seats just barely above the ground. It was incredible how nimble they were and how fast they could scurry about.

One guy wearing a wooden beak strapped to his nose and feathers on his arms and legs was strutting back and forth on stilts three feet off the ground.

Another man covered by ceremonial paint and leaves and a long leathery tail was crawling around on all fours. His ability to mimic a four-legged creature amazed me. Either his legs were too short or his arms were too long or he had been born with a knack for four-footing. It was absolutely uncanny. He could scramble over the riverbed faster than a dingo and even leap high into the air.

He was wearing a mask, a hideous thing with a longish snout and snake-like eyes.

I ignored him as soon as I'd spotted the two other men. They were lashed together at the waist, both facing the same direction. The smaller of the two was in front. His legs were bound to the taller man's so that his feet were easily a foot off the ground. His head was below the bigger man's chin. They were wrapped by hides and cloth so cleverly that only with an effort could I see the form of the small man beneath this covering. All that protruded were his arms held outward and cloaked by paint and fur so that the two of them looked exactly like a single tail-less animal with two legs and four arms. The bigger fellow's mask was different, and so were the clawed mittens on all four hands, but it was undoubtedly the monster I'd seen on the train. I hadn't any doubt of it now.

As I watched, the battle went on and on. It looked to me as though the six-limbed beast usually got the better of the four-limbed one. The crowd was definitely against him. From the sidelines tribal members joined in. They hollered. They hooted. They howled like dogs in the night. Every once in a while and for no apparent reason one would stand up and run into the circle of fires, scoop up a fistful of riverbed and hurl it at a performer—more often the four-armed fellow than the four-footed one—before dashing back to the safety of the high ground.

Across the amphitheater were the musicians. Drummers seated themselves before hollowed-out logs while the string section stood, plucking at tall lute-like instruments. The cadent beat was as intoxicating as it was frightening.

Three older men sat to one side, legs folded, watching the performance with expressionless faces.

And kneeling behind them, his face equally impassive . . . none other than Jim Jim!

I had to look again to be sure. He didn't look much like Sidney Poitier now. He'd taken off his shirt and put some white paint on his face, but, by God, it was him! He was trying to talk to one of the old men in the front row.

"*Nogota kai!*"

I whirled.

Alley Oop stood over me. His spear was raised over his head.

More of Black Tom's men were racing up behind him.

There was no time to think about it. I rolled to the side, got my tennis shoes under me and dashed toward the ceremony. I vaulted a perimeter fire and bounded into the circle.

The effect was immediate.

And profound.

Almost as one, the aboriginal audience sprang to their feet. Fists shook in fury and screams of outrage echoed up and down the riverbed. The ceremony came to an abrupt end. But I didn't slow down. I ran between the two pyres, dodged three of the performers trying to block my path and reached the other side before anyone laid a hand on me.

The elders had risen.

Impassivity fled from their faces—replaced by shock.

Jim Jim, too. He breached etiquette by pushing through them and coming forward to meet me but before he could utter a sound I let him have it.

"Where the hell have you been? These guys're trying to kill me!" I cried. "You've got to stop them!"

He didn't hear me. "You must not be here!" he said. "It is not good; it is forbid."

An angry mob surrounded us. When I looked behind me I saw Alley Oop and the others coming in for their share.

"That man!" I pointed him out. "He killed the policeman and Maggie. Look at him! He's still wearing Inspector Hawthorne's hat!"

But no one was listening.

Rage, indignation and fury closed in around me. A guy on my left got pushed into me. I fell against a man on the right and he shoved me back. The next thing I knew a flood of anger was pounding my head and shoulders; the last thing I knew Jim Jim's huge arms were wrapping me up and carrying me through the

crowd with no thoughts of playing possum—in fact, no conscious thoughts whatsoever—in my mind.

"Black Tom is wrong," said Jim Jim. "I know about the sacred
cave. Where it is. I have been there."

"You have?"

"Yes. The day my father and Black Tom left to settle their
differences among the spirits. I watched them go. . . ."

"Just watched. . . ?"

"Then . . . I followed them."

We were sitting on the dirt floor of his humpy. There was only
one chair in the whole house—a garish monster upholstered in
purple and green—because aborigines prefer to sit on the floor,
and Jim Jim had offered it to me but I had declined since he'd
taken the floor at my place and I could do the same now at his.

He had two younger brothers and three younger sisters asleep
in the next room. Once a little black face with big eyes and
pigtails had poked through the curtain but Jim Jim had ordered
her back to bed in a firm tone and she had gone and Jim Jim had
lowered his voice. I'd wondered if this was that one night of the
week his family wasn't bedded down in the yard; he said no, after
what had happened to his father and the others, everyone in the
village was sleeping indoors at night.

"What did happen, Jim Jim?"

"They went to the mountains. To the cave. I followed them
down the river and then watched from a big rock across the
riverbed when they went inside."

"I know the rock you mean. Those two bodies Black Tom
showed me. They were beneath it. Did you go in the cave?"

"Oh no! It is forbid."

"What happened?"

"I waited for a long time. Hours. Darkness came and I could
not even see the cave. I was frightened."

"Who wouldn't be?"

"Then I heard a cry."

"A man?"

"Yes. I think."

"Your father?"

"Maybe. I never heard him scream before that day. Not like that I never did. Now I hear him. Every night. Every night he screams."

"What'd you do?"

"I . . . I was very scared, Doyle."

"Anybody would have been scared, Jim Jim."

"Not like me. I was too scared."

"What did you do?"

"I ran."

He lowered his head, waiting for me to say something. But I couldn't think of anything to say.

"I ran back to the village," he said. "Later, some men found his . . . my father's body in the riverbed at the base of the rock. Had I only stayed—"

"There's no point in torturing yourself. It's over now. Who knows what would have happened if you'd stayed. Didn't you make up for it by going to Sydney?"

Jim Jim shook his head.

"At that council meeting. The elders said the gate to Gol's abode had opened. They asked me to go into the cave. To close the gate. Two other men would go to Sydney to try to stop that man from showing the pictures."

"Two others?"

"Yes. But I would not go into the cave. I told them I would not go."

"So they sent you to Sydney instead."

"Yes."

"Only Black Tom can enter the cave!" he said suddenly. "No one else may enter. The spirits are angry because the white men have desecrated the forbid land. Black Tom and the others . . . they are angry too."

"How about that guy? The one wearing Hawthorne's hat?"

"His name is Russell. He's one of Black Tom's Dongos. He was there on the road. I told him that you were not one of Killian's men. That you are a fair man. A newspaperman who comes to see for himself what goes on, and would report the truth to the whites. Russell wanted to take you to see Black Tom. They want you to understand that blacks are not killing; we are being killed."

"Then those bodies. . . ."

Jim Jim lowered his head.

"Ularus."

"Not Hawthorne and Maggie?"

"No. I would not go into the cave to close Gol's gate. Two other men were sended. Those were the two men you saw."

"Oh."

"Now I must hear their screams too."

"But the hat. I'm telling you that guy . . . Russell, he's wearing Inspector Hawthorne's hat."

"You can ask him about it," he said. "He will meet us near the waters."

The little settlement was not a town as such. It had a central tin structure with at least four doors that appeared to be a kind of community building. Small single-family tin shacks flanked this—a dozen or so on each side; all of them surrounded the spring. It looked like a crater. One left by an explosion. We couldn't see the water until we stood right on the edge and looked straight down, because the surface was more than twenty feet below, twice as deep as the crater was wide, and as black as a pool of crude oil. A frame of poles had been constructed on one side with a lever for lowering a bucket. Even in the hours before dawn aborigine women had queued up to fill plastic jugs and metal cans with fresh water. It looked like a daily routine but today it was no occasion for gossip. As fast as the containers were topped off, the women lugged them back to their homes under the watchful eyes of several warriors carrying knives and clubs and looking eager to use them. With so many angry faces in the area, I had to look twice to spot Russell. Only Hawthorne's hat gave him away.

When Jim Jim called out, he came over to us, leered at me but didn't say anything. As it turned out I didn't have to say anything to him either because Jim Jim did all the talking.

Then he translated.

"Russell says the hat is a gift of Tobraka. Two days ago when he was getting water, he found it in the bucket."

"He's lying. You don't believe him, do you?"

"Maybe."

"He could've killed them himself and thrown them down. How deep in the bottom, anyway? Do you know someone who'd be willing to go down there? To look around?"

"There is not one."

"Nobody?"

"No bottom. The water comes underground from the mountains. It moves too fast. Whoever goes in will be sweeped away."

"I see. No bodies, huh?"

"No. Gol drags them back to his abode."

"The problem, Jim Jim, is that there are too many guys around here, black and white, who know how to dress up like monsters and kill people or scare them to death. I'll even bet you've worn the Godzilla get-up a time or two, huh?"

"Yes. But we do not kill."

"Maybe you don't. I'm not so sure about Black Tom and Russell. I don't suppose he's seen anything of Hawthorne or Maggie around here."

Jim Jim posed the question.

Their conversation lasted quite a few minutes.

Then: "He says, no. He sees nothing of the whites."

"All that for a no? Does he know anybody who has seen them."

"No."

"Any of their clothes, besides the hat? Their gear?"

"No."

"What about their vehicle? They must've come here in something. A truck, a four-wheel drive. They couldn't've gotten a car down that hole without somebody hearing."

Jim Jim pursed his lips. And scowled.

"What is it Jim Jim?"

"Well. . . ."

"Well? That's just a hole too. What's at the bottom of this one?"

He jerked his head at Russell. "He says he has seen a car. In a ravine near the forbid land. I know this place. We can go there as soon as it's light."

13

White Blokes

I got my first look at the sacred valley shortly after sun-up. It wasn't exactly inviting. The road was the same pair of ruts with a hump in the middle. The desert was the same endless sweep of red dust and random grass clumps, and the mountain range that divided the valley from Ularu lands was the same impassable escarpment. But I didn't see these until later. The first thing I saw was a barrier across the road, a framework of oil drums and four by fours holding up a sign as big as a billboard.

ROAD CLOSED
The Killian Development Lands
are temporarily OFF LIMITS to
all unauthorized personnel.
By order of the N.T. police
No visitors
No press
No exceptions!!

Not what I'd call inviting.

I said as much to Jim Jim but he wasn't paying any attention to me or the sign. He was too busy looking away to the north. "There!" he exclaimed.

Sure enough a faint set of tire tracks left the deeper trenches of the road and weaved wildly off into the desert. I parked the Holden and we followed the trail on foot until we came to a ravine, more like a small canyon, where the ground had split open. We couldn't see the ends of the thing to the east or west but it was barely two car lengths wide and a car length deep. The car was still down there in case we chose to verify those dimensions. A yellow compact. We spotted its rear bumper just sticking over the edge, and when we got closer we could see its front bumper—more compact now than before—halfway across the bottom.

We climbed down together.

A layer of dust several days thick had settled over the car. It wasn't buried, not yet, but it was well camouflaged from either the ground or the air.

There wasn't much to see through the windows. Three of them were starred and the windshield had shattered. Even so, we could see there was no one inside. The driver's side door was hanging open.

The front end had taken the worst of it. However, when I brushed dust from the right side panel I found a number of uniform scratches gouged into the body paint as well as some suspicious dents and I knew that these hadn't come from the crash.

"You can see what must have happened," I said: "A bunch of Black Tom's Dongos ambushed Hawthorne and Maggie the same way they did us. Except whoever was doing the driving tried to get away and didn't make it."

"No Ularu did this," he declared.

"That's what you think. Take another look. Then go up and get a load of our car. You may recognize the body work. Top quality panel beating."

I pointed out several parallel marks below the driver's window. More on the roof and hood. It looked like somebody had worked the car over with a garden rake. Gently, Jim Jim placed his outspread hand across four such lines on the side fender. Each of his fingers touched a different line. Then he drew his hand along the fender so that the marks appeared to run out from beneath his fingertips.

At the end he straightened up.

Without a word he bent his head to the ground. He made circles. He picked up a rock and sniffed it. After a while he meandered westward along the canyon with his eyes to the canyon floor.

There wasn't much for me to do but inspect the wreck. I clambered inside.

On the seat I found a small puddle of dried blood. More on the steering wheel; more yet on the dashboard.

In the glove box I found a car rental agreement between one of the agencies at the Alice Springs airport and someone whose signature I'd seen before. It matched the one on that letter in Hector Boyle's desk drawer. There was a map of the Northern Territory too with the route—the only road, by the way—highlighted from Alice Springs all the way to Killian's property. And a wallet. It contained enough identification to satisfy anyone who didn't recognize Brock Allitt's signature on sight. The thumbnail picture on his New South Wales driver's license confirmed it. I had to admit the guy really did bear a passing resemblance to mother Mulligan's beloved. Our physical descriptions and build were remarkably similar: height, weight, hair, eyes, and so on. Even his face looked a little like mine. More forehead; eyes a bit higher maybe. Nose not so straight. But aside from that, amazingly similar.

I pocketed these and crawled out to wait for Jim Jim.

Pretty soon he rejoined me. He was moving faster now, ignoring the ground.

I asked him if he'd seen enough.

He had.

"We must go, Doyle." He spoke hurriedly too, running his words together. "Come on."

"This isn't Hawthorne's car," I explained. "An estate agent named Brock Allitt rented it Sunday morning. That's the character I was supposed to meet that night I ran into you at the Morisset Building. He told me he had somewhere to go. Apparently he was coming up here. To see Killian."

Without a word, Jim Jim went to the incline where we'd slid down and started climbing.

"What's your hurry?"

"We must go," he shouted over his shoulder.

"What'd you find?" I shouted back.

He didn't answer. I climbed up after him, followed him back to the road, finally catching up to him at the Holden. I grabbed his arm and spun him around.

"Let's have it, Jim Jim, what did you see out there?"

"We must go away from here now."

"Tell me what you found. Was it Allitt?"

"Only sign."

"You mean tracks?"

"Yes."

"Which way did they go?"

He gazed wordlessly off to the west.

"How far did you follow the trail?"

"Not far. There is a tree. Everything beyond the tree is forbidland."

"But he may be hurt. Or dying. In fact he must be; this happened four days ago."

"Not dying. Dead. Four days ago."

"How do you know that?"

"I know."

"How?!"

"The signs say."

"But his footprints—?"

"Not man prints. Only spirit sign. Gol taked him back to his abode. We must go, Doyle. We must go now."

There was no point in arguing with him. I said:

"Well, we'll have to notify somebody. Killian's people are the closest and that's where we're going."

"Oh no!"

"Huh?"

"I cannot go there."

"But you told Cockie you'd stay with me!"

"You cannot go, too. It is forbid."

"Well I am going. I've got to. Jim Jim, please, the people who are looking for Hawthorne and Maggie are there. Allitt too, if he is still alive. He knows what's going on. We've got to find him. Before it's too late."

"It is too late."

"Please, Jim Jim. As a favor to me, huh?"

"They will not let you enter. The policemen said so. The sign says so."

I flashed the wallet.

"Maybe they won't let Doyle Mulligan in," I said with a grin, "but I bet they'll welcome Brock Allitt with open arms."

"If you go . . . you will not come back."

"I will if you come with me."

But it was no use. He was every bit as stubborn as I am steadfast. His head swung from side to side and at the same time he backed away saying:

"It is death."

He couldn't even stand still. Before I could think of anything else to say, he turned and ran.

I watched his backside grow smaller and smaller as he loped off in the direction of Ularup until finally he became just a black spot on the horizon. Resignedly I climbed into the car and started it up. I felt a bit queasy going around the barricade but once the wheels settled back into the ruts the road and the car took control and I was all right again.

When I'd passed south of the mountain range, the desert was the same as before. The same broad expanse of red dust. The same stunted vegetation. The same rambling dune-looking hills. The same sun.

It was like that for mile after mile for more than an hour. I felt really alone then. I had only the Holden for companionship, and cars and I don't speak the same language. I can change a tire all right. But that wouldn't do me much good if the carburetor seized or the oil pan boiled over and I was wandering around with a jack and a tire tool trying to figure out which corner of the damned thing to elevate. Fortunately, that didn't happen. It let off steam now and then when midmorning sent the temperatures soaring and it rattled like it was coming apart whenever the going got rough.

By eleven o'clock I'd reached the site.

There was no activity anywhere in sight. No excavating or drilling. No building or plowing.

Nothing.

The first thing I saw of the worksite as I pulled up to the front gate was the gate itself, and the fence, a twelve-foot-high barbed-wire monstrosity topped with a twisted roll of concertina; it completely encircled the property. Distant buildings were visible but other things caught the eye, such as the board with bold script which indicated that the fence as well as the gate was charged with "High Voltage—Danger!"

A bigger sign announced:

Killian Development Field Headquarters
No Admittance Without Authorization

The Holden scrunched to a stop. I got out to look the place over and as I did so, a dust cloud thirty miles long, my backtrail, drifted back down the road toward the border as though it were running for safety.

I still felt alone and I still didn't feel welcome.

In addition to being charged, the gate was chained and locked with a padlock. We're talking heavy duty. Killian might not have bought his first cow yet but he'd certainly beefed up his security.

The electrified fence was strung about six inches apart near the ground, closer to a foot at eye level and eighteen inches or so on the top. It looked as tight as piano wire, but I didn't strum it to find out because I don't play the piano and, quite frankly, I've no interest in taking up the harp.

There were upright poles every twenty feet and on each one was a sign that warned: PRIVATE PROPERTY—KEEP OUT! and below that, TRESPASSERS WILL BE SHOT.

Between the barbed wire and the first of the buildings was a strip of bare ground two or three hundred yards wide. It was like that all the way around the site. I didn't see any guard towers but that was the tone. Two guys with guns and guard dogs were walking the inside perimeter about half a mile off to the north. I didn't waste my breath shouting since they were already heading my way. Instead I went back to the car and hit the horn a couple times to let them know I wasn't a man to be trifled with. Ten minutes later I got out to join them at the gate. The dogs were big Dobermans, not barking but straining at their leashes. The guards were big too and the guns were semi-automatic rifles, not aimed at me but slung over their shoulders where they'd be handy in case the wire and the wattage and the watchdogs failed to impress me.

Neither man showed any inclination to friendliness.

"No 'un's allowed!" snarled one between strands of wire. "Cayn't ye read? The 'ole plyce is awf limits."

"Ye'll 'ave to turn round an' go back," said the other.

I stood my ground.

"I'm here to see Rush Killian."

"Nothin' doin'. 'Ur orders are to let no 'un in."

"Tell him Brock Allitt's come all the way up here from Sydney. He'll want to know that. You'd better tell him."

They exchanged words with one another and then one of them went to a telephone box on the inside gatepost while the other eyed me suspiciously. I watched the first speak into the receiver but I couldn't hear what he said.

Presently he called out:

"The captain says ye're four days lite."

I remembered Allitt's reaction to that and decided to jump

into character. So I shouted back, "Tell him I'm not late. Brock Allitt is never late. He can ask anybody."

In another moment:

"Ye gawt 'ny oi-dee?"

I fished Allitt's wallet out and flashed his driver's license at the other guard. "No, hand it through," he said, adding the warning: "watch out fer the metal . . . she's 'ot!" While he studied the specs and the pix I turned my back on him. I held my breath. Shortly the guy shouted okay to the bozo holding the phone to his ear, who relayed the message and then hung up.

A Captain Digs, they informed me, was on his way out.

I went back to the car again to wait.

The two ruts of the road extended beyond the gate and across the clear strip of desert into the site. I watched until a plume of dust rose off the ground. It grew bigger and bigger and blew nearer and nearer.

When a Toyota utility truck braked on the other side, a cloud of desert swallowed it up. The cloud wafted right through the gate. It engulfed me and my car and then moved on down the road, replacing the dust that my car had sent farther downwind.

In the meantime a tall rangy specimen in outback shirt and desert tans had climbed out of the vehicle. He stood like a drill sergeant. He used his bushy hat to slap dust from his clothes and put it back on his head before walking to the gate. He walked like a drill sergeant too.

He watched me all the time he was talking in low tones with the guards. Eventually he sent them on their way down the inside perimeter of the fence but not before taking possession of Allitt's license.

I went over to meet him.

Having produced a key, the guy went to work on the padlock. Once he got it unlocked, he pulled the chain through. Apparently he'd shut off the electricity. As he pushed open the gate he barked, "Brock Allitt?" exactly the way my drill sergeant used to say "Mulligan?" back in boot camp—or would have if I had gone to boot camp, that is, which I hadn't, of course, for the same reason I hadn't played football.

I offered a hand. "Captain Digs?"

He ignored it.

"Forget the captain," he said handing over the license. "Some of the men served under me. You can call me Digs. What happened? We expected you Sunday."

"Something's happened all right," I said, "but not to me. There's been an accident. A man's wandering around out in the desert. He might be hurt. He might even be dead."

"Man? What man? Who is he?"

"Just a guy. Does it matter?"

"We heard a reporter was coming up. Name of Mulligan."

I tried not to react.

"Where'd you hear that?"

"Never mind. We have our sources. Was that the man?"

"Oh, he's up here somewhere, all right," I admitted.

"Mr. Killian will have to be told." He pointed a blunt finger at my face. "You had a deal with him. No reporters. Not until after the two of you'd come to an understandin'."

I grinned.

"Don't worry, Mr. Digs. I haven't said a word to Doyle Mulligan. I wouldn't. In fact I'll lay you odds that Killian talks to him before I do."

He grunted.

"Let's get something straight, Allitt. As far as I'm concerned you represent nothing but trouble. Like the heat. Or them heathens over there. Trouble that could slow down our assignment. It's my job to overcome problems like you."

I tried to look overcome.

"Follow me to the visitors' quarters," he said. "Don't leave the road. Don't slow down or stop. Stay right behind me, is that clear?"

"It sure is. You think I already know too much, huh?"

"Just stay behind me."

Under his watchful eye I went back to the Holden, drove inside while he held the gate open and, once he'd locked it behind me, followed his vehicle's dust trail.

The place looked more like a military installation than a construction site. Quonset huts with big hangar doors sat side by side along the whole southern boundary. There was a motor pool that had as many jeeps and personnel trucks as it did earth-moving equipment. To the north, staked out over a flat stretch of desert, were several rows of canvas tents. As many as two dozen of them.

Speaking of military, I saw a lot of drilling going on but none of it for water. Work crews double-timed down the roadside in rough formations. They lacked only helmets and fatigue uniforms to complete the picture of army inductees. I heard explosions too. Not, as I thought, excavating, but demolition practice. We drove right by a rifle range. The crack of target fire echoed all over the site; it never let up.

Dozens of earth movers, graders, and dozers stood idle. I saw drilling trucks too, rotary rigs mostly, as well as two or three cable tool outfits but their derricks were down and apparently they hadn't been used in some time.

Off in the distance was a supply yard; acres and acres of construction material stacked on pallets and ready to be moved to a building location stood waiting.

Next we came to the downtown of sorts.

A quonset hut with a big wooden front that made it look more like an old Western saloon than anything else obviously served as a recreational center or mercantile store, or maybe both, like a PX.

A double-wide wood-sided structure on wheels served as an administration building. We passed that too. Unskirted mobile homes like that one but shorter and just single-wide turned out to be the visitors' quarters.

We parked the cars in front of one.

While Digs marched up to the door, I planted Allitt's rental form in the glove box. I folded mine up and stuffed it under the seat. Then I locked the car and joined him on the little wooden stoop.

"You'll have to share it with a couple other blokes," he told me. "Journos, like your friend Mulligan. It won't be long. Mr. Killian'll want to see you as soon as he gets time. He's in a meeting right now."

"I thought you didn't want me near any reporters?"

"These two work for us. They write what we tell 'em to write."

I could hear voices inside. A deep one. And another, four octaves higher and four times as obnoxious. I couldn't hear what they were saying, but I didn't need to hear words to know who they were.

"MacMutton and Geoffers?" I asked. "From the Picky?"

He nodded curtly: "Ey. You know 'em?"

"We've met. They did a story on me."

He raised his fist to knock.

"Wait a minute. How long until Mr. Killian gets out of that meeting?"

"Two hours. Three. What's it matter?"

"Well . . . what about that guy out in the desert?"

"I'll notify the law. They're out there now searching for a couple of their own who got themselves lost."

"The policeman? And the woman?"

"I s'pose."

"Have they found anything?"

"They've found something," he said.

I felt a flush of relief. Had I made the whole trip for nothing? Was I finished before I'd gotten started? I hoped it was true. Maybe I should run for the car. Try to make a break for it before Mutt and Jeff gave the whole thing away.

"Who? What did they find?"

"Dunno. They spotted it from the air. We're going out in a ute to bring in the body."

"Body?" My hopes sank.

"Yeh. And not much of that after them bloody cannibals get done with 'em. It isn't the first . . . and it won't be the last."

I asked him if I could go with him. Clearly, he didn't like the idea too much. He wanted to know why and the best I could do was say it had to beat sitting around here twiddling my thunbs.

"Besides," I added, "suppose I get into trouble? If I go with you, you'll know where I am and what I'm doing, and you won't have to worry about me finding out even more than I already know."

He had to admit that was true.

After giving me a glare I didn't deserve he nodded his head and told me to follow him.

We turned and left.

I gave myself a pat on the back for the way that went. As it turned out, the pat was premature. We hut-two-three-four'd down the road a ways to a motor pool where they were getting a couple of jeeps ready for the journey. Before we reached the entrance, the door swung wide and a troglodyte abruptly stepped through the opening—a skinny, gangly jet-black man wearing the same jeans and leather vest he'd had on before.

Everything was the same.

The flat nose, the wide cheeks and the massive brow.

Even the red marble eyes—although they didn't reflect sunlight the way they'd reflected the firelight last night—still looked like cats' eyes to me.

The skull still dangled from around his neck.

I froze.

Black Tom fastened those eyes on mine. He recognized me the same instant I recognized him, which was instantly.

I looked quickly away.

Not a word passed between any of the three of us. Tom stood aside and together Digs and I went in without a backward glance. The door swung shut.

It took another fifteen minutes to outfit the two utes. It dragged like fifteen hours. I spent the whole time on a hook.

Someone would come for me at any moment. I just knew it. The jig was up. What was the worst they could do to me I kept asking myself. Of course the answer was simple: They could kill me. Just like they killed Arthur Copley and maybe Hector Boyle, Mickey Fine and Nevil Cross too. Inspector Hawthorne and Maggie McDowel? I didn't even want to think about that. If one of them was dead . . . maybe the other was still alive.

Anyway, no one came.

Fifteen minutes later Digs and I in one dune-buggy-like vehicle and two other military types in another were heading east toward the mountains. We stuck with the road until we came within several miles of the border but there we left it and turned north across open desert.

It was already boiling out there. The utes had canvas tops but no windows and the breeze blasting us in the faces felt like a hundred hot air blow dryers.

Our ute took the lead.

Digs was a good enough driver, I guess. Anyway better than Russell. We didn't trade more than ten words in the hour it took us to get where we were going. That's five words for him and another five for me.

At one point I said:

"Watch out for that gully!"

He replied:

"I know what I'm doing."

That's the lot.

There was plenty I wanted to ask him about but I didn't know how much Brock Allitt already knew. So I didn't dare to ask. Digs didn't know how much I knew either, but he wasn't about to fill in any gaps.

A bleached slab of sheer rock three or four stories tall turned out to be our destination.

When we were virtually in its shadow—the sun was now almost directly overhead—we came upon a small single-engine

airplane with police markings, parked on a small rise. Where the
pilot had set down or how, I never found out.

A bushy policeman flagged us down.

The four of us dismounted. Digs spoke to the cop while his
two men shared a drink from a canteen and I headed for a slope
of loose rock at the base of this cliff. That's where all the activity
was, about halfway up. Two other cops were milling around
some object on the ground.

I scrambled up, but with Digs's long legs he was right behind
me when I got there.

I had my eyes on the object.

I heard Digs saying: "We got here as fast as we could—is
it. . . ?"

"It's not the Scotland Yard man," one of them answered. "Or
the woman. Who it is, we've no idea."

I took a deep breath.

I looked up.

And I'll be darned if I wasn't standing toe to toe with Vic
Tanny. The bad cop with the narrow skull and his brains in his
fists. Unlike his ears—which were too big—his eyes were too
small and—like his ears—too close together. They were burning
two holes in my face.

"I brought someone along . . ." Digs said casually, "he'd rather
look at corpses than sit about twiddlin' his thumbs."

Ek harumphed loudly.

"Ey, he's not one for twiddling his thumbs. Ears maybe, but
not thumbs."

This caught Digs off guard. "You know Allitt?"

At that point Ek's brows went up.

"I know him, all right!"

What choice did I have but to open the bag and dump the
whole thing in Ek's lap? The charade couldn't have gone on
much longer anyway. Since Black Tom had seen me and Mutt
and Jeff were prowling around the camp, I couldn't go back.

But before I could confess, I heard Digs suggest I give the corpse a closer look.

So I did.

As the man said, there wasn't much left. Every stitch of clothes had been ripped from the body. The chest cavity had been opened up. The skin had been ripped from the trunk and arms and huge hunks of muscle had been removed from the thighs with sharp-edged weapons.

It had been a man, that much was obvious. A white man. But shorter than Hawthorne. Thinner too. Around a hundred fifty pounds. Five ten. Red hair. Blue eyes. They'd been a bit higher than mine, I knew, even though only one of them was still in its socket. The high forehead had been crushed and the curved nose was gone completely. Even so, I hadn't any doubts about his identity.

"How about it?" said Ek. "D'you know him?"

I found myself nodding.

"Well?"

"It's that nosy journo. Ain't it?" asked Digs.

I let my head rise and fall again.

"Yeah," I said. "It's him all right. It's that nosy journo Doyle Mulligan."

Ek waited until everyone else was away and then motioned me over.

"Let's hear it, yank," he murmured.

"Now?"

"I'm all ears."

"Maybe," I said, "but you don't look so bad in profile."

"Enough of that. Who was this guy, and what's all this about you being Brock Allitt? Who's he?"

I lowered my voice.

"A real estate agent. He got the commission when Rush Killian bought this land from the federal government. Also he knew Hector Boyle and Arthur Copley and he was there at the opera house the day of the fire. He tried to get in to warn Copley. You remember. He was the guy who looked like me. He came up here to talk to Rush Killian."

"I see. And you've taken his place?"

"It just worked out that way." I told Ek about finding the rental car in the ravine with Brock Allitt's license and lease papers. "He didn't make it to the construction camp," I said. "Allitt bragged to me he'd never been late a day in his life. And he wasn't, even though Killian's men expected him four days ago. Not late a day in his life . . . get it?"

Ek indicated with a little nod the body being conveyed scrap by scrap into the bag.

"So that's him?"

"That's Brock Allitt," I replied. "Of course, now he's the late Brock Allitt."

Ek glared.

"You think it's funny?"

"No, I think it's scary. Don't you know a frightened man when you see him?"

"Then what are you up to?"

"I'm looking for Superintendent Hawthorne. And Maggie McDowel. I'm going to help them if I can—if they're still alive. Have you found them? Do you know anything?"

"Haven't turned up a trace of 'em yet."

"I'll help you. I'll do anything you tell me to."

"Anything?"

"Try me."

"All right. Tell me everything you know. Forget the wise-cracks, keep your voice down and make it fast."

I didn't have any choice but to tell him. I opened up and dumped the whole thing in his lap. Everything I'd seen and done since the cops had turned me loose. In the end he stood there silently, giving me his narrow gaze and pushing his hands deeper and deeper into his pockets.

"None of it makes any sense," he snarled.

"Some of it does."

"Like what?"

"The way I've got it figured, Arthur Copley started it all by talking Black Tom, or paying him, into revealing the location of the sacred cave of the Ularus. That's when this whole mess started. I think Copley saw something he wasn't supposed to see. Or he photographed it. I think Copley told Hector Boyle about it. The geologist and surveyor. The two men apparently knew each other; they had offices in the same building.

"What was it Copley wasn't supposed to see?"

"I don't know. But Hector Boyle knew or he wouldn't t've been given the surveying job up here over Killian's regular surveying crew. Boyle got bought off with a contract."

"Boyle got killed."

"Right. But so did Copley. Brock Allitt was in on it too because he got the commission from the sale of the land over a bunch of bigger, better land agents. It's my theory the three of them set out to cash in on the deal themselves but when they saw it'd take a lot more cash than they could scrape together they went to Killian and offered to cut him in."

"And now Killian's cut them out?"

"That's my theory."

"What about them aborigines? Them Ularu. They're the ones so good at dressing up like beasties. And they're the ones with the stomach for this kind of thing."

"Black Tom, yes. Their mulla-mullung. He's the guy I chased from the opera house that day it burned down, remember? Well, get this, I just ran into him at Killian's camp. He's working with Killian."

"Then you think he's doin' the butcherin'?"

"With Killian's help."

"You're sure?"

"MacMutton and Geoffers killed Arthur Copley, I'm sure of that, and they did a good enough beastie on that train to scare the hell out of me. They're working for Killian, too. Digs told me

so. Those stories they're sending back to the Picky about the
Dongos . . . about the Ularu admitting to the killings . . . I think
they made up the whole thing. The Ularu have had some of their
people killed the same way, and most of them believe it's ancient
spirits. I think Black Tom is trying to scare his own people into
doing what Rush Killian wants them to do."

"Show me some proof."

I inclined my head toward the corpse.

"Allitt had it. He called me Saturday night . . . wanted to give
me the whole story. To be printed in the event of his death.
Anyway, that's what it amounted to. Insurance. I was his policy.
And his beneficiary too. After talking with me Allitt came up
here to negotiate with Killian. He wanted his share but he didn't
want to get murdered to get it."

"I thought you knew a little too much."

"Think again. I never got to read the letter. It went up in the
Morisset Building fire the night you and Hawthorne left Sydney."

"So you've got nothing."

"Nothing much. But I've done better than you, I found a trace
of the superintendent."

"What?"

"His bushy hat. The one he bought to wear up here."

"Where'd you find it?"

"On the head of one of Black Tom's Dongos. He said he
pulled it out of the spring in Ularup."

"He's lying. The superintendent never went to Ularup."

"How do you know?"

"He and that reporter went with one of Killian's men to see
where Hector Boyle's body was found. And those two ENA
journos too. The bloke says they wandered off and got lost."

"He's lying, too."

"Prob'bly. But Killian's man couldn't have got them on the
aboriginal lands without a fight. We'd have heard about it."

For several seconds we watched in silence as the gruesome
remains were transferred to the body bag.

"And him?" asked Ek. "Killian's people didn't do that or they'd've known you wasn't Allitt, wouldn't they? So who killed him?"

"I don't know. Maybe they thought he was me when they killed him. They knew I was coming up."

Ek considered everything I'd said. "It doesn't wash," he observed. "Some of it's all right but not all. If it's Black Tom doing all the butcherin' on Killian's orders, why the fences around his camp? Why are his men running around armed to the teeth to defend themselves? They're ready for trouble. Why bother if it's all their own doing? What's he afraid of?"

"I don't know. Bunyips maybe?"

"Well there's one way to find out what he's afraid of," said Ek. "From Killian himself. Have you met him?"

"Didn't I tell you? Killian can't stand reporters. He doesn't give interviews. He keeps an army of bodyguards and guard dogs around just to stop reporters like me from coming too close. Did I mention he's got some kind of a lion dog? It's got a mane and everything."

Ek nodded.

"You told me. I asked around. It's one of those silly Chinese hairless things."

"The Chinese hairless isn't a guard dog. It's a toy."

"Right. And Killian doesn't know you're a journo. He thinks you're a blackmailer by the name of Brock Allitt."

I could see what he was up to.

"Maybe. But Black Tom and MacMutton and Geoffers are all there; they know me. If they see me I'm done for. Why don't *you* go back and interview Killian if it's such a good idea?"

"I've tried. He won't talk to me."

"Let's go together. Good journo, bad cop—"

"I'm going to puck around here. This is the place the superintendent wanted to see. Boyle and those two mates of yours were found close by. And now here's Allitt. See the fall at the foot of that cliff over there?" I said I did. He said it looked as though someone had been blasting. "Not long ago either," he added. "I'm gonna have a look around. You said you wanted to help. Well? Do you or don't you?"

"Forget it."

"I'm not forgetting anything. I'm certainly not forgetting what's going on in this country. Or what day this is. It's Wednesday. Three hours ago in Canberra the High Court announced its decision."

It's true. I'd forgotten all about that.

"So who. . . ?"

I knew the answer before I'd asked.

"Who d'ye think?"

"Killian."

"That's right. He's won the legal right to do whatever he wants to this land."

"Then . . ."

"The trouble's already started. We can't see the fires from out here . . . or hear the gunfire . . . but it's there. This country is coming apart at the seams and it's up to us to do something about it."

"Us? You mean me."

"Ey, you're going back. Why do you think I played along when Digs introduced you? Why do you think you're not under arrest right now? Anyway, you want to go back; you know you do." For the first time since I'd met him, Ek smiled at me. "Just keep the wisecracks to yourself and you'll be foine."

As he spoke the procession of blankets and bags passed by us. Doyle Mulligan on his way home and a dune buggy for a hearse.

"Don't sweat it," said Ek, loud enough for the bearers to hear. "You're better off than that poor Mulligan sponger, aren't you?"

"Poor's roight," said one of the bearers. "This bloke wasn't worth killing if you ask me. Too skinny to be mucha meal even for cannibals."

"He wasn't skinny," I growled back; "he was thin."

14

Bad Blokes

Killian's office was furnished lavishly and decorated by professionals. I recognized the motif; it was hang-the-expense. Soundproofed, too. The crack of target fire died the moment the outer door closed. But the real treat was the air. Twenty degrees Centigrade. And scented. I took a whiff. Either lilacs or sandalwood. Deliciously cool.

In spite of this—and despite Sergeant Ek's advice to the contrary—I was sweating.

I stood there looking around.

"*This is just in from Broken Hill: A couple of tourists were dragged out of their car and beaten by aborigines. The car was found later in the Darling River. In Melbourne, an estimated three thousand blacks were marching on Government House when they were pelted by rocks and sticks from whites who lined the streets. The army's still trying to pull 'em apart. They're patrolling the streets of Sydney too, but I can see the smoke from several fires to the north and west. Just a second. . . .*"

A massive walnut desk with gold inlay occupied the far side of the room but there was no one behind it. Likewise, there was no one at the built-in bookcases or file cabinets which filled the wall to my left. The third wall, to my right, had a crystal wet bar with captain's-style barstools and half a dozen white leather chairs around a walnut table with a top of inch-thick glass.

"*. . . that was Jermey. He says a small force of radical whites swept into a Wagga Wagga tribal town the first thing this morning and beat a bunch of gins and old men to death. Tribal leaders are threatening retaliation.*"

There was an opening midway between the wet bar and the sitting area. As I got closer I saw it was another room, an addition, off the side of the trailer. Beaded curtains fell across the opening. The words grew louder as I entered.

"Excellent. Excellent."

"Here's an update on Darwin. The whole town's engulfed by smoke now. Seventy-eight dead or missing. A twenty-four-hour cur-few's been cancelled so people can evacuate. They're saying now destruction might exceed the five thousand houses and five hundred buildings destroyed by cyclone Tracy. It's a bloody mess."

"Lovely!"

I spread the curtains and stepped through.

That's where I found him.

Them.

The dog was there too.

It had a lion's head with a full mane of shaggy, straw-colored hair. A blood-red mouth with vicious incisors came open, snarled once and then snapped shut.

When it got to its feet, I froze.

What a beast! Its huge shoulders were fully three feet off the floor. Once you got over the shock of all that hair on its head, the first thing you noticed was the lack of hair everywhere else. It had a tuft on the end of its tail and a shaggy boot on each foot, but the rest of the dog's body was covered with nothing but skin and fuzz. It sounds silly. I swear it wasn't. Not on that hound. Its muscles bulged from its furless hide like a body builder in Speedos. Worse yet, its eyes fixed on me the way a rattlesnake looks at a mouse it's about to gobble up.

"Anything else?"

"I'm expecting a call from Perth any minute. Our people in Brisbane and Adelaide went into action forty minutes ago. The first communications should come by fifteen hundred."

"That can wait until your next report."

"Yes, sir."

"Alert all units we're on for tonight. I repeat—we're on for tonight."

"Right."

I risked a look around.

The addition was actually a little communications room. There were no windows; the walls were covered by maps of the Northern Territory in various scales. The radio set itself, as miniature as the room, perched on a pedestal table in the very center. It didn't look up to transmitting a signal to Sydney by way of a communications satellite in geostationary orbit above Australia, but these days, anything's possible.

Rush Killian sat facing me in the only seat, a pedestal chair which—like the table—seemed to rise right out of the floor. He was holding a microphone in one hand and with the other, manipulating the radio controls.

"Alter your scrambler code accordingly."

"Will do."

"Killian, out."

He reached over and threw a switch. The speakers went silent. Then he turned on me, locked his eyes on mine, and grinned.

The grin was a savage one. His teeth were too long and too sharp. A tailored blue silk suit concealed his big body and his big hands were neatly manicured. But he was really just an animal, with teeth that looked too much like his dog's. That was what Maggie must have meant when she'd labelled him a "pseud." If he hoped to fool people for long he needed to shut his mouth or get rid of the dog.

After an eternity he growled:

"You're dead a long time, mate."

"Huh?"

"What I said. You're dead a long time."

"I won't argue with that."

He regarded me for several seconds in silence. Then he barked, "Your voice sounds different."

"Than what?"

"Over the telephone."

I felt my pulse pounding.

"I wouldn't know," I replied. "I only tried to call me once and wouldn't you know it—I was too busy to come to the phone." It didn't occur to me until after I'd said it, but this was exactly the kind of thing I shouldn't say.

Killian studied me.

"About being dead a long time. That's Major's department. I wouldn't get too close to him if I were you. He's trained to hold a meter from his target. Springing distance. He won't like it if you get any closer. What do you think of 'im?"

"I'm trying not to."

"Purebred Chinese Crested Hairless," Killian growled. Everything he said he either barked or growled.

"It's kinda big, isn't it?"

"The Chinese developed two varieties. The one preferred by the so-called modern breed fanciers is the Treasure House Guardian. The miniature crested. This is the other variety. The hunter. Major is the end result of several hundred years of Han family selective breeding. I got him from a Chinese outfitter in Laos who used him to hunt tigers."

He paused, giving me a chance to indicate how impressed I was.

"Tigers, huh?"

"The Chinese say of the Crested Hunter, they'll do anything any other dog can do. And when they're done, they'll kill the other dog. You don't whistle for a Crested Hunter; according to the Chinese, you 'invoke the demon.' Would you like to see something?"

I would've liked to see the dog on a chain.

But naturally I didn't say that.

"Major," he said, firing his words at the dog: "Go on!"

The Crested Hunter sank onto all fours. Still he didn't take his eyes off me for an instant. A rumble came from his throat. A purr. But not like a cat. Not a contented purr. More like a distant stampede.

"Now watch," said Killian. He whistled. There was no reaction. "Come on, Major. Come on, boy."

Nothing.

It never even glanced around.

"Why doesn't he come?"

"Because if he had," Killian either barked or growled, "I'd have killed him and the man who trained him."

I let a few seconds pass.

"So what's the trick?"

"It's called *Defend*. He only knows three tricks. This is the first one. He's on watch. Even I can't take him off without the right signal. You can move around, talk, do what you please so long as you don't threaten me. But if you were to raise your voice or make a threatening move or just come too near me, he'd show you his second trick."

"Oh, yeah? What's that?"

"Go ahead and try something and you'll find out."

"No, thanks."

"Don't you want to see it?"

"Maybe you could just tell me about it."

"It's called *Detain*. When Major's on *Detain* he won't let you move. He won't even like it if you utter a sound. But you'll have to goad him if you want to see it. Pretend to threaten me. Otherwise, he'll just wait for me to give him the word."

"Oh, yeah. What's the word?"

"That's my secret, Allitt. Would I tell secrets to a black-bloody-mailer?"

I let that go by.

It merely confirmed my suspicions about the relationship between Killian and Allitt.

"I can hardly wait to see his third trick," I said. "What do you call that one . . . Devour?"

"That's good. I like that. And you're close, but not exactly correct. He won't eat you. Not completely, anyway. I like to call it *Destroy*. Of course the result's the same."

"You mean I'd be dead."

Killian grinned savagely.

"Ey. For a long time."

"You don't dare kill me," I said, "or let Major do the job for you."

He closed a cover on the radio, stepped away from the table, swept by me without slowing down, and kept going into the office. The dog stayed where it was. At least it stayed until I, moving cautiously, followed him back in and at that point it got to its feet and stalked me, carefully maintaining the distance between us. I stopped in the middle of the room. Major crouched down a meter behind me.

Killian settled in behind his desk.

"You're pretty sure of yourself, aren't you?" he said.

"Why not? I've got the goods on you."

"Do you now?"

"I know everything."

He didn't chuckle this time, he threw back his head and laughed. It was a locker-room laugh—too loud and too nasty— and it occurred to me this would probably give him away even if you couldn't see his teeth.

"What d'you know about me worth a million dollars?" he growled.

A million bucks! I tried not to show my surprise.

"I know you're a killer," I said.

"Balls!"

"Is that a denial?"

"No. Nor an admission."

"You killed Arthur Copley, didn't you?"

"Would I tell you if I did?"

"I already have all the proof I need," I said easily.

Killian shook his head.

"I wasn't anywhere near Copley when he got it."

"No, but you hired MacMutton and Geoffers to do the job for you. You're just as guilty as they are."

He nursed a thought before answering.

"The fool was going to display those bloody photographs of his. I warned him against it. I won't have all my plans ruined now. Not after all I've done. I'd offered to buy his entire collection but he wanted too much. His notions about value, like yours, were way out of line."

"How about Hector Boyle. . . ?"

"Friend Boyle became too curious for his own good. It doesn't pay to get too nosy out here."

"And those two ENA reporters?"

With a sweep of his hand he waved Nevil and Mickey away like two bothersome mosquitoes. "Did anyone ask them to come sniffing around? I figure they got what they asked for. If this is all you have. . . ?"

"It isn't."

My plan was to keep him talking. I hoped he'd say something about Hawthorne and Maggie. But he hadn't so I'd have to. "There's that policeman, the British CID superintendent. And the woman reporter—"

"Enough!"

Killian pounded the desktop with his fist. At the same time the low distant rumble in Major's throat got louder and nearer.

Then he drew open a drawer to activate a hidden switch. I hoped he was readjusting the thermostat on the air system because suddenly I was sweating more than ever. I heard the hum of a servomotor and when I looked back, the radio room table had begun to drop. The chair too. Their pedestal legs telescoped until they were just off the floor. Then the floor started down. With hydraulic smoothness, it sank to about a foot below the office level before stopping. Meanwhile the overhead lights withdrew into the ceiling and the ceiling was rising. After that, several things happened at once. The floor, flattened table and radio together slid slowly under the office. The ceiling

crawled over our roof. At the same time the two side walls of the
radio room began closing, drawing the outer wall in behind
them. The pictures on the side walls—each half of a large water-
color of a bush scene—matched so cleverly that once the wall
came together I couldn't even tell where it had split. Finally, the
sheer curtains automatically drew themselves back.

"Do I care what happens to a bunch of stickybeaks? You can't
bail me up over nonsense like this!"

I spoke quietly but firmly.

"The cops don't think it's nonsense. Murder and arson. You
did a million dollars worth of damage to the opera house and I
can tie you to the fire."

"So what! A million dollars? Why, I could write them a
check."

"Write it to me instead."

Killian spat air.

"Better yet," I told him, "make it cash. You know how boring
it is standing in line at the bank."

He stared at me the same way Major had. As though the
desktop which separated his hands and teeth from my throat
represented no more than springing distance.

"I wouldn't pay you one dollar for anything you've told me!"
he said. As Killian levered himself up I sensed he was about to
give Major the word. The secret word.

"Don't forget, I've written everything down."

I said it quickly. "I left it with . . . someone," I added. "It'll be
splashed across the front pages of every paper in the world if
anything happens to me."

"Do you expect that to save you?"

"I'm counting on it. The man I gave the story to is a reporter."

"So you told me."

"Did I?"

"Yes, but you neglected to tell me which one."

"I'd be a fool to tell you that."

Killian shook his head from side to side.

"You can't give the press what you don't know. Frankly, I don't think you know much."

Pressing another button, he started around the side of the desk.

I heard more servomotors and whirled around. What the first wall had just done, the opposite wall was undoing. A twenty-foot section of the bookshelves began opening French-fashion, exposing a hidden wall behind them and driving it slowly outward. When the two sections of shelves were parallel to each other and perpendicular to the outer wall, they locked. Then the ceiling settled into place and the floor rose until it was flush with the office.

At that point I was looking into an adjoining room ten feet by twenty.

The back wall of the room was taken up by a bold full-color floor-to-ceiling topographical map of the continent. But as big and bright as that map was I didn't even notice it until later when Killian pointed it out. The only other thing in the room was too eye-catching.

With the walls, ceiling and floor in position the last metamorphosis took place. A tiered platform pushed up from below. The top was about four feet wide and eight feet long and maybe three inches thick. The second tier was smaller. The third smaller yet. By the time it was tabletop high off the floor, the base was barely one foot by two and the whole thing looked like an upside-down pyramid. The upper surface was covered in green baize like a pool table but since it didn't have any pockets or bumpers it wasn't.

Anyway, pool tables don't have the kind of displays on them that this table had.

I followed Killian over in a kind of a stupor.

On the platform was a scaled mock-up of a magnificent metropolis so modernistic it looked like a science fiction fantasy come to life. A 2001 World's Fair.

Killian stood back and basked while I got a good look.

The city would've looked right at home on the surface of Alpha Centauri. Tall parabolic-curved towers rose over the downtown. Rows of inverted pyramidal skyscrapers got bigger the higher they went until they finally met one another. They appeared to have gardens and trees and even a golf course across their roofs. Spherical office buildings—or maybe apartment houses—stood on pedestals like golf balls on tees. There were miniature skyways and aerial walkways connecting each futuristic structure to the others. There were parks, and a lake surrounding a frisbee-shaped thing on an island, that was either a building or a flying saucer. Everything was modeled of mirrored plastic which reflected the baize and made the whole display glitter green.

I stopped when I came against it; I looked around and found Killian standing beside me and Major three feet away on his haunches.

Killian waited for me to speak first.

"Let me guess . . . Emerald City?"

He surprised me by smiling.

"That's good, Allitt. I like that. What's more, it's precisely correct. Emerald City, right in the middle of Oz. I call it Killianstown."

I'd been fighting darkness for a long time but suddenly a little light shone through.

"So that's it!" I whispered.

"That's it, mate."

"You never had any intention of setting up any cattle stations."

"Bah! This country's overrun with cattle and sheep."

"You're building a city."

"Ey, but not just any city."

"I'll say. Disneyland Down Under's more like it."

He ignored that.

"I'm going to do what the yanks tried to do in Washington, D.C. and screwed up with obsolete construction methods and

centuries-old architecture. What the Brazilians tried to do with
Brasilia, but didn't have the money to do right. What we tried to
do at Canberra but didn't have the brains to do right. To mold
a city from the wilderness."

"What's wrong with Canberra?"

He snorted.

"Do you know what Canberra means? It's abo for tits!"

I said I didn't know that.

"Neither did the idiots who named it. Is that planning? Worse
yet, the chief architect was a yank. A bloody seppo! The place is
nothing more than a collection of mausoleums, a soulless city.
Tits up, I say!"

"You're going to do better?"

"I'm going to build this country a city in its interior such as
no nation has ever seen before. It will be the city of the twenty-
first century and beyond. A city-state, self-contained, self-
sufficient, self-governed. It will be a safe city without crime or
slums . . . an efficient city, where business prospers and people
will beg to come, to live and work. Soon, it will become the
country's heart. The focus of her agricultural, mineral and industrial might. It will be—"

"Yours."

"Of course it'll be mine. I'm going to build it. But it will also
be—"

"Immensely profitable."

"Careful, Allitt." His tone warned me to watch my step. So did
the animal look in his eye. I looked down at Major—his look
looked the same.

"But why out here?"

"That's an odd question coming from a man in your line, isn't
it?"

"You could do all the building you want to in New South
Wales. Or Victoria or Queensland for that matter. Why come to
the outback?"

"I don't have to tell you what land costs on the coast. No one could buy enough or own enough to build a city. Anyway this is the site and you know why as well as I do. It'd be the right place even if it weren't for that. Look at the map. It fairly shouts at you."

He indicated the back wall and for the first time I saw the large geographical map.

With a flourish he snatched a baton off the table and pointed the tip at the right hand shoreline.

"Australia was first settled along the east coast just like the United States. America's population shifted to the west, the same way ours did. Sydney, with three and a half million people, claims a fourth of our population. Melbourne is close behind with three million." He indicated Victoria's southernmost city and its capital. "Brisbane and Adelaide," he pointed to the coastal capitals of Queensland and South Australia, "about a million each. Again like America's, our population began a westward shift across a land mass remarkably similar in size. You could call Perth on the coast of Western Australia—with a million residents and growing—our southern California."

He turned and pushed the stick in my chest.

"But there's one major difference. We made the shift across country without any significant development of the interior. There are no major cities between east and west from Canberra to the Kimberley. North and south, there's nothing between Adelaide and Darwin—"

"Alice Springs."

"Bah! Eighteen thousand people! From one coast to the other the central region is dominated by a watering hole . . . a village not much bigger than an abo settlement. Australia's the size of the continental U.S. Can you imagine the American interior without a single population center larger than Alice Springs? Not so much as a Chicago, Dallas or Houston. No Kansas City. No St. Louis, Omaha, Minneapolis/St. Paul, or Atlanta. No Des Moines, Denver or Phoenix. Five million square kilometers of uninhabited land between New York and L.A. Bloody absurd!"

"You're overlooking something."

Killian held his stick, one end in each of his hands. He flexed it like an epee.

"An' what's that?"

"The interior of the country was never settled because there isn't enough water. You can't build a city smack in the middle of the desert unless you've got a good source of water."

The millionaire contractor grew strangely silent.

His eyes narrowed and I felt as though he were trying to look through me.

"There's water out there," he said at last.

"If you can find it. And find enough of it to supply a whole city."

"I can solve that problem," growled Killian. "Nothing is going to stop me. And no one."

He was showing me his savage smile. It occurred to me that all he'd done was give me more ammunition to blackmail him with. He wouldn't have done it if he'd any intentions of letting me go.

"I don't want to stop you," I said. "I just want what I've got coming."

"You'll get it. Allitt, you're a fool. You said you'd be a fool if you told me who you'd given your story to but, the fact is, I've known for days now. It's that ENA journo Doyle Mulligan, isn't it?"

"How can you. . . ?"

"I had all your office telephones tapped."

I was frantically searching my memory. "But I didn't take the call in the office. It was over a pay phone."

"Not *your* office. Hector Boyle's. We tapped them all. But by the time we got to the Morisset Building to grab the letter it was already gone. Mulligan had it. However he was still in the building, so I ordered it burned to the ground."

It seemed the only thing Killian didn't know was who I really was. But I didn't see how telling him could help me. Just the opposite. If he knew that!

I said:

"But they didn't get m . . . Mulligan or the letter."

"No. They didn't. But those abos did. Digs tells me you identified Mulligan's body out on the desert." He spun to the hound.

"Wait! That police sergeant. He knows I'm here!"

Killian merely smiled.

"Does he? Bad luck for him. Major! O-kay now!"

The dog lunged.

It came forward so fast I fell back against Killian's display. I almost went down but gripped the edge of the platform and held on. This time Major moved within inches of my chest. He didn't crouch. He stood there, snarling, the saliva running down his chin, and his lips pulled back from twin rows of knife-like canines. His eyes flamed.

"I've taken Major off *Defend,* Allitt. I've put him on *Detain.*"

I started to say something. Killian's palm in my face shut me up fast.

"Don't make a move. Don't even think about it. Don't say a word. If you do anything . . . anything at all," he said, "Major will go to stage three. *Destroy.* He'll rip out yer throat. Don't move, don't speak, don't breathe, don't even piss your pants. Just hear what I'm saying and believe me."

I believed him.

I didn't move.

I didn't speak.

I didn't breathe.

I didn't piss my pants either, but to tell the truth I did think about it.

While the dog and I held our positions Killian went to the door. I heard it open but I didn't turn to see. I heard more people coming back in.

Killian's bark sounded first.

"Wait until dark. Then take him outside the barrier. Have him meet with an accident. You know the kind I mean."

The voice that answered surprised me. It belonged to my old munchkin pal Jeff.

"Outside the barrier? After dark?"

"Yes after dark. Think, man! Those search planes are still up there. Do you want some police spotter to see you?"

"It ayn't safe, Mr. Killian."

Mutt was there too. I caught his bass asking if a few of Killian's men oughtn't to go with them.

"My men will be engaged. Take Major along," he replied, "if it'll make you feel better."

"I dunno," said Mutt. "If ye ask me that damn bitser's as likely to kill us as help us."

This was a mistake (and an ironic one), Mutt's calling Major a bitser—Australian for mutt, "Bits o' this and bits o' that."—because Killian took it as an insult. "Major," he pointed out with a growl, "is a purebred, and takes instruction considerably better than the two of you."

At this point in the conversation they moved around the corner of the alcove.

"By gawd!" squeaked Jeff. "It's the seppo!"

Mutt drew up his great height.

"What's 'e doin' eyer?"

"What are you yakkin' about?" growled Killian.

Mutt jabbed a finger in my direction.

"This ayn't Allitt."

Killian whirled.

"Who is he?"

"He's a nosy yank reporter named Doyle Mulligan."

I hadn't said a single word throughout.

Killian pushed over and gave me his most savage glare. "I've got a good mind," he barked, "to take you apart right here and now."

I thought about telling him it didn't take a good mind to come up with that. After all those two halfwits had had the same idea five days before. I thought about saying it, all right. But naturally I didn't.

15

Good Blokes

Take a baseball bat. An ax handle will work just as well if you happen to be someplace—Australia for example—where they play cricket instead of baseball and use a sissy paddle instead of a real bat. Next get some spikes. Forty penny stuff. Barn nails at least six inches long. Pound a dozen of these through the business end of the handle until the points stick out the other side. Do this all around the end. That's it. What you've got is a makeshift mace and a wicked weapon. I noticed that Jeff had wrapped the grip of his with electrical tape and Mutt had filed his nail points to needle sharpness but even without these refinements they looked brutally efficient.

Of course I didn't see them right off.

Killian had ordered me locked into a trailer rig until nightfall. I sat for hours in complete darkness. When the trailer doors swung open, twin headlights blazed in my eyes and my night sight erupted in flames.

"Com'on, seppo!"

It was Mutt. He was silhouetted between me and the car but there was no mistaking that huge frame. He held a short-barrelled revolver in his right hand. Then I spotted the spiked ax handle in his left. I stared at it, squinted my eyes, and shaded them with my hand until I saw what the thing was. A shudder ran down my spine.

"Move," said Jeff. The headlights caught him in profile. He had a similar weapon. The mace. Instead of the gun he held a flashlight. The beam struck a lethal-looking creature between them. I recognized that too, the Chinese Crested Hunter.

"Get in the car," Jeff screeched.

"Look, you guys. If you—"

"Move!"

"Just listen a minute, will ya?"

Mutt snickered.

"I told ye he wouldna be so lair the next time we met."

"Ey, you told him."

My palms were out.

"You won't get away with this, you know. I'm working hand in glove with the cops; they know who I really am and what I'm doing here."

"Is that right?"

"That's right. It was Sergeant Ek's idea, me talking to Killian. I also told him about you guys and what I saw at the art show. If I disappear like Maggie and Hawthorne you're the first two he'll come looking for. Is that what you want?"

"Ek? That flat-'eaded sergeant?" Mutt's head wagged side to side. "He won't be lookin' for no one."

"He won't if you take me to him. Come clean with him; turn state's evidence. You could still get out of this mess in one piece."

"Maybe I will tayke ye to him."

"Don't do it, mate!"

"Why not? The yank's askin' for it, ayn't he?"

While I stood stock still, Mutt stepped to the trailer rig beside mine, threw open the latch on the back doors and pulled them open. I fully expected to see Sergeant Ek come stumbling out with his hands shielding his eyes as I'd done. No one came out. At least not until Mutt reached inside and pulled out a heavy-duty plastic bag. It was a garbage bag. The same kind of bag they'd put Brock Allitt in. It hit the ground like garbage, too.

Then he reached in and pulled out another just like it.

And another.

Mutt produced a pocketknife and slashed one of the bags from end to end as though he were gutting a deer. The way a deer's insides spill out when it's gutted. . . ? That's how the body came out of that bag.

It spilled onto the ground.

"You got something to say to the sergeant, yank?"

I guess it was Ek. My hopes hit my heels when I went over to see. He was just like all the others. As shocking as that was, even more shocking was how many bags remained in the trailer.

I stood there in shock.

Mutt spoke to my back. "If you got any more ideas for gettin' outta this mess in one piece better save it for yerself, seppo."

Jeff had remained by the car. Now he urged us to get going.

Mutt prodded me with his mace. He just brushed my arm and yet the nails slashed my skin like razor blades. "You heard him, let's go, seppo!"

There wasn't anything else for me to do.

I turned around and staggered to the road.

Captain Digs's rover, headlights blazing, was parked facing the trailer.

"No, not that one! Yer own car. Back seat."

By then my eyes were accustomed to the darkness again and I could make out the Holden parked behind the rover. Its engine was turning over and its interior lights burned; both headlights were out for the simple reason they'd been bashed in the previous night by Black Tom's Dongos.

I got in.

Major leapt in beside me and sat facing me on the back seat. Meanwhile Mutt had crawled behind the steering wheel and Jeff was moving out in the lead vehicle. Mutt took off after him, hugging his rear fender so he could see where he was going.

"Who . . . who are they?" I stammered. "All those bodies? What happened?"

Without turning around, Mutt muttered:

"Drillers and equipment operators, most of 'em. Night crews before Killian stopped working at night—dragged into the desert by those abo friends of yers. There were others who never

got found. As for what happened to 'em, it's the same as what's
gonna happen to you."

He'd laid his makeshift mace on the seat beside him and stuck
the pistol in his belt. I leaned forward to peek over the seat back.
Major, the Crested Hunter, flew into a frenzy of barking. He
nearly bit off my head. Mutt spun around and cried, "Try that
again if you wanta DIE!"

As soon as he said it the dog calmed down and I leaned back
against the seat cushions. I was almost too scared to think and
yet I couldn't help but be puzzled by the animal's reaction.

Bumper to bumper we drove through camp.

For a while Mutt was able to back off a little because a solid
line of other vehicles had been parked off the road with their
engines idling and their headlights burning and the whole place
was lit up like Wrigley Field. There was a lot of activity too.
Something was up. Men running around in desert camos were
loading equipment and arms into trucks. Killian hadn't stopped
all night work. However, nobody paid much attention to us
except one guy.

Black Tom.

He was standing at the side of the road as we drove by. His
black eyes bore through the glass of my window.

I never saw an unfriendlier face.

When we passed the last of these vehicles, Mutt closed up to
the rover again.

Soon we reached the front gate.

Two guards keyed the padlock, pushed open the gate, and
waved us on with hardly a glance in the windows; they wasted
no time in closing and locking it up the instant we'd passed
through.

Our two-car convoy started down the road.

"Why are you doing this, Mutt?"

"The nyme's MacMutton and why don't you cork it?"

"What do you get out of it?"

"I git to kark you, don't I?" he smirked.

"Sure. To keep Killian's hands clean." I tried to keep the nervousness from my voice. "But after that? What's in it for you and Jeff once you've done all his dirty work?"

"Plenty."

I forced a laugh and let him see my grin in the mirror. "Like your buddies, Copley, Boyle and Allitt, huh?"

"I don't wanta hear none o' yer yabber!"

"Shall I tell you?"

"No!"

His anger didn't go unnoticed.

Major began emitting a low-throated growl.

I continued in a casual voice. "Killian needed you and your dwarf friend to write his stories for him. And to kill people who got in his way. But now, he doesn't need you any more. In fact, *you're* in the way. And it's only a matter of time before your organs, yours and Jeff's, show up in Sydney in garbage bags."

"Shut up!"

I shut up long enough to catch Major's growl gathering volume. I was sure the dog felt no more affection for Mutt than it did for me; I was hoping it wouldn't obey him any better either. And I was betting that, having been trained to recognize a threatening manner, it would see the angrier of us as the enemy.

I looked straight into the dog's eyes and I said in an undertone:

"Major. Die!"

It gave me a queer look. I leaned forward again, just enough for a test. Sure enough the growl intensified. But not as much as before. And it didn't snap at me this time.

"An' don't talk to the dog either!"

I sat back and shook my head in amazement.

The rover led us down the road only a couple kilometers before leaving the ruts. It headed north across the desert; its speed took Mutt by surprise. He hit the horn a few times in a vain attempt to get Jeff's attention, but there was no slowing the little munchkin. His brake lights never came on. Mutt didn't dare stop for fear of being left in the dark and he couldn't pass Jeff, so the two cars bounded over the rough ground banging their underbellies on every upturned rock.

"Are you gonna let the dog do it? Or are you gonna do it yourself?"

"I wouldn't give that bitser the pleasure."

"Also you don't know his code signals, huh?"

"And you do, I suppose."

"I might."

"Ayn't you clever?"

"Did you know Major comes from China? And that it was trained by a Chinese to hunt tiger?"

"So?"

"So the commands he knows . . . *Defend, Detain* and *Destroy*. They were never intended to be used against people. They're hunting commands—stalk . . . subdue . . . kill."

Mutt was so busy eyeballing me in the rearview mirror he almost ran into Jeff's bumper. He slammed on the brakes just in time.

I smiled to myself.

"Killian told me, they don't call the Crested Hunter, they invoke the demon. That's Chinese. *Mey* is Chinese for demon or spirit. *Juh* is invoke. Major . . . *Mey-juh*. To invoke the demon. Get it? That's its name and Killian doesn't even know it."

"You speak Choinese?"

"Oh sure, I spent several years in Hong Kong. So does Major. It was already trained when Killian bought it. All the commands it knows are Chinese. I just told it to die. *Dai* is Chinese for 'stay.' And guess what? It did!"

If I'm any judge of expressions, Mutt was suddenly lost in thought, which was unexplored territory for him, which was why he was lost. I gave him a little time before continuing:

"Killian doesn't speak it though," I went on. "When he put Major on stalk he used the command: Go on. Maybe that's what he thought the command is, but it isn't."

"Oh, yeh?"

"Yeah. It should sound more like this. . . ."

I turned to the dog.

I told it distinctly:

"Meyjuh. Gu-an."

Major regarded Mutt ferociously and I had the pleasure of seeing Mutt's eyes suddenly widen.

"I told you to cork it!" he said through his teeth.

The hunter grumbled audibly.

But, for the first time, not at me.

Meanwhile the rover approached a steep ravine. Jeff took off along the rim instead of trying to cross it and we stayed right behind him.

I kept up a running monologue.

"And then later, when Killian put the dog on subdue, he used the phrase: Okay now. The Chinese words for 'apprehend and subdue' are Keh Na. Here, I'll show you; watch this. I eyeballed the dog—*"Meyjuh, keh-na."*

At that point I didn't know which of them was more lost in thought, Mutt or the dog.

And who knows what would have happened if Jeff's brake lights hadn't come on. We came that close to plowing into his bumper. At the last second Mutt jammed his brakes and whipped the wheel. We stopped beside the rover at the edge of a shallow ravine.

Mutt looked warily over the seat.

"All right," he demanded, "get out!"

Jeff was already out. He was anxious to get started. Nervous, I decided, and eager at the same time. His eyes were as big as silver dollars. The way they were that day at the opera house when I'd mistaken his and Mutt's excitement for fear. He was afraid now . . . but that wouldn't stop him from doing what he'd come here to do.

I climbed out.

Major jumped out right behind me.

We waited while Mutt released the clutch and sent the Holden rolling into the ravine. The bonnet dipped and the boot rose. The car hit bottom with a raucous collision of stone and steel.

Mutt joined us near the edge.

The little munchkin was playing his flashlight in a big circle. At first I believed he was looking for a good place to do it. I was wrong. I think now he was just making sure there was no one around to see.

Because something was bothering Major.

Jeff put the light on it. The dog had his nose in the air. It was taking samples and didn't like what it smelled.

I glanced off to the west.

A steady stream of headlights lit our backtrail through the desert. All those vehicles we'd passed leaving the camp were now following us out. It was this, I decided, that was bothering Major.

"Careful of the dog," called Mutt. "The yank can speak to it in Choinese."

"Choinese?"

"Ey. He knows its signals."

The two of them stood there, unsure.

"Never mind. Let's do it, mate," Jeff urged him.

The two of them closed in.

Mutt cocked the ax handle over his shoulder. Jeff did the same. It was a race to see which could get in the first blow.

My back was to the ravine. I had no place to go and no weapon. No word to Mutt and Jeff would save me. But to the Crested Hunter. . . ?

The problem being I knew at least a dozen words in Chinese for kill. I didn't have time to try them all. It had to be the right word the first time. And it had to be now. The dog wouldn't defend me in any event. It wouldn't attack them if I didn't know the right command. I knew that. But I couldn't believe those two half-wits knew it.

"*Meyjuh!*"

Mutt and Jeff froze.

"Shitzi!" I cried. *"Shi-tzi!"*

There is only one word in Chinese for "Tiger!"

The dog stiffened.

His chest went out, his lips pulled back and a guttural snarl erupted from deep within his throat.

Mutt turned, saw the dog all set to attack and guessed incorrectly what was about to happen. He raised his weapon. That was a mistake.

At that point Major reacted instinctively.

He leapt.

The ax handle caught Major across the back in mid-leap. This only enraged it. As Killian had promised the dog went straight for the throat and his weight took the two of them down together, growling and screaming.

I squared off with Jeff.

He experienced a horrible moment of indecision.

If he helped Mutt, I might get away.

If he didn't help. . . .

He'd be alone against me.

As I say, it was a bad time for Jeff but it only lasted a moment.

Even as I spun to face him it was almost over. Had I turned a second later I'd have missed the whole thing. As it was I saw little enough.

I heard a grunt.

A shapeless blackness, like a ragged piece of the night but moving at lightning speed, pulled Jeff down. One second he was right there. Just three steps away. The next second he wasn't. Sand flew everywhere. I shook my head, and when I looked around again Jeff was gone.

His mace and his flashlight were thrown to the ground.

I heard a scream from out in the darkness and I knew it was Jeff. It didn't sound like Jeff. It didn't sound human. It was though. I knew it.

The sand was still flying.

I heard more growls. A vicious, savage snarling.

Major, I thought. By this time my brain was going like a top. I was on the edge of blind panic and almost too dizzy to stand. Somehow I managed to turn back to my left because I couldn't understand how Major could still be fighting with Mutt if he'd just tackled Jeff.

I picked up the fallen flashlight and pointed it at the ground.

All that remained of the man and the dog was a shoe . . . just one. And a pair of furrows cut in the sand. I aimed the light along this trail. Ten meters off the beam picked up Mutt's feet—one of them shod and one bare—still moving away. He wasn't walking. He was being dragged by the head.

I couldn't see the thing pulling him. It was too near the gully. His legs, first the shod foot and then the bare one, vanished over the rim. And then he was gone too, like Jeff.

I wasn't on the edge of panic, not then.

I'd plunged headlong, kicking and screaming, over the side.

I turned and ran. North, south, east or west . . . I don't know. I just ran. Into the darkness. Somewhere, anywhere, it didn't matter, I just wanted to get out of there. But I'd only covered a few yards when I stumbled and fell on my back on a pile of rocks.

I recovered the flashlight again. I pointed it at the thing I'd fallen over.

It was the dog.

The great Crested Hunter.

Major's underbelly had been opened up. His insides were scattered all over the desert along with a quantity of blood and his big lion's head, hanging onto his shoulders by a mere scrap of fur, lay off to one side.

I started up.

A clatter of stones stopped me. Footfalls.

A grunt over there.

Another there.

The grunts became snarls.

I scrambled on hands and knees to an outcrop of stone. It had a niche on one side just big enough for me to get my legs into. I managed to squeeze in until only my arms and shoulders were exposed.

Savage snarls closed in around me.

I swung the flashlight out in front of me like a sword. I swung it like a maniac because that's what I was. Though I sliced the darkness to pieces the source of the snarling somehow remained just out of sight.

I turned off the light, buried my head in my arms and closed my eyes.

Nearer they came.

I heeded without really hearing the low-throated wail. It was a call. And a cry. The noise filled the air like a keening wind and yet I couldn't swear it was a sound at all until it became so loud it drowned out the snarls.

I felt without really touching the figure that rose up before me. It was a part of the night sky, as high as that and as black . . . a cosmic black nebula in the shape of a man. His form masked the stars that burned beyond him. His arms reached high over his head, as high as the highest constellations. I whirled on him with the flashlight. Even fully lit he was still just a blackish figure and all I could see was his back. But he held something aloft. Something that glowed in my beam as white as he himself was black. It was a skull! A human skull. The man was standing on the outcrop above me—he facing forward, his skull watching behind—the two of them confronting the horrors that lurked all around.

I sensed without really seeing the other more sinister shadows gather about us. The shadows froze.

At that point the wail became a voice.

"Togla ani motogai nulu!"

And then again:

"Togla ani motogai nulu kadi makara alu!"

There was more. Much more. It continued for several minutes.

"Jim Jim?" I hissed, "Is that you?"

It didn't sound like him. This voice was stronger and older and it rang with more assurance than Jim Jim's. When he shouted, his words hammered the air like thunder. Still I couldn't be sure; my voice didn't sound like me either.

"Jim Jim?"

"Motogalu nulu kadi makara. Gouna gol anka!"

When he stopped shouting the night turned preternaturally quiet. The snarls had died. For the moment at least. I heard a strange howl and an answering yip from across the gully and then nothing.

Suddenly a hand came under my arm and pulled me out of my hole. "Come!"

"For Chrissake, what are those. . . ?"

"No talking! Move fast."

He got me to my feet and took most of my weight as we stumbled together back over to Jeff's rover. Not a moment too soon.

Even as I fought through the driver's-side door I could sense the night coming alive. I could hear heavy breathing. Feel the pounding of many feet on the ground. See the swirl of shadows around us.

I fumbled for the ignition switch. The key was in it.

"Hurry!" shouted the black man.

Something threw itself against my door. The car shook like it had been slammed by a bus. If the thing had struck the window instead of the panel it would have come through. Another landed on the roof and I thought it would collapse with the weight. Iron claws raked the body. By the sound of it they could slice through the steel as easily as a can opener through tin.

"What the hell's out there?" I cried.

"Don't talk. Drive. Hurry!"

I cranked the motor, slammed it into gear and stomped on the throttle. Our wheels spun momentarily, then caught. The rover lurched forward. Toward the ravine. I tried to turn too sharply and lost control, smashed against a boulder and then caromed into a sand pit, burying the car up to the rocker panels. I threw it into reverse. Something bolted through the headlights but at the same time the rear tires threw a ton of sand over the hood and the thing—whatever it was—disappeared.

With agonizing sluggishness the rover edged back. All the while I kept crying, "Come on, come on, come on," until the front tires finally came free, and then I crashed gears until I found a forward one and headed away from the ravine.

When I looked back I saw them chasing us. Their huge eyes reflected our taillights. A dozen reddish balls flew in pairs above the desert behind us.

Soon the speedometer showed forty kilometers. But we still hadn't lost them. Every time I slowed even a little they attacked the bumper or the fenders, or tried to smash through the back window.

Finally they fell behind.

The last time I looked back they were gone. I guess I was still screaming even then because someone called "Stop!" at the top of his lungs and I barely heard it above all the shouting.

Anyway, I didn't stop.

I had no intention of slowing down until we got to the nearest city. Maybe not even then. It depended on how big the place was and how well lit up.

A black hand reached over and pulled out the key.

The rover coughed to a halt.

I turned on my passenger. Believe it or not that was the first time I'd looked at him since he'd showed up.

"You!"

Black Tom was already piling out his door. He closed it behind him, walked around the front, opened my door and handed over the keys.

"You must go to Ularup," he commanded me, "Tell them—"

"I'm going to Sydney!"

"No. Go to Ularup. Tell the council—"

"I'm not getting out of this car until I get home!"

I made to pull my door closed but he forced it all the way open and aimed a bony arm and an even bonier finger off to the west. I looked. A few kilometers away and coming nearer every minute was that stream of headlamps—dozens of them—the convoy from camp.

"Who. . . ?"

"They come to attack Ularup," said Black Tom. "Unless you warn my village, all . . . all Ularu people will die. Tell the council this. They must get ready to fight. They must send women and children into the desert to hide until it is safe."

I laughed.

It must have sounded more like a shriek. "I've got a flash for you—it's not safe in the desert."

"They must leave the village."

"I'll go to the highway. I'll tell the cops there to do something."

"No. They will not help. They will not believe you. You must warn my people." He pointed over the hood. "The road to Ularup is that way."

He didn't give me a chance to argue.

He closed the door, turned his back, and sprinted off in the direction of the convoy.

The darkness swallowed him up in a second.

I didn't hang around to watch.

I threw the rover into gear and stood on the throttle with both feet.

Then I was flying across open desert. I have a clouded memory of boulders, sand dunes and scrub vegetation whipping into and out of my headlights too fast to see clearly.

I remember the ground opened wide.

I sailed out into space.

The engine screamed.

A surprised herd of animals bedded down in the bottom, kangaroos or maybe they were wallabies, bolted in every direction. Their eyes turned upward in horror.

I recall seeing the other side so far away.

For a moment—before the rover plunged headfirst into the gorge—I actually thought I might make it across.

I saw two dreamlike black figures. They appeared over the top of a distant hill and came toward me. Half a mile away they stopped. They saw me. They must have. But for some reason they wouldn't come any closer. I called out to them. I waved my arms over my head but they didn't call back or signal. They just stood there waiting. For some reason I couldn't understand at the time, I had to make it on my own to them.

As is so often the case in a dream, I couldn't seem to get anywhere. I had no energy. None at all. I moved in a kind of slow motion and I tripped over things. When I fell, which I did a lot, it took me a long time to get up again. I wasn't too sure what I was trying to do or even where I was going. My vision was fuzzy and everything I saw looked like it was at the end of a tunnel. Of course the only way to break free was to convince myself it was really all just a dream and eventually I'd wake up and be fine.

The only problem being, I wasn't dreaming.

When you dream in the day and you're awake at the time, they call it hallucinating.

If you hallucinate in the desert they call it a mirage.

But mirages don't bend over you when you fall and speak some strange gobbledygook in your face.

They don't prod you with a stick.

Neither do they heft you onto your feet, wrap your arms over their shoulders and drag you off between them like some fresh-killed kangaroo they're planning on eating for dinner.

The sun was straight overhead when they dumped me unceremoniously onto the sand. One moved to a bush with spiked leaves and red flowers and began shoveling with his fingers. He returned moments later with a mud-caked frog—or maybe it was a toad. He held it over my mouth and squeezed the thing until liquid oozed off its back and ran down my throat.

If I'd been awake I'd have gagged, but since I wasn't I didn't.

Things like that don't happen when you're awake so my mind put it down as part of the dream.

Soon afterwards the two aborigines hefted me up again and carried me off and I was free to go back to sleep.

"You walked out of the forbidland," said Jim Jim.

His black face hovered above mine.

He wasn't hazy, not really, and he wasn't at the end of a tunnel so I figured I'd finally woken up.

"Did I?"

"Yes. They found you on the edge of our lands. What happened, Doyle?"

"I don't . . . I know I crashed a car near Killian's camp. It wasn't my car though. It was one of . . . wait—I remember! Something attacked us. Those things . . . those spirits . . . the ones you warned me about—they're real!"

"Yes."

"They attacked us. Me and two others. Mutt and Jeff. They're dead. They almost got me too. I had to wait until daybreak to start walking."

"From Killian's camp?"

"Just east of it."

Jim Jim nodded approvingly.

"Thirty kilometers."

"I don't remember most of it. I guess I'd have died if your friends hadn't found me."

"They have never saw anyone walk out of the sacred land before. Your shoulder has been bad cut. They knew you were attacked by the spirit of Gol. But you were alive. All the Ularu people are much impressed with you, Doyle."

"Where am I now?"

"My house."

I looked around. Sure enough, I could see through the doorway the living room of his house where we'd sat on the floor talking two days before. Now I was lying on his bed.

"Do you want some more water?"

"No thanks. There was something. . . ."

Suddenly I bolted up.

"Killian! Has Killian come yet?"

"No."

"He hasn't attacked the village?"

"No."

"He's coming. Black Tom told me to tell you Killian's on his—"

"I know, Doyle; you talked of this. You were not awake but you talked. The council of ten came here and listened."

"But Killian didn't come."

"Not yet. It is light. The council thinks he waits for darkness. He will come tonight."

"You believe me?"

"Yes."

"What are you going to do?"

"We are going now. All the warriors are preparing to meet them. They are going to wait for Killian and his men to come up the road."

"You're going to fight?"

"Not me. The others will fight."

"What about the women and children?"

"The men will try to hold Killian's soldiers until our families have hidden in the desert."

I grabbed his shirt with both fists.

"They can't, Jim Jim! You know why . . . what's out there. There is something . . . something horrible. You can't send any of your people into the desert. Not at night. They'll be killed. All of them."

"I know. That is what the council agreed."

"Then. . . ?"

"As long as Gol is free. And with the spirit gate open, none of my people are safe. It would be useless to fight the white man. The council decided someone must go into the cave. He must close the gate."

"Who'd be stupid enough to try that?"

He was standing very straight.

Very proud.

"You mean. . . ?"

He said, "Even a brave man needs help."

"Oh, no you don't . . . !"

"Yes, Doyle. I'm going with you."

16

Bump in the Night

Jim Jim and I hiked up the riverbed, the same riverbed I'd run down the night before with Black Tom and his Dongos hot on my trail.

We stopped when we came to the spur of rock that over-looked the entrance. This was the same boulder Jim Jim had hidden behind waiting for his father and Black Tom to come out. It was here Black Tom had shown me those two mutilated bodies.

The ogre-ish black maw of a cave was the same too.

Side by side we crouched behind the boulder. "Are you scared?" I asked him as he surveyed the haunted hollow. He didn't reply. But moments later when I sneaked a glance at the spot where the bodies had lain he murmured, "The Dongos taked them back to Ularup to be buried," and I knew he was thinking the same thing I was.

I said:

"Those things, those evil spirits or wild beasts, whatever they are . . . they're in there now, waiting for nightfall. When it gets dark they'll come out to hunt. Is that right?"

He nodded.

"Unless we close some sort of gate somewhere in there to keep them from getting out."

"Yes."

"How much time have we got?"

He looked up. The sun had already settled behind the mountains.

"One hour. Maybe less."

"That's not much time."

Again, he didn't reply.

I tried to tell myself it wouldn't really matter if it was day or night out here; it would be totally dark once we were inside.

Just thinking about it was enough to make me shiver uncontrollably.

"Is this the only way?"

"The only way in," he replied; "or out."

"No, I mean, isn't there another way? Maybe we should talk about this."

Jim Jim moved out from behind the boulder and began to climb the slope to the cave.

"Well. . . ?!!"

"Yes," he said over his shoulder.

"Yes? Yes, there is another way?"

"No."

I hurried to catch up to him.

"Should we talk about it?"

"No."

"Yes what, then . . . it isn't much time?"

"Yes, I am scared," he said.

First his head and then mine came over the edge.

The last time I'd been here the wind was blowing out of the cave; now it seemed to be blowing in. I told Jim Jim so.

"The cave is alive," he replied in a shaky voice. "It breathes."

It seemed to make sense to him.

The cave breathes.

Therefore the cave is alive.

"What's that smell?"

"Bad spirits?" Jim Jim hissed even though there was no one but me to hear him.

Seconds later we stood together at the mouth.

It wasn't big—Jim Jim could've stood on his toes and touched the roof with his fingertips if he'd wanted to and I could've touched both sides just by stretching my arms.

If I weren't around I doubt if he would have gone one step closer. If Jim Jim weren't around I know damn well I wouldn't. But it was the two of us together. And we were stuck.

A hellish howl pressed against our backs.

Miasmic fingers tugged at our clothes.

I swear that cave sucked us in. How else can I explain it? I don't remember taking those first steps. By the time my brain figured out what I was up to we'd already developed enough momentum to keep us going.

Planets whirl through the void.

Continents drift over the earth.

Mountains erode into deserts.

And fools rush in where angels fear to tread. I guess it's all just a matter of gravity.

The first thirty feet weren't too bad. The going was easy and the light was okay. But soon the easy-going went and the light lit out. We scrambled down a shoulder-width corridor that descended at twisting angles into utter darkness. When we reached the end of the corridor, I felt the walls open up. I must have felt them because I sure as the world couldn't see them.

I stood there waiting for my night vision to kick in. There wasn't a candella of light in the whole place.

At first the darkness lay against me like damp, dirty laundry thrown over my head. The air was oppressive. Hot as well as humid. If the light quotient was near zero the heat and humidity had to be a hundred. Just standing there I was soaked with sweat. It ran down my forehead and chin. I could taste it in my mouth. Even the stench of the cave stank of sweat. Until I heard someone or something moving around, sweat was the sum total of what my senses detected.

But I heard something.

"Jim Jim, is that you? What are you up to?"

". . . that you? . . . up to?" My own voice came booming back from a distant wall. We were in a big chamber.

With both arms outstretched I took a single exploratory step forward. My foot dislodged a stone and it rattled down a slope.

"Do not move!"

I stopped.

"What's the big deal?"

"Wait!"

"What for?"

"Listen."

I listened. A second passed. Another and then another. The silence was mind-boggling, broken at last by the merest crack in the distance. Beyond and below me.

"I heard it. What was that?"

"Stone."

I froze. The cave floor was a pool of utter blackness. It remained a pool of blackness even while the rest of the cave, the walls and ceiling, became suddenly illuminated by firelight.

At first I thought Jim Jim had started a small campfire near the entrance but when he came over to me, the fire came along. He had a makeshift torch of dried grasses and sticks in one hand, a box of matches in the other, and more torches under both arms.

His black face was hideous in the flickering light.

"There's no bottom to this place."

"Doyle, please." He spoke quietly, earnestly, giving me one bundle of torches to carry. "This place is bad; we must stay together. One man will be lost and without light there is death."

"Where'd you find those?"

"Near."

I demanded how he knew they were there and he shrugged and asked where else would they be? It was easy for him to say. He'd lived his whole life in a world with no electricity or running water. He handed me one of the bundles and said, "You will take half."

"In case we get separated?"

"No. We must stay together."

"I know. One man will be lost and without light there is death."

"Your torches are for coming back."

As he turned and held aloft the torch, I looked around.

We were in a big chamber, all right.

Big wasn't a big enough word to describe it.

It was the size of the Sydney Opera House—not the hall used for opera but the larger symphony hall. The view from where I was standing in the hundred-dollar balcony seats was something to see. The roof was vaulted like a rotunda. The walls formed a rough circle and were almost perfectly sheer. But the floor . . . it was still cloaked in darkness. Even when Jim Jim held his torch over the edge it wasn't bright enough to reveal what lay below.

Finally he gave up and walked away and the darkness intensified a hundredfold.

He went to the wall behind us.

I followed him because one man will be lost and without light there is death, and since he had the light, I'd be the man. I found him standing straight and stiff with the fire held high to illuminate the side of the cave.

Once there I saw what he was seeing and I froze too.

Over the smooth limestone surface, from foot-level to as high as the flames of his torch could shine above our heads, were the paintings Arthur Copley had photographed.

We'd found Rolly Melsum's prehistoric camera. A photo montage that spanned the millennia of Australia's past.

The wall constituted a phenomenal mural. Perhaps the largest in the world. If it had been done as a succession of paintings it was impossible today to say where one work ended and the next one began. A thousand different styles of aboriginal art were represented and twenty thousand different artists.

I started down the wall to my left. So mesmerized was I by what I was seeing I nearly walked over the cliff again when I came to the main body of the room. In fact, I would have walked over if someone hadn't cut a ledge in the walls that completely encircled the abyss.

The canvas circled the abyss too. It was occasionally broken by cracks or outcroppings but with those exceptions art occupied every square inch of wall space.

Before I could stop him, Jim Jim began working his way out. I had to follow.

We walked carefully all the way round. When we were nearly back to the ground on the other side of the entrance the torch had burned down to nothing and Jim Jim started up a second one. In the stronger light, we saw that the ledge didn't rejoin the entrance at all. It sloped down at about forty-five degrees. There was nothing to do but go down to explore or go all the way back round. He started down without asking my opinion; I would have rather gone back.

After about ten feet the ledge flattened out again and continued around. It was a scaffold to the next level of paintings.

If the upper level was the earliest millennium of aboriginal history then this next tier was the second thousand years but, to tell the truth, I didn't know if we were going backward or forward in time.

We made a slow circle. We had to. The ledge was barely a foot wide and in places it was badly eroded.

After another three hundred degrees it angled down to another level ten feet lower yet.

By then the walls were no longer straight up and down. They sloped more and more the deeper we went, as though we were descending into a massive funnel made of stone.

"This can't go on forever," I said, looking down.

But my voice lacked conviction. I sensed my own doubt when my words echoed back from the floor. Jim Jim held the light out and down and it wasn't bright enough even then to illuminate the end of the trail.

We continued around.

Around and down.

If Arthur Copley had limited himself to photographing paintings on the upper levels he'd gotten hardly a fraction of what was here.

There were black tracings, crude sketches of emus and kangaroos, lizards and snakes and other animals I couldn't begin to name. Jim Jim played the torch over landscapes in three colors, elementary portraits of aboriginal and spirit beings, stick figures of men using every conceivable rudimentary weapon from stones to spear throwers and boomerangs. Some of the paintings were as basic as hand outlines while others were complex pictographs that were completely indecipherable to me.

However some things were becoming clear.

We were descending through the eons. If every painting represented one year and the paintings had been drawn in the same order we were now traveling, we were witnessing eons of prehistory emerge before our eyes.

By the fourth level I couldn't even see the ceiling any more. It lay in darkness. But I wasn't interested in what lay above or below. My mind was completely absorbed in the wall.

We were watching evolution at work, documented year by year, century after century, by people who had never heard of the term.

Earlier there'd been several pictures of a big dog-like creature with stripes on its haunches and peculiar shortened shanks on its hind legs. Shown beside aborigine figures for scale, the thing seemed to be the size of a German Shepherd. But as we descended the Tasmanian wolf got smaller, more the size of a cocker spaniel. The stripes reached farther along its back and its shanks grew longer.

There were several early paintings of a wallaby-looking animal which was always depicted down on all fours. I never saw it after we reached level five.

A bird with a rat's tail appeared on level seven. Not before. And never again. I'd be willing to bet the museum people had never heard of it.

Twenty or thirty paintings on level eight were all done by the same hand. One mulla-mullung. One painting a year for a lifetime. He was a talented artist with an incredible eye for detail. Frogs, lizards, snakes, even trees and flowers. He drew them all and with astonishing skill.

He'd rendered one creature, an emu, that made me stop and stare. It showed an aborigine balancing on another's shoulders standing beside the beast which looked eye to eye with the upper man. The heaviest bird to walk the planet. Extinct for the last thousand years.

By then I knew we had to be nearly a hundred feet below the room level and the shaft was barely twenty yards across. As the shaft inexorably narrowed, the wind increased in speed and volume. Two more levels down our torch illuminated both sides of the shaft at once and I felt I could have leapt the distance between them. But I didn't dare try it. The force of the wind being drawn into the bowels of the mountain was so powerful it was all we could do to cling to the walls to keep ourselves from being sucked in.

We had to be near the end.

It ended. But not the way I'd thought it would.

Finally Jim Jim's torch, his fifth, revealed the base of the shaft. It took a sharp bend, angling down at about thirty degrees and becoming a tunnel.

I asked him if that was the gate because I didn't know. I had to shout to make myself heard over the rush of air.

His eyes were already large, wild with fear. Like me he hoped that it was the gate but when he shook his head I knew that he simply didn't know.

"Don't you have any idea what it looks like?"

"No," he shouted back.

"How will you know when we get there?"

"Don't worry, we'll get there," he cried, lighting a sixth torch as he said it.

"That takes a load off. Now all I have to worry about is getting back."

As the fresh torch burst into flames I saw something on the wall I'd have otherwise missed.

I grabbed the burning branch from his hand.

It was a particularly distinctive painting. I held the light closer. The wind whipped the ashes into my eyes. The flames blew every which way.

"Look!"

"Yes," he bellowed. "This is Black Tom's work."

"I've seen it before."

"That man took a picture."

I shook my head. "No, I never saw Copley's photographs. But I saw this one. So did you."

We stared at the drawing.

It showed a river and an unusual bleached cliff face in the background, an aborigine to one side, and the monster in the center.

"It's the Great Goanna painting," I said.

"No," said Jim Jim.

I reminded him of the negative we'd developed in Arthur Copley's darkroom. "He must have made it all the way to the bottom. Which means he undoubtedly looked through that hole, too."

"No."

"He didn't look through?"

"This is not Great Goanna."

"Sure it is," I said, but I looked again, and suddenly I wasn't so sure.

I'd known something was wrong the first time I saw it.

The tail, I'd felt then, was too short to be Melsum's giant reptile . . . that *Megalania*. The head didn't look a bit like a crocodile head, more like a bear or a cat; the teeth especially the two front teeth, were far too long; and skin that appeared to be fur instead of scales in the negative looked even more like fur now.

However, there was no getting away from the leg count. An extra pair coming right out of its belly.

"It's got six legs," I insisted. "Count 'em. This is the source of that aboriginal legend, isn't it? Isn't this what that two-man get-up of yours is supposed to represent?"

"Yes."

"Well, that's Great Goanna, isn't it?"

His big head, damn him, wagged back and forth.

"No, Doyle."

"Maybe," I observed with a frown, "you're just not up on your aboriginal legends."

His head was still wagging in the torchlight. Then he said something about the Great Goanna being a reptile. "Reptiles," he said, "have only four legs."

I stared at him.

"But no animal has six legs."

"Mammu."

"You mean mammals? But mammals. . . ."

"Have pouch."

Marsupials. Excepting the dingos, which the aborigines had brought to Australia with them, Jim Jim had never seen a mammal that wasn't pouched.

"God!"

"Yes."

"I know what this thing is," I said abruptly.

"Gol."

"I've seen it."

"Black Tom, too. He drawed it."

The full truth was just starting to hit me.

"They're supposed to be extinct. Died out ten thousand years ago."

Jim Jim didn't utter a sound.

He didn't shake his head.

He didn't have to.

"They're not dead, are they?"

"No, Doyle. I told you, Gol is still alive."

I looked dumbly around. Down the hole.

"And it's in there?"

"Yes."

He relieved me of the torch, turned, and began working his way around to the hole. I followed in a kind of trance. A few yards farther on we passed the last of the paintings. For the first time the wall was free of art. Meanwhile the ledge narrowed to mere inches.

Jim Jim stopped abruptly.

The wind had kicked up again. All the air in the cave had to blast through the one tiny opening and the resulting gale threatened to puff out the torch like a match.

He eased through. By the time I got there he'd disappeared down a twisting tube of a tunnel. All I could see was the glow of his torch reflecting off labyrinthine walls.

I called for him to wait up.

I crawled on hands and knees down a maze. Down to the left. Right and down. Then left again. And down. Always down—we didn't complain though because gravity was the one thing on our side.

The tunnel dumped us into another chamber. This one, nothing like the size of the first, was even more astounding for its subterranean architecture. Jim Jim had just lit a seventh torch from the sixth and light from both burning at the same time illuminated the chamber like a bonfire.

The whole place had been molded of flowing stone. It gushed from the ceiling, oozed over the walls, poured down waxy pillars and slumped across the floor. Every step I took I expected to sink to my knees but I didn't. I didn't even leave impressions on the surface.

Textures and colors from one side of the room to the other varied widely. On the roof, stalactites had the look and color of icicles. Over there an alcove appeared to have been gunnited in place . . . blasted with concrete and left to cure. Nearer yet I found sea-coral-like columns I couldn't have wrapped both arms around and a wall exuding honey by the barrel. Only it was hard as stone.

We passed through this chamber into another tunnel yet, mercifully larger than the last one, for I could walk upright, and straighter, too.

By this time east and west, north and south, had long ceased to have any meaning to us. I was pretty sure about up and down, though. We were going down.

The farther we went the more the ground fell away and the hotter it became. I was sweating freely in spite of the wind. We'd already descended three or four hundred feet at a steeper and steeper grade. Some slopes were so difficult we had to drop the spare torches first before lowering each other down.

Finally the floor flattened and we found ourselves on the platform of an immense underground train station. The tunnels to unfathomed destinations disappeared to our left and right. The train tracks themselves were a mysterious strip of blackness several feet below; they extended for a hundred feet or more to another platform on the other side.

Such a rushing, roaring sound sprang to our ears that I knew a whole fleet of trains were only moments from pulling into the station.

I stood waiting. Watching.

The roar continued unchanged. It didn't grow louder; neither did it diminish.

"It's water!"

"A river," said Jim Jim.

We couldn't see across it. The rushing black ribbon extended to the limits of my vision.

"It's the one on the painting," I said.

"Yes."

"You knew it was here all along."

"The legends say Tobraka, the goanna fish, dug these tunnels through the mountains. The waters are a gift for my people."

"But there's water enough here for . . . a whole city."

His torch was about gone—he had only two remaining—and when he'd lit the next to last torch I took the dying branches and hurled them as far as I could into the void. The meager flare arced over the river and finally plunged with a hiss into rapids that carried the embers swiftly downstream.

Jim Jim began exploring the platform for another way out.

I had to shout for him to hear me.

"Don't you see, Jim Jim? This is what Arthur Copley discovered. A river in the middle of the desert. He and Hector Boyle and Brock Allitt were going to use the knowledge of this water for their own profit. It's what Rush Killian hopes to exploit. He knows about it, too; and he knows . . ." I stopped. "By God! Jim Jim?"

He couldn't even hear me.

"Jim Jim!"

He'd already explored the outer wall of the platform. There were no other caverns. Now he was investigating a narrow trail that followed the tunnel upriver just inches above water level. I clambered over to him.

"Jim Jim, where does this go?"

"The water comes from the land of the Rainbow Serpent."

"And flows under the desert?"

"Yes."

"To Ularup."

"Yes."

"It feeds the spring."

"Yes."

"Jim Jim; don't you get it? Inspector Hawthorne's hat. Russell told you he found it in the spring at Ularup? This river flows under the desert to the spring."

He stopped.

"Your friend was here?"

"As far as I know he's still here."

About that time the ledge abruptly ended and as it did another tunnel opened up into solid rock at right angles to the river.

Here the walls narrowed to only a few feet across and we had to step over a pile of sticks, poles and crossbraces scattered over the floor. In the light of the torch I could see that some of the poles, though torn apart now, had once been lashed together with some sort of crude twine. If the pieces were reassembled they ought to make a framework about the same width and height as the tunnel at this narrow spot. The spaces between the uprights wouldn't be enough for even a child to squeeze through.

Jim Jim knelt down to examine the remains of the sacred gate of the Ularu.

What had destroyed it?

Time?

Heat?

Humidity?

All of the above?

Maybe even high water washing against the rocks.

Much of the tunnel here looked pretty unsafe, as though it could be dislodged with a good swift kick. I guess it was possible some of the roof had broken loose and shattered the wooden framework.

But it was none of these. Jim Jim held up some of the pieces of twine for me to look at. It didn't take any woodsman to see they'd been sliced. Cut with a knife or ax.

Probably the latter. He pointed out ax marks on a few of the poles too. Clean marks of the type made by a factory edge.

"Your friend?" he said.

I shook my head. "I don't think so. Probably Arthur Copley or Hector Boyle."

"There is not enough left to repair."

"You don't have to. With a couple of these poles as levers you could bring the whole tunnel roof down. That should block it permanently."

"Hold the light, Doyle, I will do it."

"Wait."

"There is no time, Doyle. It is nearly night time. Soon Gol will come out."

"Where does that tunnel go?"

"No one knows. Except Black Tom maybe."

"What does the legend say?"

He looked into the waiting hellhole.

"The legend says the tunnel leads to Gol's abode."

Gravity.

I was still going down, still being pulled by gravity. Things couldn't get any more grave than this.

"All right," I blurted, "I'm going in there."

"Doyle, you cannot!"

"I've got to."

"It is death."

"That's what you said when I went to the sacred lands. I'm going to see what's in there."

"No."

"Inspector Hawthorne. And Maggie. What's left of them is in there. I'm not going to leave until I've found them."

"Doyle, please. You are my friend."

"Thanks, Jim Jim, but I'm their friend too."

I took his last torch, lit it from the one in his hands and returned his. I then handed over the bundle of torches I'd carried. They should see him back to the entrance if he didn't get lost.

"If I'm not back by the time this last torch burns out, bring down the roof."

"You will die."

"Just do it. You've got to, you know you do, it's the only chance for your people."

"What about you?"

"I'll be back. Just wait until your torch burns out to cave in the tunnel, understand?"

He said nothing. If he nodded I never saw him.

I'd already ducked through. My time was limited since his torch wouldn't burn for more than another few minutes.

I moved in a crouch down the shaft. After a couple of bends I couldn't hear the river any more and I couldn't see Jim Jim's light either. I was alone.

A dozen meters in, the tunnel forked. I took the larger branch but a few meters later it forked again. Later, again. Twice it even bifurcated—forked in the other direction—and I decided they might be the earlier forks rejoining the main branch. I never learned for certain. The only thing I knew with any certainty was the reason Jim Jim's ancestors placed the gate where they had. No barrier in this maze could ever ensure the way out was blocked; and although they could have barricaded the tunnel nearer the entrance, that wouldn't have kept Gol from traveling the waterway through to the outside. Twelve thousand years ago, that river might have been a mere trickle and Gol could have followed its course beneath the desert all the way to Ularup.

The meters passed and so did the minutes.

My torch burned down to a glow.

Eventually I was left with a bundle of black coals in my hand but before it happened the last meager light saved my life. I was moving along fairly flat ground when I heard again the rush of water. That made me slow down. And when the torch's last flickers of flame illuminated a black zone across my path I stopped altogether.

It wasn't the river . . . not right in front of me. It was the brim of a precipice. Some rocks I kicked over the edge took a long time hitting bottom and the bottom they hit sent back an almost inaudible splash. So I'd rejoined the river. Temporarily. But I'd come close to joining it permanently.

When the torch gave up its last lumen of light I found myself in darkness of the most unimaginable totality. I had spent an hour in torchlight and my eyes should have been accustomed to the night but this was absolute opacity.

I screwed my eyes shut.

I opened them wide.

No difference.

There was no point turning back. If my torch was gone so was Jim Jim's and so was he. What's more he'd have caved in the tunnel before he left. However, I'd have to retrace my steps at least as far as the last fork that led me here, try the other way, and pray.

I opened my eyes.

I'm not claustrophobic. And I'm not scared of the dark. I was scared then. I left the edge of the cliff on hands and knees. Nothing felt the same as it had. All the directions had changed. The turns were all wrong, the grades were all steeper, the angles were much sharper.

It seemed to me that I crawled for an eternity although it couldn't have been more than a quarter mile, and probably wasn't even two hundred yards.

I left the sound of the river behind me.

I left everything behind me, in fact, except the heat and the humidity and the hateful smell.

That seemed to grow more intense.

I must have banged my head a thousand times. I cut my arms and shoulders on sharp stones and wore the skin off my knees. I didn't know whether to pray like an Anabaptist or swear like a sailor; I suppose I did a little of both.

I was crawling along with one hand held in front of my face when I saw it.

Light.

Not a lot of light. But a lot of little ones.

The ceiling seemed to glow with them.

I stood up, for the glow was far, far over my head.

It wasn't enough illumination to light my path but it was

enough to show the size of the chamber I'd entered by the distance between the glittering walls.

I crossed to one shining stone on the roof and looked closely.

They were tiny threads suspended from the uppermost rocks. Droplets of luminescence seemed to hang like beads down the length of each thread. And there were millions of them. I came to the conclusion they were some extraordinary species of glow-worm. The luminescent string dangling below their bodies probably attracted tiny flying bugs which found their way inside the cave.

The farther I went, the more of them there were and the lighter and bigger the chamber seemed to get.

I was still stumbling along, still banging my head and my arms and still letting out an occasional profanity, when I heard the rumble.

It sounded to me like a distant gristmill, like huge stones rolling slowly over one another. Maybe even . . . like a stone doorway being opened up. It's sounds crazy, I know, but not to me, not then, it didn't.

Then I saw the two red balls off to my left. Red balls that seemed to glow and moved slightly as I moved, following my path. I stopped. The red balls stopped too.

I moved closer. Another form of glowworm? What else could produce its own light in here?

Suddenly the rumble turned into a growl and I realized the growl was coming from the same precise spot as the red balls. I stopped. But the balls moved toward me.

Slowly at first and then faster and faster.

I was petrified with fear.

Literally frozen.

The balls vanished for an instant and at the same time a feeble spot of light shone onto the floor where I'd last seen them glowing. The light spot moved until it found the balls again nearer me and held them.

The light must have been coming from somewhere behind me but I couldn't bring myself to turn around.

As the thing got nearer to me, nearer the light, I could see more.

It was a huge furry head with extraordinarily big eyes and even more extraordinary knife-like canine teeth.

Without warning the beast sprang to its hind legs. It stood there, batting the air with its forepaws.

And as it did I saw clearly the third set of legs swinging from beneath the huge furry belly.

"Gol!" I said aloud.

The thing landed on its front feet and bounded at me.

"Mulligan?"

It came from behind me and high over my head.

I recognized my name and the voice too and yet I didn't turn around even then.

It came again.

"Mulligan, you damned fool . . . jump for it!"

17

Prime Evil

It leapt.

I saw that much before the flashlight winked out—wild eyes, jaws wide, two sabre teeth. Six sets of claws reached out for for my throat—

Darkness!

I whirled.

"Up here, Mulligan! Jump!"

I launched myself blindly into the air. A stone wall smacked me in the face. My fingers scrambled for a handhold. My shoes skidded over the rocks.

A pair of heavy and powerful paws with ginsu knives for claws dug into my leg.

But then a hand grabbed my right wrist. Two other hands took hold of my left.

They tugged while I thrashed like a madman.

Somehow I pulled free of the beast. Its claws raked my thigh. It grunted and snarled. I'd heard the same savage sounds twenty-four hours before but my mind had blanked out the horror of it as the only hope of maintaining my sanity. Now it was back. And I was mad with fright.

Before I knew it, I was sitting on a rocky ledge eight feet above the floor of the cave.

The tiger sprang at us. Its claws raked the limestone and its jaws snapped at my feet. I could only imagine the six-inch canine teeth furiously slashing the air.

Again and again it threw itself, snarling and spitting. But when

I pulled my legs under me and hugged the back wall there was nothing for it to do but give up.

I heard it fall back to the floor far below. I heard it growl in exhausted frustration.

I lay back, closed my eyes, and expelled a dry bushel of air.

"Are you all roight, Blue? It didn't get ye, did it?"

I shook my head. But of course they couldn't see that. "It just. . . ." I stopped, took a deep breath and went on, "it just scratched me."

"Ye don't know 'ow glad we are to see you."

"It took you long enough," said a very matter-of-fact Superintendent Hawthorne, although his voice was weaker and more gravelled than normal.

"Ey," added Maggie. "We were wonderin' when you'd be along. But we knew you'd come sooner or later. Anyway Lew did. He kept saying, Mulligan'll come."

"I said he'd be later than sooner," snapped Hawthorne.

They were surprisingly calm.

Not me. I was shaking like I had the D.T.s. My pulse hammered in my skull at pneumatic speed.

"I never expected to find you guys alive."

"How did you find us? Who told you we were in here?" asked Maggie.

I said, nobody; I'd seen Hawthorne's hat at Ularup. "An aborigine found it floating in the spring."

"You went at once to the authorities and informed them of this, I trust."

"I went to Sergeant Ek. I informed him."

"That's something."

"Not much. He's dead now."

"Perfect! So you're alone and unarmed."

"He was a lot less cranky back in Hong Kong," I managed to get out. "Maybe he prefers saving people to being saved."

"Saved! You call this being saved? I'll bet you've no more idea where you are than we have."

"I found you, didn't I?"

"But you've hardly saved us. Does anyone know you're here?"

"Certainly. Do you think I'd be stupid enough to come alone?"

"Where're the others?"

"I've got an Ularu native with me."

"Where is he?"

"Back down the tunnel."

"What's he doing there?"

I sighed hugely. I said, "I almost hate to tell you."

"Let's have it."

I told him about Jim Jim.

"He's doing what!!!"

"Caving in the tunnel. In fact, he's already done it. He should be halfway back to the entrance by now."

"Mulligan, you fool!"

"What else could we do? We didn't have any reason to believe you were still alive and if he doesn't seal off the tunnel that monster will go out tonight hunting his people."

Maggie broke in:

"Monster is right," she said. "What is it, Blue? I've never seen anything like it."

I took one long breath and caught up for the moment.

"It's a coelacanth," I said.

"Rubbish." I sensed Hawthorne's hatchet face swinging back and forth. "That's a fish."

"It's a dinosaur. Of a sort. It was supposed to have died out sixty million years ago. Until they fished one out of the ocean back in 1938 off Madagascar. Now they've found whole schools of them."

"You're saying this thing's a bloody dinosaur?"

"Not exactly."

I told them about my trip to the Dreamtime courtesy of the

Powerhouse Museum. And about my inspection of the cave paintings on the other side of the mountain.

"There are drawings of this same creature on the walls. Not just high in the cave where the early Ularu painted, but low, all the way to the bottom where they're still painting today. Black Tom drew one; he knows all about it. He must have spent a lot of time in here watching and studying them. He can communicate with them somehow. Even control them to an extent. They were about to tear me apart last night and Black Tom was able to hold them back for a while."

"But what are they?" Maggie's voice was harsh and dry.

"That depends on who you talk to. To Black Tom and Jim Jim and their people it's an ancient spirit named Gol. He's supposed to be banished to the far side of the mountains but he found his way through this tunnel."

"I mean—"

"According to your friend Rolly Melsum, it's called a *Thylacoleo*. A kind of sabre-tooth tiger."

Hawthorne's growl came again.

"There are no giant cats native to Australia. Never were."

"This is a marsupial cousin of the sabre-tooth. A marsupial lion. That's the part that threw me. The six legs. The small ones hanging from its belly belong to a fair-sized youngster in the mother's pouch. That's a female down there. If it had been a male I don't think it would've hesitated as long as it did."

"A bloody sabre-tooth tiger!"

"The experts thought they died out ten thousand years ago but apparently all of them didn't. At least a few are still alive."

"Not a few," she replied.

"There's dozens. Maggie and I—that is, Miss McDowel—we've seen as many as fifty pass through here every night."

"Can't you sneak out when they've gone?"

"They don't all leave. A few always remain. Occasionally we'll have a chance to explore, find a better spot, but we haven't found

a way out. This place is a bloody maze and there are pockets of
them everywhere."

"You've been in here since Sunday?"

"Getting deeper and deeper. For two days we were holed up
near a river. We had plenty of water then. Miss McDowel used
my hat for bringing water back to me until the current carried
it away."

"How bad are you hurt?"

"Lew's leg is pretty bad," offered Maggie. "One o' them took
a chomp out of it before we got up here. 'E thinks the bone's
broken above the ankle but it's been too dark for me to even
tayke a look at it."

Hawthorne remained quiet.

I knew from experience that if Maggie hadn't been able to do
anything for him, I wouldn't either. All the same, he sounded
weak. We couldn't get him medical help soon enough.

"How'd you find the cave in the first place?" I asked.

"We were taken."

"By the Ularus?"

"No. By Killian."

"He took you onto the Ularu's Occupied Lands?"

"Listen, Mulligan, we came from Killian's land. If you entered
the cave from Ularu Occupied Lands there are two entrances."

This is what the Ularu legend had told, that the tunnel went
all the way through the mountain. From the traditional land of
the Ularu to Gol's sacred land.

Hawthorne obliged me by recounting what had happened to
him and Maggie. As I'd guessed, they'd gotten a look at all the
firearms and hardware Killian was stockpiling and become suspicious. The two of them were taken into the desert with one of
Killian's men for a guide. He led them straight to a cave on the
west side of the mountain range, telling them it was near here
the bodies of Hector Boyle and the two ENA reporters had been
found. Only once Hawthorne and Maggie were inside the cave
their "guide" blew up the entrance, trapping them within. Fortu-

nately, Hawthorne had a flashlight. They wandered for hundreds of yards, perhaps a mile or more, into the cave before the batteries began to go and they found out they weren't alone; and that they'd gone from the frying pan to the fire.

"The lions go out every night to hunt," I explained to them. "They hunted kangaroos on the sacred land until Killian's people moved in and scared most of the game away and then they hunted men. Some even found their way through to the occupied lands when an old barrier was torn down by one of the guys who explored this place. After Killian's people blew up the western entrance the lions had no choice but to come and go through the eastern side. They've been raiding the Ularu camps ever since."

"The guy who explored the cave? You're talking about Copley. The man who was killed at the opera house. Right?"

"I think Arthur Copley paid Black Tom to show him the way to the sacred cave," I said. "But once Copley was here he must have seen more than pictures. He might have interpreted the paintings and figured out that there really was a river flowing through the cave . . . or maybe he did a bit of exploring and found it for himself. Either way, I think he took his discovery to Hector Boyle, the geologist-surveyor, to see if there was any money to be made of it. A real estate agent named Brock Allitt came in too, but how much he knew we'll never know now. Apparently the deal was too big for them. They ended up going to Rush Killian for the cash. I thought Killian was knocking them off so he wouldn't have to split with them or to keep them from spilling his scheme but I guess I was wrong. He killed Art Copley to stop him from showing his pictures but the lions killed Hector Boyle and Brock Allitt. And Mickey Fine and Nevil Cross, too."

"What's his scheme?"

"It's more of a dream than a scheme. He plans to build a futuristic city in the middle of the desert."

"Insane!"

"I'm certain he is."

"What about a water supply—?" When Hawthorne broke off suddenly I knew he'd answered the question for himself. "You mean, the water here. . . ?"

"He bought the neighboring property hoping he could tap into the underground river but his wells came up dry. Even this cave was of no use to him. The mountains belong to the Ularu. Which left him in the unfortunate position of owning worthless land with neighbors who owned what he craved, but whom he'd outraged by moving into the neighborhood."

I told Hawthorne about the bodies in the refrigerated truck.

"He must have thought it was the Ularu. So he built an impenetrable fence and began stockpiling weapons and men who could use them; he turned the place into a fortress."

"Why didn't he call in the authorities? If he had evidence to show them, bodies. . . ?"

"Because he doesn't want the Ularu in jail. He wants their land. And he doesn't care if he has to kill them to get it. With what's going on in the rest of the country, a few more dead aborigines aren't going to matter. That's what he figures. The man started a race war to justify murdering several hundred people in cold blood."

"Do you know that for a fact?"

"He's out there right now," I said, "waiting for nightfall to raid Ularu. I saw his convoy last night."

As I reached this point in the story I sensed movement on the floor below us. More than one. Two, three or four. I could hear them prowling around. Hear them grunting. We couldn't see anything. At least not until Hawthorne turned the waning power of the flashlight on them. The beam was so feeble it did little but make their eyes shine like rubies. Their coats were too dark to show. I thought I saw canines unsheathed below the eyes but maybe this was my imagination.

When one clawed at the rocks right below us Hawthorne aimed the light down and what it illuminated was beyond my powers of description.

"That's a male," said Hawthorne.

It was the size of a grizzly bear though longer and a whole lot leaner and meaner looking. Its coat was brown to black and the fur was rough, scabbed in places and not very thick. It easily weighed five hundred pounds. The slabs of muscles along its flanks and shoulders made me shudder.

Hit by the light the beast turned its face upward to snarl.

Never have I seen such a terrifying thing.

His mouth opened so wide that if it weren't for those teeth he could have sunk my chest between his jaws. I could look right down his throat.

Then his mouth closed and he glared at the three of us with an expression of ungovernable savagery.

The mere thought of a dozen of those behemoths dragging at a man's body and tearing him to pieces was enough to send my mind reeling.

I didn't wonder for a second why Hawthorne and Maggie had spent the last four days in a hole or on a ledge. Anything— anything at all—was better than going down there.

For no apparent reason, the big male turned and bolted. One after another, the others followed him out.

"It must be dark outside, huh?"

Hawthorne's voice showed interest, "They've never left in quite so much of a rush."

Maggie was the first to see it.

She braced herself upright.

"There's someone coming," she said.

Sure enough an infinitesimal flicker of light reflected from a distant tunnel. In the same moment we saw it, it disappeared.

"A search party!" hissed Hawthorne.

"We've got to warn them!"

I gripped Maggie's arm to keep her quiet.

"Wait!"

"What is it?"

I was standing now too, holding her back. "Those are Killian's men."

"How do you know, Mulligan?"

"You two came through an entrance on the western side. Killian's coming through the same way. That's what he spent all last night and today doing. Digging out the tunnel they blasted in."

"Why?"

"To keep the cops from finding it."

"But why dig it out? To kill us?"

"He would if he knew we were here still alive and that we know what we know, but he doesn't."

"Then. . . ?"

"They're taking a shortcut through the mountain." As I spoke the whole thing became clear in my mind. "The Ularu are guarding the southern approach to Ularup. Killian's cutthroats will sneak in from the west. Once through the mountains they'll slip down the riverbed and attack Ularup from behind—Jim Jim's people won't stand a chance."

Hawthorne didn't sound too impressed.

"Those fools could be months finding their way through this maze of tunnels."

"Maybe. Maybe not."

"Anyway, your Ularu friend has already caved in the only passage."

"Killian's men will have plenty of digging equipment."

A short silence elapsed.

"There's nothing we can— Now, I say, Mulligan, hand that back!"

"What?"

"The flashlight!"

"I didn't take it."

At that moment something brushed by me. I heard rocks rattling on the ledge and then the sound of someone landing on the floor below.

The light winked on.

Its pathetic beam swung over the floor before dashing off in the direction we'd seen the distant flicker of light.

"It's Maggie!" I shouted.

"Go after her! Stop her!"

"But she's—?"

"She's working with Killian, dammit! She's going to warn him we're here."

I landed badly. My left leg collapsed, then didn't want to get up. I'd already lost a lot of blood. The pain wasn't too bad yet— adrenalin had saved me for a while, or maybe it was shock—but pain was hitting me now.

Hawthorne shouted for me to get moving.

I picked myself up, stumbled off in the right direction and crossed the chamber without actually falling or running into anything. It was sheer luck. And it didn't last long. Once on the other side I banged into a wall with my shoulder only to carom down a shaft which, lucky again, turned out to be the right one.

With hands outstretched I hobbled down it, patting the air like a blind man. Blind I was. My eyes were operating perfectly, dilated to the size of silver dollars, no doubt, but no light was reaching my brain for the simple reason no light was there.

I stopped to listen.

Footsteps. Far. Faint.

Slowly I moved in that direction.

Did I dare call out to her? Would she answer me?

In my mind, the events of the past week replayed themselves like a movie that was too confusing the first time I'd seen it but clearer once I knew the ending:

Maggie chumming with Mutt and Jeff at the opera house. Then quizzing me. *What was I doing at the art show?* Word for word what Mutt and Jeff had wanted to know because they also knew I was supposed to be working on the Killian story. It was Maggie who'd told me to throw the talisman at Copley. Then she stuck with me all the way across town and onto the Indian Pacific. Did she want the story, or did she want to make sure that I didn't get it?

Black Tom and the others. Maybe they hadn't overheard Maggie and me talking at all; maybe she'd told them about me. And later. Could it be I was the only one who was supposed to be thrown off the train? Not both of us. She'd ordered most of the drinks, gotten me intoxicated enough I couldn't be sure what I was seeing. She'd been adamant the creature was a bunyip until it served Killian's purpose for it to be an aborigine trick, then suddenly her story to Hawthorne and Rolly Melsum changed.

I came to a stop.

The footfalls had faded. She'd stopped, or I'd taken the wrong tunnel.

I started back.

Then I heard something else.

Not footsteps. The thing never made a sound when it walked. But I heard it breathing. And hugging a wall, I heard it grunt.

If a blind man can dash, I dashed.

I scuttled sideways deeper into the tunnel desperately searching the wall surface with my outspread fingers.

They found a recess.

It was just big enough for me to crawl into. However, it didn't end. It kept going. So did I. A growl erupted from behind me. Claws scratched at the rockwork. But I was already moving fast, worming down the hole that was far too small for that lion. Very nearly too small for me.

It was just good luck, or maybe another prayer answered, that my hole didn't dead end. I snaked through it for quite a ways until it suddenly dumped me out in a chamber which I had never seen before. I'd been here—but I'd never seen it before. I was seeing it now only because of the flashlights. Not one light. Not Maggie's. At least a hundred beams were arcing over the roof, walls and floor. I didn't recognize it at first—not all lit up like that—but this was the chamber I'd crawled to after leaving the river. Then, a few million glowworm hairs had subtly, quietly illuminated the overhead; now, the whole place was a circus of sight and sound.

I dodged behind a stalagmite.

One by one they appeared, marching in single file with automatic weapons unslung. All were dressed in camouflage fatigues. Except for the second man. Black Tom. As they entered the chamber their line broke and they gathered in a rough formation in the center. Meanwhile more soldiers kept coming until their number had reached battalion strength of a hundred or more.

More than enough.

And if Black Tom was leading them through, there was little chance they'd get lost in the maze.

"Listen to that . . . do you hear it?"

I tried to stop breathing. If I could have managed it I would've stopped my heart from beating too but I couldn't, as evidenced by the fact it was exceeding the safe limits by twice. Sweat was running off every inch of my bare skin; at least this was done quietly.

"You blokes, 'old it down. Quiet!" Little by little the thunder of boots settled down.

I recognized Captain Digs's rangy form and drill instructor's baritone at the head of the column.

I could hear it now too. The rush of water nearby.

"That be the river," said Black Tom. "Not much farther. We're now half way to the other side."

"All right, let's move," Digs commanded, "I want this over with before dawn."

As I watched the men working back into file, the light was sufficient for me to see the arsenal they carried. All wore side arms but sported sniper rifles in bolt action or semi-automatic with powerful flashes affixed to the barrels. They all carried ammunition belts and backpacks.

I was still watching them go by when Maggie appeared.

She entered the chamber off to my right, between the tunnel they'd come through and mine. Without a word she was climbing down to join them.

I darted out from my place of hiding.

Maggie saw me coming. She hesitated for a moment, then hurled the flashlight. It missed only because I moved aside. The lens shattered on a rock but the sound was lost amid the footfalls of boots echoing back and forth off the walls.

"Maggie, wait!"

"Mulligan," she cried, "don't try to stop me!"

"You can't do it."

In the chamber below, the column had halted. The line broke and men began spreading out once more.

I thought they'd seen us. Or heard us fighting.

But it wasn't us.

At the front, Black Tom was standing on a rock, holding something over his head. I recognized that, too—it was his human skull. He directed it in a circle around him.

His voice was a high-pitched wail that seemed to fill the chamber. It reverberated down every tunnel and shaft.

This is what the men were watching.

"It's not too late, Maggie. Come back with me."

"With you?"

"Please."

"Don't myke me laugh."

"*Togla ani motogai nulu!*" Black Tom's voice, stronger and louder than ever before, rang through the cavern.

"You're a fool," Maggie hissed. "Go back."

"Not without you."

"Why should I?"

"I'm trying to save you."

"Ha! I'm the one who saved you. They wanted to kill you, those two. On the train, remember? I talked them out of it." She looked down and saw the armed battalion still entranced by Black Tom's performance. Digs was endeavoring, without much success, to get him down. " 'Just scare him,' I said. 'Knock him off the train. He won't bother you after that.' I saved your life. If you want to stay alive, Blue, you'd better go back." Maggie broke off as Black Tom's wail again hammered the air.

"Togla ani motogalu nulu kadi makara! Gouna gol anka tolo Nai!"

That's the best I can do. His words sounded a lot like those he'd spoken the night before.

But somehow different.

It was nothing he said, for I didn't understand a word. It was something I sensed. A feeling.

All I had was a suspicion.

A beam suddenly spotlighted us. Through the glare I saw one of the soldiers had leveled his weapon in our direction.

Shouts went up.

There was an explosion.

A heavy caliber bullet slammed into the wall behind me and shards of rock sprayed us like buckshot. Instinctively, I covered up. When I looked up, Maggie was gone.

She raced toward the soldiers waving her arms.

"Maggie! Maggie, stop."

She didn't stop or even slow down.

I took one last look at Black Tom. His wail was like a siren.

It was no longer a feeling.

I didn't suspect.

I knew.

"He's not holding them back, Maggie! I'm telling you! He's calling them in!!!"

Another shot hit the cave wall beside me.

I leaped behind a boulder.

More shouts rose; more shots erupted.

But they weren't shooting at me. When I looked around I saw darkish forms emerging from every part of the chamber. From every hole. Like ants in a disturbed hill they poured out of the walls. Stragglers, those straying from the main body of men, were the first to be dragged down. They never knew what got them but their screams panicked the rest. In seconds the beasts must have slipped inside the formation.

I started running.

I didn't stop running until I reached the far side of the chamber. From behind a rock I witnessed the carnage.

Flashlight beams were arcing helter-skelter through the darkness, illuminating everything and nothing.

Orders were shouted.

Ignored.

They were drowned by a sudden barrage of gunfire. The explosions muffled the screams, too.

The din became deafening.

Spent bullets ricocheted everywhere. It was madness. In those conditions even trained soldiers were more likely to shoot one another than the savage shadows that streaked among them bringing down one victim after another. One by one the weapons fell silent; one by one rifles fell to the floor, their beams transfixed upon some spot upon the wall, there to remain until the batteries died.

The shrieks of fear and pain were ghastly. I thought once I heard a woman's higher-pitched scream, but of course it was impossible to say for sure. I know I never heard a cry I could say was Black Tom's. His would have been just one man's cry among many others.

They sounded louder now than before but they weren't. Now there was no other sound. No gunfire.

One by one the screams died too.

I saw some still trying to find safety where there was none. A few fled back down the tunnel they'd entered with the lions in pursuit.

The whimpering of the wounded assaulted my ears as the beasts roamed among the bodies, finishing off anything which struggled and dining upon human flesh as they pleased.

No one was spared.

No one.

I couldn't stand any more.

I broke from my cover, scampered over a spew of molten-looking rock and made a dash for the end of the chamber.

It was rough going because most of the flashlights had been extinguished on the rocks or were pointed in lifeless hands at some obscure corner and I was virtually feeling my way along again.

I sensed as much as I heard the grunt behind me.

As I turned to face it the thing took two large steps and sprang into the air. He struck me square in the chest. I was knocked off my feet. His claws gouged into my sides. His massive weight pushed me back and back and. . . .

We were falling. Several seconds passed which seemed like a minute or more. The lion's claws drew away from my chest.

I plunged into water. The beast fell right on top of me. We went down. Down and down. I batted at the water. It was doing the same—I felt its powerful legs thrashing. When it started up, I pushed away.

Then I kicked upward for a breath of air.

I'm no swimmer under the best of conditions and these conditions were far from ideal.

The surface was a wild chopping sea. Waves smacked my face. Currents tugged at my feet. I was back in a darkened tunnel, the same black totality as before, but this time I was racing through at a breakneck speed, just seconds from slamming my head into a low-hanging stalactite. Assuming I could keep my head above water, that is. I slapped my arms in a fruitless attempt to tread water. I came up, heaved a deep draft of what turned out to be half water, tried again and got mostly water this time, and went down for the count. I felt something slip past me. A line of some kind moving with me through the water. Not a vine or a root. A rope?

No matter.

I was a drowning man.

I grabbed on.

Waves broke just over my head. Spume filled my useless eyes. I threw my head back and inhaled.

Air.

And light!

The tunnel was lit by fire.

I could see the bank coming closer; see the torch that silhouetted Jim Jim's soaring frame on the river's edge. He stood there unmoving. Unmovable.

In both hands he held a wicked piece of gatepost like a makeshift spear.

I tried to call out but my lungs heaved only water.

As the rope drew me ever nearer he raised the pole over his head. He remained like that, a statue hacked in coal by a miner's pickax. Finally I washed right up to the bank and when I had, he plunged his weapon into the river beside me. Once. Twice. Again and again. I clung to the rocky shore, my face turned away and my eyes closed, till I felt his hands take hold of my arms and lift me up.

Thirty Dash

Golden Australian-style sunlight flashed over Sydney's glass towers which rose into a cobalt Australian-style sky.

It was the kind of day when you take a deep breath and tell yourself it's great to be alive, that it's great to be me. Of course, that's what I tell myself. I *am* me. Everyone else, I suppose, has to settle for just being alive. It was still June, still winter in Oz and still very warm. Yet no horns sounded as I jaywalked across town. The Dry still reigned. But the heat wave had passed. I looked people in the eye when I met them and they looked back. Many smiled. They didn't even know who I was or what I'd done. To them, I was just another guy, black or white.

The war was over:

> (Alice Springs, N.T.)—The last survivor of the Ularu cave massacre returned to civilization today courtesy of the Royal Flying Doctor Service. He was flown here for treatment before going on to Sydney.
>
> British CID Superintendent Llewellyn Hawthorne was found clinging to a ledge in a cavern deep within the mysterious Murtchison Mountains. Heavily armed searchers were led by another survivor, ironically the Ularu native who was wrongfully accused of complicity in the burning of the Sydney Opera House and the historic Morisset Building. An R.F.D.S. physician declared the superintendent to be in excellent condition.
>
> Hawthorne is largely credited with bringing the

recent civil strife to a quick end through his investiga-
tion of Rush Killian's activities on the Ularu sacred
grounds. Ushered into the turmoil by the Governor-
General the British detective offered this comment
when informed that an audience with Her Majesty
awaits him upon his return to London:

"To have the fires of turmoil be extinguished from
this beautiful land is reward enough for all of us, I'm
sure."

In the Black Stump, things were as cool as ever.

Alvin Cockie and Percy Newman and a bunch of the boys
seated at ENA's assigned table were shouting in turns—for
frosties, of course.

To see them, to hear them laughing, no one would have
guessed that their country had very nearly engulfed itself in
flames. In pubs like this across Australia, oases and bomb shel-
ters in one, they had weathered the firestorm.

What's more, they weren't even sweating.

I decided, not for the first time, that it must be the beer.
Aussies won't drink their beer warm as their British brothers do
and they've gone their American draft-drinking cousins one
better. By upping the alcoholic content of the brew they're able
to keep it fluid at temperatures far below freezing. And that's
how they drink it.

Several "Oi's" rang out when they saw me.

"Welcome back, Doyle," said Newman.

Cockie set down his mug.

"Bluey!"

With a warm smile, he beckoned me over, then made room
on the seat by sliding his big lap aside.

(Biggawindi, N.T.)—The once-feared, unjustly ma-
ligned Ularu aborigines took a courageous step away
from centuries of isolationism this week by inviting a

team of zoologists to enter the ancient cave of their spirit gods.

The invitation was quickly accepted.

"We intend to go as guests," said Powerhouse Museum director and paleozoologist Rolston Melsum. "As guests we will respect their taboos."

The dinosaur hunters hope to capture a living specimen of the species *Thylacoleo Carnifex*—the marsupial lion thought to be extinct for more than eight thousand years. Plans are being made to study the creatures in their natural habitat, the caves which honeycomb the Murtchison Mountains. This particular species of the lion has been named *Thylacoleo Melsum* because of the museum director's work in identifying a large slain specimen dragged from the cave by an aboriginal named Jim Jim.

To the Ularu, the lion represented the totems of an ancient and evil Dreamtime spirit named Gol. It was responsible for the brutal deaths which had been blamed on the Ularu. Jim Jim's slaying of the animal assures his place in Ularu—not to mention Australian—folklore. The young aboriginal is the tribe's new mulla-mullung. Promising to lead his people on a path respecting both old and new ways, Jim Jim was reportedly instrumental in the invitation being extended to zoologists.

"For our part," said Melsum, "we intend to do what we can to see that the Thylacoleo's habitat—and this includes their hunting ground to the west that was bought by Rush Killian—is placed under a federal mandate of protection. The sacred lands," he vowed, "will remain sacred."

"I'm sorry, Blue, but you quit, remember. If it were jist me and Percy you'd be back but Seattle sees things differently. You quit twice. You went up there against orders. You brought back a bloody magnificent yarn, but Seattle says it'd look bad for the rest of the boys if we was to overlook what you did?"

"So I'm out, huh?"

"It's not like that, Doyle." Newman was conciliatory. "In view of the story you broke, Seattle isn't about to let you get away. But they can't just welcome you back either. They've decided to reassign you."

"Back to Hong Kong?"

"No, they couldn't send you back there. That'd be a death sentence."

"Where then?"

"They said something about sending you to New Delhi."

"India?"

"It'll just be for a few months."

"Why India?"

"Who knows why Seattle does anything?"

"How much time have I got?"

Newman passed over a ticket folder. "Your plane leaves this afternoon. Can you be ready?"

Cockie looked sheepish.

"No hard feelings, Blue."

> (Sydney, N.S.W.)—Two Eastern News Association reporters will earn a posthumous reward for their gallantry in bringing the recent controversy that threatened Australian order to public light.
>
> Nevil Cross and Mickey Fine have been named Foreign Correspondents of the Year and their story detailing Rush Killian's alleged efforts to foment civil war as a diversion for him to assume control of Ularu Occupied Lands has been forwarded in nomination to the Pulitzer committee.
>
> The story, which hit the ENA wires three days ago and made banner headlines in member newspapers

throughout the world, was written by Percy Newman and Alvin Cockie. They pieced the facts together after the two reporters were killed in the Top End earlier this week. Former ENA reporter Doyle Mulligan was the source for most of the material. However, Mulligan's name could not be submitted for the annual prize as it is open only to members of the press.

For their part, Percy Newman and Alvin Cockie declined kudos. "Any honor this story earns," they declared, "belongs to the memories of Nevil Cross and Mickey Fine."

On any given day of the week Kingsford Smith Airport is overcrowded with travelers, overrun with tourists. On this particular day, the airport was also overcast with clouds. I wondered if minimum weather conditions were responsible for the planes running late or if they were just overbooked. They couldn't land and take off fast enough to keep up with the demand.

When two more legs walked up to my chair in the Qantas lounge I didn't think anything about it. Not until I noticed the cane and the cast did I even glance up.

"Superintendent!"

"Mulligan."

I stood.

"What are you doing here?"

"I'm on my way back to London. My flight leaves any minute. Your friend Cockie told me I could find you here."

"I'm leaving too."

"Yes . . . so he said. India."

"Yeah."

"It's a grand place, Mulligan. The opportunities for adventure and excitement are extraordinary for a man like you."

I could see he was trying to make me feel better.

"Thanks anyway."

"I mean it."

"You know, superintendent, I never had a chance to ask you. How did you know about Maggie? That she was working with Killian?"

"I spent four days in a cave with her. How could I not know what she was like?"

"But I'd spent two days in the outback with her. I've known her for six months. I never suspected a thing."

"I'm a trained investigator."

"I'm supposed to be an investigative reporter. . . ."

"Yes . . . well. You know, Mulligan. She was really quite a woman. Very fond of you." I said really? "Yes, she was. She spoke very well of you. Not by name, of course, but she had very many nice things to say about her young man; I knew she was talking about you."

"That's good to know."

"There's just one thing."

"Yeah?"

"What is this nonsense about you holding your breath when you kiss?"

I blew up.

"That's not me! That's Don—!"

He was laughing.

It was only a chuckle, with just a hint of a smile, but for the superintendent it was positively a guffaw.

"Okay, you got me."

"Yes. Too bad, really." He let a little silence come and go. "You didn't make out very well, did you? All things considered."

"I'm not complaining."

"Certainly not. But I must say . . . that is, I wanted to tell you. . . ." He had jammed both hands in his pants pockets. For the first time since I'd known him Hawthorne was acutely uncomfortable.

"Yeah?"

"Well . . . you've got one thing you may not know about."

"And what's that?"

He withdrew his right hand from his pocket and thrust it in front of me. There was nothing in it—or rather there was. I reached out and shook.

"If ever you have need of me," he said.

I was speechless.

"Same here," I replied lamely.

He released his grip, turned, gathered up his cane and his bag and walked to his gate.

I was still standing at the window when his flight took off. It disappeared through overcast skies to the north and east. But off to the northwest there was a patch of cobalt. Scintillas of gold beckoned me. To India.